Praise for *The Favor*

"A celebration of the unexpected paths and lasting power of female friendship... A gem of a book."

—Rebecca Serle, *New York Times* bestselling author of *In Five Years* and *One Italian Summer*

"Adele Griffin is a compelling new voice in literary fiction."

—J. Courtney Sullivan, *New York Times* bestselling author of *Friends and Strangers*, *Maine*, *The Engagements*, and *Saints for All Occasions*

"Beautifully written and charming and funny and real."

—Jennifer E. Smith, bestselling author of *The Unsinkable Greta James*

"A wise and sparkling story about how we connect and where we belong."

—Jenny Han, #1 *New York Times* bestselling author of The Summer I Turned Pretty series

"Warm, bright, and funny. I cheered for Nora every step of the way."

—Abbi Waxman, bestselling author of *The Bookish Life of Nina Hill*

The Favor

The
Favor

a novel

ADELE GRIFFIN

sourcebooks
landmark

Published by Sourcebooks Landmark, an imprint of Sourcebooks
PO Box 4410, Naperville, Illinois 60567-4410
(630) 961-3900
sourcebooks.com

Cataloging-in-Publication Data is on file with the Library of Congress.

Printed and bound in the United States of America.
WOZ 10 9 8 7 6 5 4 3 2 1

For you, Mom

favor *(noun)*

1. an act of kindness beyond what is due or usual
2. friendly regard shown toward another, especially by a superior

PART ONE

One

The woman appears just as I'm about to lock up. She's a sudden force, pushing so hard on the other side of the door that I have no choice but to open it.

"I'm in!" she says as she swooshes past me. She's younger and more glamorous than our usual customers, with coppery curls that offset the drape of her pale cashmere coat. I note her diamond studs and the irreverence of a slip dress, which is paired with chunky biker boots she wears as easily as her astonishing beauty.

I check my watch. "Can I help you with something?"

"Yes! I'm here for your Ferretti dress. I saw it on your website." She plants her bumblebee-yellow Birkin—not a fake—on the counter. Her voice holds the sweet and smoky flavor of the South.

"We keep our best things upstairs," I say. "Our boss lives over the shop." But Barb is upstate at her home in Rhinebeck, and I tend not to enter her apartment without asking.

"Ah, I figured it was *your* shop! You've got that whole retro classic thing." She waves a hand to encompass me.

"I'm about to lock up, but if you want to stop by tomorrow, I'll have the dress ready for you."

"My flight's in three hours. I'll be quick—promise!"

I've been on my feet all day, and I *really* need to get home to Jacob, but I can't figure out how to say no to her expensive-looking teeth. I check my watch again. "It's late..."

"Sigh!"

Did she just say the word *sigh*? But she doesn't move. I don't move either, and now we're locked in a sudden game of upscale-retail chicken.

"Nora, I can hang out," says Frankie, coming in from the storage room, where he's been unboxing padded hangers. He drops into the club chair outside the dressing area. I give him the side-eye—*it's so late*—but he ignores it. "If you get me Barb's key, I'll take over." Frankie and I work most shifts together, so he knows all about my plans to swing by Whole Foods and pick up ingredients for chickpea meat loaf. I read him the recipe during our lunch break, despite his yawns. Dinner with my husband is my favorite part of the day, and I'm not about to blow it for Kentucky Elle Woods.

"Let's get at it, then!" The woman tosses her coat onto the hook of our hat tree, then spins in a circle, taking in the fusty charms of our thin-skinned salmon silk carpet and cranberry velvet curtains. "I've lived six years in the East Village and passed right by this shop, oh, must be a thousand times—till now!'" She beams at me. As if I'm the key to her fate instead of an attempt to escape it. "Such a sweet name for a vintage shop, too. I'll Have Seconds—how do you say no? I'm Evelyn."

"Nora," I say.

"Frankie," says Frankie. "Take your time." Seth is traveling for work, and Frankie doesn't like to be alone. I could leave right now if I wanted to, but I scrabble for the key in the register drawer. My mind is scrabbling too. If we're both on the floor, Frankie and I split the 10 percent commission—and minus our hourly, we've made no more than a hundred dollars today, combined.

The Ferretti costs almost two thousand dollars.

I could double my day off this sale alone.

"Herringbone, am I right?" Evelyn reaches across the counter and gives the end of my braid a teasing yank. "Nicely done too. Spelling bee chic. Who taught you?"

I'm surprised by the question. I need a second. "My mom."

"So sweet. I adore tradition—and a braid is one of the best. It's like a puzzle that solves a bad hair day. Thanks, Mama." She says this so gently, like she knows my mother. "And is that beaded Valentino upstairs? Let's bring that one down for a spin too."

The Valentino is three thousand dollars.

I find the key and fish it out.

It's not like anyone was begging for chickpea meat loaf.

"I'll get the dresses," I call to Frankie, and before he can say anything, I duck through the back door that leads up to Barb's apartment.

Given where this sale appears to be heading, she'll surely forgive the trespassing.

Two

Upstairs, I text Jacob. He writes back, You got this, plus a chef and a heart emoji, and I send back an xoxo.

My breath is quick as I pull both pieces. I'll Have Seconds is mostly high-end evening-wear consignment, but a real couture sale is a rare coup—let alone two. Frankie and I'll need to upgrade our celebration from the usual overpriced cocktails at Death & Co.

On my way out of Barb's with the gowns—which are so heavy I have to sling them over my shoulder like a couple of slumbering prom queens—I catch a dim view of myself in the hall mirror. My spearpoint collar and knife-pleat pants. My walnut-brown eyes, the same shade as my hair. *A braid is one of the best.* My mom died when I was a senior in high school, twenty years ago this spring. But whenever my fingers plait a fishtail or a waterfall, I can feel the bite of her plastic Goody comb dividing my part. Her singsongy "Sit still, sit still."

I'm singsonging it under my breath to an imaginary daughter, binding the end of her imaginary pigtail, as I head downstairs.

On the floor, Evelyn has peeled herself to her lacy bra and underwear. She's got our Balenciaga pencil skirt crimped up around her waist and is studying herself in the mirror.

Frankie is on his feet, releasing our mannequin from a couture '93

Versace coatdress with gold Medusa buttons as big as quarters down its front.

"I'm trying on a mess of other things," says Evelyn when she sees me. "Forgive me, but I'm taking over your shop!"

"Okay." I am mostly speechless, looking at her.

Evelyn's body is as inked as a treasure map. There's a band of Gaelic encircling her left bicep, a butterfly spans the small of her back, and a trellis of wild ivy climbs daringly up her inner right thigh. Tiny scripted words whisper messages across her wrists, arms, and hips. She's a living canvas. And so spectacular. Voluptuous and warmly suntanned, with curves like old-timey porn. The tattoos are a surprise, though—like cayenne pepper on a sweet potato pie.

"It goes on easier from the bottom." I gesture, mimicking how to get into the skirt. "And there's a blouse."

"Aha. Thanks, Spelling Bee! Did you win all the spelling bees at school?"

"I won a few," I admit, smiling. It's an apt nickname; I'd been that student—a bookworm, a chaser of ribbons, stickers, and stars.

"You look smart like that," says Evelyn. "I wasn't too much for school, but I've always loved the smart girls. They make me brainy by association." With a last yank on the skirt, she starts prowling, an apex predator in her luxury-boutique habitat. I pull the blouse and stand there holding it while Evelyn picks up cigarette boxes and opera glasses and sniffs into the perfume bottles lined up along our bookshelf. "I was in the fragrance business," she says. "Highly unprofitable—do not recommend. And what's up with these books?"

"Rare books," says Frankie, who has plugged in our upright clothes steamer to give the Versace a quick once-over. "Nora finds them."

"So sweet," says Evelyn. "And this Murano glass lamp...and your funky Biedermeier cabinet."

"Yep, that's all Nora," says Frankie. "Before Nora fixed it up, Barb had it looking like a brothel."

"See? You *are* the boss." Evelyn's laugh is low and rich with mischief. She slides a book out from the shelf. "Frieda Bergessen was a friend of my great-grandmother's."

"Seriously? She's my favorite," I say. I'd nearly had a heart attack when I found that first edition in Charleston a couple of years ago. It was some unexpected enchantment, that trip. Jacob and I got one deal on JetBlue (two center seats, not together) and another deal at the Riverview Inn (free breakfast, no Wi-Fi, no river view). We spent the weekend walking the harbor and eating our weight in deep-fried pickles at the Swig & Swine. I discovered *Way to Find Me: Poems by Frieda Bergessen* in a juice crate at a porch sale off King Street.

The copy is shabby. Its corners are foxed, the pages brittle, though Bergessen's observations on love and friendship continue to stick around, recrafted for the virtual world in quotes and hashtags.

"Back home, my family's got Frieda treasures spread out like a cold supper," drawls Evelyn as she flips through the book. "I even have an evening cloak created for her specially by Christian Dior."

"Dior himself? That's incredible," I say.

"I guess so. She wore it to her last public appearance at Carnegie Hall."

"Why've you got it at all?" asks Frankie.

"Because she left a lot of her things to my great-grandmother when she died. Great-Gran liked sponsoring the arts and arty types and such."

I trade a meaningful look with Frankie. *Money*. We watch Evelyn put down the book and finish her loop of the shop. Then she yanks off the skirt—"Ready!"—and unhooks her bra. Her large breasts plop out like a couple of beached jellyfish. I try not to look surprised, but casual topless isn't a thing here. Our shoppers are well-heeled, discerning women—Frankie refers to them as the Discount Dowagers—who don't want to spend the maximum for luxury labels but aren't afraid to pay for quality.

I move to shut the storefront curtains as Evelyn slides into the coatdress.

"That looks absolutely dreamy on you," pronounces Frankie, who tends to be excessive with client compliments.

"It might be a bit snug," I add because it is.

"Formfitting fits me fine," says Evelyn. "I'll take it."

"I'll put it up front," says Frankie. He's trying to remain calm, but I can hear the thrill in his voice. Our Versace, at seventy-five hundred dollars, is our prized floor piece.

"'Way to Find Me' is my favorite poem ever," says Evelyn as I reshelve the book.

"Mine too," I say.

"'Of sweeter moments, far and few.'" She quotes the second verse. Is this a test?

"'There will never be another you,'" I finish.

Evelyn's staring at me with surprised pleasure, as if I'm something she's discovered that might bring her good luck. It's a startling feeling, no less strange than if she'd kissed me. "My favorite," she repeats.

"Who is this schmaltz ball we keep talking about?" asks Frankie, whose reading leans more toward fashion and design magazines, along with his subscription to *Variety* so that he can "stay in the loop."

"Frieda Bergessen," I tell him, "was the daughter of—I think they were Scandinavian immigrants who settled somewhere in New England after the First World War. She was a prodigy—only seventeen when she wrote 'Way to Find Me.' That's the poem she's most known for. It's so passionate and personable—and if Frieda gets hold of you young, she keeps you forever."

"I scratched the line 'My way to you was not a lie' on Alex Jaffe's locker after he cheated on me with Liz Knoll," Evelyn says. "Frieda had good words for a wronged heart."

"For me, that was Amy Winehouse," says Frankie.

"There's no doubt Amy was up on her Frieda," I say.

"Clock is ticking. Let me try my Ferretti." Evelyn is shrugging out of the coatdress.

I hold up the gown like a shield to protect myself from her soft-core Bettie Page breasts. Once she climbs in, Frankie darts around to fasten the hook and eye.

"Now *this* auntie is a win," says Frankie, meaning it.

"You're like some kind of a rock star–Viking goddess," I blurt out. Really, I can't stop looking at her.

Pleased, Evelyn stares at herself in the mirror. "Who's Auntie?"

When Frankie explains that our best pieces belonged to Barb's long-dead aunt, Evelyn claps her hands. "Rustle me up the rest of the aunties!"

This time, Frankie makes the dash upstairs and returns with a haul, and Evelyn's game to try them all. Something about these campy diva Las Vegas–style gowns, with their plunging necklines and glittery batwing sleeves, fits with her burlesque beauty.

She's the perfect client—the woman who turns a dress into a story.

"Let's take a break," Evelyn declares as we release her from a heavily structured Scassi, "while I decide what I want to buy." She must see some flicker of concern in my eyes, because she dips into her Birkin for her wallet, then hands over her thick, battle-ready Amex Platinum. "For real."

I smile, relieved. "There's Taittinger in our mini fridge."

"Will Barb care?" asks Frankie.

"Only when she wants it and sees that it's gone." I find the champagne and pop the cork while Frankie gets plastic cups from the stockroom.

When I take the love seat, Evelyn jumps next to me, sloshing our drinks. "Do you have Sonos? I'm putting on my playlist!" Her knees bump compatibly against mine. Like we've done this a hundred times before. It's strange but not unpleasant.

Frankie gives Evelyn the Wi-Fi network and password, and now Lana del Rey intros soulfully through the speakers. Evelyn nudges in closer. I let it happen.

"To Ferretti? Versace?" Frankie raises his cup as our eyes trade another *woo boy*. Even if Evelyn purchases a fraction of what she likes, we've made our entire week.

"To me, of course!" sings Evelyn. "Your rock star–Viking goddess!"

We laugh and tap cups, and over the next hour, Frankie and I are a captive audience to whatever Evelyn wants to talk about next; it's her money, of course, that gives her permission to have the most to say. We learn that she's thirty-five years old, an only child who grew up all over, but mostly at her family home in Tennessee, before attending boarding school in New Hampshire—"for some spit and polish"—followed by a single semester at UC Santa Cruz, where she met Jurgen, a Swiss DJ who soon became the father of her son, Xander. She has her scuba diving license, she's been to Base Camp One and Timbuktu, and she would have been part of the U.S. National Equestrian team if she hadn't taken a fall that fractured her collarbone; one of her most heartfelt cause célèbres, she tells us somberly, is the care and rehabilitation of retired racehorses. She cochairs the annual Frick Young Fellows Gala in the fall and the Watermill Center's Summer Benefit. She's six years married to an artist named Henry, and they live downtown.

She shows us photos of Xander, whose sprinkling disruption of eighth-grade acne can't hide that he is beautiful like his mom.

"You were twenty-one when you had a baby?" I ask carefully.

"A new twenty-two. Xander was the last thing I thought I wanted." Evelyn puts away her phone. "And prepare to be shocked, but it turns out DJs don't make the most exemplary parents. Thank goodness I've got Henry. He's such a great big hug of a stepdaddy."

"That's so lovely," is what I intend to say, but what comes out is "That's so lucky."

"We are," says Evelyn. "We're a real cozy little family."

"I was asked to be in a threesome at my friend's bachelorette party," says Frankie, with a quick glance at me, as he deftly shifts us to sex anecdotes for the reward of Evelyn's laughter. We're all getting tipsy, which is probably why Frankie and Evelyn now decide to recreate some TikTok dances. On Evelyn's urging, I recite a few stanzas of "Way to Find Me" before she's suddenly on her feet in a bounce. She pulls her phone from where it fell into the velvet cushions. "My bottom buzzed me! It's my driver. My flight's leaving—quick, pack it all up. I want everything."

"*Everything*, what?" I laugh. "You're kidding."

"Aw, Spelling Bee, I'm not sure that's a winning sales strategy," says Evelyn. "Yes, every last thing."

"Will you come back for alterations?" Frankie looks stunned.

"I have my own tailor. My driver's almost here. Point me to the ladies'?"

We can barely keep our cool, and as soon as Evelyn vanishes to the bathroom downstairs, Frankie and I grab each other's hands and start spinning.

"When did we ever do a sales number like this?"

"The lady with the Q-tip hair? Who bought all the dragonfly stickpins?"

"Nora, I'm pretty sure this is bigger than our whole June!"

It's such a rush, all this money. I'm already imagining how I'll tell the story to Jacob.

"And the books," says Evelyn as she reappears. "Are they worth a lot?"

"The books?" I shake my head. "The books aren't for sale."

"Why not?"

"Because they..." Because they're mementos from Jacob's and my road trips. Crackerjack prizes pried from flea markets and swap meets. I pick up *The Alice B. Toklas Cookbook*. "This copy is water damaged, see? I got it for her hash fudge recipe."

Evelyn's breath is on my cheek. "How much?"

"They're not—"

"Two K for all of them," calls out Frankie, but he doesn't even sound serious; we both know the books couldn't be worth more than fifty dollars.

"The thing is," I say, "just because I picked these books doesn't mean—"

"Nora worked at Lineage Holdings," says Frankie grandly. "A boutique auction house," he adds. "Very prestigious."

I try to think of something to add. "But they aren't valuable, I wasn't—"

"Two thousand, done," says Evelyn.

"Except I'm not—"

"Oh, no!" Frankie presses a finger to his chin. His eyes twinkle. "Nore, have you already placed these books with another client?"

"No," I answer. "Not...at this time."

"Then finders keepers," says Evelyn.

It feels too easy. Money—my evergreen worry—is just falling into my lap.

"Poor you," says Evelyn when, books packed, I meet her up front.

"Poor me, why?"

"I'm adopting all your book babies."

"They're going to a good family." I try to match her breezy tone. I feel dazed by my windfall. But she's right—I'm sorry to give up my books.

"Promise I'll make it up to you." She takes one of my hands, binding our fingers so tight that it feels like she's stitched them together. "I owe you."

Here's when I should assure this almost-stranger she doesn't have to promise me anything. At the same time, I can't shake my sense that whatever she believes she owes me, it's real to her. Maybe it's the champagne talking. Or the way Evelyn is staring at me, like I'm her long-lost family. But now I've got an ache in my throat, and so I keep silent. Holding her grip. Allowing the moment, whatever she needs, until she lets me go.

Three

She's magic, obviously. She could read my mind." I blow out the match I've used for our tealight candles and look over at Jacob, who is busy in the kitchen. "How else would she know how I feel about the books?"

"Dunno." Jacob slides two turkey burgers from the skillet onto our plates and brings them out to the table in our front room. "She sounds like a lot."

"Did I tell you she was flying to *Italy*?"

"You did."

"Did I tell you she was going for only three days?"

"You mentioned."

"But I don't think it's the last I'll hear from her. What do you think?"

"I think, *What a day*." We sit, and Jacob raises his beer—he's even poured it into a pilsner glass.

"Including you making everything perfect. Look at this, and with flowers—so special. Thank you."

"Hey, it's worth celebrating. Cheers to your biggest commission ever."

As happy as I am about that, even better is how Jacob lets me keep circling Evelyn. Like a seventh grader with a first crush, I've related pretty much everything—but I don't want to stop talking about her just yet. She's too deep in my head. So I tell him again about her low, dirty laugh. The way she sailed around in her lingerie. Her wonderland body. The seven nautical stars scattered down her lower back to mark Xander's seventh birthday. The winged St. Mark's Lion at her pubic bone, from after she spent that month in Venice.

"She's like someone from another era, but I don't know if I mean from the past or the future. Frankie said she's like if joie de vivre were a person."

"And no chance she's coming back tomorrow, a la Marjorie Gangle?" Jacob smiles as I give him the look of anything but Marjorie Gangle, aka "I'll Have Sevenths" because of her penchant for returning everything she bought the day before. But we're both reveling in a conversation about money that, for once, isn't tense and depressing. This past year, debts forced us to sell our Honda Accord, Jacob's Peugeot racing bike, and the emerald earrings he'd given me on my thirtieth birthday.

"Evelyn doesn't have that excess-spare-time Marjorie energy," I say, "so I'm counting on the whole forty-five-hundred-dollar commission."

"What's her family fortune, anyway?" Jacob's tipped so far back in his chair I used to panic he'd fall over—athlete that he is, he never does. "Guessing you and Frankie went online sleuthing. Gold, oil, Big Pharma? Rock, paper, scissors?"

"Steel! She's descended from some railway mogul. T. Rutherford Fitzroy."

"Now that's a name. T for *Tycoon*."

"Yes. Deep tycoon roots." On our respective subway routes home—Frankie zipping up to Chelsea, me tunneling the East River to Gowanus—Frankie sent me a link to an interview in *Southern Lady* that featured Evelyn's mom, Evelyn "Bitsy" Fitzroy-Boyle, talking up her century-old trees. I sent Frankie the article about Evelyn's dad showing off his Colt and Winchester collections in *Garden & Gun*. We also traded images of Evelyn's silver fox husband, Henry, a dashing presence on her arm at their upmarkety-downtowny social events.

"Evelyn sleeps naked," I remember as we clean the kitchen the way we always do: Jacob steady on the dishes while I orbit him, drying and putting away, then setting the counter for breakfast. "She says everyone should."

"Agree." Jacob drops a cleaning pod into the dishwasher.

"But you'd be devastated if I gave up my gray sweatpants."

"I would. It's tough to pull off sexy baby elephant. But night after night, you nail it."

We're in the couple-mood I love best—lighthearted and a bit fizzy. As Jacob replaces the detergent on the high shelf, I steal up behind him, twining my arms around his chest. He turns and presses his lips against my mouth, kissing me along my throat as I tug up his shirt along with his undershirt.

We break to throw a liver snack to Nick, our scrappy terrier-mix chaperone, before we move to the bedroom. We're taking our time, mutually delivering each other's bodies the earned confidence of knowing what works, what works better.

Tonight's zing of the unexpected also might be reactivating something deep within us. Reminding us of the fun sex we used to have, way back when we were fun-sex people.

Jacob even says it afterward, as we lie together in bed in the dark, listening to our breath and the late-night traffic and sirens off Atlantic. "You know what?" He traces a finger down the side of my neck. "That was dating sex."

"Did we do that?"

"I meant, you know, if we'd dated."

In truth, we did date—but not much, since we were engaged seven months to the day we met. An instant connection, although we crossed paths only because of some shared midtown-office real estate. At the time, Jacob was at Hoopla, creating new tech platforms for educational games. Seven floors up, I worked in the parallel universe of Lineage Holdings, a traditional auction house specializing in fine watches and jewelry. The two companies shared a cafeteria—and, as it happened, a moment of old-fashioned good luck.

I remember my first sight of Jacob in storybook detail—his unhurried walk, his lanky boyishness, the graceful way he balanced his lunch in one hand as he spoke with a friend in the checkout line. I can picture his thumbs-up to the cashier, the smooth slide into his seat at the round table. His smile for everyone. And when his direct and curious gaze landed on me, I had an immediate sense of him all at once, and our connection felt as electric as it did predestined. Like I'd lived my whole life to be here in this molded plastic chair, with this lunch of Harmless Harvest coconut water and my turkey and cheese on wheat, plus a pickle, waiting for Jacob Hammond to saunter around that corner.

We didn't speak then, but he made a point to catch up with me the next day as we cleared our trays after lunch.

"You always stared at me like you wanted to see me naked," is Jacob's teasing take about those early meetups. Embarrassing, but I never had much of a poker face. Our first dates were a breathless rollout of drinks, movies, dinners, and sex that blew up our life into a wreckage of nights with no sleep at his place or mine, and days lived in a countdown of hours until we could be alone with each other again. I've never been a party-drugs type, but Jacob might be the closest I ever got to an addiction, as I was in perpetual need of a hit.

Luckily, he was on a similar drug.

"You sure you're okay with someone else's engagement ring?" he'd asked me that night in bed as we inspected it—platinum filigreed Edwardian, with an emerald-cut diamond. "I know you love antiques, but I can't stop thinking about how it's over a hundred years old. You sure it doesn't feel jinxed? Dead people's jewelry?"

"It feels more like I have custody of somebody's history." I stretched my fingers. "Which is always the story of vintage."

"I just don't want to get you wrong."

"You never get me wrong."

At the time, it all felt so true and easy.

The memory of those early years, and all the sun, moon, and starry dreams for us, can feel overwhelming when I look at Jacob now. There are so many things that I love about him. The freckle on the tip of his right ear. The furrow in his brow when he drives. The way he mouths along with dialogue from old *Star Trek* movies. The baby photo of his nephew, Oliver, he keeps in his wallet. This very notch I'm tracing with my fingertip at the bridge of his nose, from where he broke it playing lacrosse at Hobart.

When I get to his mouth, he crocodile-snaps it.

"Best day," he whispers. A thing we started saying when we felt sabotaged by too many worst days. Hormone-injection days. Embryo-transfer days.

No-more-IVFs-because-it-was-breaking-us days.

We couldn't un-worst the lows of those days, and so we searched for their antidotes.

"Remember New Paltz?" I whisper. "When I found a hardcover of *Iggie's House* at that rummage shop?"

"Next door to the tapas grill with the chili prawns."

"Another best day."

"It was."

"Evelyn has *Iggie's House* now."

In answer, Jacob yawns.

I'll make it up to you, Evelyn told me. She felt guilty about the books, was all. It's more likely I'll never see Evelyn Elliot again. A stray thought that depresses me past any sense of reason.

"Nora, that's the great big sigh that wants me to ask what's bothering you."

"It's just." I sigh again. "The books always reminded me of our getaway weekends, and now I won't get to see them anymore."

"'But the memories are ours,' he said cheesily," says Jacob. "Anyway, we can always do more road trips." He is whispering now, his lips on my shoulder. His chest hair is a prickly comfort against my back. I find my eye mask under my pillow. I slide it on as Jacob tucks me into the crook of his body, like Superman rescuing Batman.

Also, it's a known fact that spontaneous sex has a high pregnancy-success rate. This was the parting-gift wisdom of every specialist we ever saw, after every failed in vitro cycle.

Not that I'm focusing on that part.

But still.

Four

For a while I cling to this absurd hope that I'll hear from Evelyn. But after a few weeks, I let it go, and she starts to feel like someone I invented. Summer pushes through its hottest, slowest hours. Frankie gives me his Fridays and Saturdays so he and Seth can spend weekends in Nantucket, and Barb closes us on Sundays per the summer schedule. One late and lazy Sunday morning, Jacob and I are home, sitting at the table with our iced coffees and laptops, when FedEx buzzes.

"Expecting anything?" I press the panel-door open button.

"Nope."

"Me either." My hunch is that my stepmom, Gabi, has dispatched a box of treasures from Sarasota. Gabi tends to buy everything in doubles on the Home Shopping Network, and that's why Jacob and I own a bottle opener shaped like a set of dentures, an Ostrich Napping Pillow, and a switchblade spork.

"Don't come down," calls the FedEx guy through the intercom. Heightening the mystery. "I'm gonna get on the freight elevator."

Jacob looks up. "Did you forget you ordered a NordicTrack?"

"I wouldn't put it past me. But I don't think so."

We're both standing at attention, with Nick growling from a safer distance in the living room, when the FedEx guy wheels up a wooden box on a dolly. In the kitchen, Jacob gets his toolbox pliers to remove the staples. I open the card.

"What's it say?"

"'Bequeathed to Spell. Wear it when her spirit moves you. XO, Evelyn.' Oh!" I feel wild in the quick grip of knowing.

"*Spell?* This woman has a *nickname* for you?"

I thought I'd told Jacob all of it, but I guess I'd forgotten that part. "It was just silly. We were all so buzzed on champagne," I tell him— though now I remember that's not true. She'd given me that nickname, *Spelling Bee,* almost as soon as she'd walked in. But do I need to share everything about Evelyn with Jacob?

He looks at me, skeptical. I return his look with a shrug. Together, we pry open the wooden box to reveal a cardboard wardrobe container.

I peel off a length of tape like a banana skin. And then I stop.

"Nora. The suspense is killing me."

"Hang on. I'm relishing the moment."

"You know what it is?"

But I can't say it out loud. Just last night, I'd stayed up late listening to Frieda Bergessen's performance for Carnegie Hall's "Night of the Poets." Wrapped in my mother's old lazy daisies–pattern quilt and using my headphones so I wouldn't wake Jacob, I blasted through the digitalized radio broadcast of mostly unfamiliar poets until I got to Frieda. Her voice was like a low bell through the staticky crackle. Listening to her read from her own work hypnotized me.

I also found a photo in the online Library of Congress archives of Frieda wrapped in her couture Dior, alighting from the depths of a Chrysler Imperial.

Jacob is itchy, but I take my time, unraveling the last length of tape so I can pull the handles that open the box.

What strikes me first is how there's so much of it. A wall of black velvet lined in cherry-red silk, weighted in silver frog-tie closures and a dense drizzle of beaded embroidery work. I feel almost reverential as I kneel before it to locate the hand-sewn couture label at the hemline. *Automne-Hiver Christian Dior 1957.*

"I was right!" I stand up to breathe it out and take it in.

"Golf-claps for you," says Jacob. "So it's that poetry lady's cape, right?"

"Cloak."

"What's the difference?"

"The length. A cloak hits below the knee."

"My last FedEx was the Nike Vaporflys you got me for my birthday. I still think I win." Jacob crosses his arms at his chest and squints at it. "What's it worth?"

"No idea." I bump my fingers along the pointillist beadwork. "Vintage is too idiosyncratic. You can sell a piece for a nickel or a fortune. All you need is that one buyer."

"So it's hanging with us now?" asks Jacob. "Aren't there poet safe houses that keep track of this stuff? A sanctuary for Robert Frost's toothbrush? Emily Dickinson's galoshes?"

"We can protect her ourselves." I use both hands to pull the piece from its hanger. It feels almost sacrosanct, like a priestess lifted from her tomb. What a creature. Created in Paris, a place I'd never been, by artisans I'd never know. A history passed from Christian Dior to Frieda Bergessen to Evelyn Elliot...to *me*? The responsibility of ownership is a chill through my body.

"What's the resale value, do you think?"

"Hey. It's been here two minutes," I chide him. "I'm not ready to get rid of it." Though I don't totally blame Jacob. All year we've been selling everything worth anything, and as an object, it's enormous for our small space. I inhale the fabric, its dry musty-attic top note. Its earthy base of pressed leaves. I examine its tambour Lesage sequins, the spiderweb needlework courtesy of Dior's famously dedicated atelier *petit mains*. "It's like a time capsule," I say. "Frieda's never been so close to me."

"Right, but where do you wear five hundred pounds of *cloak*?" asks Jacob. "Disney's wicked-stepmother ball? Your semester at Hogwarts?"

"Romantic date with my husband?" Carefully, I spin the cloak out and let it fall over my shoulders. It feels like a portal. "Evelyn Elliot didn't give me this gift so I can *flip* it. She wants me to have it because we connected." Is that true? Hope ripples inside me.

"Maybe we could write Dean for an outside estimate?" Dean Nicholson was my very first boss at Lineage, until we were both let go due to downsizing, and he also introduced me to his friend Barb post-downsize when I was in need of a job. A couple of times a year, the three of us will get dinner at The Odeon, where Dean and Barb regale me with stories of New York in the footloose '80s and show me pictures on their phones of their young round-faced selves in fluffy mullets and raccoon eyeliner.

"Sure." I don't want to speculate on estimates. Not now. The pin-tucked, pleated heft of the velvet is as balanced as a sonnet against the drape of the folds. I pace the short length of our hall and back, feeling the drag of the train over the floorboards. I'm in Paris in the '50s. I'm Frieda, standing before the fitting room mirrors in my waxy red lipstick and poodle perm while Dior's seamstresses flutter around me like besotted moths.

Whenever a Frieda Bergessen line is tagged on social, it's usually accompanied by hearts or broken hearts—or a smiling cat with heart eyes, as Bergessen's cat poems occupy a whole other corner of the internet. She's an emotional reaction, a moment I can still recall in my seventh-grade self, when we'd been assigned "Way to Find Me" for English class. I wasn't expecting my skin to ice, my heart to leap, or my soul to burn with yearning and connection. I wasn't expecting how poetry ignites a human self.

"So, five thousand, ballpark?"

"Seriously, would you stop pushing? Not everything we love is for sale, Jacob!" I sound more biting than I mean, and Jacob raises his hands in a back-off.

"I'm gonna head down to the pier and play hoops."

When he leaves a few minutes later, he semi-slams the door.

There are so many things Jacob and I aren't talking about when we talk about money. I'd never grown up with much of it, but the bills we've racked up and the credit card Tetris we play every month to carry the balance deliver a new kind of stress. I'd supported Jacob's pay-cut move from Hoopla to codeSpark a few years ago so he could jump into the educational sphere of ad tech, and he supported me when I chose Barb. It felt good at the time to find jobs that we like, but it also edged us out on a financial tightrope that began to fray significantly once we started our adventures in reproductive technology.

Perhaps it was inevitable that the wild excess of this gift would strike a sour note between us. But right now I don't care. I'm too thrilled by it. I find space in my closet. Tuck it in with my own clothing, where it feels like a souvenir of Evelyn. The glass slipper that fits us both.

Five

Jacob's gone, but our argument lingers in the room. Nick is panting to go out, so I take her around the block, then pick up a Hale and Hearty tomato soup for lunch while mentally composing a thank-you note to Evelyn. I'm glad Jacob's still out when I get back so he can't witness how long it takes me to draft it. The right thank-you note reminds me of fine needlework—a small space that calls for patience and precision.

Evelyn's Instagram is set to private, but she has two other contact points. On her LinkedIn, I finally press Send on a note that I hope hits a breezy, off-the-cuff sweet spot, even though it took me the better part of an hour to write. On her Pinterest, I discover that Evelyn's mood board of rare old perfume bottles links to a website called Find My Fragrance. The site holds a chill of neglect. I take a chance and paste in a copy of my LinkedIn thank-you to hello@findmyfragrance.com. This time with:

> PS: Since I'm on your (inspiring!) site, I hope you could help me. About 25 years ago, I bought my mother a bottle of Libre d'Orange at Bamberger's off the Woodbury Parkway (MA). She died many years ago, and I've been trying to find another bottle ever since. If one even exists?

An evening at the Woodbury Parkway mall was my mom's favorite thing. We always made a night of it, window-shopping the expensive stores until we'd made our way down to the cheap end and the Half-Penny Exchange with its dollar deals. During one excursion, I traded a dollar for a Lisa Frank sweater while Mom found another prize, a men's wide-wale corduroy sports jacket in dark purple.

Next door at Calico Lane, she bought a length of black braid trim.

"I'll cut this down and restyle it into the most elegant coat you ever wore," she declared. "It makes a difference, a fine coat. Even when you're not wearing it. It tells you something about yourself."

My classmates sometimes teased me for my elaborate homemade clothes, but I was always thrilled to see my mom get swept up in a project. Now I imagined my new overcoat enshrined in my closet, softly telling me things about myself—all of them good.

"It'll be a dress coat," my mom decided, rubbing her hand over the bunny-soft fabric. "A real piece of work. Because you never know if you'll run into the princes, visiting the States on a royal tour. And you're just William's age!" Being royals-ready was always a little bit my mom's goal.

Afterward, at the food court, we ordered TGI Friday's blackened Cajun chicken sandwiches. It didn't take much coaxing for my mom to open the bottle of Libre d'Orange, an early Christmas gift from me. We both loved its TV ad, on heavy rotation that holiday, where the orb of the perfume bottle turned into a crystal ball, offering a view into glittering parties.

"Nora, you spoil me!" She was radiant with pleasure as she unscrewed the curled-leaf stopper and daubed first her wrists, then mine with its bright citrus scent. "I'll use only a smidge. You'll need it when you go to parties in the city that never sleeps!"

I squirmed whenever my mother envisioned me showboating around in a place she knew almost nothing about beyond how easy it was to stay up all night in it. She loved telling me about my future invitations to cocktail and dinner parties, where grown-up me "had a seat" in a life bigger than anything she'd ever known. Even as a kid, I sensed her naivety, but also because I was a kid, it felt like the dazzling truth.

We split a Friday's caramel-apple pie, and since we didn't want to go home just yet, we walked to the in-mall movie theater to see *That Thing You Do!*

"Tom Hanks is such a comfort!" my mother gushed as we left the theater, and he did feel like the coziest way to cap our orange-scented caramel-and-corduroy evening.

When I outgrew the coat, I reclaimed the braided trim and eventually used it to upcycle a straw beach bag that I keep to this day.

But I can't find another bottle of that perfume.

It reminds me of her. I know it's a long shot.

If Evelyn still checks in with her site—somehow, I doubt she does—maybe she'll be intrigued by this note? I send it, listening to the swoosh of no return, just as Meg's name lights up on my phone.

"Hey, you." As I take the call, I bring my mug to the kitchen for a coffee refill and some best friend catch-up time, but I can barely hear Meg's voice above Hailey's screaming.

"—and then type six, seven, two, Peony Avenue, in Short Hills," I hear Meg yelp above the shrieks.

I sit down again and tab into Zillow.

It's Meg's and my forever-favorite game, cruising sites like Zillow and Redfin in search of the ideal home for Jacob and me. We're always getting crushes on bargains, debating how to remodel a bathroom or convert a basement. Meg doesn't know that my savings is wiped out, and I'm too devoted to our fun to end it. Today she's found Jacob and me a cute and quirky upside-down Victorian.

"You'd have to gut the Carmela Soprano kitchen. But isn't it the sweetest?"

"Two working fireplaces... So gorgeous."

"Now go look at the midcentury Cape Cod revival on Lark Lane in Bronxville—jeez, Hailey, all I'm asking is a minute of peace!" Then to me: "Can you believe I'm shouting at my newborn? She's driving me completely nuts! Did I tell you it was colic?" Meg swears under her breath. "Stay on, Nora. I need a bit of grown-ass company. I'm just gonna warm up a bottle."

I stay on, re-clicking through the Bronxville property. I paint the door heather blue. Then hunter green. I build out a side deck and admire, then reject, my digital design work.

Minutes pass and Meg doesn't come back. I hear Becket, my god-daughter and Meg's oldest girl, screaming that Reed, her middle girl, has spilled Cheerios and now their dog, Duke, is eating them. I shout Meg's name and Becket's name, but I end the call when I hear Jacob climbing the stairs. Mooning around Zillow and houses we can't afford will only stir up more tension between us.

Just as I'm logging off, I see a new message in my Gmail tab.

It's a response from hello@findmyfragrance.com. I pounce on it.

Thanks for your query. We're in-scentivized!
We'll issue a ticket and see what we can do!
—Find My Fragrance Group, LLC

Six

⫷⫷⫷⫷⫷⫷⫷⫷

All week through the next weekend, I sit tight. Willing Evelyn to write me back. She never does. By the next Monday, I feel a little silly about it. I can't even picture us past being squeezed up on the love seat at I'll Have Seconds, drinking champagne. Where Evelyn is always exactly, extravagantly Evelyn, and I'm this glamorous, amplified Nora, spouting off on-the-spot witticisms I'd never come up with in real life. A girl can dream.

I want to talk to Frankie about her, but something's up with him. We've been less in sync than usual. He traditionally covers the morning coffee run, while I do afternoon beverages—but these past few weeks, Frankie almost never texts me the question mark that means do you want your small extra iced with a splash of two percent? And even when we're on the floor, Frankie seems distracted, less prone to enchant clients with his quirky anecdotes—"This yellow coat dress is identical to the one Linda wore when she married Paul McCartney!"

Frankie's also taking his personal calls outside, across the street from the storefront. Like he can't even chance that Barb and I might try to listen in.

Is he speaking with his therapist? Maybe. Is Seth leaving him? That seems impossible. Seth Tanaka is a lovebug of a civil rights lawyer, who's been nothing but a good influence on the Frankie who strolled into I'll Have Seconds four years ago, looking for some work to plump his erratic sometime-actor's paycheck. Anyway, if they'd been having problems, Frankie would talk it out with me. Wouldn't he?

At the window, I flick the curtain to watch Frankie pacing Orchard Street. His face is clenched, and he's gnawing the edge of his pinkie cuticle. Seth does travel a lot for work. Last weekend, Frankie was in Nantucket with his mother-in-law. Just the two of them. That's a lot of tea and shogi. What have I missed?

"Nora!" I turn.

Barb is at the counter, holding the rotary-phone receiver and looking annoyed.

At seventy-eight, Barb is part of an old-school New York, whose members feel forever entitled to their food truck pastries, their lunchtime smokes, and—no matter how many telemarketers barrage us pitching free cruises to Belize—their liver-spotted landlines.

"Sorry. I didn't hear it ring."

"It's *personal*," adds Barb meaningfully as I take the receiver. "Tell them that's the business number."

I nod in acceptable deference as I say, "Hello?"

"Hey, Spelling Bee? It's me—Evelyn Elliot. I don't know your cell."

"*Evelyn!*" I cough out the squeak in my voice. "You're back from Europe?"

"Ages ago. I'm just leaving Montauk. Did you get the gift I sent?"

"I did! I sent a thank-you note to your LinkedIn. I just didn't know—"

"*LinkedIn?*" Evelyn's laugh is a great big burst. Barb's cinder block eyebrows raise over her Edith Head glasses.

I can feel myself blushing. "I couldn't find your—"

"No, no—it's just...a thank-you note on LinkedIn? Anyway, I need to ask you a favor. My assistant, Poppy, just quit on me. She was my absolute right hand. Travel, shopping, scheduling, the whole caboodle. But she's got this cooking channel, and it's really taking off. Which is divine—nobody wants to stay a PA forever! But it also puts me in a pickle."

"Sure," I say, trying to wrap my mind around an assistant named Poppy who is now cooking-channel famous, and also Evelyn's ease with the word *caboodle*.

"Didn't you say you did house call alterations? I've got an absolute pileup."

Did I say that? I don't think I did. "I can! When's a good time?"

"Sunday's my only night in."

"I'm so sorry," I tell her. "Sunday I've got plans with Jacob."

"Jacob the husband! Bring him on over! I'll host a dinner. How's seven?"

"Ah..." Jacob and I like the rhythm of our Sunday nights. Even if it's just paying bills and coordinating our calendars. We have an unspoken deal that we don't mess with Sundays, don't let anyone in. I hear myself tell her seven is fine.

Evelyn hoots a hooray and recites her Bowery address; then, with a final "Big squeeze! Now let me let you go," she's off.

I'm on my phone, watching an episode of *SnapCracklePoppy*, where Poppy—a bright-eyed, toothy moppet—fixes on-the-go meals using a single measuring cup and a Mason jar, when Frankie comes back inside, cracking his neck, his other stress sign after cuticle-chewing. "Want to grab lunch?"

I look to Barb, who shoos us off in a way that makes me think Frankie's precleared this event with her. On our way out, she double-pats his shoulder. Did he already tell Barb about Seth abandoning him? Am I second to know? I could be. It's been lucky for Frankie and me that Barb tacks smoothly between boss and mother duck, redirecting from mom-guide to mentor with her signature unruffled ease. I guess I'm next in line to hear.

We decide on Double Dragon for takeout spring rolls. Then we sit on our bench by the basketball court in compatible silence. Frankie still hasn't plunged, even after we've packed the empty containers into the paper bag and are taking another walk around the court, the sun on our faces.

"Talk to me," I say. "How's Seth?"

"He's great." Frankie's got a gorgeous leading man's smile. "We're both really great." He looks radiant. I can see I've been way off about whatever is coming. "We have news."

Anything but baby, don't tell me you and Seth are having a baby. I feel dizzy. "Did you win the scratch-off?"

"No, no. Nothing like that." He reaches a hand to his neck and gives it a crack. "We've contracted with a carrier—a surrogate. We just got a positive. We're due in June."

"Frankie, wow! This is news!" *This is shocking news.*

"I know! And I'm totally springing it on you! I'm so sorry, Nora."

"What? No! Don't be sorry! It's wonderful!" *It's excruciating.* My limbs are tingling, my stomach is in free fall, my smile is hanging open like a scream. I close my mouth and cover it with my hand.

"I know!" Frankie stops walking to face me, arms wide. I step into his hug and press my leaking eyes into his shirtsleeve. We stay clamped together. He gets it. He holds on tight. I let go of my breath when he releases me.

"Wow, Frankie. A baby. Congratulations!"

"Two babies, actually? Twins!"

Twins. I am nodding. "That is just terrific! The bee's knees!" I'm so discombobulated that I've turned into Daisy Buchanan. "Really, Frankie. The best news in the world."

"It is. It is." The heels of his hands brush the outside corners of his eyes. No doubt he was dreading telling me. He looks overcome with relief and sadness that it's done.

"I'm thrilled. For real, I am literally crying from joy, Frankie! I'm so happy for you both!" *I am a friend, I am a good friend, I will not drag down this moment.*

"Okay. I know—thanks, Nore."

We walk in step. Frankie slings an arm around me. "And Barb?" I ask.

"I told her yesterday. Seth and I are still circling how to tell my parents." He tightens his grip on my shoulders. "I *know* you said you and Jacob are done with all this and weren't looking at carriers or any of it anymore—but it's a lot of news for you."

"It's not a lot!" Except it's too much. I might topple over.

"I hate to think it hurts you."

"You know me better than that."

"It's just that people have random reactions about the surrogate thing. I really need my safest crew around me right now."

"I am here for all of it. Tell me everything."

"Okay. Okay! I guess the first thing is it's a real leap! You know Seth, he's so organized; he handled the business end, the contract. So I feel like I'm catching up to it emotionally in a way? Also, we don't even have any idea if it's my genetics or Seth's—we just mixed it up and spun the wheel!"

"Spun the wheel! Love that!" *Spun the wheel and got twins I want to die.*

"Lisa Ann was harder to find but worth the wait. You've got to meet her. She lives in Maryland with her husband, Russell, plus their little Jedi, Aiden. She temped at a fertility clinic. So it's like she knows the whole conversation. Obviously, it's a huge spend for us. Every day I'm kind of freaked about the money. But it also feels karmic, Nora. It really does."

I am bobble-heading my yeses.

"So, yeah, we signed the papers, wrote the checks. Boom."

"Boom!"

"Can you even? Me, with kids? I barely started noticing them until about three months ago. But babies are everywhere!" Frankie pauses. "Sorry. I'm trying so hard not to say the dumbest, most insensitive shit right now. Should I stop talking?"

"No! I want all the details. And look—it could still happen for me and

Jacob. They never even figured it out with us. It's all very who-knows-if-or-when, you know?" I give a shrugging eye roll, as if we're just chilling through Murphy's Law of unexplained infertility, where everything goes from bad to worse, and jeez, there's simply nothing you can do about it.

"Crazy life changes," says Frankie. "I'm trying to get my mind around it all. My new reality in wet wipes." He smiles anxiously.

I'm feeling out of energy. "Can we sit?"

"Yeah, sure." We find a bench. Joy and worry fight for space in Frankie's eyes. "I'm not losing you, Nora, am I?"

"Oh my gosh, *Frankie*. Never." *Except maybe? No, never. I love Frankie!* I press my hands against my navel. What if this is my month? A pregnancy this month would mean a summer baby! So close in age to Frankie's twins!

Frankie's twins. It doesn't feel real. I'm still light-headed. "Do you have names?"

"We're between Daddy and Papa, or Dads and Daddio?"

"I like those, but for the babies."

"Ah, right. Seth wants to name them boat names. Caspian and Cali. Fisher and Sailor. I hope it's a phase. I'm waiting him out."

"I'll come to that intervention, if you need me."

"Thanks. He's also pushing nursery nautical. Whale patterns, rope-and-anchor murals. But I want nursery gnomes and fairies and tasteful toiles to feel welcome too."

"Remember that basin and washstand we saw at Waterworks? Or who's the Irish lady we met at that last roadshow who does the woolly animals with the faces?"

"Nora, exactly!" Frankie takes my hand. "Can I send you the link to our registry before we go live? We're at Bed Bath & Beyond, but that's mostly a jump-off."

"Send, send."

Frankie is tapping on his phone. He looks up, his eyes bright. "Thanks for being so you about this. Now I feel like I'm officially on cloud nine."

"We are totally on this cloud together." *Get me off this cloud.* "Really!" I add, too loudly, to drown my thoughts. "I am beyond happy for you guys!" I bump my shoulder into his. "Oh, and here's something—Evelyn invited me to dinner next Sunday."

"Seriously?" Now Frankie looks shocked. "Southern-fried fortune Evelyn?" He flaps a hand in a fanning motion. *"Why?"*

I'm doing her clothing alterations sounds dreary, so I say, "Who knows? She even sent me a present—that Dior evening cloak that belonged to Frieda Bergessen."

"The couture Dior? Are you for real right now? I need evidence."

I have photos. Frankie is enamored, staring at them. "That is next-dimension fabulous," he says, passing back my phone. "It's like the Bentley Continental of evening wraps."

"Ha!" But then I say, "It's one of the nicest gifts I've ever received. I peek in on it every night. The fact it was Bergessen's feels almost mythical."

"I guess you and Evelyn did have a quirky chemistry," he says. "A friendergy."

I feel a rush of heat in my cheeks. This is so exactly what I want to hear. "Do we?"

"Not to mention how you look alike."

"Really, you think?"

"Less style-wise. More like Gwynnie in *Sliding Doors.* Evelyn's the one with the really, really good life, just to be clear."

"Got it, thanks."

"You *one hundred percent* need to become best friends with heiress Evelyn," says Frankie. "I see our whole future in private jets to Turks and Caicos; then it's just a matter of time before she gets attached to Port and Starboard and gives them ponies and Bitcoin on their birthday."

"Hooray, our whole diabolical plan is coming together."

"Evelyn Elliot." Frankie shakes his head. "I love that you're in her orbit now."

I'd been feeling intimidated about the prospect of dinner with

Evelyn ever since she called, but Frankie is so genuinely impressed that now I feel ignited by it. Yes, bring it on! Okay, it's not twins—it's not even in the same universe as twins—but let me circle this bright planet of Evelynworld. Let me catch her like a gold balloon and hang on tight. Let me float out on her big heiress energy and find a little fun.

Back at the shop, Barb smiles uncertainly.

"Seth and Frankie, dads-to-be!" I exclaim. "This is so exciting!"

"It is," says Barb as she lifts an imaginary champagne glass. "If only we still had that bottle of Taittinger, we could toast."

Seven

"Martiniello's is back to doing football-season happy hours till seven," Jacob mentions as Ursula Thakor, PhD, PsyD, buzzes us into her third-floor walk-up off Union Square. "They've got that free bruschetta." Jacob is all about the post-therapy treat, which usually involves draft beers and small bites.

"I'm down for that," I tell him. We've been doing twice-a-month couples therapy Wednesdays for a few years now. Like vegetables and exercise, we know that it's good for us, but it's also a habit that's nicely bolstered by reward.

Upstairs, in Ursula's office/living space, we both take the couch. Ursula, with her frizzled gray bun and flowing tunic, along with her usual offering of ginger tea in thickly glazed, grandchild-made ceramic mugs, sets a loose, holistic mood. We're so used to these Wednesdays that our sessions feel more like office hours with a favorite professor of a problem subject, and we settle into our usual resigned readiness for the next fifty minutes.

Jacob launches hard into the small talk, a skill he's developed from working so many conferences with tech introverts. He tells Ursula about the rumors that codeSpark might merge with MindBop, and so it's anyone's guess what the new mash-up name might be. He runs her through our plans for a possible road trip to Lake George if we can make the dates work. He describes Nick's recent weigh-in at the vet that proves *someone* is still feeding her peanut butter crackers—in fairness to Nick, she is at least 10 percent happier with this snack in her life.

Then I tell Ursula about Evelyn's invitation. Playing it all very low-key. Jacob wasn't wild about this shift in our Sunday routine, but he doesn't let on to Ursula. Neither of us wants to be the dud partner, the one who can't roll with an unexpected dinner invite.

Ursula listens and affirms everything with her practiced, professional calm. "And did you speak with Meg this weekend?" she asks, gently moving us toward the broccoli-and-push-ups part of the session.

"Yes!" I say brightly. "Hailey *still* has colic. Meg tells me they're all exhausted."

"Have you been out to see everyone yet?"

"Not since the hospital visit. Soon." My body is clenching up. I feel awful that I haven't been to see baby Hailey, even though she's had all her shots and Meg keeps inviting us. "We've been busy...with things."

"And of course Hailey is tied to a sense of loss," Ursula reminds me. Like I might have forgotten. Last year, in a gesture of loving and poorly timed kindness, Meg stepped forward and offered to carry for Jacob and me. Unaware that she herself was already a few weeks pregnant with Hailey.

"I hope I'm better than that," I say, with a levity I don't feel. "Hailey didn't do anything wrong, right?" Except maybe I will always twig to some hidden grief that there is a Hailey—and that Meg's preeclampsia during that pregnancy put a hard-stop ending on our fragile, hopeful plan. "I'm so glad there's a Hailey," I say emphatically.

"I'd like to talk about Meg's phone calls." Jacob glances at me, then sits forward. "Last night, she must have kept Nora on for an hour."

I'm surprised to hear this, since Jacob never mentioned being bothered by Meg's calls. "She calls me late at night because Hailey takes forever to get down," I say. "I mean, Meg's got three young children. Three under seven is a lot."

"Three under seven *is* a lot," says Jacob. "Seven years trying to conceive, ten rounds of IUIs and IVFs, no pregnancies, and more debt than we ever imagined we'd need to handle—that's a lot too, right? But then Meg sucks up an hour of Nora's time to talk about Becket's kindergarten homework and Reed's allergies and Hailey's gas." He glances at me. "I think Meg could read the room better, is all."

"She's too exhausted to read rooms. And I like hearing about the girls. But if I'd known you were eavesdropping," I say lightly, "maybe we'd have changed the subject to something more interesting for you."

"It's a small apartment," says Jacob. "It was more like my ears work and I was hearing."

"Do you feel upset by Meg's calls?" Ursula asks me.

"No," I answer. "There's not much else on topic right now. Sleep and children."

"I feel protective of you, Nore," says Jacob. "That's all I mean."

"She's my closest friend," I say. "I can't drop every friend who becomes a parent." Even though I tend to do that. Or they drop me. It often feels gently mutual. People's lives change. Babies can be a lot for the people who have them and sometimes even more for the people who don't. I know in my heart that Meg and I—best friends since college—could weather a dozen colicky newborns. But right now our friendship is nourished on phone calls, real estate links, and our mutual love of sending each other Harry Styles reels.

I'll visit soon. I love Meg's girls. Even Hailey. Meg knows this.

Then I blurt out, "I'm really looking forward to this dinner with Evelyn."

"Ah." Ursula perks up. "Why is that?"

"That night," I say, "when Evelyn came into the shop, she zeroed in on the tiniest details about me—the way I braided my hair, the kind of student I'd been—and we talked about poetry we both loved. I felt like she was discerning all of these secret, half-forgotten things about me. It was so refreshing, being this other self, in her eyes." I pull a tissue from the box at my elbow. "We've been stuck for too long in this horrible experience," I say to Jacob, "and we pay so much attention to sad us. Therapy us. It's diminished us, I think."

Jacob shifts to re-angle his body toward me. "We might be stuck," he says, "but we're not lost. However we move forward, I'm right here, Nora, and I know we'll survive it."

I agree with a nod as I blow my nose—though Jacob tends to talk like this in therapy, folksy and earnest, like a character in *Our Town*.

"And this was a hard week," he adds. "Frankie's news and all that."

"That's true." I blow again and add another tissue for reinforcement. "I was overwhelmed at first—it was painful. At the same time, I was also thrilled for him." I nod. "I was. I am."

"Frankie's news? Frankie's having a baby?" asks Ursula.

"Twins," Jacob and I say together. Then Jacob glances at his watch. He's remembering Martiniello's and all that free bruschetta. Sometimes it's the hour post-Ursula—shaking out the shared hard experience of remembering another shared hard experience—that feels best.

Eight

In an old digital issue of *Architectural Digest*, I find a photo spread of Evelyn's penthouse apartment. It's a jaw-dropping residence. I picture the four of us—arty Henry, good sport Jacob, alluring Evelyn, and me—having the time of our lives at her *quartet of midcentury chrome chairs that serve as a frisky foil to the couple's Art Nouveau high-lacquer Wolfmann dining table.*

"Am I watching you get ready for a date?" observes Jacob after I've rejected my third Sunday-dinner outfit. "I thought this was more like a work thing."

"It is. It is...mostly!"

"Can we bike?"

I'm not wild about the thought of us arriving for dinner with sweaty bike faces. But I also know that no matter how he played it with Ursula, Jacob isn't thrilled I've swapped our comfy Sunday of takeout Chinese and sci-fi dystopia.

"Sure," I tell him. "I'll pack my flats and wear my sneakers."

The mini spare room where we store our Treks is a hold-all of everything we didn't sell on Craigslist but aren't ready to donate to the curb. From Jacob's bachelor beanbag chair to our broken-handled Yeti and my Singer sewing machine jammed in the corner, we've made the space into nothing by cramming it with everything. But we can't quite dodge the feeling of the nursery that it isn't.

"I'm done with this crappy apartment," says Jacob as we unhook our bikes from the wall.

"At least they didn't raise the rent this year." I'm not bothered by Jacob's highlight reel of gripes: the scratched kitchen linoleum, the ceiling's possible mold issue, or the bathroom's plastic stall with its wall-mounted nozzle head that Jacob says feels like showering in a hospital. I grew up in a fixer-upper that never got fixed up, and I tend to experience the term *gently used* as a comfort. Our apartment also feels like the story of our marriage: The club chairs we found upstate at Brimfield Flea. Jacob's grandmother's French oak trestle table. My mother's scrolled brass headboard.

"Ichabod Cape is also using up some real estate." Jacob plucks the edge of the Bergessen cloak, which is draped on a headless mannequin that Barb let me take from storage.

"We won't be here forever."

"I hope it moves out before we do. Did you ever send that note to Dean?"

"Yes. I'm waiting to hear back." Though I have a hunch the cloak is worth a fraction of Jacob's pipe dream. In his final decade, Christian Dior churned out such an excess of outerwear that his best pieces are worth only a few thousand dollars, tops. While even one thousand would help, I desperately don't want to sell, no matter what we could get for it, and so my current strategy is silence.

The Elliots live on a cobblestone street off the Bowery. The doorman lets us put our bikes in the mail room. I change my shoes, re-swipe my lipstick, and smooth my outfit, Classic Hits of Vintage finds: a mid-'90s Agnes B. cream blouse, Claire McCardle wrap-waist olive pants, and a lavender pearl-button Barney's Warehouse cardigan.

"How do I look?"

"Lovely. Tell me now if you're leaving me for this woman."

"Stop. She's our best new client and worth an effort, is all."

The elevator shoots us up to the penthouse, and the doors slide open into the Elliots' spectacular great room with its full-length casement-window views of the East River.

But it's all been completely redecorated. For a moment, I think we're in the wrong home, and it catches me off guard. All that *Architectural Digest* black lacquer and nickel finish is gone, exchanged for minimalist textured neutrals. Looking around, I feel anxious, like I've lost my feel of the night before it's even begun.

"You made it!" Evelyn sails in from around a corner, a glamorous apparition in billowing pink Miyake, Henry behind her. Her skin is tanned golden, like she's just stepped off the beach, and she's warm like sunshine too, as she brushes a kiss on each of my cheeks, then pivots to kiss-kiss Jacob, which he's not expecting. "You're such a jock! Not at all what I imagined."

Jacob laughs but looks mildly crestfallen. "What did you imagine?"

"More like your wife, maybe? But you're the straight man."

"Am I? Sorry to disappoint."

"Don't be sorry. You know what they say. In every couple, there's the garden and the gardener." Evelyn winks at me. "FYI, we're gardens."

"I'm only the gardener when it's time to weed," says Henry, an almost-joke that nobody quite gets, but we all laugh because it's kind of an icebreaker. Henry looks even more like a Eurovision rock star in person, with light-blue eyes that would be the first thing you'd note to describe him, and a shock of silvering blond Beethoven hair.

Jacob hands off the wine from his backpack. I bought the wine myself, using cash so Jacob doesn't know how much I paid. I'm glad Henry doesn't ask about the label since I've already forgotten everything the wine lady told me.

"The clothes are in my dressing room," says Evelyn. "But I'm in the middle of finishing up dinner—my chef, Tabitha, left me mixing and heating instructions, which is as close to home-cooked as I can imagine. Let the guys go."

As I trail her into her galactic kitchen of cast-iron beams and columns, Henry and Jacob strike up a conversation—I hear the words *Coltrane* and *Casamigos*—as they head off into a zone past the archway that flows from the great room.

"We can start with rosé," said Evelyn. "We'll have your red with the paella."

"Evelyn, I love my gift! It's breathtaking. It felt like my birthday, opening that box."

"Oh, sweet." Evelyn looks pleased. "I almost donated it to a museum in Vermont that has a few of her things. But it's better off with you."

She opens the lower-oven door, releasing a spicy smell. "What is it?" I ask.

"You know what! Hash brownies, from that cookbook you sold me that mixes up recipes with long stories like my great-aunt Sis used to tell at parties after her third sherry." She uses a fork to poke at the lumpy batter. "I added twice the THC. Too much?"

"No way!" I declare, though the last time I ate a hash brownie was never, and when Jacob and I vaped with my dad a few New Year's Eves ago, we both got thumping headaches.

Past the kitchen, I peer into the massive open dining room. A slab of dark marble table surrounded by fat bouclé chairs. White gardenias in crystal bowls. Not an ounce of *frisky midcentury chrome* in sight. Where is her other furniture? Donated to Goodwill? Stored in that ultra-modern Hamptons house that I found featured in last July's *Elle Decor*?

Evelyn delivers my glass of wine. "Go on and have a look around. I just redid it. Out with the old! But I need to finish my secret-family-recipe vinaigrette."

I take myself on a tour. At least Evelyn hasn't changed the paintings. I comment with casual wisdom on the Katz, the Walker, and the oil portrait by Faye Creasy of a quietly smoldering twenty-something-year-old Evelyn with ombre pastel-pink hair.

"Wow, where'd you study art again?" Evelyn calls from the kitchen. "Or did you just google all my stuff?"

My cheeks flare—that's exactly what I did. "No, I just really love art," I say, ducking away from oil-painting-Evelyn's knowing eyes.

There's a muddy watercolor—possibly a child's—over the fireplace. I don't recall this piece from the *Architectural Digest* article. "This covered bridge painting is lovely," I say. "Who did that?"

"Yours truly!" Evelyn sings. "My semester at Estudio Nómada, in Barcelona."

"It looks really...professional." I sense this is a word she wants.

"Right?" I feel her pleasure radiating from the kitchen.

On the mantel, I pick up an ormolu-framed daguerreotype of a stiffly posed Edwardian couple who look like they've never experienced the joy of good news. "Whose ancestors?"

"They're nobody! I found that frame in a market in San Sebastián. The photo came with it. Such a mousy little pair, bless their hearts. Maybe they needed to be adopted."

She'd spoken that way about the books. I don't see them anywhere. Would she have tossed them? *Out with the old.* But I'm also relaxing, notch by notch, into Evelyn's easy mood. Even the air smells bakery friendly.

I drift in and out of the pocket anterooms—a lounge in tasteful neutrals, a formal paneled study—before circling back to join her in the kitchen, where she's whisking her vinaigrette. "Do you go to Europe often?"

"The usual amount. Four times a year, maybe? Why, when were you there last?"

"Oh, me?" I swallow some wine. "Not lately."

"I scooped up a whole mess of bellissimo vintage in Florence. I've been on a real kick."

"Clothes?"

"Cars," says Evelyn. "A Fiat for my dad and an Alfa Romeo cute as a bug's ear for me. I had 'em both shipped over to our farm."

Old Orchard. The family estate. How my mother would have loved everything Evelyn. *She ships cars. She has a country estate, like a duchess.* "Antique Italian sports cars. Dreamy."

"Right? There's just so many beautiful things in this world, I never want to settle for less."

"So true." I think about everything in our apartment that feels complicit with less, which is most of our things since I trend toward sentimental value. "Is your son here?"

"Xander's with his tutor at chess practice. Hey, Anya," she says, as a uniformed woman materializes—where did she come from? "Let the boys know we're ready."

Anya opens and decants the wine, and then leaves. Moments later, Henry and Jacob arrive in the dining room, looking relaxed on top-shelf tequila.

We sit. As Anya moves around us filling our waters, I hear my mother's voice in my head: *Crystal water glasses and pressed linen napkins!*

"Oh, quick question," says Jacob, with a finger snap, as if he's remembering something. "Do you have papers on the Dior? Just for insurance purposes?" Avoiding my glare, Jacob now fixates on buttering the entire surface of his bread roll.

"Papers, no—but I've got some history," says Evelyn. "My great-gran and Frieda traveled a lot back in the fifties, and they both loved Paris."

"Paris!" I exclaim to shift the subject.

"But for insurance purposes, Ev," says Henry. "What did we pay in luxury-gift tax? Evelyn's family has a whole team of accountants," he tells us, "and I think they estimated the cloak at fifteen thousand. A touch high, but there's the celebrity—"

"Henry," says Evelyn, "that's not how I want to talk about a gift."

"Right," says Henry. "Sorry."

"Sorry," echoes Jacob, apologetic but also shooting me a look of shock for this wild number, *fifteen thousand.*

"I collect concert T-shirts," Henry says, his voice a crisp reset. "I've got Led Zeppelin from Knebworth '79. Your shop sell any of that, Nora?"

We don't, but the rest of dinner is a flow of topics from the value of rare ratty concert T-shirts to how the Bowery has changed to the best hacks for a tasty paella and the origin story of our shelter mutt. How I'd had my heart set on a boy dog we'd call Nick Charles since my mom named me after glamorous Nora Charles in *The Thin Man*, but the second Jacob and I saw our woebegone girl, with her stumpy beagle legs and upright ears, we knew she was our one true Nick Charles Hammond.

Evelyn loves this story. She tries to coax out their cat, Shade, who is slinking around somewhere but, on brand, never appears. We eat creamy burrata with fig balsamic, farmers market salad, and a smoky, garlicky paella that's the best I ever tasted.

I didn't know what to expect of tonight, but it's pure enchantment, the kind of evening I hope will get us another invite, even if this number, *fifteen thousand,* is also zipping around like a minnow in my mind. Every time I've glanced at Jacob, I know his own head is swimming with it too.

Anya slips back in to clear the place settings. Then she brings out the platter of hash brownies cut into squares. Mine tastes like sweet dirt.

"You can cook out the potency," says Henry.

"I hope so," says Jacob. "We have to be up early."

"Quick game of pool first?" suggests Henry, and rack-'em-up Jacob can't resist.

"I'm glad we did this. It got Henry out of his head," says Evelyn once we leave the dining room for the lounge, and the guys are gone. "He's been working on a new idea, and he's so modest about his art—but let me show you his books!" She darts off and soon returns with a stack of children's picture books.

Red Fox. Blue Wolf. Orange Fish. Green Frog. Yellow Duck. Gray Cat.

"Ooh!" I slide *Red Fox* from the top like I've never seen it, though I used up my lunch break one day last week to hit the Mulberry Street Library so I could study all of Henry's books ahead of this dinner. "These are so charming!"

"Aren't they? His strength is animals," says Evelyn proudly.

"Was he always an artist?" I also know Henry's history. I've stopped by his website and his publisher's page, and I've read all his interviews. Not that I would admit to this. But am I so stoned that I'm in danger of ratting myself out as a creepy online sleuth? I need to be careful. Especially since Evelyn already guessed I tracked her art.

"Actually, no," says Evelyn, pleased that I've asked. "Henry was an elementary school art teacher for years, and after he and his ex split up—their girls were almost grown—he decided to try something new. His series took off like a bottle rocket; he even made a *Sesame Street* video with Scarlett Johansson that went viral. It's just about the sweetest thing you ever saw."

The *Sesame Street* video showed up first when I searched Henry's name. I've watched it multiple times. "I'll have to look for it."

"After *Sesame* came the Nick Jr. animated show. Xander was obsessed! So that's why I bid on an art lesson with Henry at a fundraiser for Xan's school. He was such a dad with Xander. Right from the go. Nothing like the hedge fund cowboys I'd been dating. Henry was different." Evelyn flips to the back-jacket image of Henry looking a man-bun kind of handsome. Her voice goes soft. "We pretty much raised Xander together." She tilts her head, attuned to a noise I don't hear. "Speaking of."

The elevator pings, and Xander lopes in, his skateboard crooked under an arm, followed by a string-beany college-aged woman in tortoiseshell glasses. "Thanks, Kristen," calls Evelyn.

Kristen waves as the elevator doors close.

"Xander, this is my friend Nora," she says as Xander kicks off his shoes. "Did you eat?"

"Hey," says Xander to me. "Sweetgreen, plus Five Guys."

"Maybe a shower now?"

"Nuh." Headphones readjusted, Xander backs away from us, heading off any further adult conversation as he moves fast down the long hall on the other side of the elevator.

"I have friends with packs of kids. As soon as they lose one to Minecraft, they go off and make another. Teenage boys are their own universe; I'm just happy Xan still talks to me, even if it's mostly to remind me of my parental failings. But I'm one and done." Evelyn sighs, as if talk of Xander is a meal that satisfies her. I brace for the next question, but instead she says, "Tea?"

"Sure." My brownie high, a vague premonition only a few minutes ago, is announcing itself. My bones are jelly. The squish of the settee makes it hard to stand. I manage to pad behind Evelyn to the kitchen, where I watch her spoon loose leaves of Earl Grey into mesh infusers. She sets out cookies with hard icing.

I take one. Everything here tastes magical, like it was made by fairy folk and sprinkled in gold dust. I contemplate saying this out loud, but is that too loopy?

When Henry and Jacob come through, Jacob gives me an eye signal that I miss on purpose. He looks the same stoned that I feel.

"We'd better get going," he says. "This has been great, folks. Thank you."

"But we haven't done my alterations yet," says Evelyn.

"Take your time. Jacob and I'll have port on the roof," says Henry. To Jacob, he says, "It's a '67 Fonseca. No curfew, right?"

"Wish I could, man, but like I said, work tomorrow," says Jacob. "So, yes curfew." He sends me a look of entrapment that I pretend not to understand as Henry claps him on the back.

"But there's not a sitter to get home to, right?"

"Nope." Jacob emphasizes the *P* as he lobs me a warning with his face. I mouth, *Soon.*

When they're gone, I dip Evelyn's bee-handled teaspoon into its hive-shaped glass honeypot. The question is hovering. I might as well plunge in.

"We froze an embryo," I say. "We've been through a lot of in vitro."

"Aha," says Evelyn. "So you're all teed up. Are you planning for this year?"

"That's the thing," I say. "We've tried it all—hormone modulation, immune therapy—the full buffet. The short story is nothing attaches. Our doctor thinks the next step is a surrogate."

"So do it. Hire some help." Evelyn's advice sounds like something she says a lot. "You know, a sturdy gal who breezed through it and who'd be an old hand at incubating. Someone like me, right?" She makes a joke of flexing her biceps, and the muscles of her arms are thickly chiseled, the friend who can open the jars. "My friend Libby had *triplets* through her surrogate. She picked up her babies in July, moved to Maui in September, and now she does a Substack newsletter about climate justice."

"It's a little pricey." I say this the way I might comment on the cost of veal chops. I don't want Jacob and me to be Evelyn's new daguerreotype sad sacks. "We're saving for it," I add, for bonus optimism.

She shrugs in affirmation as she takes the plate of cookies, then motions for me to follow her into a nook on the other side of the pantry. A plump couch offers itself up for continued relaxing. As we settle in, I select another cookie. I can't believe I'm still eating.

"Baby-making problems seem to catch up to just about every other friend of mine," says Evelyn as she tosses me a featherlight throw and tucks up in one of her own. "I know I feel lucky I dodged it. Anyhow!" She yawns it off. "Tell me what happened to your mother—was she sick?" The question is a whiplash change of subject I'm not expecting. "You wrote to my website, remember?" she adds at the puzzled look on my face. "FYI, I rarely check that mailbox. I don't do the fragrances anymore. These days I'm thinking more about creating a lifestyle platform. I even picked out the name—Evvie Does It. It's fun, right?"

"It is," I say.

"But I'll keep an eye peeled for your perfume."

"I mean, only if you have any time. She had breast cancer," I say awkwardly.

"Oh, honey. I'm so sorry. What was she like? Were you close?"

So few people ask about my mother these days, but Evelyn's eyes are all in. Talking about my mom feels like unfolding a blanket from some forgotten childhood chest. "We were. Really close. She also loved clothes—she taught me everything I know about fabric and sewing. How to cut a pattern, basting, fine-needle stitches. She was incredibly resourceful."

"And even before upcycling got trendy," says Evelyn. "You miss her."

"I do." I try to focus on Evelyn, who appears liquid. I am so stoned. I am so stratospherically high. "She would have been infatuated with your home," I add. "We didn't have money, but she was starstruck by beautiful things. I guess she was kind of a kid that way—she loved palaces and princesses, Wallis Simpson and Grace Kelly, Diana." Suddenly, I feel my mother—her warm, soft-waisted presence—next to me on the couch, our box of Pepperidge Farm Classic Collection tucked between us as we watched the funeral. Diana's boys marching behind their mother's coffin. My eyes sting.

"I had a sister," says Evelyn. "Alexandra. She died before I was born—crib death." She takes my hand, bending her fingers through mine and pressing hard. "I always knew when my mother was thinking about Alex, and it made me feel so helpless. Poor Mama, she still wears the same lace dress every year on Alex's birthday." Evelyn is squeezing my hand as hard as an orange for fresh juice.

"My mother and I wore black for Diana. She made us special hats with veils. We had tea and cookies while we watched the funeral on television."

"Spell," whispers Evelyn after a moment. Her eyes widen—and that's when I see the brownies have hit her hard too.

"What?"

"Hats with veils for a TV funeral? That's about as crazy as a soup sandwich."

"Hey," I say. "Spooky lace birthday dress?"

We take a minute, absorbing what we've said to each other. And then we're laughing, a little teary, overwhelmed by our mothers and our childhoods and the heady dream-mood of these memories, and I'm still woozy with homesickness and tender around the edges when the guys come back inside.

Nine

The next morning, I wake up with pain in my fingertips and a hangover pinging in my temples. My kneecaps burn. It was after midnight by the time I'd measured for Evelyn's alterations and spent an hour kneeling with a mouthful of pins, in her rose-gold dressing room that could have swallowed our apartment whole.

This is also where I discovered the books, tucked into a bookshelf behind her chaise. "Aha, so *that's* where Anya put them," Evelyn said happily when I pointed them out, but for a moment I wanted to bundle them up and spirit them away. Evelyn could never value the books the way I do, purchased as they were on her casual champagne-fueled impulse.

But I can't afford to buy them back either. The money's all gone, in a single payment to Auntie Visa.

Jacob and I didn't even get home until almost 2:00 a.m.

I leave the bedroom to find Jacob pouring us glasses of green-olive smoothies as thick as aspic. "What a night," he mumbles. "I feel like I walked into a wall." He drains his drink and makes a face. "Are you ready to discuss how the Caped Crusader is worth fifteen thousand dollars?"

Here we go. Last night, wobbling home at one mile per hour on our bikes, I told Jacob I felt too queasy to talk about money.

I'm not feeling much better now, but Jacob looks as alert as a meerkat. He hands me my glass. I take a tiny sip, all the proof I need that it's terrible. It's an effort, but I finish it. "First off. Barb could never sticker-price fifteen thousand for that piece and expect it to sell."

"Can we get an outside appraisal?"

I hold up my phone. "Dean wrote me back this morning."

"What'd he say?"

"Bring it by his apartment anytime next week."

"Great, let's set it up. Could be a nice surprise."

"Right, except it won't be."

"Nora, even if we got half. Seven grand. Imagine deactivating the Fleet card."

We'd put our last round of IVF on our BP Fleet fuel-plus card. A distinctly ironic move, given that we'd sold our car.

"What's that face?" Jacob is staring at me. "I'm just thinking out loud."

"I don't want her to know if we sold it."

"We don't need to tell her."

"But what if she's over here for a visit," I say, "and she wants to see it?"

"Here, as in this apartment? She'll never be here. If she needs you, she'll summon you. Evelyn lives in a whole different dimension from us."

There's no way Jacob could have enjoyed last night the way I did. He didn't know I was twirling around inside my very own Libre d'Orange commercial.

I begin to unload the dishwasher.

"You can't get too cranky." Jacob moves to the closet to get Nick's dog food. "You told me she planned to donate it." He shakes kibble into Nick's bowl. "She clearly doesn't feel precious about it."

"Evelyn donating the cloak is different from us selling it."

Jacob stands, grimacing. His fingers massage the sides of his head. "Advil?"

"Bedroom dresser." My voice is tight. "I just don't want to upset her, is all."

"Evelyn had you pinning her clothes when we couldn't walk a straight line." In the bedroom, I hear Jacob pop the Advil cap. "I'm sure she likes you fine. But you work for her. She's not coming over for sweet tea and peach cobbler."

"I don't work for her. I did some work for her."

"Nore."

I look up from where I'm sorting forks into the utensil drawer. Jacob is planted in the bedroom doorway. "If that thing is worth real money, we need to know."

This is true. While Jacob and I like to remind each other that, as long as we stay on our budget tightrope, we're doing okay—we're both employed, there's food in the fridge, and we can spring for the odd treat—no way can we keep a fifteen-thousand-dollar anything.

I rinse and add the smoothie glasses to the dishwasher. I try for neutral, but my tone is guarded. "Let's agree on an offer price. The number where we sell. Same strategy as Craigslist."

"My Peugeot bike sold for thirty-five hundred." Jacob adored his Peugeot. It was harder for him to sacrifice that bike than to sell our Passat. "How about three thousand?"

"How about four?" I counter. "It's a major piece of vintage, it belonged to my favorite poet, and it was given in a spirit of—" My phone buzzes with a text from Evelyn. My heart leaps to read it. "Oh, listen to this! Evelyn wants us to join her party at this art exhibit tonight. It's in Long Island City. She's got a friend who's an installation sculptor."

"You can see the Elliots all you want," says Jacob. "Leave me out of it."

"But this is us trying new things together. This is Ursula's advice."

"I didn't think *new things* meant all in on one couple. "

"It might be fun. And see, you're wrong!" I shake my phone like a castanet. I feel joyfully reaffirmed. "She'd so come here for cobbler."

"Or how about a date night, just us?" Jacob pulls out his own phone. "I'm on OpenTable." He goes quiet a moment, looking. "Want to go to Casa Nostra? Seven thirty? Be my date."

"What am I not getting here?"

He puts away his phone and shrugs on his jacket. "I'm here to rescue you from sacrificing yourself to weird art exhibits in the name of something new."

My eyes narrow. "What is this really about?"

He shrugs. "This isn't who I am. Friends with the superrich."

"Why not?" I ask. "Is there something you don't like about the Elliots personally? Or do you mean more like *ideologically*?"

I'm kidding, but Jacob looks thoughtful. "Last night, when I told Henry how Dad and I bring a cooler up to Tanner Lake Park for some catch-and-release, Henry sent me contact info for an Alaskan fly-fishing resort. Like maybe I was a guy who flew across the country to fish at a private lodge."

"So?"

"So, I let him think it. Easier than telling him I could never spend that kind of cash. I even looked up the website. Five days, ten thousand bucks—not including plane tickets."

"But is that the worst thing?" I ask. "To pretend a little?"

"Two nights of the Elliots, back-to-back, is pretending *a lot*," says Jacob. "Come on. Let's do our own thing tonight." It's true I'd rather enjoy a quiet evening with Jacob than trek out to Long Island City to stare at incomprehensible sculptures. On the other hand, I don't want to wreck my chances of being asked on future dates with Evelyn. Last night was like slipping into a ball gown and dancing a romantic waltz all around another life. "What if I don't want to eat the rich so much as sometimes dine out with them?" I ask. "You're really making me choose?"

But now Jacob's holding his smile like it's a hand he really needs to win. Any itch on my end doesn't come until later, when I text Evelyn that I can't make the show, and she only writes back k.

My itch stays with me right up until later that evening, when I see Jacob in the doorway from where I'm sitting in the dining room. He's managed to get in a haircut and shave today, and he looks so casually gorgeous as he moves through the space to our table that I can't take my eyes off him.

Last time we were at Casa Nostra, a sweetly rustic Northern Italian hideaway in Williamsburg, was for our anniversary two years ago. It's a bright, happy memory that beams through the fog of what sometimes can feel like the lost years of our IVF era.

Casa Nostra hasn't changed either. It's charming but not fussy. Pricey but doable.

We get the littleneck clams and a bottle of red to split, just like last time.

"This does feel like a bit of a rescue," I tell him.

Ten

Come with me to this on Friday? Henry's out of town to see his daughters this weekend.

Anticipation turns me weightless even before I check Evelyn's link. It's her first invitation since I declined the Long Island sculptures two weeks ago. No matter that she texts me almost every day and calls me most nights after she gets home, with breathless recaps about people out and behaving badly. She enjoys spinning a yarn, and I'm always ready to hear it.

If I'm on with Evelyn, Meg's night calls go right to voicemail.

Up? she will text me after she's left a message.

I'm up but not for colicky-Hailey talk. Always for Evelyn talk.

I click the link. Her invite is to a Broadway play in previews.

Love to!

Yay! And can you find me something to wear for it? Cocktail vintage?

While Evelyn hunts down a new assistant, she's entrusted me with her Platinum card and some of her former assistant Poppy's old responsibilities. I've relished being her personal stylist. Easy.

You're the best!

The shop is busy all morning, so I can't start looking until my lunch break. It's 10 percent challenge but 90 percent fun hunting down the Thierry Mugler cocktail dress in pale silk and glittering silver panels, available at Retrospect, an online retailer in Philadelphia. Next, I snap up a pair of heart-stabbing laser-green stiletto Zanottis at Vestige-Vintage in Los Feliz, California.

My best find is a Kieselstein-Cord gold-alligator cuff bracelet.

The dress and shoes top out at $7000, with $12,500 for the bracelet. Charging so much money leaves me woozy although, according to Evelyn, I don't have a limit. Her unique line of Amex numbers are more valuable than a Mega Ball ticket, and when I send her the ModernMirror file, I feel like someone with all the answers. She's going to look spectacular. This is my expertise and delight. I check my phone every few minutes. Her reply comes when I'm in the subway station.

I'll keep it all! You're an angel puff!

There's a ping from my phone as three hundred dollars hits my Zelle.

Evelyn, you don't have to pay me.

Honey, I know you're saving up! She sends a kiss-blowing emoji, and while I'm embarrassed about the money and the meaning behind it, I'm touched by Evelyn's empathy. I was pretty sure she'd forgotten most of what we'd talked about in the stoned soup of that night.

Thank you.

Want to do these too?

It's a pair of links: An invitation to a preshow cocktail party at the Lotos Club. A private room at Hearth for a small dinner afterward.

I get to be Evelyn's date for the entire evening. I float home.

"Just so I understand. Evelyn's paying you to be her stylist?" Jacob holds out a spoon for me to taste. He's made curry, which is his passion but not exactly his specialty. The sink is full of pots and pans, and there's no Anya to make them disappear.

"It's just a one-time thing, Jacob. It's something I'm good at."

"The worst negotiations are those that are unspoken."

I make a Vulcan sign. "Thanks, Mr. Spock."

"Solid advice, no matter who said it," says Jacob. He ladles the curry into bowls of rice.

"It's also your favorite *Star Trek* quote. Anyway, I'm not in negotiations for anything. I'm just happy for a night out." We each carry a bowl to the table. "It's nice to break patterns, right?" I don't mean it to sound like our dinners are a pattern in need of a break. But now Jacob looks hurt and guarded, like I told him exactly that.

"We were out last Monday," he says.

"I know, and I loved it—but this is dress-up! 'A whole to-do,' as Evelyn put it." Also, come to think, the last time I've gone anywhere lavish was Frankie and Seth's wedding in Nantucket. I get that Jacob's gloomy only because he can't deliver this night himself. I cheer him up by telling him this too-spicy curry is an improvement on his last overly spicy curry, and I save my excitement for Barb the next day.

Barb hops right into fairy godmother mode. The store is my oyster. I borrow a pale gray Moschino sheath with a steel metallic Oscar de la Renta bolero jacket.

On Friday, Frankie covers my lunch while I splurge on gel tips.

But that evening, as I walk alone through the door of the Lotos Club, reality catches up. Everyone's so crusty and conservative, with too many old men who look like the critics who boo Kermit. I'd bet I'm the only person in borrowed finery. How did I think this would be fun? I feel like a lost sock. Minutes drag by. I'm hiding behind a potted fern in a back corner, clutching my warm glass of prosecco and pretend-studying my phone, when Evelyn finally sweeps in.

She looks incredible—a vision in the Mugler and the Fendi baguette bag I found for her yesterday. She makes her smiling way toward me, and when we stand eye to chin—giantess Evelyn has me by at least five inches—I'm jolted by our physical similarity, which feels more apparent now that I'm dressed for an Evelyn-style occasion. We've both got our hair up. Should I take mine down so we aren't like a pair of Rockettes?

"Well, have a look at us!" Evelyn exclaims. She clearly doesn't mind the twinning. "We're a sister act tonight!"

It seems she means this literally. I try not to feel too scorched with self-consciousness as she locks elbows, wheeling me around the club, presenting me to all as "my big sister, Nora."

A few faces register surprise, but nobody is spoiling to contradict Evelyn, either. Mostly it's the opposite.

"A pair of stunners!" creaks a doyenne in a chocolate-brown '80s Bill Blass—I actually think it's from the shop, but I decide not to ask and out myself as a lowly pay-stubber.

"Nora! Lovely to finally meet you," says the thicket-bearded director of the play.

Their collective delight doesn't surprise me half as much as how I begin to feel about it. It's a peculiar thrill to be introduced as Evelyn's sister. A bold, smirky shortcut for telling everyone, *Yes, I do belong here.*

On those rare moments that Jacob and I find ourselves in social settings, we work hard to putter away from each other, to prove we can go it alone for ten-minute stretches of solo mingling. But tonight, with every handshake or double kiss, I ease into my new alter ego. The air feels buoyant with goodwill. What's more, wherever Evelyn and I go, our admirers move with us, the room tipping to whichever side we're on, pressing into Evelyn's attention and offering us extravagant praise. Eventually, I learn why. The Fitzroy Foundation underwrote this play and—since Evelyn's parents aren't here—we are the faces of the Fitzroy fortune.

Until tonight, I had never attended an evening that came anywhere near my mother's fairy-tale objectives. Not in college, and not when I moved myself and my seven cardboard packing boxes to the city, where Meg and I shared a one-bedroom. Our space was so tiny that we spent most of our off hours at whichever club happened to be trending in that week's issue of *TimeOut.* In crop tops and boot-cut jeans, our goth nails gripping Solo cups of overpriced Skyy Peach, we danced until our ears bled from house music and our eyeballs were seared by strobes. Once I'd met Jacob, my weekends became about our couple-hood, easy evenings followed by peaceful mornings with the Arts and Leisure section, enjoying our coffee-and-bagels breakfast. It's still how I prefer to sail around the town—by reading about it from the privacy of our Brooklyn walk-up.

But this evening is elevated. I'm gliding through my mother's fantasy city that never sleeps, all dressed up and in the center of the room. The attention cracks me open into a more extroverted, Evelyn-y self. By the time we get to the theater, I've got the hang of socialite Nora. I don't even correct people when they send regards to Beau and Bitsy, and I graciously accept thanks for the Fitzroy Foundation's unfailing support.

The one thing I can't copy is the way Evelyn throws around her opinions. She's so easy with her take on everything—the mayor, the Cotswolds, Beeple. I'd be too worried about being tasteless or hurtful or wrong. Is it her money that emboldens her? It must be her money. Even when she's wrong about something. In conversation with the director about his trip to the Falklands, Evelyn thought the Falklands were somewhere in the UK, and then she'd recovered the flub by insisting she was making a joke. The director played right along.

Backstage after the play, I meet a movie star whose name everyone already knows and who acts like he's met me before since I'm clearly just another member of New York's social elite.

We even run into some paparazzi outside Hearth.

They're taking your picture, Nora! I can hear my mother's voice, hushed and awed in my head as Evelyn and I swan into the restaurant. *You might even wind up in* People *magazine!*

There's security everywhere, probably due to all the bold-faced names, and I feel valuable by association, like one of Queen Elizabeth's corgis. Afterward, when we leave Hearth, people practically stand to salute Evelyn, loading her up with send-off praise as if she wrote the play herself. I get the spillover smiles. A television actress who knows Evelyn from their neighboring Hamptons homes says she loves my bag, and we should all go shopping together. I agree that would be a fabulous plan.

The entire evening feels unreal—a glittery spin inside the glass kingdom of Libre d'Orange.

"Sigh! I sort of think it might have been a mistake, to produce a play about September Eleventh," says Evelyn as we kick off our heels, Evelyn's chauffeured town car slaloming down empty, late-night Seventh Avenue. "Or maybe this was just the wrong play about it."

"It wasn't bad." Though yes, it was. I search for an acceptable opinion. "It was loud."

"They tell me what they think I want to hear, but the early reviews are mixed—and then to suffer through all those depressing *where were you* stories, good gravy."

I was upstate and in college when the towers fell. Classes were canceled, and Meg and I hunkered down in our dorm with our friends, slurping takeout ramen, our eyes ablaze on the news. Tonight, I learned Evelyn was with her parents on a luxury cruise, skipping her first week of boarding school to do "The Crossing" of the Atlantic Ocean from England to New York. They'd been about to dock when the ship was diverted to Boston.

Every time I heard Evelyn tell that story tonight, I felt slightly embarrassed for her. Obviously, nobody would call her out for being spoiled. But shouldn't somebody let her know it might be perceived as out of touch? Wasn't that the job of a friend? Like the way Meg once told me my heels were dry and cracked as pony hooves. Or when I had to check Meg's self-tanning habits when her skin started to look like a canned peach. I feel like an eighth grader, all fidgety, lip-chewing doubt.

"Oh, and that story of yours, Evelyn." I shake my head. "A cruise ship! Not exactly the most relatable anecdote."

She looks so startled that I regret this comment as soon as it's out. Of course, nobody criticizes Evelyn. Too much opinion from me! "I wouldn't wish it on anyone," she says, her voice cool.

"I didn't mean it that way," I say quickly.

"We had a front row view, and it was terrible." Her lips press together. "I'm the same amount of human as you, Spell."

"I'm really sorry."

"Aw, sugar, I'm only messing with you." She bursts out laughing. "And it's not like I was telling my luxury liner story over at Dave and Buster's. You can always tell la-di-da stories around la-di-da people." She sounds like she's speaking to convince herself. "I'll have Max drop me at my door. Then he'll take you over the bridge and home, okay?"

"Ha, great, yes. Thanks." I exhale into a laugh, though my heart is beating at a hard clap. Like the Falklands moment, I'm not sure Evelyn was working on her gotcha moment, but I'm not going to call her out on it. In a world that keeps telling her how right she is, maybe it's hard for her to admit when she's wrong.

"You keep me real, Spell," she says. "Nobody wanted to say to my face if that play was just as awful as all get-out. Sometimes I can't breathe from these things, and I'm only here on account of the Foundation, which really means to please my parents. But every time I looked over, I could see this was a kick for you."

"I had so much fun," I tell her honestly. "And I loved being your sister tonight."

Early the next morning, I'm buzzed with a Zelle notification from Evelyn Elliot for five hundred dollars.

I bolt upright in bed. What's this for?

Can you style me for the French Heritage Society's Proust Ball next Saturday? Your usual magic—source the outfit, style the bag. I wouldn't ask except you're good at it!

Jacob and I were planning to head out to Lake George that same weekend.

Thought you might want the job. She adds the pregnant woman and the wink and the cash stack and the heart emojis.

I can sense Evelyn's trying to make this transaction less awkward and more intimate, but it feels mortifying, as if she's helping me stuff money into my baby savings cookie jar.

In the kitchen, Jacob hands off my smoothie, and I show him my Zelle.

"What's that about?"

"To style Evelyn for a fancy party. How is this so bitter?"

"Because of the kale. Or maybe the apple cider vinegar. Do it in one big gulp."

"The money's not nothing."

"I'm not in your way," Jacob says after a moment, and I can hear that he's trying to sound casual and cheerful while probably feeling neither. But it's good money, and we need it. "We can go to Lake George another weekend."

"Then I'll do it," I decide. "Since she's already Zelle'd me. And then I'll talk to her about not dropping cash on me like this. I want to establish some boundaries."

"I doubt Evelyn needs any clarity on boundaries," says Jacob. "She's good to act like you two are sisters one minute, and let you get down on your hands and knees to hem her skirt the next."

"That's a little brutal," I say. "I just don't want the money part to matter."

"Nore, don't kid yourself," says Jacob. "The money part always matters."

Eleven

Dean Nicholson's apartment in Chelsea reminds me of him—spare, elegant, and discreet. He's got an alfresco lunch waiting for Jacob and me. We spread the cloak in a swoon across his couch, then enjoy Greek salad and pear tartine in the postcard Shangri-La he's made of his small outdoor space.

Dean is recently retired, and he catches us up on his life with the ease of someone luxuriating in a newfound abundance of free time. After he refreshes our iced teas, he brings out a tin of shortbread cookies and a book.

"I found this for you at The Strand, Nora," he says. "Though I'm sure you've read it."

"Thanks—yes, I've read it, but I don't own it." I take the book he's offering, an out-of-print biography of Frieda Bergessen. I turn it over in my hand. Its crackled Mylar jacket is Scotch-Taped across the front, bisecting the hand-tinted photo of a baby-faced Frieda just before her catapult into fame.

"A big twenties and thirties," I say, "and a quiet everything after."

Dean nods. "Her popularity didn't survive the war, but she spent her happiest years up in the Berkshires, observing the seasons and finding poetry in everything from her calico cats to her walks in the woods. I also marked where it mentions Evelyn's family connection."

Dean's stuck a Post-it to a photograph of Frieda squashed between a couple on a porch swing. The man and woman are laughing and turned toward Frieda, who is erect as a puppet. Her stare into the camera is atomic.

There's a joke happening here. I certainly don't get it. But what I can tell is that Frieda's not enjoying it.

"I'm sure I looked at this photo when I read this book before. It's a fresh context now that I know Evelyn." I read the caption out loud. "'Bergessen, pictured in the summer of 1946 with Evelyn Stoker Fitzroy and her husband, Theodore Fitzroy, Jr., at the family farm, *Old Orchard*. Bergessen had a lifelong regard for the Southern socialite.'"

"The piece you've brought is a cleaner spin on Dior's cut," says Dean. "But anyone looking for haute Dior wants his New Look. The fox trim, the soutache, the mink extending down the front. All the bells and whistles."

"What about the fact that an almost-famous poet wore it?" asks Jacob.

"There's a photo of her wearing it too," I add.

"That helps. Nora, remember Joanne Speck?" asks Dean.

"The tank watch." I groan. "How could I forget?"

Years ago, I'd gone along with Dean, a senior appraiser, to meet Joanne Speck in her studio apartment in Lenox Hill. A former model, Joanne showed us photo albums from her days palling around with Brigitte Bardot and Gunter Sachs in Capri, and she informed us that her Cartier watch, a pink-gold face with a cordovan leather strap, was a gift from Babe Paley.

The watch itself was gorgeous. But with no monogram or proof of provenance, all we had was a fun story. Joanne sold it reluctantly for fourteen thousand dollars, a lot less than she'd hoped. Then, a few years later, a photograph circulated of young Paley wearing the same watch.

Sotheby's scooped this image and—with some flashy copy evoking the glamour of that bygone era—used it for the inside front page of its catalog when they obtained the watch as part of their International Fine Jewelry Auction. They resold the watch for a quarter million.

Mrs. Speck was not amused. She left Dean several spiteful messages, using shocking, inventive combinations of very bad words.

"The needlework is stunning," says Dean. "These vermicelli stitches. The tubing and paillettes. That gold thread. You need a special buyer who recognizes its worth."

"But who's that special buyer?" asks Jacob. "Count Dracula?"

"One rich count will do the trick," says Dean. "But I don't see anyone bidding past twenty-five hundred. Three, best case."

We leave with promises on both sides to reconnect soon for an Odeon night.

"You've been quiet," I say to Jacob on the subway. "But I hear your mind whirling."

"What if we put it up on this site?" Jacob thrusts his phone at me. "Curiosity Corners? It sells vintage weirdness. Elvis Presley's Bible just went for ninety-four thousand dollars."

"That's because of dedicated Elvis superfans."

"The Aston Martin from *Goldfinger* sold for seven million."

"Intense James Bond people crossed with rabid antique-cars people."

"For five thousand you can own scraps of Charles the First's beard. Snipped by his personal physician after he was beheaded. It's DNA certified."

I shiver. "I don't want to think about people who buy beheaded beard scraps."

Jacob is still scrolling. "Guess how much Marilyn Monroe's *Seven Year Itch* dress sold for? That subway grate dress..."

"Hollywood's not my specialty."

"Humor me."

I sigh. "It's a known dress, a known costume designer, William Travilla. Mint condition since the dress was always famous. Six hundred thousand?"

"Thanks for playing." Jacob's eyes dance. "Five point two million."

"Wow, okay. Was not expecting."

"There are over thirteen thousand Bergessen hashtags on Twitter," says Jacob, deep in his phone again. "Huh. So she's not as stone-cold obscure as I thought."

"Frieda Bergessen was a one-hit wonder *poet* from a hundred years ago," I say. "She doesn't have Marilyn Monroe's star power. Or Sylvia Plath's star power. She doesn't even have Elizabeth Bishop's star power. There are zero intense Frieda Bergessen people."

"Let's put it on Curiosity Corners for a week. See if we get any bites."

"I don't want bites. You wanted an appraisal. Dean, who's a certified appraiser, guessed three thousand, tops. I know that's different from what Henry told us, but the estimate on a luxury-gift tax write-off isn't the same as how you'd price it in the commercial marketplace. We made a deal, and it's still worth less than your Peugeot bike. So we get to keep it."

"It's just like the Paley watch—we don't know what we've got," he says.

I try another angle. "Since I'm currently earning some money working for Evelyn," I say, "I'd prefer to focus on that instead of looking for ways to mess up my relationship with her." It's a thought that I speak before I have time to process it. But it's true. I've never earned more money than Jacob until Evelyn began padding my income, and along this line of reasoning, I feel a new twitch of power—and I don't mind it.

Even if it drives a wedge into this conversation.

Even if we are silent for the rest of the ride home.

Twelve

Evelyn calls me at the shop the next day to see if I can come over to her apartment and sew a bird's-eye back on the Galliano that I've couriered for her to wear to the Proust Ball.

"It's too gorgeous to save," she says, "so I'm wearing it to Bryce's tonight. I'll Zelle you another five hundred if you hunt me down a new dress. I know, I'm such a pain!" She laughs off her confessional truth-telling.

I agree to come see her after work.

And now I need to reschedule tonight's date with Frankie.

"Will we ever hang out again in this lifetime?" he asks as we close shop. "Also, I've got a request. I'd planned to do it at drinks."

I stop buttoning my coat. "Ask me now."

"All right, well." Frankie's hand is at his neck. "Seth and I want to appoint you and Jacob to be the twins' legal guardians."

I freeze.

His eyes widen, mirroring mine. "If it feels like a lot, Nore, you don't have to do it. But we can't think of a better couple to take the twins if we die in the proverbial fiery plane crash."

"Frankie! We'd be honored!" Though I feel short of breath, picturing

Jacob and me like a traumatized childless couple in a German fairy tale, catching those orphans as they fall from the sky. Our good fortune at a terrible price. It's moments like this when I realize I haven't moved past my grief at all; I've just hidden it, like a drop cloth thrown over a pile of broken glass.

"Can we get a date on the books for real talk?" Frankie asks. "I miss you."

"Me too." These past few weeks, I've ducked three of Frankie's invitations for drinks or dinner—mostly so that I can avoid listening to his topic of choice, impending fatherhood. But I'm becoming a bad friend, the person I swore I wouldn't be. Irish goodbye-ing my way out of his life when he needs support most. The only family who came to Frankie's wedding were an aunt and uncle and his little sister, Trix.

Frankie's big brown eyes are unblinking on me, and there's a seriousness in his face. He's feeling the rumble of change in his life; he's nervous and determined; he wants to talk about it and he wants me to care. I do care. I can do better.

"Next week. Pick your night," I tell him. "We'll go to a very Frankie place with cocktails that take at least twenty minutes to prepare."

"I'll drink to that." He smiles. "And before you go—look. Sixteen weeks." He hands me his phone.

The twins are a pair of melon-head aliens suspended in the grainy weather forecast of their ultrasound image. I'm rapt as Frankie points out knees and noses, but when he takes back his phone, I keep my head down. Intently watching my fingers buttoning my coat. Winding my scarf up and over my chin like a mummy so it hides anything raw and pitiful printed on my face. I need to get to Evelyn's. I need to make sure she's still mine.

Thirteen

S angria?" Evelyn asks the moment I step onto her roof deck. "I got the recipe from Hotel Xcaret in Mexico."

"Wow. Thanks." I hold up my sewing basket. "I came prepared."

"You're the best." Evelyn reaches for the pitcher as Anya, who delivered me here, now leaves us. Evelyn's hair and makeup people have come and gone, serving her with this evening's loose waves and eyelash extensions. "And how drop-dead gorgeous is this? You've got a real jeweler's eye for what works best on me." She indicates the Meng robe she's wearing that I also found for her this week. It's a light piece, silky and breathable, a watercolor-blossoms print with dolman sleeves and a delicate ruffle around the hem. Each detail of the wrap is a small victory for me—the ruching that doesn't pinch her middle, the banded sash that adds weight but doesn't hamper the drop.

"Now come take a load off," she instructs, pouring me a glass.

I drop into the chaise next to hers. The clouds are just beginning to lift on a Manhattan sundown when Anya reappears with a tray of tidily compartmentalized dried fruits, nuts, and olives. Listening to Evelyn chat about her impending dinner party, I feel the pressures of my day dissolve. The confused but mostly cranky old guy who returned a smoking jacket that he'd in fact purchased at Decades, a vintage shop in Los Angeles. The Hunter College girls who tried on everything; turned the dressing room into molehills of wrinkled, discarded clothing and then left empty-handed—or so we thought until Frankie discovered the detached ink tag in the bathroom's wastepaper basket and our black velvet Azzedine Alaïa catsuit missing.

But now I'm in the kingdom of Evelyn. Where her smile and this delicious sangria make me feel cared for.

Monogrammed tumblers too! trills my mother's voice. *Greek olives as big as malt balls!*

After we've drained our drinks and the sun has sunk, I follow Evelyn downstairs and along the hall to her dressing room. But it's all different. I step back, confused. The rose golds of the dressing room are gone, replaced with heavy creams and shiny brass that evoke a feel of Old Hollywood.

"Cute rethink, right?" Evelyn lifts onto her toes and twirls. She looks so tall and yet graceful, like an exotic bird. "This room needed a glow-up."

Did it? The bookshelf with the first editions is gone too. But to ask where they went might rupture the mood. Evelyn disappears into her walk-in closet and returns with the navy Galliano slip dress I'd sourced from Elle Encore Couture, its sheer-tulle back scattered with an appliqué riot of hummingbirds and flowers. She finds the ruby bird's-eye where she's kept it in a ring box in her dressing table drawer. I open the basket and search out the right needle and thread.

"I'll be quick."

"Take your time. You know Bryce, so type A. I think I almost *want* to be late, just to get under her skin."

Bryce Appell was a couple of years behind me at Phelps College, and Evelyn always assumes I know her, but I don't. None of my friends did. Bryce, granddaughter of cosmetics mogul Opal Appell, mostly orbited our collegiate life in sightings and rumors.

Her family foundation is putting twenty-five kids through Phelps every year.

Britney Spears performed for her tenth birthday party.

Her grandfather is cryogenically frozen in Zurich.

Bryce and I intersected once when we were getting to-go, on-campus coffees at Wake-Up Café. She asked me to pass her the soy milk, and we shared a moment about how the lids never fit. I attended Phelps on a Pell Grant and half a dozen other stitched-together loans, plus all my mother's savings. I balanced classes with a full-time work-study library job, and most of my meal plan was Cup Noodles. Bryce had a Lamborghini and a bodyguard.

The bird's-eye is a droplet of ruby, surrounded by tinier beads of jet-black.

I squint, choose a thinner needle, and thread it.

"Bryce and Jorge tell us eight," says Evelyn as she sits at her dressing table and screws a gumdrop-sized diamond into each ear. "But they don't even serve until nine. When they hosted the Friendsgiving last year, we were snoring in our vichyssoise."

"Friendsgiving... Is that a tradition?" I ask.

"It's more like my reaction to a tradition. It's inspired by the show *Friends*. Bryce and Pauline and I rotate who's the Monica. It's me this year." Evelyn takes a pavé-diamond necklace from her jewelry box. "Help with this?"

I put down my sewing and move to stand behind her, arranging the necklace around her neck. It's my *Downton Abbey* moment, where I'm the lady's maid in black bombazine, dressing glamorous Lady Evelyn for dinner.

"Look at us," says Evelyn, and I glance up from the catch and hoop to see Evelyn staring at our reflections in the mirror. Our physical similarity is like a shared electrical current, though Evelyn is all glossy hair, glazed makeup, and sparkling diamonds.

I look down to fasten the necklace's clasp and then its safety catch. Evelyn is still staring at us in the mirror. "I've got an idea—why don't I bring you on for my Friendsgiving? Then I know it'd be special. Poppy was fixing to do a whole Gatsby thing. You could manage that, Spell. You'd find me a fun outfit, and you'd be so clever at decorating the table, scouring around for all those antique-y little party favors."

"Do you mean plan your Thanksgiving for you?" I'm already shaking my head. "Don't you go see your family?"

"My parents use Thanksgiving to do a couple's detox at their favorite ashram in Miramar," says Evelyn. "It's the one holiday I don't have to hear my dad preach about ethics and capitalism and football."

"We always go to Massapequa," I say as I return to my chair and the sewing. "Every year since we got married."

"Just saying, it can be fun to spend one holiday with people you choose. Xander loves to drop his Gen Z wisdom on me, telling me how Thanksgiving is next up to be canceled. But *Friendsgiving*, I tell him, now that's just chitchatting and pie à la mode. And if I had you, then you'd make it your own quirky special Spell-thing, and you'd keep everything well managed."

"There's no I way I could miss—"

"I'd pay you too, of course. I know a little extra in your pocket helps the dream along." She winks.

Evelyn means well, but the phrase *a little extra in your pocket* feels humiliating, like I'm an urchin selling peanuts from a handcart.

"Evelyn, I'm touched that you're thinking about Jacob and me, and our financial situation," I say, "and I'd do this job for free, as a favor for a friend, if I could—but I can't."

"How about don't give me an answer right this minute," Evelyn says, even though I just did, "and help me get into my dress?"

And so I retrieve the Galliano and finish helping Lady Evelyn dress for her dinner party.

Fourteen

"A re you kidding?" Jacob stares at me for a second or two. "Tell me you're kidding." I've waited until Sunday when we're at the dog park. A good place to deliver big news. Jacob can't slam out the door if he's already outside.

"I'm not. I said I wouldn't do it. But then yesterday she Venmoed me—and she wrote me a very kind note about it, too, thanking me."

"*Very kind* note? Who *very kind* gives a crap? She's *paying* you to handle her *Thanksgiving*. It doesn't even make sense. Thanksgiving is just cafeteria food. Nobody cares if you burn the green beans." He's shaking his head. "I don't get it."

"We don't have to do it, obviously," I say, "but it might be interesting to spend one holiday with people we choose?"

"But I didn't choose the goddamn Elliots," says Jacob, pulling his hands through his hair so that it sticks up like grass. "I barely know them! And I thought you liked visiting my folks."

"I do!" Though in recent years, our visits coincided with a couple of IVF-related hormone crashes, and one of my less-joyous Hammond holiday memories is when I hid in the powder room, hissing "Get it together, Nora!" at the mirror like I was giving some psychotic TED Talk.

Jacob pops up from the park bench. He's got Nick's ball knuckled. "Is this because of last Thanksgiving with Dad?"

"Okay, now, just hang on a minute. Last year, that was *you* who got into it with your dad. The whole baby-racket conversation? That was you, Jacob. Not me."

"It's not like I'm holding a grudge. We were fine by Christmas."

"I'm not holding a grudge either," I say, "but it's been harder at your parents' lately."

"We can't just exile ourselves from them."

"It's nobody's fault that we want to try new—"

"Try new things. Gotcha," snaps Jacob. "Except these days *new things* means *Evelyn Elliot*, and to be honest, I think it's effed up. She's clearly glitched on how to have a level-playing-field relationship with a non-socialite person, so she's put you in this other category where she bankrolls PA jobs because you can't do the rich-lady things with her, like race speedboats or eat truffles and blowfish, or whatever she gets up to with all her little trust-fund pals."

"She gives me the jobs because she thinks we're saving for a surrogate," I tell him.

Jacob throws me a pained look. "Okay, that doesn't make it better. Dangling the money in front of you because she knows we need it? The whole thing is nuts. Including her stupid, stage-managed Thanksgiving." He pitches the ball so far that it arcs past the dog run and drops deep into the soccer field.

Nick blasts off as a pack of bigger dogs all barrel ahead of her, mowing her down.

"I'll Venmo her back the money."

"How much was it? Another five hundred?"

"Fifteen hundred, actually."

Jacob gapes, starts to say something, then shakes his head and decides to sprint across the green. I watch him wrestle the ball from the teeth of a Great Dane. I whistle for Nick, who's no longer interested in the great ball chase and is now sniffing around a trash can for possible snacks.

She trots back diligently, but Jacob stays on the run to play catch with the big dogs and maybe get his mind around the money.

When Jacob and I got married at his parents' house nearly eight years ago, it set a comfortable tone for a relationship with my in-laws that I've always been happy about, even if our at-home wedding dashed Jacob's dreams of a Hyatt packed with all his buddies performing badly executed flash mob dance moves to Bruno Mars's "Marry You." With Meg as my maid of honor, I descended the staircase in a bohemian '70s-era dress I bought off Etsy and met Jacob at the living room fireplace as his dad, Phil, joyfully banged out the "Allegro" from Vivaldi's *The Four Seasons* on the Steinway upright. Our backyard reception was picnic tables set with checked gingham tablecloths and a wheelbarrow stocked with Dad and Gabi's favorite longneck beers. Lunch was sandwiches and wraps, cold cuts and cheeses, fruit salad and ice cream, and Sandy's three-tiered raspberry-jam cake.

The Hammond-family wedding photo abides in a silver frame on the piano. I've never seen evidence of a bigger smile on my face; on that day, I felt as complete within a family as I'd ever been since my mother died.

But the house of Hammonds was a big change for me. Even before she got sick, my mom was a homebody edging into recluse. She'd grown up a foster kid, bumped indifferently through the system, and for as long as I could remember, she'd been a loner, deeply mistrustful of the outside world. She didn't do field trips or adventures—she didn't even like to answer the door. She could imagine no better company than just the two of us at home, watching old movies and sharing a box of butterscotch Tastykakes, our knitting needles clacking in compatible rhythm. Now I was part of a rowdy bunch who loved lawn football and show tunes, the latter led by Phil, who teaches music at Massapequa High, where he also plays piano for their theater productions. When they were boys, Jacob and his brother, Peter, were neighborhood-known for their backyard bouncy castle in July and their light-up roof Santa in December.

A smile is the curve that sets everything straight is the first framed needlepoint you meet in their foyer. It's a Phil and Sandy Hammond quote aesthetic that feels exactly them.

As newlyweds, Jacob and I told everyone we wanted to have kids right away. It just seemed foregone that within a couple of years, we'd be adding another member to the happy Hammond household. We made giddy plans about how the first thing we'd do after a positive test was to get Pinkberry and a cup of Frosty Paws for Nick—who was brand new in our lives, so it seemed important to include her in our family-building milestones. We picked baby names and preschools and hypothesized how our combined DNA might shuffle and merge into all different possibilities of this new exceptional human.

Two years later, Peter and Marisol were married. Oliver Luke Hammond was born one year after, a complicated pregnancy that secured Ollie's place as an only child.

But still no positives, no Pinkberry, no Frosty Paws.

About a year after Ollie arrived, Phil and Sandy began to speak up.

"It was the same month we stopped trying that it happened for us."

"Champagne and Bing Crosby, and let the night take care of itself."

"It'd be good for Ollie to have a cousin. Especially if he's not getting that sibling."

From Phil, I learned, "Sometimes when you want something so bad, it pressurizes your whole system. I'd roll a squash ball under my feet at night. I carry all my stress in my feet."

From Sandy, "When Phil and I were, ah—trying? My doctor recommended Epsom salts. Epsom salts are lovely, and I just saw they've got a deal on two-pound bags on Amazon."

When squash balls and sitz baths didn't light the path to grandchildren, the Hammonds went quiet. But then, last Thanksgiving, gathered on the porch before Jacob and I left for the train, Phil and Sandy emboldened themselves to ask for an update.

We were frank. We told them about our year in failed in vitros. Our doctor's advice.

"How about putting that money into a real home?" asked Phil. "Lots of better places for your savings than the baby racket."

"All right, Dad," said Jacob. "I don't remember hiring you to be our life coach."

"It's just common sense. More sense than pay this doctor, pay that lady," Phil grumbled. "In my opinion? A couple having a baby should be the most natural thing." He cut his eyes at me. A micro-moment, and yet I felt instantly ashamed and defensive.

Jacob saw it in my face. He stood. "Okay, folks. We need a lift."

"I thought your train wasn't for another couple of hours," said Sandy.

"And when are you two buying another car?" asked Phil.

"You'll be the first to hear when we do," said Jacob.

"I'm sorry about Phil," Sandy said to me at the station. "He worries, and it comes out scrambly. Your luck will change. I know it. Remember, no winter lasts forever, and no spring skips its turn."

She was quoting her own cross-stitch from a pillow in their den, but I knew Sandy meant well. She always stood by her embroidery.

A few weeks later, Jacob and Phil got together for a father-son lunch, and this was the start of smoothing things over. When we went out to visit them last Christmas, there was no talk about in vitro or the fact that we still don't have a car.

We probably owe them a visit, but it's just been easier not to engage for a while.

Fifteen

"You really don't mind working on the holiday?" Jacob asks that night in bed.

"I don't mind the fifteen hundred. Evelyn wants you to come too, of course."

After a minute, Jacob says, "I think Mom and Dad will survive."

"If we put that money toward our Citi Cash card," I say, "we almost clear it."

"Yep."

"And you'll come with me?"

"Yeah." Jacob lightly knocks his foot against mine. "We're in this together."

When I text Evelyn that I'll handle her party, she sends me a string of turkey and heart emojis, plus her Friendsgiving to-do list, along with another task list of must-have fashion items—both vintage and contemporary—that she wants me to track down.

The next day, she pops over another to-do; this list detailing her personal travel schedule, along with some errands.

Please deal? Just a teeny bit of PA work.

Is the "teeny bit of work" included in the original fifteen-hundred-dollar payment? I'm not sure how to ask or how to say no, so I tap a thumbs-up.

Evelyn is on a lot of planes this month, often in service to the family foundation, alighting into board meetings and dropping off sacks of the Fitzroy fortune like a philanthropic stork. I coordinate her travel to Miami and Los Angeles, and her trip to Montreal to attend a friend's birthday party. I style her for the Fashion for Action dinner and the UNICEF Snowflake Ball.

For her Friendsgiving, I find an authentic 1920s Jean Patou–couture glass-beaded rose-motif dress with a scalloped hemline.

Nailed it! I'm sending you something fun to say thanks.

Later that afternoon at the shop, I sign for a messaged delivery of a brand-new Celine tote bag. That evening, I photograph and post it for sale on Fashionphile. I don't let myself feel guilty about it; I know it's not a sentimental purchase on her end. Evelyn routinely sends out expensive, impersonal birthday and thank-you gifts. But I don't need a Celine tote. I need money.

The bag sells that week. For $1840.00.

Jacob and I pay off the last of the Citi Card debt, and another old bite stops itching.

Frankie and I make a date for Wednesday at Temple Court, the bar at the Beekman Hotel, though by the time we get down there—after a detour to look at baby-changing tables at Babesta—we're up for one cocktail, maximum. It's been a day. A few weekends ago, Barb went rogue at an estate sale up in Millbrook, and this morning her purchases arrived at the shop in several large dress boxes for Frankie and me to unpack in horror.

Neither of us criticized Barb in the moment—she didn't even seem to remember what she'd bought, then insisted the spangled, crinoline-choked formalwear needed only some love and industrial steam cleaning before she retreated to her apartment for an afternoon nap. But it will be next to impossible to sell these gowns.

"I feel like we just spent an afternoon backstage at the Ice Capades," says Frankie once we're ensconced at the bar and have ordered a pair of aviation cocktails—we're both curious about this mysterious ingredient crème de violette. The drinks arrive in martini glasses and we touch them before we sample-sip what looks like—*don't think it*—lavender hand soap.

"Just to be clear, this is not a celebration drink for the warehouse of Bob Mackie that just got dumped on us," says Frankie.

"Poor Barb, what was she thinking?" I sigh. "I love Mackie, but he's a lot."

"I can't imagine any client who'd be down to wear her weight in Swarovski crystals," says Frankie, "except maybe your Evelyn."

"Not even Evelyn," I say.

"Are you still moonlighting as her stylist?"

"Yep." I try a sip of the drink, picturing delicious violets.

He sips too. "Is this drink bad? I can't tell."

"It's maybe good? As for the Evelyn jobs, I'm not complaining," I say. "Jacob and I aren't out of debt yet, so every little bit helps."

"Yeah, I'd hold on to that side hustle. If Barb loses the rest of her marbles and keeps buying leftovers from the costume department of *My Fair Lady*, you and I could find ourselves out of a day job." Frankie's downplaying it for the cocktail hour, but we're both unhappily aware we haven't enjoyed an Evelyn-style binge buyer in the shop since, well, Evelyn. The cash flow at I'll Have Seconds is at an all-time trickle.

"I like the extra work, but Jacob is skeptical of Evelyn," I admit. "I think the power of her money unsettles him."

"Jacob doesn't give off threatened-masculinity energy," says Frankie.

"I agree," I say, "but Jacob and I never snipe at each other the way we do about her—which is odd, considering we've been through a lot more turmoil than Evelyn."

Frankie tries another mini-sip of the drink. "You two ever think about adopting?" he asks. "Or is that one of those taboo questions I'm not supposed to ask because obviously you've thought about it, and also it's none of my business?"

"Ha, it's fine," I say. "It's a reasonable question—and sure, we've talked about it. But that's an expensive, multi-step path." I take a second sip. It's not what I expected, and not in a good way. "Right now, we're paying eight hundred dollars a year to keep an embryo banked at NYU Hospital. That's real money for us, but I think as long as we're clinging to this one specific possibility in the physical world, it holds us back from other choices." I shrug. "You could say we're in frozen-embryo limbo."

"*Frozen-Embryo Limbo* sounds like the name of all the bands I saw in the East Village in my twenties," says Frankie. "But that's a hard one. Seth and I got four blastocysts with our egg donor. We used two on the first round with Lisa Ann, and neither took. Next round, both did— but thank God we don't have any extra embryos to consider in all this. Shopping for double strollers is surreal enough." On his next sip of the aviation, he shakes his head. "Is it a *pigment* of my imagination, or are you tasting notes of church and old pocketbooks?"

"*Hue* know it," I say theatrically. "I think I can also taste why crème de violette got left behind in the Gilded Age."

Frankie pushes the drink away and signals the bartender. "Let's see if we can exchange these for a couple of craft beers."

Sixteen

Thanksgiving Day, I go one more lap around the table for twenty that Evelyn called out of her storage. Bryce and Jorge Appell's two boys, plus Keith and Pauline Chen's three children are grouped at the smaller round table. I recount forks and spoons, wine- and water glasses, the pressed Deco-mosaic napkin rings—all part of Evelyn's "Gatsby" theme—along with every piece of Evelyn's own '20s-era gilt-edged Minton English china.

In the kitchen, I check in with Tabitha, who is chopping garnishes and setting glazes.

"Fun to connect with some of my odds-and-endsies I haven't seen in a while," is how Evelyn explained her guest list to me. She's also folded in some of Henry's odds-and-endsies, including his two grown daughters, down from Boston, where they're both in school to become teachers—Claire for history, Ann-Marie for special education—and Ann-Marie's fiancé, Dave, who's got a sniffle. Claire and Ann-Marie tread carefully around their stepmother, as if they know they're violating the fun of Friendsgiving by being plain old boring family. But if the point of the day is untethering from traditional obligations, both Elliot girls seem to get it. They are all polite, understated sweetness when I look in on them downstairs watching television in the games room along with the younger children and a stonily expressionless Jacob, who has his eye trained on the football.

We trade brief, tight-lipped smiles that we're in this together.

As soon as I get back upstairs, Evelyn signals for me to come say hi to Bryce, who pretends that she remembers me from Phelps. If Bryce lacks Evelyn's dazzle, she's held on to her own delicate brand of femininity in her bias-cut ballerina-pink satin that calls to mind a Jean Harlow–style dressing gown. She asks about my outfit that I'm passing off as attributed Chanel when really it's an old Gunne Sax dress I bought years ago at Antiques Depot in Jersey City.

I'm talking to Bryce Appell instead of about her! It's a wild thought, and I'll have to remember details for Meg.

Then Bryce and Evelyn pick up their talk about weekend plans to stay at Bryce's lodge in Ketchum. It's a shift in topic that is not my reality, and so I quietly excuse myself for another check-in downstairs.

"How's it going?" I ask Jacob.

"Still going," he answers, with a look that conveys both his annoyance to be down here with the children and a reluctance to move upstairs where he'd be expected to talk with the husbands.

Upstairs again, I restock the ice and guest towels, and then I move Dave's place card so that he and his contagions are sequestered toward the end of the table. Once everybody's seated, there's excitement about the table gifts—engraved playing cards for the men, driving gloves for the women, checkers and tiddlywinks games boxes for the kids.

"I'm obsessed with the twenties," says Bryce as she flaps her gloves at me. "How did you find all these cute things?" From the head of the table, Evelyn jumps in to tell the story of the day we met, the tucked-away enchantment of I'll Have Seconds, and our Bergessen connection. This prompts Bryce to launch impromptu into the first line of "Way to Find Me." "'Born twice at sixteen. Caught fire, caught up!'"

"I remember that one," says Pauline. "We had to study it for school."

"Like 'The Jabberwocky,'" says Ann-Marie. "Or that one about fences."

"Not sure I know 'Way to Find Me,'" says Keith Chen.

Evelyn points down the table at me. "Spell, could you do it? Please?"

Dave is tapping his spoon against his glass. I fight my embarrassment as I begin reciting the poem, and I'm relieved when other voices immediately join in, until everyone who knows it roars the last line—"And you who know the way to me/My way to you was not a lie!"—followed by a smattering of good-natured applause.

Next, Claire and Ann-Marie recite "The Jabberwocky." Then Keith and Pauline's sixth-grader son, Louis, procures a cardboard paper towel tube and uses it as a microphone to give us Captain America's "Whatever It Takes" speech from *Avengers Endgame*. Louis hands off the paper towel tube to Dave, who meets the moment, reciting a poem about taking a night drive—which afterward he confesses are just the lyrics to "Standing Still" by Jewel.

"I love that song," Dave says.

Evelyn catches my eye and winks. She is incandescent with approval. Here's the easy-breezy, low-stakes, quirky, and well-managed Friendsgiving she'd wanted.

"My grandmother adores the history of American fashion," Bryce tells me later as the guests are gathering themselves to go. "She'd adore you too."

Opal Appell's possible adoration of me feels like a little shake of snow globe glitter over the night. It's not until later, outside and heading down Broadway to pick up the Q, that I feel like I've landed back inside my own body. Jacob puts his arm around me, and we bump compatibly against together as we walk.

"The dinner party was, by all accounts, a smashing success," he says in a plummy English accent.

"Not too sad to miss a day with family?"

He shrugs. "All things considered? It was fine."

"So you'd do it again?"

"No! *All things considered* meant I was considering only the money," says Jacob. "But I'd cohost Thanksgiving with you. At our place, with our own family."

"I like that! We'd squeeze in everyone who wants to come—and we'd make it a potluck, and we'd cool the pies on the living room windowsill."

"And Nick Charles finally gets her big chance to recite a selection of her favorite dog poems."

"Yes, it's time she shared her talent with the world." But I hope Jacob isn't fully kidding, because it captivates me, this notion of Thanksgiving with Jacob's family and mine. Of course, we've got only one bathroom. It might even be a fire hazard, having nine people in our apartment.

"You've gotta be feeling wiped out," Jacob says when we're riding the train, Gowanus-bound. It's one of the older models, squeaky on the tracks. Multicolored seats and hard ocher light. "Making things perfect for Evelyn and her fancy friends."

"We're friends too, Evelyn and I," I say.

"Kinda sorta," he says. "The money friends are different. Like that one guy who runs a hedge fund and lives on his plane. And the other guy, what's-his-name in the plaid shirt—he's got an indoor basketball court. That's not exactly a dude who's gunning to shoot hoops with me down at Pier 4."

"Maybe he would if you bothered learning his name."

Jacob's quiet a minute. "And aren't they all off skiing together this weekend?"

"We could have gone to Ketchum too," I say, my voice tight. "If I'd asked."

"Except we don't ski," Jacob snaps.

"Why is it always like this with us when we talk about the Elliots?"

"Couldn't agree more. Let's stop." Jacob pushes back in his seat and folds his arms across his chest, closed for conversation.

The Q car is empty, ghostly, and feels bound to nowhere. I won't even get to see Evelyn next week, since she'll be at Art Basel Miami.

"I'm looking forward to Florida and spending some time with Dad and Gabi," I say. "Even if it's just so we can go somewhere." I sound cranky. I need sleep.

"Then you'd better give Evelyn a heads-up," says Jacob. "Before she hires you to create her Christmas."

Seventeen

The rest of the weekend is quiet. On Saturday, Jacob takes the train out to Long Island to see his parents, but since Peter and Marisol didn't visit this year, I stay behind to enjoy a day for myself. I remove the cover from my long-neglected Singer and start a project embroidering tea towels as holiday gifts for friends and family. Homemade gifts for all since Jacob and I don't want to put a dollar's weight on our newly liberated credit line.

Evelyn is away for most of the month, but she checks in with me as she travels from Ketchum to Miami to Los Angeles. She's briefly in New York to attend the Botanical Garden Winter Wonderland Ball. Then she's off the next morning to spend a few days at Old Orchard for her mother's annual black-tie to support the Exotic Avian Emergency Sanctuary. Followed by a week in the Hamptons. I keep a lookout for her texts and late-night phone calls, or the occasional Zelle-boosted task to book her a facial or hunt down a loofah—"Just till I get my new Poppy!"—or source an outfit. Her requests are like a bright silk ribbon woven through the plain cotton fabric of my day, and I'm thrilled when she's back in town and wants to make an in-person plan.

Shopping Tues? I don't leave for West Palm/Bahamas till the day after.

I'll be only window-shopping, but yes!

Reserve us a dinner somewhere nice.

Tuesday after work, Evelyn and I meet at Gorsuch, where she's already sashaying around the store and egging the commission-sniffing sales staff to find her every latest style of riding boot. Sixteen thousand dollars and three pairs of boots later, we're all warmed up for Fendi, Hermès, and Issey Miyake in quick succession.

By now, I'm so fluent in Evelyn's taste that I know just what to pull for her—a Gucci envelope bag, a silky wide-collar Chloe blouse, and a distressed faux fox–trimmed Stella McCartney jean jacket on reserve. Evelyn buys everything she wants—which still has the power to jolt me.

At Prada, she treats me to an acid-orange hooded raincoat that is as impractical as it is overpriced.

"I shouldn't take this," I say out loud, to convince myself.

"You should! Merry Christmas!" She purchases the same raincoat for herself, and we wear them out together like two fashionable traffic cones, protected from the damp chill that's crept in with the night. We head over to Lafayette Street for dinner. There's a glow in Evelyn's face and a hype to her chatting that I'm familiar with as the high she gets from spending. I feel a little worked up myself, coming off the whirl-wind of luxury stores, with their complimentary drinks and excessive packaging, to land here at Le Coucou.

"But I can't drink half a bottle of wine! I can't drink half a bottle of anything," I protest as the sommelier presents us with wineglasses big enough for a goldfish to live a happy life.

"We're celebrating! You found me so many pretty things today. Cheers!"

Half doubting, wholly charmed, I tap the thin crystal of my glass against hers.

"I love New York in the holidays," Evelyn drawls, gazing with rap-ture around the crowded restaurant. "Wanna hear something fun?" She leans forward conspiratorially. "Six months!"

"Six months what?"

"Is how long we've known each other!"

"Hey, and that's three and a half years, if we were dogs," I joke—but Evelyn's own mood is serious.

"You're a gift to me, Spell," she says. "Always so steady, and you gave me such a leg up on my little Friendsgiving, and of course you're always so good for a hoot on a late-night call. I've loved you in my life." She reaches across the table and twines her fingers through mine. That tight Evelyn interlock, before she lets me go and leans back. "And finally you can breathe easy because I went and found myself a new assistant. Her mom is Ina Son; you remember her, the nineties model? And her dad was some pop star I never heard of. Raquel Son-Rojas. She's right out of Fordham, and she's finishing an internship doing content promos for Rent the Runway. January, she's all mine, and you're off the hook." Evelyn winks. "No more me bothering you with eight jillion things I need by tomorrow."

"Never a bother," I say, feeling a squeeze of disappointment and maybe a touch of envy for Evelyn's brand-new pedigreed personal assistant.

"Meantime, I've been thinking about something to give you."

"Please, are you kidding? You already bought me—"

"No, wait." She swipes a hand, brushing off my words. "Not a store-bought thing. I did want to sit down with you about this since we're off to Nassau next week and not home again till mid-January."

"Mid-January!" My squeeze turns sour. A month without Evelyn.

"Yep, and it's a gift I need to give in person. Heck, you might even know what it is!"

I shake my head. *Three guesses*, I'd said to my mother that night at the mall. Her bottle of perfume had wiped out all my babysitting money. I wanted to stretch the special of that night for as long as I could hold it.

Give me a hint, my mother said. Happy to play along.

"Give me a hint?" My hunch is that Evelyn is offering her house in Montauk for a week next summer. She's been asking about Jacob's and my vacation schedule. It would be incredibly generous of her, and I know Jacob would love it, too.

But I don't want to dilute Evelyn's fun by guessing correctly.

"Ooh, a hint." Evelyn presses a finger to her chin. "Sooo, first hint. It's nothing I *got* you, since it already exists—ooh, ta-dah!" She claps as our three-tiered shellfish platter and a carafe of blanc du blanc are delivered. "It's not Christmas till you eat your weight in raw bar, right?" She selects a crab leg and goes to battle with it using a silver nutcracker.

"'Already exists'?" It's Montauk. "Art lessons with Henry?"

"So sweet! But no. Hint two." She pauses dramatically. "You want it *and* you need it."

My heart upticks. Is it money? Money is something I always want and always need. Evelyn's money is something that already exists. Would she give me a chunk of money for Christmas? It would be weird and embarrassing, and not outside possibility.

It also feels tacky to guess money. "A trip to the Azores?"

"Spell! You're not even trying. Hint three—it's as much for Jacob as it is for you." She looks at me, and then something—a flex of her jawline, the glint in her eyes—sends a dart of anxiety shooting through my chest.

Evelyn discards the crab leg and unfurls a hunk of meaty lobster flesh from its tail. She twists it free, dunks it in cocktail sauce, and pops it into her mouth.

"Jacob and I don't need anything," I say at length. "We have everything."

She takes a sip of the white. "Almost everything." She chooses a doll-sized crab fork and spears a stack of littlenecks up the tines. A mini shish kebab. "You know all this. Not one bad day. Not even my delivery. I was Miss Beach Bohemian, didn't give so much as a holler when Jurgen went back to Switzerland. Xander was all me."

Yes, I'd heard all these stories. I'd seen Evelyn's Ibiza-Madonna pictures, too. Red flags are batting multiple warnings in my brain. The most important thing here is to hold on to myself. To control these next minutes, no matter where Evelyn wants to lead us. "So maybe I'm out of guesses," I tell her.

"It belongs to me. Then to you. My fourth hint." She downs the kebab.

"Evelyn, I'm not saying this out loud."

"But it's a guessing game!"

I shake my head. I can't indulge the guess. I won't.

"Why not me?" Evelyn enjoys another long sip of wine. "Right? Why not? The other day I was thinking, maybe this is why Spell and I connected in the first place. I could carry that baby—I'm a badass, as we both know. Aren't you always saying that to me?" Her voice is loud and coaxing, like someone in an icy pond telling you it's okay to jump in.

"Evelyn, it's an incredible thing to offer." I take a deep breath. "I'm so moved that you'd even consider it. I'm so touched. But there's a lot to this."

"Honey, I should know. I'm the one who's already had a baby, right?" But then Evelyn picks up her handbag and fidgets with it. Pulls out a tube of lipstick, opens the top, and blots her lips. How long has she been thinking about this? Five minutes, five days, five weeks? I watch as she replaces the lipstick and then, from its shell, prongs a dripping oyster with her fingers and pops it in her mouth. "Are you shocked?"

"I think we're both shocked," I say. "Maybe we could talk about this somewhere else. Another time. Not at a restaurant."

"No, no, I'm *serious*, Spell," she says. "I read this piece in Buzzfeed about a sister carrying for another sister, and it just about turned me inside out, the love between those sisters."

"I read that story too," I tell her. I've read them all. "But that article didn't go into the details. None of them do—not really. The tests and hormones and blood work and injections, the doctors and technicians who monitor your every move."

Evelyn rolls her eyes. "What, you don't think I could do any of that?"

"All I'm saying is you'd have to give up so much. Things you might be thinking about"—I gesture at the shellfish, the wine—"but also things you might not be thinking about? Like your travel, your social calendar." But surely, *surely* Evelyn, capricious as she is, already thought about these things? Some of them? I feel so uncomfortably itchy, like caterpillars are crawling on the back of my neck.

Evelyn purses her lips and lifts her wineglass. She keeps a grip on it. "Dr. Browder asked me not to say anything to you until I'd sat on it a month," she says. Then she signals the sommelier, who hastens over to top her off. "Growing up, I took such good care of my horses. Even the hard parts. Nobody had to ask me twice to muck a stable or soak the currycombs. And you see how I connect with Henry's girls. What I'm saying is that it's in me, you know? To care." Her shoulders droop, as if she's trying but maybe failing to win an argument. "Money has a way of making people into something they're not. But I've also got human capital—I'm not just an ATM. I'm not just the lady with the checkbook."

"Evelyn, you are so caring. I don't perceive you as the checkbook lady at all."

"I *encouraged* Poppy to leave her PA job," she says, but I sense she's speaking as much to me as to herself. "Because I *recognized* the extra special twist in her. I recognized it because I see it in myself."

Though I've never met Poppy, I nod in agreement and then ask, "And what does Henry think?"

"Oh," says Evelyn. "You know. Henry's on board with everything I do."

"So, this was a discussion or a declaration?"

"Ha." But now Evelyn picks up her phone and scrolls it, as if searching for her and Henry's text exchanges about surrogacy, just to refresh her memory. I feel a dizzying sense of plummeting from a high altitude. She puts down her phone and frowns at her plate of broken claws and legs and shells. She looks up and clears her throat. "We could talk about it again in January, if you want."

"Okay." I nod, smile. *Deep breaths.*

"Because now that I'm thinking about it—not that Henry isn't all in—but it's a whole separate conversation with him. Maybe a few." She laughs. "You know me, Spell; fire, ready, aim."

I nod again.

"So we'll park it here. Then we can run it up the flagpole," Evelyn says in her joking impression of corporate speak. "We'll stick a pin in it for mid-Jan. We'll circle back."

"Right," I say. "Of course."

"I mean, you're my dear friend—I *do* think about you." A tear breaks from the corner of her eye; she swipes it with the back of her hand. "Like I just got you that raincoat, right? I truly want you to be happy and have the things you want."

Don't cry, don't cry, don't cry. I know Evelyn means every word. I know she couldn't realize how hard they are to hear. It will take a Herculean effort to sound calm and assured, and my voice surprises me when it's both. "You know what would make me happy? If you two came over to our apartment in January. We owe you a dinner. Come on over, kick off your shoes. Have some pasta and meet Nick."

Evelyn's smile lifts her face. "Love it! Dinner at your place—no matter what," she says, and her voice holds an unmistakable note of relief.

Eighteen

>>>>>>>>>>>>>>>

I eat the cost of an Uber so that I can have a meltdown in private. We hit bridge traffic, so I'm in the long-shuddering-breaths part of my weep session by the time I turn the front door key to the apartment. As do memories of all the other bad days and worse nights, the tears also feel oddly comforting.

"What happened to you?" Jacob is already up from the couch, where he and Nick are watching box lacrosse on TV.

"You don't want to know." My voice, as calm as an air traffic controller the whole time I was with Evelyn, is now part screech, part croak. I hadn't texted Jacob either, so he's not expecting my bedraggled spirits or that I'm wearing what looks to be—in this light, anyway—a raincoat the color of a hazmat suit.

"Try me."

So then of course I tell him, blundering my way through it, and ending with "But do you want to know the worst, *worst* part? It's how quickly she stepped it back after I asked about Henry." There's a bar rag on the counter, and I use it to blow my nose in a vicious honk. "I think she just tossed it out there to see how it felt and then—'On second thought, yeah, maybe I should talk it over with Henry. Let me get back to you!'"

"Ah," says Jacob. His eyebrows push up worriedly, like a basset hound.

"I'm not even sure she discussed it with him at all. After she told me how important I am to her and how easy it would be." I tug off the raincoat and fold it over the kitchen bar chair. I hadn't removed the tags, so it's RealReal ready. "I mean, even for Evelyn, that's some grade A thoughtlessness, right?" I hold up my finger when Jacob starts to speak. "Listen. I get it. I do. A lot of what you've been saying is true. She's self-centered, she's slightly manipulative—and okay, maybe I'm not my most genuine version of myself when I'm around her. But for about fifteen seconds, I also thought... I really believed..." Fresh tears gather in my eyes. "You know what? I need a hot shower."

Jacob nods. "Good plan."

Later, when I'm out of the shower and wrapped in my robe, Jacob knows better than to take me through his personal back catalog of Holden Caulfield–like suspicions every time he'd thought Evelyn was being a phony. He's just here, and when I tell him I haven't eaten anything tonight, he heats me up some tomato soup and even toasts some bread to go with it.

Nineteen

All that next month, Evelyn doesn't mention her almost-offer. She doesn't send me her usual friendly-imperative assortment of tasks and payments either. Or even texts and photos. Nothing.

Is she embarrassed? Regretful? Honestly, I hope so. I go dark on my end too. No calls or texts to Evelyn. By the next week, she's off to the Bahamas. I follow her stories on Instagram, but I never comment on them. Every time I think about that dinner, I turtle so deep down in my emotions that I want to hide from everything. But especially from Evelyn.

Maybe we need this time off from each other.

The Friday night before Jacob and I leave for Florida, we take a train to Old Greenwich for dinner at Meg's house, a multi-gabled Tudor on a chunk of prime Connecticut shorefront. Hailey is adorable—another curly-top, scrambled-egg blond to match her two older sisters. I'm touched by the family's efforts to make the evening special, from the Christmas crackers at our plates to the Irish wool scarf, long and thin as a necktie, that Becket hand-knit for me.

As Jacob and Banks clean up dinner while Meg and I remain in the dining room, picking at syrupy slubs of what's left of the toffee cake, I tell her about the Evelyn dinner.

"Nooo. This is not the usual delectable Evelyn story by a long shot," says Meg. "Though I'm sure she meant well, right?" She hesitates. "Not to say it's the thought that counts, when it comes to surrogacy."

"We'll get past it," I say. "The holidays always make me feel extra sensitive, but obviously in the long run I don't want to lose Evelyn as a friend."

Meg's eyes are soft. "I know it's tough for you to come out here and see the girlies. No matter how much we love each other. I wish it were different. I wish I could make the holidays less crappy for you and Jacob. But I do get it."

She does. And it's a relief to board Nick at Rover the next morning before we fly out of the tourist trap that is New York City in December. I need to get away from families, families everywhere. Families crowded into subways, trundling up to see the tree at Rockefeller Center. Families blowing on mugs of hot cocoa in the windows of restaurants.

Even at home, our mailbox overflows with holiday photo-cards of ever-multiplying family members—including Doug Knight, one of Jacob's colleagues from codeSpark, who was engaged when I met him during Jacob's and my third or fourth year trying for kids. Now he and his wife have two children of their own.

How did we get on Doug Knight's stupid mailing list, anyway?

Every year, these cards come in, as if expressly designed to highlight what Jacob and I don't have and want most, and it gives me a bittersweet satisfaction that the last thing I do before we lock up and leave the apartment for the airport shuttle is to throw out the whole entire stack.

Twenty

Standing in line in the torpid heat of the Tampa Hertz Rental, my phone vibrates. I've missed a call from Private. I stare at the transcription.

Hi Noah it's price of pal I have a question for you but I me to be does grit also I'm an ass so time zones might be the rent depend on where you are anyway call me thanks.

"Back in a sec." I leave Jacob standing in the line. In the Hertz ladies' room, I hold my phone to my ear.

Hi, Nora. It's Bryce Appell. I have a question for you, but I need to be discreet. Also, I'm in Aspen so time zones might be different, depending where you are? Anyway, call me? Thanks!

What kind of a discreet question? And why do I have the answer?

Jacob and I decide to use all our Gold Plus rewards points to splurge on a convertible. We'll pack in the fun where we can get it since my dad prefers a laid-back version of the season to be jolly. If not for Gabi, he probably wouldn't bother with the holidays at all.

I didn't spend much of my childhood with my father, who met my mother when he was stationed at a Navy base near the Cumberland Farms where my mom was working the register that summer she turned twenty.

The way my mom told it, she was smitten with my courtly, uniformed dad because he called her *Miss* and walked her to her front door after dates. She followed him to his next naval assignment—a three-year stint in Patuxent, Maryland—but when my adventuring father accepted orders for a tour of Guam, my homebody mom decided to head back north.

"I lost him but got you" was my mother's take on that era, and as far as I ever knew, she was happy with her trade.

In Guam, my father met, then married Gabi Santos, who was working at the USO Naval Base blood drive. He stopped in to donate a pint of his best B positive, and she was the nurse who drew it. Gabi, with her relaxed intuition on the presets of our fractured family, won my heart with her steady presence in those weeks after my mother died. She also attended my graduations, my wedding, and came to stay with me in the city the week I had to have my wisdom teeth removed. An ever-reliable giver of gifts on birthdays and anniversaries, she also invites us down to Sarasota every year—and she's probably the reason we go.

Our Ford Mustang with fins is a time-hop that fits my capri culottes, sleeveless bandanna blouse, and glossy black-straw sun hat, and zips us right into a vacation mood. Motoring down Route One, we binge on gas station snacks—pomegranate Vitamin Waters and Funyuns. With the wind on our cheeks and our mouths tangy with artificial seasonings, Jacob finds a station called Let's Groove, which delivers all the Fugees and Biggie he could want.

"Are we still bangers if it's a rental on plus points?" Jacob asks, breaking from his harmonies with The Gap Band's "You Dropped a Bomb on Me." Jacob's got his dad's smooth baritone, though sometimes he'll stop mid-note if he thinks I'm listening too hard. Which I always am.

"Medium bangers? Let's swing by Publix. Beer, weed, and tacos are the only guarantees. Remember last time?"

"Taco Bell on Christmas Eve." Jacob shakes his head. He can never get over how Dad and Gabi's retirement remade them into teenagers who live on junk food and live music. But my heart tugs when we see them waiting for us on the patio of their conch bungalow. There are deepened sags and pouches in Dad's face, and Gabi's thick new black-and-yellow bifocals make her look like a rockabilly bumblebee. She greets us by fishing out two Sunset Ales from the cooler between them as Dad gives out hugs. He's lived by the beach for so long he feels like the human version of driftwood—lean and knotty, a little washed up.

Their place is the same as always. For the holidays, they've strung multicolored lights through their dwarf palms. Gabi shows us their new wind chimes and their bedroom, which has been repainted a sleepy shade of sun-dried tomato.

Then Dad jangles the keys to his Chevy Spark. "Anyone up for the beach?"

"Think I might need a nap first," says Jacob.

"All right, I'll go on. You..." Dad's nod is a slow wave through his body. Jacob once pointed out that my father's thoughts tend to vanish midstream, but I think it's his way of expressing an ease with any plan left unsaid.

"Hit the beach," I say. "We'll figure out dinner."

"Oh, right. Dinner," says Gabi absently.

Dad takes off and Jacob heads in for his nap. I unpack our Christmas gifts and wedge them under the living room's snow-frosted tree, propped up from underneath with the gifts that Gabi's been collecting all year.

In the kitchen, Gabi is puzzling out a grocery list. Her thumb pushes the clicker of her retractable ballpoint. "I know you two like healthier stuff. Veggies and whatnot." Perspiration dampens her hairline. "The thing is, they've got a twenty-four-hour ornament sale over at Sam's Club, these little blown-glass alligators in Santa hats."

"Go get 'em, Gabi. Jacob and I'll do the shop."

Gabi immediately sets down the pen and slides over the list. On it are the words *apple juice, peas*. "Or we can get a bucket of wings. Your dad and I don't mind."

I take the list to the bedroom, where Jacob, stripped to his briefs, is sprawled in bed. "Dinner is peas and apple juice, plus hot wings, unless we take over."

Jacob flops a pillow over his head. "Publix after my nap."

Twenty-One

Left to myself, I roam the rooms. Unlike Phil and Sandy's tight ship, Dad and Gabi's place is a nestled-in mess of Gabi sparking joy with pretty much everything. Their bookshelves and wall shelves display her collections of thimbles and carved owls, along with their beach finds—conch shells, chunks of coral, glass bottles, polished stones. I gather stray cups and plates for the dishwasher, then kick back on their lumpy sectional. The breeze through the living room window stirs up a pleasant scent of patchouli and cinnamon.

Listening to my message again, Bryce's voice nudges my memory of us at Wake-Up Café. How cowed I'd felt, being around Phelps's most famous coed.

I'm a flutter of nerves even now as I'm dropped into her voicemail.

"Bryce, it's Nora. It's so nice to hear from you. Hope you're having a nice holiday season. We're in Florida at my family's place, but I'm around anytime."

I hang up, cringing. I talked too long. Used *nice* twice, and said *my family's place* like I'm presiding over my oceanfront estate instead of tucked up in QVC Command Central.

Nervously, I tap into Instagram and Evelyn's profile. The recently renamed @EvvieDoesIt is Evelyn sticking a toe into the influencer waters, and from what I can tell, she's making a splash, with multiple fashion brands and friends with last names like Getty and Guinness already among her growing base of followers. Evelyn said herself that she's inspired by Poppy, now a full-fledged cooking star on Twitch. And if her adorable ex-assistant gets thousands of people to watch her make overnight muesli, why wouldn't they enjoy adorable Evelyn as she sunbathes on *The Weatherly*, her parents' yacht, currently en route from Harbor Island to West Palm?

The boat is spectacular—no matter how Evelyn tinkers tastefully with the shot. There are also some glamour photos of Evelyn and Henry, and a boomerang of Xander diving into the sea in scuba gear, per the family's daily expedition to search for Incan treasure sunk somewhere off the Florida coast. It strikes me as odd that a family already feet-up in one fortune would spend any time hunting down more of it—but I guess it beats swabbing the deck.

Evelyn just posted a new photo of a long table set on the beach for a formal dinner. As I press the heart icon, I see that I'm like number 343—an uptick by double from Evelyn's last post of herself attending the Wonderland Ball.

There are several comments already, most of them about the size of the boat.

Should I add a comment? A heart? The longer Evelyn and I don't communicate, the more it feels like a grudge, though by now I've had time to consider my own role in Evelyn's impulsive offer. Specifically, a sense from that night when Evelyn flexed a bicep and told me I needed a hearty gal like her to take the job, some part of me has been hoping she truly might be that gal? That every time I sourced her a dress or braided my hair in a style worth comment or found her some small gift—an antique snuff box or hand-sewn coin purse—I've also been presenting a version of myself that would be most worthy of her extra favor and attention?

What I do know is that I miss her.

I type the geeky phrase a feast for the eyes!, then just as quickly delete it, and I shove my phone into my culotte's pocket.

In the guest room, I crawl in next to Jacob and watch the late-afternoon sun slant its carroty reds through the mini blinds. I google *Aspen,* which leads me to scrolling through photos of Goldie Hawn bundled in large, astonishing fur coats. I feel like I'm activating my mother's old habit of overdosing on the lifestyles of the rich and famous. It's a hit of sugary emptiness, like eating a bag of candy canes before dinner. I put down my phone and close my eyes, and when I wake up, the room is a cool mineral blue, and Jacob and I are folded into our usual intimate spoony sleep position.

My phone is pressing against my thigh. I slide it up from my pocket and check in again on Evelyn's Instagram. She's put up a reel of Henry, windblown and handsome. Against the ocean horizon, his eyes are hypnotic but kind, and don't remind me of Hitler youth, that forever problem with pale blue.

Then the camera flips, and I'm looking at Evelyn smiling back at me.

It hurts my heart. She feels so far away she could be vacationing on the moon.

"Whatcha looking at?" Jacob mumbles on my side.

"Nothing," I say, and I drop my phone onto the bedside table before he can see. Another outcome of Evelyn's and my friendship hiatus is that Jacob and I haven't experienced one moment of Evelyn-related tension. I ought to take that as a win.

Christmas morning, I wake up and grope, first thing, for my phone to see if Evelyn's sent any special messages. She has. I've been included in her What's App group: a happy holidays message, along with a portrait photograph of Evelyn, her tanned and toothsome parents, Henry, and Xander all dressed in fluttery linen and standing in front of a spruce tree decorated in white starfish with touches of silver. I send a heart before I can second-guess it. When I check my phone again, Evelyn has put a heart on my heart, and I exhale my relief.

After a Dunkin apple-fritters breakfast, Jacob and I exchange gifts with Dad and Gabi. Our tea towels and artisanal spices are swamped by Gabi's overabundance: quilted wine totes, an electric nut grinder, a collapsible wire laundry hamper, bamboo wind chimes, Gabi's home-made bath salt scrubs, a mini cornbread pan, a foot massager, a blown-glass alligator in a Santa hat, and an assortment of outdoor smart plugs that she takes back only when Jacob reminds her that we don't have an outdoors.

We spend the afternoon walking on the beach, looking for shells and stones to add to Gabi's cluttery collection, and then Dad and Jacob catch some waves. I leave my phone behind so that I'm not looking to see if Evelyn texts. If Jacob is aware of all my phone fumbling, he doesn't mention it.

But the truth is, I don't want to lose her. While I'm grateful for my life—my real life—with Jacob, and even this week with Dad and Gabi in their bungalow of owl statuettes and shag carpeting the color of dried pasta, I miss the high-volume exuberance of Evelynland. I miss her dazzle and the way she turned me into a giddier version of myself. I miss the fairy tale of everything Evelyn—her wild stories, her sparkly entertainments, her dispatches from society that could spring me out of my ordinary life.

For Christmas dinner, Dad and Gabi made reservations at their favorite, the Hogwash Grill, for burgers, followed by live music courtesy of Antz Marching, a not-terrible Dave Matthews cover band.

This time, I do take my phone, though I try to limit my compulsive, surreptitious glances at it.

But Evelyn doesn't write me.

And Bryce doesn't return my call.

Twenty-Two

<<<<<<<<<<<<<

Holiday over, home again, I helm the shop. Frankie and Seth are in Maui through early January, and Barb is spending her annual two weeks in the Hudson Valley with her family. Out of loyalty to my past self's enthusiasm for working solo this time of year, I dig into projects, like redoing the front window. I decide on a green-and-neutral palette to suggest a New Year's balance of calm and growth, and I dress Gigi and Bella—our haughty, plastic storefront mannequins—in two different leaf-patterned Von Furstenberg wrap dresses.

Nice display! Reel in those youngsters! Frankie writes when I send him a photo of my efforts. He thumbs-downs my next photo, a box of garish shoulder-padded blouses that Barb has purchased and might as well have been labeled *Worst of the '80s*.

It's unsellable. At some point, Frankie and I will need to sit down with Barb and explain that some of her favorite esprits in clothing genres just don't have the wings for time travel.

At least Barb's given me the go-ahead to give over some sales space to Lollipop, an eco-friendly toiletries company that just opened in Greenpoint. The pop-up is an experiment, and so is our selection of affordable front-rack items curated to bring us more foot traffic. The thick hand-milled soaps and body balms, sustainably wrapped, twine-tied, and adorned with a dried lavender sprig, offer customers a way to leave the shop with a bag even if they can't afford a multi-hundred-dollar Max Mara blouse.

I'm arranging the Lollipop bottles for a post when my phone buzzes in my cardigan pocket. It's from Evelyn.

We fly back next Friday are we on? Henry & me?

Reading it, I drop to sit cross-legged on the carpet.

YES, I type.

"Nooo," says Jacob when I tell him at home later. "I thought we were confidently uncoupling with Evelyn."

"Consciously, not confidently."

"I might mean both. That last dinner? That was really tough for you, Nore."

"Evelyn and I made this plan a month ago," I say. "Let's think of it as a reset. I want to put that dinner behind us."

Jacob's expression is pensive, like he's shuffling through his rebuttals. Then he surprises me with "So let's do that farfalle with the broccolini we made the other time. With a salad. A couple of cheeses from Trader Joe's."

"Olives," I add. "Evelyn likes olives. But nothing fancy."

"Got it," he says. "Nothing fancy, except for the guests themselves."

Friday evening, Evelyn and Henry burst through our door looking awards-show dazzling, if a little out of breath from walking up four flights of stairs.

Their presence feels splashy for our seven hundred square feet. All the carefully casual preparing Jacob and I have done this week feels wrong too. We should have made our place look more special. We need prettier flowers than these underthought, biblical purple stalks I picked up at the corner deli. I contemplate taking half a Valium from Jacob's stash from when he got a root canal last fall. The bottle's still in the medicine cabinet. Maybe I should put a blur on this evening.

"Happy duty-free New Year," says Henry as he delivers both a bottle of rum and a large pink box of Veuve Clicquot rosé champagne into my hands. When Evelyn hugs me, I catch the familiar fruity peach-and-cedarwood notes of her shampoo.

"Missed you," I say.

"Me too—so I have one extra little something for you." She lifts a small silver-wrapped gift from her bag. "Go on, open it."

I unwrap the paper to find a hinged box, then I gingerly lift the glass orb from its tissue paper nest. "What in the world?" I blink. "No! I can't believe I'm looking at this. Where did you find it?"

"I got my ways," Evelyn says, her voice all Southern sass.

I set the bottle of perfume on the counter, speechless and marveling, before I finally pick off the seal and lift the delicate curled-leaf stopper to test the scent. "This is it," I gush. "This is Libre d'Orange."

"Same exact?" asks Jacob.

"Same exact." I touch a drop of perfume to each of my wrists, then check in with the scent on my skin. It immediately unlocks the glow of that night in my over-burnished memory. "Thank you," I tell her. "I'm overwhelmed."

"I'm really glad then," she says, smiling. "Henry'll tell you how much I wished you were with me for some of those dreary parties Beau and Bitsy pushed on us, with all the windbags and blowhards they call friends."

"Luckily, you had your fine husband for company," quips Henry in a princely voice. Henry's shirt has not one, not two, but three unbuttoned buttons. His caramel suntan highlights the silver in his hair, and his expression seems to say yes, he *knows* how good he looks. I've never sensed him feeling himself so intensely. Dreary parties aside, it does feel like some of this vacation—the Henry-plus-Evelyn part of it—worked out well.

"Spell, what a precious space." Evelyn is already midway through her very small exploration of it. She opens the door to the spare room. "Frieda's cloak, on display!"

"Of course! It's my prized possession."

"White wine or Pellegrino," says Jacob.

"Or I could open the rum and make daiquiris," offers Henry.

"We've got limes," says Jacob.

"Lead me to your kitchen and I'll take care of the rest," says Henry grandly, and two steps later he is standing in it.

The daiquiris are delicious and kick off the festivities as we settle into the living room, where we trade stories: Evelyn and Henry overlapping their sentences as they tell us about diving for treasure and snorkeling with manta rays. Then Jacob recounts the time we went to the Poconos a few summers ago and coyotes got into our garbage dumpster, and Evelyn remembers a riding camp she attended one summer in Buck Hill, where she first sampled the high of a horse tranquilizer.

But it's not the stories that matter. It's Henry's poise. It's Evelyn's pleased attention when Henry speaks, and his when she does. The four corners of this evening could be Jacob and me, plus Meg and Banks. Or Peter and Marisol. Or Frankie and Seth. There's an ease here, a nonstick surface that's smooth and reassuring. Maybe Jacob and I aren't Teflon-coated in wealth, but we aren't a pair of saddies hoping for Elliot handouts, either. The whole evening is cradled in the comfort of friendship.

We clear the dinner dishes and regroup in the living room with plates of carrot cake. Evelyn and Henry double up in our armchair, while Jacob and I take the couch, and Evelyn tells us about Xander's new friend and how they play Sims together until four in the morning. I settle back, lulled by the inconsequential conversation, the hiss and pop of our living room radiator, the burbling snore noises from Nick, curled up in her doughnut bed in the corner. I'm still in a happy fog when the Elliots get up to leave.

"It's a fake, you know," says Henry as he holds up Evelyn's overcoat for her to slip her arms inside. "The perfume."

"Henry!" Even as Evelyn laughs, I sense she didn't want him to tell her secret. "There's no reason to spoil things."

"Is it really?" I ask.

"Sigh! Yes." Evelyn swats Henry with her cashmere beanie. "I had it specially made. There's a perfumier in Grasse who can replicate anything. I got the bottle customized in Switzerland. He told me it was made on the cheap in China, not France. I mean, you've got to scratch your head about that name—what French perfume is called *Free Orange*?"

"Could have fooled me," I say, and now I do feel a little bit fooled and foolish.

Later, after they're gone, I keep hold of the bottle in both hands until it's warm, like an enchanted elixir, the way I used to do when I was a kid, before I knew it was mall perfume with a fake French name. "It's exactly like the original. It smells the same; it feels the same. If she hadn't told me, I'd never have known."

"Maybe it's also Evelyn's *no thanks* to surrogacy second-place prize," Jacob says.

"That did cross my mind."

"To be honest, I started thinking they were going to announce they're having a baby themselves." At my expression, Jacob adds, "Don't tell me you hadn't thought about it."

I hadn't. "They'd never," I say. "They have Xander! And Henry's got two grown girls."

"They don't want one until they want one."

"Henry's fifty-two."

"So is Elon Musk, and that guy's got a new kid every year." Jacob shrugs.

Henry and Evelyn, off by themselves, lost to the bliss of their own parenting paradise, is a thought experiment that leaves me feeling physically winded. In bed, I'm bug-eyed and restless with it. Eventually, I snap on my lamp and pick up my phone and search Elon Musk, though it feels like the wrong way to end such a lovely night.

Twenty-Three

C ome with me to this, Evelyn texts me a few days later.

The link is to a promotional event for Poppy, who is introducing a line of measuring cups sponsored by Baker Miller, a kitchenware shop in the East Village.

It's happening tonight, right after work.

Sure! I've looked in on her show and Evelyn gives me regular updates, but I'm curious to meet the real-life Poppy.

Great, I'll pick you up in the car!

Baker Miller is warm with bodies by the time we arrive. In the back, Poppy is signing her measuring cups and posing for photos. She's just as casually beguiling as she appears on her show, with an endearing overbite a la Freddie Mercury and a sweetly adolescent *aw, shucks* quality.

As soon as she sees Evelyn, her face splits into a big toothy grin. She hoots and jumps up and down. "You really came! I feel like a star!"

"I wouldn't miss it," says Evelyn. And while it's true that Poppy is thrilled to see Evelyn here, it's Poppy's night. It's not long before Baker Miller is packed and panting with the wolfish energy of food rangers; bloggers and vloggers and podcasters—*oh, my!* Everywhere I turn, I feel like I'm bumping into another content uploader, phone raised in front of their face like a Hamlet skull.

After Poppy signs our measuring cups, Evelyn and I step aside, releasing her to a new influx of admirers.

"Let's escape," I say, pointing to the second floor, where there's a balcony café. Upstairs, we order lattes from the barista, then take a table with a bird's-eye view on the event.

"Just look at Poppy," Evelyn says as we look down on the crowd. "She's got all this attention, and for what? Wearing a striped boatneck and breading things in panko? I could've done a cute channel like SnapCracklePoppy." She looks wistful. "Why didn't I?"

"Because outside of pot brownies and vinaigrettes, you don't really cook? Anyway, you've got some fans now that you've opened up EvvieDoesIt to the masses. Everyone enjoys a yacht."

Evelyn pulls a face. "That's just me falling into the wealth niche, letting people gawk. It's not real. It's not the same as what Poppy created." She pauses, watching Poppy pose for photos. "Jeez, I think that's Sunny Anderson from Food Network." She frowns. "There's gotta be some way for me to monetize my brand."

"*Monetize* your *brand*?" I laugh. "Why do you want to make money, Evelyn?"

"Why, just to see if I could! People are always asking me, 'Where did you get that darling bag, Evelyn?' 'What do you use to give your skin that glow?' 'How did you find that restaurant in the Philippines that's built right beside a waterfall?' And my answer is always, 'My network.'"

"Do you really think that's your twist?" I ask. "A network? Lots of wealthy people have networks."

"Spell! Be nice!"

"What I mean is, you're so many other things too. You were on the U.S. equestrian team," I say. "You've traveled to countries I've never heard of. You climbed Everest, and that other one."

"Aconcagua." She laughs. "You're always so impressed by those mountain climbs."

"Because they're *impressive*."

She smirks. "I know, I know. So if I'm such a badass, should we give Dr. Browder a sit-down?" Over her latte, she flutters her eyelashes at me. "What's that face? Didn't we put a pin in mid-January, you and me?"

"It's just, that was a strong pivot." I try to do an impression of casual laughter, but I'm sure I look as shocked as I am. "We haven't talked about it at all."

"You mean *you* haven't," says Evelyn pointedly. "*I've* talked it up and down with Henry. We really connected on it, as a matter of fact. Spell, your eyeballs look just about ready to pop out of your head."

"I guess I'm surprised?" In fact, my body has gone rigid with it.

"I don't know why. He's very nurturing, Henry. It's one of his lovelier traits. Anyway, you were right, about last month," she says. "I told you I'd spoken with Henry, but it wasn't until December, when we were away, that we had time to talk it through. He's so supportive about it too—he said it sounded like performance art." Evelyn waggles a hand to stop me from speaking. "Honey, I'm only talking about a meetup. Browder's been my ob-gyn since forever and she's sharp as a whip. She'll take the time we need to answer questions."

I'm holding my mouth in the shape of a smile, but I'm numb. "That could be something interesting," I manage.

"And you'll speak to Jacob."

"Yes, of course."

"He'll be all in, right?"

"Yes," I say. "No doubt. Jacob thinks you're wonderful, whatever you do."

She nods confirmation. It would not occur to Evelyn that Jacob wouldn't think that, though of course it's occurring to me.

"She didn't even go to chef school," says Evelyn, her gaze flickering back down to Poppy, who is signing a cardboard wall of boxed measuring cups. "That's what gets my goat just a tiny bit. But who needs chef school if you've got a TikTok?"

Twenty-Four

I wait to tell Jacob, though it feels more like paralysis than a decision. Even when, the very next afternoon, Dr. Browder's assistant calls to set up the appointment for the following Thursday. I add the date and time into my calendar. No matter how serious Evelyn was in the moment, I can hear a whooping siren in my head, knowing that at some point this week, there's a good chance she might remember she has to attend a wine-tasting fundraiser in Napa Valley, and so let's put a pin in this idea for never. But I'll deal with my disappointment when I get there. If I have any real hope for the meeting at all, it lives like a tiny spider under the porch of my mind, and I let it spin its fragile webs of possibility only in the darkest hours.

Evelyn's next communications have nothing to do with Dr. Browder. Later that week, she asks me to send over a selection of silk scarves from the shop with a description of each. By the next day, she's created a clip of herself in quick cuts, showing how "old-fashioned granny scarves" can be twisted into a one-shoulder top or tied into a flower blossom around a bag handle.

She looks gorgeous, her movie-star smile as inviting as her fashion hacks.

"It's really good," I tell her when she calls me that evening. "Friendly but professional."

"Raquel did the edits. She's got a real knack for—what's that ruckus?" Though Evelyn's own voice through the phone is so loud it sounds like it's bouncing off every wall.

"We're giving Nick a bath." I'm more like the dog-bath assistant, sitting on the toilet while Jacob takes a wide stance on his knees outside the shower stall as he rinses down our trembling captive with the hand-held showerhead nozzle. "So Raquel's working out?"

"She is. She can do my whole schedule backward and in high heels, plus run my social with me, telling everyone what's good. You confirm with Browder? We already had the sweetest phone call—there's nothing she doesn't know about being a surrogate."

Caught, I glance at Jacob. "Yep. Her office called the other day."

"She'll put you right at ease—hooray for this, right?"

"Yes, hooray," I answer quickly, but once I'm off the call, Jacob sits back on his heels and looks at me, incredulous.

"Are you shitting me?"

"What? It's just a meeting."

"What about last time? What about you coming home utterly wrecked because of Evelyn's offer-not-offer? What about you saying you don't even know how to be yourself around Evelyn?"

"If I can't be myself around Evelyn, I guess that's on me," I say. "It's something I personally need to work on. But at least we know each other, right? At least we're in this thing called a trusted friendship. That already puts us ahead of any complete stranger that you and I'd meet through an agency."

"What I really mean," says Jacob, "is why is this idea back to bite us at all?"

"It's only a meeting," I say. "That's it. Maybe Evelyn really does feel abjectly sorry for us. Maybe she also wants to brand herself as some badass surro-babe who could do this better than anybody. But nobody offers to do it unless they're pretty freaking confident they can. So, that's what I'm showing up for," I tell him. "That's why I'm going."

"Surro-babe," says Jacob. "Is that a real term?"

"Does it matter? More to the point, do you have any other options?" I toss Jacob the bottle of oatmeal pet shampoo; he needs to dive slightly to catch it. "You know anyone in the sales department of codeSpark who wants to have a baby for us?"

"Just—give me a second." Jacob squeezes out a shampoo blurp and lathers Nick up with it while she whimpers. "Because our friend Ms. Evelyn Elliot is, how do you say, a lot."

"This would be a lot, no matter who," I say. "Meg would have been a lot. The whole concept is a lot."

"Meg was different," he says. "You've known Meg for decades." He finishes sudsing and then picks up the shower nozzle again, adjusting the spray to hit Nick's undercarriage. Her whining notches up a decibel. "We don't have that same history with Evelyn."

"You said she'd never come to the apartment. The other week, she and Henry were here for two and a half hours for dinner. She's real, Jacob. She's invested."

"Not to be crass, but if she's so invested, why does she feel she needs to insert herself directly into our problem? Why can't she just help us hire someone? Or better yet, hand us the money?"

"Because this is validating and meaningful for Evelyn too."

"So we're like, what?" Jacob snorts. "Her charitable experiment?"

"Listen to you," I say. "Here's a woman *possibly, maybe, potentially* offering to carry our baby for us and taking no money for it. We'd be responsible for only the medical—and even that part's not small change for us. So, sure, maybe we are Evelyn's charitable experiment, if you want to put it that way, but when you *do* put it that way, you also kind of sound like a dick."

Jacob keeps his focus on Nick and doesn't respond. He shields Nick's eyes with one hand as he grips the nozzle with his other for the rinse-off. Soaking wet, Nick's head is the size of a tangerine. Then Jacob sighs. "Let's not do this."

"Not do what?" My jaw is so clenched, it hurts. "You are coming to meet the doctor with me, right?"

"Obviously, yes, I'm coming with you," says Jacob. "But I don't want every Evelyn conversation to be this hard for us."

"I don't either."

"Yet here we are."

"But you enjoyed that night they came over," I say. "And I was definitely me."

"I did," affirms Jacob. "And you were."

We're quiet together. I know this is hard for Jacob as someone who intuitively prefers to keep his personal life private. The image of himself and me and Evelyn and Henry all pushed into this doctor's meeting could not feel more counter to Jacob's desire to handle sensitive life issues from the inside. "We just don't have lots of options," I add softly. "As much as I wish we did."

He doesn't answer. The bathroom holds the echo of Nick's whimpering, Jacob's tongue-clicking efforts to soothe her, and the deeper sound of water rushing through the pipes. "Also, let's figure out how to talk about Evelyn," I say. "Because if this happens—big if..." I put my hands over my face for a moment. Suddenly, even speaking hypothetically about it feels like too much. "I can't even wrap my head around how lucky we might be."

"Nora, it's me," he says. "I know how it feels. I lived it with you. You don't have to sell me on everything this means for us. But just to note, we're in better shape now than we've been in a long time. We've cut our debt down by half—next year, we could even be in the black. There's better days ahead for us, right? With or without Evelyn."

"I know that," I say.

"The two of us, out from under, maybe even looking for a new place to live? Not just as some real estate fantasy league you and Meg play?"

"That would be nice," I say.

"That would be incredible, and it would be enough for me." Jacob turns off the tap, and Nick starts to shake off water, spraying it everywhere. "A good life, being the chill, happy people Nick already thinks we are. Right, girl?"

Nick pants anxiously in answer.

"It's one meeting," I say. "If it feels wrong, we'll know. I'm not getting swept up in the—the *Evelyn* of it all, okay? But there isn't a day that goes by when I'm not thinking about the last chancer." It's our old private name—"the chancers," we'd cheerfully designated all of our embryos, back when we'd banked multiple chances—and chancers—and felt generally optimistic about our outcome. I haven't used the term in a while, and it gives me a pang to say it out loud. It's memories, and I sense in Jacob's face that he's feeling them, too.

"All I'm asking," says Jacob, "is that you and I stay connected. We're the team, Nore."

I nod. "The Intended Parents, even," I say, raising the towel while Jacob air-lifts Nick from the shower. I wrap her up tight. Her enchilada body is trembling bone-deep, like she's just been rescued off an ice floe. Jacob gets the hair dryer, and we center Nick between us on the floor, me with the rake brush as Jacob takes command of the blow-drying action.

Once she's dry, Nick tunnels between us as we settle in to watch a movie. When Jacob's and my hands meet at the scruff of her neck, we exchange a smile. In this snug apartment, our dog cozied in between us like a warm loaf of bread, it seems absolutely insane to want anything more.

PART TWO

Twenty-Five

D r. Browder's resting smart face inspires confidence, and she gives us over an hour to talk through our every question. She also schedules us for a top-of-February appointment with her colleague, Dr. Glass, the division head of Reproductive Endocrinology at Weill Cornell. Dr. Glass agrees she'll take us on. A week later, when we're back for a follow-up, she asks us please to call her Sharon. Like Dr. Browder, Dr. Glass—and her wall of diplomas—is daunting, and I might need some time to ease into first-name basis.

In her sunny office of floor-to-ceiling bookshelves and four chairs already half-mooned around her desk in preparation for this meeting, Dr. Glass has all the time in the world. There might be a reason for that. A few years ago, the Fitzroy Foundation donated twenty million dollars to Weill Medical College at Cornell.

I feel the long arm of that goodwill extending right into this room.

Jacob and I spent years in the desperate choke hold of overcrowded IVF hospital bookings, our calendars rejiggering out to three or five weeks at a time if I made the mistake of ovulating on Presidents' Day or because transfers happen only on Thursdays. We'd count down obsessively in our calendars for our coveted fifteen-minute bracket of in-network expertise, just to be offloaded into the next month or onto another specialist.

Now money pushes us to the front of every line. Each meeting is like a golden breadcrumb that leads us effortlessly to the next one. Evelyn puts me in charge of the scheduling, and her name is the password to the glide path. I'd never factored in how a bottomless bank account and the interconnected system of high-powered friends and contacts dissolve any obstacle—as if the roadblocks themselves were put in place only to keep the masses in check.

But in Evelynland, there's no such thing as conflict.

Step by cautious step, we follow the breadcrumbs into March. Evelyn strides through the requisite battery of medical tests without a hitch. She has a concierge plan, where nurses arrive at her apartment like the kindly staff servants in *Annie* to check her vitals and do her blood work. Evelyn also schedules her sonogram and ultrasounds at Weill Cornell's downtown location because it's right around the corner from her Pilates class. It's the Evelyn Fitzroy-Boyle Elliot variation of a fertility workup, a reality Jacob and I never experienced, and when she tells us how simple it is—how easy-peasy—we bask in it.

We have one bump in the road when Jacob and I suggest putting a contract in place ahead of the transfer. "If my lawyers get involved, then my parents get involved," says Evelyn. "Call me superstitious, but I'd say let's get that pregnancy first before you go paying a bunch of lawyers? Though I've got every intention of handing you a healthy baby in nine months—and if you don't trust me on this point, Spell, you never will."

Put that way, it seems reasonable to wait; after all, Meg wasn't in contract, and there's no upside to no pregnancy plus a whopping legal fee.

After Evelyn successfully completes a mock cycle—a trial run to test her response to the hormones she'd take for the first couple of months of pregnancy—we move into the fast lane of the next step and the real transfer.

"This is happening so quickly," I tell Jacob. Or sometimes he tells me.

The transfer appointment is scheduled for the first week of April.

The embryo will be transported from NYU Langone to Weill Cornell where it will be defrosted and, one day later, implanted.

It feels like a very long way from the stealth copy of *How Babies Are Made* that my friend Chrissy Silva and I read in disbelief—and some horror—sitting together in the beanbag chair of our elementary school library.

It even feels like a long way from the night I told Jacob I'd stopped taking birth control pills, and who knew, maybe we'd run into some beginner's luck.

While we've stayed connected as we travel at the speed of Evelyn, no matter how hard we try to guard and manage our expectations, we can't keep our hopes from creeping in. We've got about a 60 percent shot that our last chancer will stick, and these odds are all we think about.

Twenty-Six

On the cold bright early-April morning of the transfer, I wake up to the sounds of garbage trucks and street sweepers. Under the covers, Jacob finds my hand.

"You good?"

"I am." But then I say, "I guess I don't know exactly what to worry about."

"Maybe nothing?" suggests Jacob. "Maybe we get to be lucky, just this once."

"Maybe."

We are heading in different directions today. Jacob is in Newark for an off-site codeSpark sales conference. Pitching digital ad space in a New Jersey DoubleTree isn't how Jacob wanted to spend this morning, but he couldn't get out of it. We've been together for everything else, and work caught up with us only this one time, but being unpartnered from Jacob makes me feel awkwardly extraneous when I meet up with Henry and Evelyn in the examining room. As if for all these years, I was the stunt double, and this morning I'm only here as witness to the real show. Even the way Evelyn is sitting on the metal table, her tattoos like a layer of armor on her skin, her cashmere-socked legs swinging, her focus on her phone—feels like the right, relaxed confidence that you'd need to meet this day. By my last transfer, I was so worn out I hated even to be touched, and what I mostly remember of the entire procedure was being sick with dread, already anticipating the failure and the bad news call and the hormone crash and the weeks of depression that followed.

Easy-peasy Evelyn likes to text Jacob and me after every test and procedure, and her self-assurance and professionalism have done wonders for our peace of mind. Looking at her this morning, I feel newly awed for the good fortune of her excellent health that she's so freely bestowing on us, and my gratitude heats my eyes as I hand over her ginger-lemon tea with one pump agave.

After a couple of sips, she looks up. "Did you see my latest post? I'm getting a lot of love for my anniversary-party tips."

"I did. It's very fun." I've got to hand it to Raquel—she's clever at creating stories from Evelyn's life. Just this past week, I've watched a clip of Evelyn transform from towel-dried hair to springy curls in thirty seconds as part of her "Getting Ready" highlights reel. I've also seen a montage of Evelyn's recent trip to Newbury Street in Boston, shopping with her school friend Schuyler Cushing, in her "Faces and Places" story. I've watched her unbox and sample serums and dusts and juices and powders, and I'm diligent with my exclamation points, paying attention because I know it makes Evelyn happy—while at the same time hardly noticing it because all I'm really thinking about is Jacob's and my last chancer, and the most momentous crossed-fingers day of my life.

Did I heart and comment on the anniversary-party tips post?

I'll have to go back and check.

When Makebe, the ultrasound technician, comes into the room to start the screening, Henry—who's been in the corner, chatting with our nurse, Bianca—now repositions himself closer to the machine. I stand behind him, wishing for that warm, shared spot of comfort that is Jacob's hand on the small of my back.

Doing the ultrasound, I text. Jacob, who is keeping shark eyes on his phone, hearts it immediately. We've heard lots of tough news in rooms like this one, with their chunky sonogram equipment and posters of reproductive systems. His texts are the net to catch me if I feel overwhelmed.

But there's a lot about this morning that also feels better than those other mornings. Starting with this airy room, with its adjacent restroom and wide window view of Seventy-Second Street, and the reassuring comfort of Bianca and Makebe. Evelyn likes to stick with the same faces. No student doctors allowed in here either.

If Evelyn wanted flamenco music piped in, I'm sure that could happen too.

Makebe applies a thick aqua gel and murmurs, "Here we go."

We watch as she rolls the transducer over Evelyn's stomach and pelvis. On the monitor, she clicks through fuzzy gray images that look like a series of unexceptional angles on a lunar landing.

"Eleven millimeters," reports Henry, recently an armchair expert in analyzing uterine linings.

"Want to hit that coffee shop on Amsterdam after?" asks Evelyn.

"Let me call Barb. I bet she won't mind if I come in late today," I say, before I realize Evelyn isn't talking to me but Henry.

"We'll walk through the park," says Henry, with a rueful half smile for me that acknowledges the awkwardness of my misunderstanding.

Makebe sends the images to Dr. Glass. A few minutes later, we've gathered in her office.

"Catch me up on the weekend," says Dr. Glass, with her usual abundance of free time to chat with the Elliots. Then she swivels her monitor. "Everything looks great," she says. "The procedure is no more than a few minutes. Then we ask you to rest for half an hour." To Henry and me, she says, "So it's just Evelyn now."

Henry says he'll stay with Evelyn.

"And everyone knows three's a crowd for embryonic transfers," I joke, though Evelyn probably doesn't need me to keep looking at her as if my whole life depends on her, no matter how hard I'm trying not to do that. I feel clumsy and unwieldy anyhow—as if the very fact of my physical self, this unhelpful extra body, is a little bit of an embarrassment.

"Spell, we're really doing this," says Evelyn as she gives me a hug at the door.

I never want to stop hugging Evelyn, but eventually I let her go. It's not even another twenty minutes before I'm outside, heading to subway.

Jacob texts me a heart and I send one back.

And now we wait.

The hardest part is the hope.

Twenty-Seven

While there's no way to stop my endless *good news bad news good news bad news* chyron chasing itself around in my head all week, at least I have the distraction of the weekend's Manhattan Vintage Show. It's one of the biggest exhibitions of the year, and hands down the most eclectic. Stylists flock here to find a VIP client's next Oscar gown, but the emporium also has more denim than a rodeo roundup and vintage treasures hiding in plain sight on every rack.

A few years ago, I found my favorite black pants here—thank you, Alexander Wang—and this morning, I pair them with the cream chiffon wrap blouse I wore the day I met Jacob's parents, along with a Navy-surplus peacoat I bought on Canal Street for my first New York winter. Today's a day when everything I wear needs to feel like a close friend.

There's already a line around the block at the Metropolitan Pavilion. Every year, this show gets bigger. Vintage has never felt so timely, and it's gratifying to see a new generation prefer the thrill of a one-of-a-kind prize to pulling the trigger on a SHEIN cart.

As soon as I arrive at our stall, Frankie looks at me expectantly. I shake my head.

He waits until Barb leaves to do another lap before he asks, "But you'll hear today, right? When will you know?"

"She's getting the blood test this morning before she leaves for Cabo. We find out by early afternoon."

"Wait, Cabo?"

"It was always the plan," I say. "Evelyn and Henry got engaged in Cabo, and she decided if the test is negative she wanted to be somewhere beautiful."

"Don't we all," says Frankie. "Has she been sending you texts?"

"As a matter of fact, she texted a four-leaf clover about an hour ago."

"Okay, that's good news," says Frankie.

"That's what I thought!" I exclaim. "No text is the bad text, right?" I take a deep breath, then another.

"We were negative the first time," says Frankie, "and pre-test, Lisa Ann went silent. She said she had a hunch. Second time, she sent us smiley faces. But I'm sure she'd taken a secret pee test."

Maybe Evelyn took one, too. I'm relieved that Frankie's so emoji-affirming, and it's probably just as well that we can't get a signal in here; it saves me from obsessing over my phone, and as soon as the doors open, we get slammed. First, it's a group from Bridgeport who wants to see our grunge-era Calvin Klein slip dresses. We're sold out in an hour. Then I meet Martin, on a laser-focused hunt for early Pierre Cardin. We've got an early '60s houndstooth jacket, but the buttons have been replaced. Martin and I eke out a discount that feels fair on both ends. The next shopper hems and haws for almost an hour, debating an ice-blue polka-dot Lanvin cocktail skirt before deciding no. But a bright-eyed spender in from Dallas, Texas, drops $18,235 for the privilege of owning our best Yves Saint Laurent, whose minimalist, pan-generational pieces are the jewels of the shop.

"Oof," says Frankie. "All your faves. Nore—the pantsuit, the smoking jacket, and the lips-print dress, gone in one big *au revoir*."

"I already miss them." I watch the woman glide off, not nearly done with her spree. She hadn't been interested in the history of the pieces nor my rhapsodic Saint Laurent fun facts—the first designer to use Black models on the runway, the first living designer to be honored by the Met. She just liked the label, she explained. The label was the point.

"Looks like I saved the show," says Barb, who loves to be proven right that we are haute first, and needs the victory lap besides, since not a single one of her opulent Jackie Collins tribute pieces sold.

The minute we break for lunch, and I can pick up a signal at the sandwich kiosk in the atrium, I learn that I've missed Evelyn's text by half an hour. Call me.

My breath is coming in struggling little puffs when I leave a message on her voicemail.

"What do I do?" I ask Frankie, staring at my phone in my hands. My head is spinning.

"Nora, you can't do anything. We wait. She'll touch in."

"Wouldn't she call me back immediately, no matter what?"

"I don't know the magic eight ball on the callback," says Frankie, but then he says, more emotionally, "I'm not sure I can handle bad news."

"You'll just have to give me one of the twins." It's our standby gallows humor joke, but neither of us has the appetite to laugh.

"Hold on to that clover," Frankie says in my ear before we head out at the end of the day. When I get home, Evelyn still hasn't called, and I want to crawl under the covers and sleep. Jacob is here, and he's busied himself making a pad thai. We put my phone on the counter to keep watch on it as I toss a salad and chop zucchini for fritters; then we force ourselves through this elaborate dinner we've prepared but have no desire to eat.

My phone rings midway through cleanup. Even my finger feels numb as I press Pick Up and put her on speaker.

"Just got your messages!" Evelyn sounds far away, her voice further muffled by the jazzy strains of "The Girl from Ipanema." "We decided to go snorkeling today. We're still out on the beach. Are you both there?"

"We're here!"

"We're pregnant! Oh, look, Henry—gosh, that's gorgeous."

"You two need some Cabo in your lives," says Henry in the background.

Jacob and I have gone as still as statues. Both his hands are still plunged into the sink, where he'd been sudsing our wok. I'm holding a drying rag in one hand and the top of our salad spinner in the other.

"This cowrie shell is so cute," says Evelyn. "Hang on, Spell, I'm sending you a photo."

Slowly, Jacob and I unfreeze to come together. I don't even know what it is to live in this moment—suddenly, I'm so high in the sky that the ground is very far away. I close my eyes and lean into the warm familiar, cottony scent of Jacob's shoulder, steadying myself.

"Hello? Did you hear? It's positive," says Evelyn. "Hello? Hello?"

"We're here." I lean past Jacob's shoulder to speak into the phone. "We're here! We're here and we're so happy!"

"Sorry we can't hear you," says Evelyn. "We'll let you go. Cabo's very romantic!"

"It's romantic here too," says Jacob. "We're going out for Pinkberry."

Twenty-Eight

Just because you know there's a chance the thing you've been wishing for most in the world might come true, doesn't mean it can't completely bowl you over when it does. After the call, Jacob and I walk in a stupor of euphoria, cradling our cups of Pinkberry. Even Nick, trotting out ahead of us and slightly drunk off her own serving of Frosty Paws, seems to have caught our rapture. She looks like she's leading a parade.

"Want to call your folks?"

I think. "I'd rather wait on the second positive test," I decide. "I'll call Frankie when we get home since he had to spend the day sweating it out with me. But I'm not telling my parents or Meg just yet. Want to call *your* folks?"

"Let's go out and see them," he says. "I think we should give them this news in person."

We get a confirmation positive test the following Sunday. By then, Evelyn and Henry are back in the Hamptons, and Jacob and I toast them on Zoom with Pellegrino. Afterward, we debate if it's odd to send Evelyn flowers.

We decide yes, it's odd—and so much money besides. A frivolous extravagance.

Then we send her flowers anyway.

Later that day, we take the train to Massapequa, with Nick in her little travel crate between us. We can't stop beaming—at each other, at everybody else on the train, at Phil and Sandy, who are here to pick us up at the station. I sense they've been hurt by our slowdown on visits, and they're at us in a flurry of news and lunch, which they serve at their kitchen banquette. It's all Jacob's go-to kid favorites: grilled cheese on thick-cut sourdough, with macaroni salad and chocolate chip cookies. But now the meal is done, our glasses of iced tea drained to melty cubes and the staple-shaped crusts of our grilled cheeses lying in neglect on our plates.

Under the table, I give Jacob a subtle foot-tap prompt. "So, folks, some good news. We're having a baby using a surrogate," he blurts out nervously, and I wonder how he possibly thought he'd do a better job in person than by phone.

"What?" asks Sandy. "What did you say?"

"Her name is Evelyn," says Jacob.

"Who?" Sandy repeats. "Goodness! We need more. Who is Evelyn?"

"She's Nora's friend who's going to carry a baby for us," Jacob replies.

"She's friends with us both," I amend.

"How much is she asking?" Phil asks, crossing his arms in front of his chest.

"She's not asking anything," Jacob explains. "She's got money."

"She's an incredibly special person," I say.

"Was Evelyn at the wedding?" Sandy tips her head back and narrows her eyes to think.

"No. She's new in our lives," says Jacob.

"How well do you know her?" asks Phil. "Are you sure you get the baby in the end?"

"Obviously we get the baby in the end, Dad. There's no doubt about that. Just...trust us." Jacob's voice softens. "Be happy for us."

"To be honest," says Phil, "it sounds like one of those movies, where the mother takes the baby and runs off to Canada."

"Technically, I'm the mother," I say.

"Yes, Nora's the egg mother!" says Sandy. "It's their bun, Evelyn's oven. I just read a thing about it. It's called *compassionate carrying*." She looks at me. "Right? Is it all free? Since your friend's so wealthy?"

"We're splitting the medical," I explain. "Evelyn has concierge care, which she's paying for herself." And thank God for that. No way could Jacob and I cover Evelyn's stratospheric concierge doctor fees.

"This feels like one of those thrillers where everyone fights for the baby after you tick off the mother," says Phil.

"I'm the mother," I say, more firmly.

"Dad, have a little heart," Jacob says. "You know what Nora and I have been through."

"But that's why I'm worried!" Phil bursts out. "How are you *sure* she won't keep it?"

"Phil, I promise she doesn't want our baby," I say.

"What do you mean, she doesn't want it?" Now Phil stares at me, confused.

"No, I mean—she won't want to keep it. Because it's Jacob's and my DNA."

"But isn't it also her baby?"

"Phil," says Sandy, "I'm going to send you this thing I read."

"How pregnant is she?" asks Phil.

"One hundred percent pregnant," says Jacob.

"Well, I'm very happy for you," says Sandy.

"We're happy you're happy for us," I say to Sandy.

I'm conscious of the sounds through the open kitchen window: The drone of a lawnmower. The lift of a floral-scented breeze as it passes through the Hammonds' blossom-dropping magnolia tree. Then Phil asks Jacob if he wants to see his new electric hedge trimmer, and Jacob jumps up, eager for the change of activity.

Together, they head for the garage.

"Phil will come around," says Sandy, when the guys are gone. "He's a worrywart, but he always gets there eventually. So, is my math terrible, or is this a New Year's baby?"

"Yes, April to January. Your math works." I smile. "The due date is January eleventh."

"I'm so thrilled, Nora! And really, Phil will be!"

"We'll start getting the nursery ready this summer," I tell her. "Do you think we could borrow Jacob's old dresser—the one that's up in the attic?"

"Borrow? Just take it. And his brass duck lamp, too—I've been saving it for you. But that room in the city is tiny! What a squeeze! Aren't you thinking of moving? Especially with a growing family? You must have a piggy bank by now." Sandy is forever perplexed by our decision to choose Brooklyn over the ample homes and friendly school districts of Massapequa.

"We're going slow and steady," I say. No need to pull back the curtain on the empty piggy bank.

Before we leave, Phil uses his electric hedge trimmer to cut away an armful of branches from his prized lilac tree for us to take back to the city. As soon as Jacob and I walk through our front door, the scent of lilac thickens the air with soupy sweetness, then the petals all drop, and Nick tries to eat them, and so after dinner, we throw them away.

"Though I *do* think that was Dad's version of an olive branch," says Jacob. "Okay, ready to call your parents?"

"Let's do it."

We lie on opposite ends of the couch and put my parents on speakerphone. "Oh, man," says Dad. "Nice. A kid."

"Ohhh," says Gabi, "this means I'll be a grandmother, maybe?"

"You'll definitely be a grandmother," Jacob says.

"Because she won't put it up for adoption on the illegal market, right?" says Dad.

"Since she's your friend," says Gabi.

"Yes," Jacob and I say together.

"Yes," Dad and Gabi agree.

"We're in the car on our way to see Toad the Wet Sprocket," says Dad.

"Cool," says Jacob.

"We're turning into the tavern now," adds Gabi, apologetic.

"We'll let you go," I say.

Once we're off, Jacob says, "I kind of wish we could find someone who'll jump up and down for our news. Want to call Meg?"

"I would, but it's late," I say, "I know she's on pins and needles, but let's do it tomorrow morning."

"All right." Jacob yawns and stretches. "Even factoring in my dad's fear that Evelyn will run away to Canada, and your dad worrying that Evelyn's long game is to sell the baby, I can't seem to wipe this big stupid grin off my face." He big-stupid-grins at me. "I know it's gonna be a long nine months, but right now I'm savoring this feeling hard."

"Hey, and there was a time when *we* were asking all those skeptical surrogate questions," I remind him. Now it's my turn to yawn. "Remember way back to when we thought we'd be plain old pee-on-a-stick parents?"

"We'll be plain old pee-stick parents soon enough." Jacob says. "Like when we're pushing that stroller in the park next spring, nobody's gonna say, 'Cute baby. You must be so glad your surrogate didn't run away to Canada to sell it.'"

"I'm looking forward to that day," I tell him.

Late that night, with Jacob asleep beside me, my phone buzzes. I lean up. Meg.

87 Brook Lane on Realtor.com

I sit up and click the link.

Larger Than It Appears. Feel the warm invitation of this lovingly maintained 1908 Dutch Colonial. A wraparound porch leads into an expansive living area, a charming space for formal entertaining. Claw-foot tub in primary bathroom and hardwood floors throughout. Cozy kitchen opens into an oversized backyard just waiting for summertime barbecues. Mature dogwood, crabapple, and cherry trees. New roof installed twelve years ago. Skip to Larchmont Park or stroll to town.

I take the tour twice. Then I get out of bed and duck into the bathroom, where I sit on the mat with my back against the door, the way I did in middle school so my mom couldn't hear when I called my friends late at night.

"I figured you'd be up!" says Meg. "I know you're waiting on the test, and I wanted to send you your possible dream-come-true house. Isn't it adorable?"

"Actually, the wait is over. I'm calling about another dream come true." I take a dramatic beat. "We got our second positive today."

"Wait—what? Seriously? Nora! Best news ever! Banks, wake up!" I hear scuffling sounds. Then Banks's voice, at first a distant mumble and now a roar in the phone.

"Nora, congrats! We're so happy! We love you!"

"Thanks, Banks!" Suddenly, my eyes are full of tears. How many times have I imagined this moment of telling Meg and Banks? I wrap my arm tighter around my knees and press my phone closer to my ear, hugging the moment even harder.

"I want it to be January already!" Meg carols. "I can't wait to see you and celebrate!"

After we hang up, she sends me Harry Styles in a pink tutu.

It's so refreshing, Meg's straight-up, reliable happiness. For a few minutes, it even lets me feel like a pee-on-a-stick person.

Twenty-Nine

The week after Evelyn and Henry return from Montauk, they leave for a trip to Kahuna, and they tailgate that trip with a long weekend in the Dominican Republic. Evelyn's short and sweet post about becoming a surrogate for her "dear friend" gets so much traction that EvvieDoesIt jumps up another hundred followers. Evelyn fuels the fire with a couple of friendly-glamorous bikini photos—"First trimester, bring it!"—and a few days later, she follows these photos up with a post on tips for morning sickness.

I'm sorry to hear you're not feeling well, I text her.

She texts back a wink. bright as a penny!

"Oh, good," I say. "She doesn't have morning sickness."

"Betcha she just wanted to post the tips," says Jacob.

"Maybe so. Wow, she's got so much engagement on the posts."

Later that day, Evelyn puts up a photo of herself in a shell blouse she bought at the shop and tags @IllHaveSeconds. As a result, we get two new online sales and five new followers. All ships rise in a successful social surrogacy.

We don't see the Elliots in person until the seven-week check-in, when they're back in New York, and we're gathered in our VIP concierge examining room to listen to the baseline *womp, womp, womp* on the fetal Doppler.

Jacob's hand finds the small of my back as we stare at the bean on the screen.

"I think I might explode from joy," I say.

Evelyn's smile is the sun. "We should do a baby shower," she says.

Her suggestion startles me. Meg and I were just talking about baby showers. Years ago, I'd thrown Meg a shower for Becket—but this time, we've agreed that Meg won't host one for me until after the baby is born.

I just can't count this chicken before it hatches.

But now that it's Evelyn proposing the shower, I feel tongue-tied. I don't want to disappoint her. "Maybe in February?" I say.

"February?" She wrinkles her nose. "But then the baby's here," she says. "That's too late. How about closer to the due date, sometime in November? Or even December works. Maybe we could set up a cash fund to donate toward a few weeks of a night nurse—trust me, you'll want the extra sleep."

"Oh, that sounds very kind," I say as Jacob shoots me a dubious look.

He knows what Meg and I decided. But I don't want to upset Evelyn, not about something as feel-good and generous as a shower. The back of my neck is hot.

"We'll put Raquel on it," says Evelyn.

"Sure," I say. "But really, it's not—"

"Let's you, me, and Raquel all sit down and brainstorm everything baby later this week since I don't leave for Paris till Friday," says Evelyn. "You should meet her anyway since she's handling my life. She'll get in touch to set it up."

"Sounds good," I say, and this is how I learn that Evelyn owns an entire other apartment on the seventeenth floor of the Baccarat Hotel on West Fifty-Third.

"How did I not know about this?" I ask as Evelyn answers the door and I step through into the entrance hall. "When Raquel gave me the address, I thought it was a WeWork."

"We never use it," says Evelyn. "It's so plain vanilla and sterile! That's why we call it the 'corporate' apartment. But it's good for little meetups."

"Evelyn, it's a whole other home!" This morning, Jacob and I were arguing about whether we should stop buying so many groceries from Trader Joe's. We love their frozen pizzas and salad dressings, but Foodtown is cheaper. So maybe I won't share with Jacob just yet the details of Evelyn's apartment that looks like nobody has lived here, ever.

"It's where my folks stay. It's very parental, right?" Evelyn makes a sweeping gesture that dismisses the dove-gray color scheme, the crystal fixtures. "Bryce and Jorge must own four other apartments scattered all around the city—now *that's* insane."

The nuances of millionaires versus billionaires isn't so obvious to me. The apartment has three bedrooms and four bathrooms, and unobstructed views of Central Park. I don't stop gaping at everything until Raquel arrives a few minutes later, and then I gape at her instead. Raquel looks exactly like what you think you'd get when you cross a model with a pop star—lanky and slouchy, with excellent cheekbones and even better clothes—today, she's wearing a tiny Missoni dress and a red Courrèges jacket—and she's got a choppy haircut that looks cool but also like she just cut bubble gum out of it.

Introductions are made, then we all sit together at the high-gloss walnut dining room table that easily could belong in a boardroom, and we tune into Raquel—who looks like she's on her way to The Dome at Coachella—to chat digital surrogacy.

First, Raquel takes us through how we'll use her Slack account to connect everyone on doctor appointments and emergency contacts.

Then Raquel looks to Evelyn, in what seems to be an expression of tacit agreement. Evelyn nods.

"So we were thinking," says Raquel, in a bland voice that is the way she says everything, "there's such a lot of wonderfulness to explore here with the surrogacy for social. That first post—the one where Evelyn explains why she's doing this—totally knocked it out of the park. The latest one, when she shared the, ah..."

"Quantitative HCG beta test," I prompt.

"Right," says Raquel. "That post got a lot of attention, too."

"I know," I say. "The comments are really positive. People are intrigued."

"Go me," says Evelyn with a cheerful fist pump. "So Raquel and I just want to make sure you're on board with the fun, Spell—and that you don't mind us marqueeing some of this. And to speak up! It's all kind of a test expedition."

"We'll take our cues from your guidelines," Raquel tells me.

"But I told Raquel we better make sure you're on board from go," says Evelyn.

"Hey, I'm as happy as anyone to tune in to EvvieDoesIt." I smile. "Happier, even. As long as you don't mind leaving Jacob's and my names out of it—we can cheer from the sidelines."

"Totally," says Raquel. "It works on our end too, since we'd like to create a space of respect and intimacy around the pregnancy without opening it up for every single question ever. Really, it's better to keep it centered on Evelyn. Day in the life. Wellness and exercise."

"Mentoring too," adds Evelyn. "Bits of wisdom I picked up my first go-round, with Xander. Nothing preachy."

"Candid and relatable, and you can't go wrong," I say. Though Evelyn's life is also tantalizingly aspirational—even Jacob likes to look over my shoulder for the occasional glimpse into her dreamy mornings of curated parfaits in her breakfast nook or Pilates in her home gym, or even to note the ever-upward climb of her social metrics.

Raquel has opened her laptop, and she's studying her screen while twirling a pen like a helicopter propeller between her navy-lacquered fingertips. "Everyone loves a how-to space," she says, "so we were thinking we'd start with scheduled posts on how to make healthy first-trimester recipes."

"We'll hide Tabitha in the corner," Evelyn says with a wink. "It's not like you need to go to cooking school to rustle up a snack." She waggles a finger at me. "Also, I'm not too sure about that app you sent." She means the Baby2Me app that I shared, where Evelyn can input meals and exercise.

"Okay," I say. Then I say, "It's a good app though. Frankie and Lisa Ann used it."

"Hmm," says Evelyn. "It just feels like a lot of inputting, maybe?"

"Also," says Raquel, "we saw you sent that Dropbox file about Carriage House Birth. The doula and midwifery center?"

"Yes! I've always wanted to take a doula class," I begin, but now I feel a bit defensive, having to explain myself to Evelyn's goth-punk-pixie young digital content creator. I shift in my seat, conscious of them both watching me. "I thought it might be a worthwhile thing for us to do together," I say to Evelyn. "The center is just a few minutes from your apartment—you could walk."

"I don't know," says Evelyn. "A doula might be a little touchy-feely for me."

"Also, I checked it out, and they don't have any handle on social—nothing. Not even Facebook," says Raquel. "It's pretty old-school."

"Well, *midwifery* is pretty old-school," I say. "And not everything needs to be uploaded to EvvieDoesIt, right?"

"One hundred percent," says Evelyn. "But I'm taking things slow—after all, I'm just starting to relax into this whole journey myself."

"I spoke on the phone with Alice, the midwifery consultant," I say, "and she said we could do a first class for free. So, putting that out there."

Evelyn nods. "Keep sending me those apps, Spell. You have a good eye." She looks to Raquel. "Ooh, idea: I could rank my top five favorite baby apps?"

"Now *that* I like," says Raquel. "That's organic content."

When I get home, Jacob is comfortably stretched out on the couch, watching *The Amazing Race*, Nick tucked like a football under his arm. He doesn't look like he needs to hear about Evelyn's extra apartment or any of the specifics of how she's shaping the surrogacy for the most hearts and eyeballs on prenatal wellness social—and since I'm not feeling the energy to enlighten him, I don't.

Thirty

Evelyn leaves for Paris, where she mixes stories of the shows with updates on how she's handling some nausea, but after she texts that wink emoji again, I'm convinced the morning sickness is just more make-believe. When I watch a YouTube video about the first weeks of pregnancy, with visuals of cells doubling and differentiating into a mass that becomes a tadpole, I feel less like an Intended Parent and more like a kid retaking sixth grade biology class—still abstract, only now I'm paying attention.

The next week, while Evelyn and Henry are in Lisbon to attend a friend's wedding, I get a surprise call at work from Bryce Appell's assistant.

Bryce wants to meet with me.

I'd always wondered why Bryce never called me back in December. Had she wanted me to help with a dinner? Another Jazz Age event? I figured that whatever it was, it was nothing much.

The assistant apologizes for not knowing why Ms. Appell-Papadopoulos has asked for this meeting, which she sets for an afternoon the following week. On that day, I get off work early to head uptown. Appell Inc. is a prime slice of midtown Park Avenue skyscraper, with security inspired by *The Bourne Identity*. I'm photographed, ID'd, and cleared for the forty-fourth floor. I land in a soft-lit and intensely feminine universe, where a willowy young assistant in a headset is waiting to spin me down one card-key-coded passageway after another before we cross the finish line into Bryce's sun-drenched, pastel-hued office.

"Nora!" Bryce jumps up from her marbled-pink desk and meets me halfway across a cloud of white carpet. "Thanks for coming all this way!" She is a sprite in a size-zero lavender power suit and precarious heels, and her hands reach to clasp one of mine and press hard, like a teeny little waffle maker. "Flat or fizzy water, or iced tea?"

"Oh, anything. Regular water." And in the next moment, the Appell gazelle is offering me a slim glass—flat water, twist of lemon. Bryce nods for her to go, then indicates one of a pair of ballet-slipper-pink accent chairs.

"It's very nice to see you, but I'm curious about why I'm here," I say, giving Bryce my best sales floor expression: attentive and helpful, as we sit.

"Yes! We'll get right to it. But first, we need to address the Evelyn in the room!"

I smile. "Jacob and I are still floating."

"I saw her in—was it Milan? No, that's not right."

"Paris."

"Paris! Fashion Week is always a blur." Bryce crosses her matchstick legs. Her smile is a reminder I need to buy Whitestrips. "Anyway, it's the talk of the town!"

"Is it?" "The talk" as in "the gossip"? A defensive spike runs up my spine.

"I've known Evelyn since kindergarten. She's always been so popular, figuring out one way or another to be the center of attention. And you can't deny, she's found an interesting niche." Somehow, Bryce manages to sound admiring and devious at the same time.

"Ah, but I think it's the opposite," I say. "I feel like she's got Jacob's and my priorities right at the center. She's put such a lot of thought into her social, with all the care she gives each comment. Or when she tags her doctor for clarification. Always so generous and wise."

"Love that for you. That is so the right take," says Bryce. "I just read somewhere that it was, maybe, seventy-five thousand dollars to contract with a New York surrogate?" Bryce overemphasizes a single blink. There's a sudden challenge in the question that I'm not sure how to meet. And why is Bryce even looking up the cost of surrogacy?

"It is very expensive," I allow. "But I bet that's not why you asked me up here."

"Guilty!" Bryce puts up her hands. "I actually wanted to chat about my grandmother," she says. "Opal," she adds, as if I don't know.

"Sure." I sit up straighter, as if Opal Appell might be joining us imminently.

And who knows? adds my mother's thrilled voice in my head. *She just might!*

"Opal and I have always been super close—when I was little, I'd come over for these 'tea and toast' nights, and she'd let me call her Grandy." Bryce's hands press against her heart. "And when I saw her in Aspen, back in December, I told her about your and Ev's link with the Bergessen cloak—and do you know what she said? She said, 'Frieda Bergessen? I'm such a fangirl!' A *fangirl*! Opal's eighty-nine. Isn't that adorable?"

"Ha, yes, I hope I'm still fangirling when I'm eighty-nine." The other night, in preparation for this meeting, I looked up Opal Appell, a fragile public sighting these days in her trademark Herrera suit and pearls. It's amusing to hear Bryce speak about this formidable icon like she's a little old grandma drinking Lipton in her fuzzy slippers.

"And here's the most fun part." Bryce gives a dramatic pause. "Opal was *there*! She was *at* Carnegie Hall that night. She didn't have a ticket, but she stood in the line to watch all the stars come in. She remembers them all vividly—Dylan Thomas and W. H. Auden—and she remembers Frieda, too. Wild, isn't it? Two legends crossing in a space-time axis!"

"That's... Yes." I sip my water and try to slow down my sudden, awful premonition that Bryce wants to buy my cloak for her grandmother.

As if on cue, Bryce says, "This October is Opal's ninetieth. Would you consider selling me that cloak?"

Aha. Very, very carefully, I set down my glass of water.

"I know it's sticky, considering it was from Evelyn. But I don't have just *any* grandmother." She's speaking in a rush. "I'd like to offer you twenty thousand dollars."

I can't disguise my astonishment. "That's a lot of money," I say, but then again, what's twenty thousand dollars to Bryce? A year in Wagyu burgers? The seasonal running cost on her personal ski lift?

"Nora, you wouldn't believe how people *shower* Opal with gifts and honors. And not just on her birthday. Every day. All the time, all over the world. I don't want to call it a problem, because all that adoration is completely lovely, but what do you give to the person who has everything?" Bryce knits her brows together in woeful anxiety. "So I guess I'm really appealing to you?"

"I feel for you, Bryce," I say, though mostly what I feel is panic. I don't want to be caught in a dilemma where I'll have to refuse a big chunk of Bryce's money. I fight my flight impulse. "But it's not for sale."

"She got *tears* in her eyes when she spoke of Frieda Bergessen. When you think about it, this is Opal Appell's history, too. I've made a mistake. Twenty isn't enough, is it? I'm not good at this! What would you say to thirty?"

"I'm sure you want to make your grandmother's party special," I tell her. "But if I sold this piece, Evelyn would be crushed."

"We'd *never* say anything to Evelyn!" Bryce looks shocked. "You must think I'm the worst. Putting you on the spot like this! I hate to make such a big ask—and I wouldn't, if it weren't so huge for me." She is holding her hands close together under her chin, like a squirrel. "But if you think of it in another way—as a very *kind* thing of me to do—then we all win, don't we? I could go to forty."

"I can't do this," I say. "I couldn't even tell Evelyn we're meeting about this."

"It never leaves my office! Promise! In the vault!" Bryce zips her mouth and makes a key-turn gesture. "How about I email my proposal? I'd be willing to go to fifty. Or, if you had a price—say you did—what would it be? Maybe I could send a written offer."

"Bryce, no."

"Nora, that cloak is history. You work in vintage—don't you think it should be somewhere safer than in your coat closet or wherever you've got it?" There's a whiff of schoolteacher in Bryce's voice. "You might find that letting go of it—and knowing it's in good hands—to be more reassuring than the burden of keeping it."

"It's not a burden."

"Okay."

"Okay."

We allow few seconds of stare-off. "I'm always so curious about vintage," Bryce says. "What is it *specifically* you love? Your *philosophy* of it?"

"Philosophy?" I'm glad for the topic shift. I try to relax into it. "I guess I've always enjoyed wearing pieces that are older than me. I feel protected by these other lives. Pre-owned clothes hold a history that seems to reinvent itself in every next generation of ownership."

"And what if it reinvents itself into sixty thousand dollars?"

I'm so gobsmacked that Bryce jerked us right back to the money that I stand up in a little hop. Who taught her to be like this? While other kids were mushing Play-Doh, was young Bryce at Opal's knee, honing her cutthroat deal tactics? "I think I should go."

Bryce looks surprised that I'm closing the meeting as she also jumps to a stand. "You'll take some time to think about it?" She hesitates. "Because maybe this is the one piece of vintage that protects you in a slightly different way?"

I shake my head. "This gift has real meaning for me. Especially considering what Evelyn is doing for my family."

Bryce nods. "I'll buzz Winnie." Her gaze moves past me to her window bank—her endless skyline, the pink cherry trees down Park. I feel like I've already left the room as Bryce daydreams through other ways around this birthday gift problem that I didn't help her solve.

"You've been kind to hear me out," she says, slapped back to life as Winnie enters. Then Bryce air-kisses me goodbye in a flowery whiff of what I recognize as the company's best-known scent, *Belle by Appell*—we all wore it in college. Her manners are impeccable, but her proposal feels like the tip of an ice pick lodged in my chest.

On the subway home, I sidestep Jacob's curious texts.

It was no big deal. Bryce wants ideas on vintage colors.

Don't give them away for free! he writes back.

I'm still processing the meeting in tiny electric zaps when Bryce's email comes in.

Her jaw-dropping final price: seventy-five thousand dollars.

Is this the number she was planning all along?

Opal's birthday isn't until the fall if you need some time. It'd be a lovely tribute to my grandmother, who's someone I'm hoping you might have a soft spot for, as a feminist trailblazer of American industry.

It's eye-watering, life-changing money. My thumbs move more quickly than my good judgment, and I slide Bryce's email into the trash. I'm trembling. At least I've got some time before I need to answer her.

Meanwhile, since I can predict his response, I'll hold off saying anything to Jacob. I've never kept a secret from him, and this one will feel excruciating. But I need to think.

Thirty-One

Abraham and Claudia Mendoza-Tanaka are born at the end of May. When they all come home from Bethesda, Jacob and I are their first visitors. Abe has Seth's square ears and monkish stare, while Claudia's kitten face is a clone of Frankie's. I send lots of photos to Jacob's and my parents so they can see a real-live happy family where the surrogate didn't exchange the babies for a sack of gold. To cover Frankie's paternity leave, Barb hires her friend Tina Mendelson to help, and it's a little bit like having another Barb in the shop.

"I know you're enjoying your time, but you'd better come back," I inform Frankie one evening after work when I'm up at his apartment to visit. "Right now I'm dealing with a lot of old-broad humor and Steely Dan." We're both in Frankie's living room, folding a pile of fresh warm laundry lumped between us on the couch while the twins nap in their nursery. "Tell me now if you're harboring secret plans to turn into a stay-at-home dad."

He shakes his head. "It's too hard—these babies are kicking my ass. I've been in this shirt for two days, there's bottles all over the apartment, trash bags piling up in the kitchen that I'm too tired to take out. Don't let Barb give away my job." He yawns. "Are you coming to the shower-thing Trix is hosting next Sunday? It's small; Seth's mom, some work colleagues from the firm, some of our hall neighbors—and did I tell you my parents said yes?"

"Of course I'm coming," I say, as I refold a pair of footie pajamas so they look less wadded. "And good! It's about time they meet their grandchildren!"

"I'm not counting on it," says Frankie. "They said they'd come to my wedding too. But I'm glad you'll be there, in case things get weird."

"Evelyn is planning to throw us a baby shower, which is very sweet of her, but it makes me nervous," I say. "Not to go to my darkest places, but what if something happens, and we've got all these baby toys and clothes in the apartment? I can't imagine anything worse."

"Preacher, meet the choir," says Frankie, plucking out the match to a baby blue sock the size of a finger puppet. "I think it was because Lisa Ann lived far away and it felt so out of our control, but Seth and I were fully superstitious."

"That's the thing," I say. "Every time Jacob and I work to emotionally prepare for this baby coming to us in January, we hit the wall of our defense-mechanisms. We've been listening to parenting books on Audible, and we go into stores to look at cribs and strollers, and yet even the word *expecting* feels so presumptuous for our situation. More like *hopefully anticipating while desperately anxious*? All to say, it might not be the best baby shower energy."

"So just tell Evelyn to reschedule the shower." Frankie takes a stack of clothing from me and places it in the laundry basket.

"It's not so easy, telling Evelyn what to do."

"Are you superstitious about the posts?" Frankie asks. "Or the fact your baby is a little bit social media famous now? Or all the random content she uploads?"

"Not really," I say, "but I'm superstitious about not wanting to be an obstacle between Evelyn and what makes Evelyn happy." I pause. "And can I let you in on a secret? Something I haven't told Jacob, or even our therapist?"

"Tell me."

"I made a stealth account."

"You did not!"

"I did! I wanted to find out things I'd never have the nerve to ask her in real life."

"That is nuts, Nora."

"Is it, though? Evelyn answers even the most fringe questions in the comments section—she always wants to educate people. Like when she got that massage the other day."

"Saw that," says Frankie. "Personally, I thought it looked great. My kingdom for a ninety-minute neonatal lymphatic drainage massage."

"Well, I had questions about where the therapist was trained. So I asked under my assumed identity, at marjigangle."

"You named your social-media-stalking alter ego after our very own compulsive returner, Marjorie Gangle?" Frankie makes a face.

"I did. But I'm not stalking. The handle emboldens me."

"Did Evelyn respond?"

"She did," I say. "She listed the therapist's credentials—and even tagged her—and I felt a lot better."

"I guess that's one way to do it," says Frankie, "and your secret is safe with me. But can I invite Evelyn to *my* shower? Lisa Ann and her husband, Russell, are coming. Everyone could meet. What are the odds we'd *both* have families this way?"

I've spoken with Lisa Ann once on FaceTime. Sweet as she is, I can't imagine what she'd have in common with Evelyn. "Sure," I say, "but Evelyn's in Saratoga Springs this week. Henry's doing a book festival, and she has a farm up there for retired racehorses."

"Big heiress energy," Frankie says. "Full disclosure, I know all about Camp Champion from EvvieDoesIt."

"Seriously?" I give him a look. "I didn't know you were such a big fan of EvvieDoesIt."

"What can I say? I love Evelyn's luxe-surro-mama vibe, and it always feels like she's having a good time. She just posted a recipe with a photo for skillet four-cheese ravioli—Seth wants to try making it."

"That's her chef, Tabitha, who's also the wizard behind the one-pot lentils and the sheet-pan fajitas, and the recipe fruits of the week that correspond with the size of the baby."

"Nice trick," says Frankie. "But it must be a relief that Evelyn's so health-conscious. I used to go after Lisa Ann for her Triple-Whopper-with-Cheese cravings and all that sodium."

"I could never tell Evelyn what to eat," I say.

"Never? But that's your baby." Frankie cuts me a concerned look that makes my cheeks burn, and he must see something in my expression, because then he slaps my arm with the onesie he's holding. "Bah, it doesn't matter, as long as you're both on the same page. And it's great that she's posting health information."

"It is," I agree. "She's always creating content, and she's got a real talent for starting conversations. In fact, if there's any slight downside of EvvieDoesIt taking off, it's that I've seen Evelyn only once since the last doctor's appointment."

"That's pretty standard. Seth and I didn't see Lisa Ann more than five times, total, transfer through delivery," Frankie reminds me.

"Right, I know," I say. "And there's something charming in everyone being invited to enjoy Evelyn's pregnancy right along with her. She's getting an avalanche of support, and I know she loves the affirmation—and she deserves it." I fold the last burp cloth and press it firmly onto the top of the stack to compact it.

"So everybody wins," says Frankie.

"Everybody wins," I agree. "But still, I miss her."

Thirty-Two

<<<<<<<<<<<<<

No matter how carefully I word it, I feel like a nag when I send
Evelyn a second text that I hope she'll drop by Frankie's shower.
The first text went unanswered, and this time she sends a breezy I'll try!,
so I'm surprised to see her when I show up at the apartment the next
Sunday. At the door, I'm greeted by two enormous bobbling bunches of
balloons—one pink, one blue—over which a gold banner reads **BABIES
IN BLOOM**.

"Nora!" Trix plants a kiss on my cheek as she takes my bag of gifts.
Frankie's little sister has his star quality but goofier—the comic foil to
Frankie's svelte leading man. She checks over her shoulder as she drops
her voice. "You just missed the FaceTime drama," she whispers. "Our
parents aren't coming after all. They're saying they ate bad calamari at
Carmine's last night. They're at the hotel."

I sag. "Really?"

"Really." Disappointment hangs off her. "All Frankie wants is
things to be normal. So I'm cranking up the happy. I made a cute
little coconut cake, and we're playing a shower game called Don't Say
Baby!" She reaches into her front overalls pocket for an oversize diaper
pin that she fastens to my sundress strap. "If you say the word *baby*,

someone can take your pin! The person with the most pins wins a lulu-lemon robe."

"Oh, so fun," I lie as Trix leads me into the living room, a pink-and-blue jungle of crepe paper and balloons. She sets my bag—half a dozen cotton sleep sacks Singer-sewed by me—on the console heaped with gifts, and she shepherds me around for introductions. I meet some of the neighbors and say hi to the faces I know—Mrs. Tanaka and Lisa Ann, who introduces me to her husband, Russell... But all I see is Evelyn, standing by a far window, chatting with Seth.

She's wearing a navy Akris jumpsuit that I sourced for her last month, and in her Van Cleef pendants and Gucci gladiator sandals, she looks like a goddess of plenty.

"Spell!" she calls out and then leaps across the room to envelop me in a jangle of necklaces and bracelets. I feel the firm, warm bump of the pregnancy; a point of contact that overwhelms me and leaves me feeling slightly light-headed.

"Oh," I say. "The baby." *That's my baby. My very own baby.*

"Strange for you," she says, her eyes limpid with understanding. "Here I'm this whole other person, and it's your own precious thing."

"It's fine—the good strange." I feel Seth watching. "The nine-month babysitting job, you called it on one of your posts. I loved that."

"Well, and that's just the way to think of it, Spell. Anyway, I told Seth I'm here to scope tips for our own fabulous winter shower," she says. "I can't stay long, but I did get to meet those adorable babies."

"Baby! You said *baby*!" Trix cries. Evelyn, who is holding the diaper pin in her hand, now drops it into Trix's palm like it's something that's been stuck in a dog's mouth. "Shower games are the worst," she declares sunnily.

"Guava or lime mojito mocktails?" asks Frankie, who looks trans-fixed and elated that Evelyn is here. "Also, Trixie, stop this game." I'm pleased to see how self-conscious he feels around Evelyn. *See? Try telling Evelyn not to eat a Whopper.*

"Guava," says Evelyn. "I'll come with you and watch how you make it."

"Ooh, for EvvieDoesIt? So posh—let me get my top hat." And Frankie does his best Fred Astaire soft shoe as they head for the kitchen together.

In the dining room, Trix's blue-and-pink coconut cake is lopsided and turning emo purple where the dyes meet. I select a wrap and some roasted vegetables and join the others in the living room. Lisa Ann and Russell are sharing a plate balanced on his knee.

"Some water, babe?" Russell asks Lisa Ann.

"Oops, sorry, but you said *baby*!" Trix says as she leaps from her chair.

"He said *babe*," I correct, but Trix is already unfastening Russell's pin.

"Let's do presents," suggests Seth once Frankie and Evelyn have joined, and the next hour is devoted to exclaiming over diaper bags and sippy cups. Evelyn's shimmering, sunshiney energy is the center of the hub as she takes photos and records video clips before she says she's sorry she can't stay longer, but she's got to skedaddle to be on time for her one thirty.

"I'll walk you out," I tell her. I need to get back to Jacob, who is primer-painting the nursery today.

"It's one fifteen," says Russell. "You're not leaving much time to catch that train."

"Because it's a helicopter," says Evelyn. "The heliport is right off the FDR."

"Oooh!" says Lisa Ann. "By helicopter!"

"You can see it for yourself in my next post. It's tips about how to stay comfortable while traveling when pregnant," says Evelyn.

"We made your skillet ravioli from EvvieDoesIt the other week," says Seth. "Evelyn's a big deal on social," he tells the group.

"Oh, stop. You're too sweet, mister," says Evelyn.

Immediately, Lisa Ann finds EvvieDoesIt on her own phone. "Geez! You've got over eighty thousand people following you!" she exclaims, and now everybody's pulling out their phones.

"Nectarine salsa—that sounds interesting," says Mrs. Tanaka.

"It's because this week, the fetus is the size of a nectarine," I offer, to signal that I'm also up to speed on EvvieDoesIt, though now I feel weird that I went with *fetus*; I only said it to dodge using *baby*. *Bean*, *munchkin*, *peanut*? But nobody's listening to me, because everyone's looking on their phones at EvvieDoesIt.

When Evelyn leaves her new fans for a trip to the bathroom before she lifts off, Frankie gestures for me to walk with him to the door.

"I'm sorry about your parents," I say.

"Thanks," he says. "But Evelyn being here saved the day."

"I thought that my being here, as one of your closest friends, saved the day."

"Actually, I'm very shallow, and you don't have eighty thousand followers." But when we hug goodbye, the weight of his sunken hopes feels so heavy, and I hold strong in my best *Giving Tree* trunk support for him to lean against.

"The *Weekend Journal* is doing a little profile on Henry and me," says Evelyn as we leave the apartment, pushing into the sweltering heat as we walk to the corner to meet her town car. "It's about the surrogacy but with some focus on what I'm doing to build awareness for the horses— they come to us in such bad shape."

"Wow. And the *Weekend Journal*, that's real."

"I just hope it's not some unrelatable story—like being on a cruise ship when the towers fell." Evelyn says it good-humoredly, but *Right, because a farm for retired racehorses? Now* there's *an everywoman hobby* is the joke I know better than to make out loud.

As Evelyn puts a hand on the car door, I say, "I'm sure you've got a lot going on, but I'd love to grab lunch or a tea sometime soon."

She stops. "But you see me every day on social!" she says, sort of kiddingly—though I know embedded in that light protest is her desire to hear me tell her again how well she's curated EvvieDoesIt and what an impressive community she's building, especially evidenced in the flood of goodwill every time she posts, the hundreds of hearts, the well-wishers and comments: "With everything you do, how mind-blowing that you're making time to do this," and "You are providing a miracle," and "You are giving your IPs an extraordinary gift."

"I miss you in real life," I say instead.

Evelyn pauses to absorb this. "Spell, honey. Of course. I'll get Raquel to set it up," she says, and we exchange a hug, and the moment is like a lifeline. She pats the front of the jumpsuit. "Say bye-bye, baby."

"Bye-bye, baby." Which suddenly feels like the most depressing thing I've said all week. But I keep my smile in place as I take off my diaper pin and slip it into my pocket.

Thirty-Three

Jacob meets me at the door with a spatter of primer paint like playful freckles on his nose. But he's not in a playful mood. These past few weekends, he's been hard at work on the nursery, stripping out old gummy coats of paint to find the shape of the original moldings. Today, the priming looks like it got the better of him. His face is overheated, and his T-shirt is sweat-darkened at the neckline and armpits.

"Come look," he says, and I follow him to the nursery.

"Aha, your parents dropped off the dresser! It looks so nice!"

"How does *this* look nice? It's half the room." Jacob rarely blows his temper, but I can feel his lid is loose. "I'm taking it down into basement storage tonight."

"Great, and we can put the baby clothes in the hall closet. It'll free up space. Meg is giving us her bassinet, we'll keep my Singer, and I bet we can squeeze in a rocking chair—"

"A *rocking* chair?" Jacob slumps to sit against the wall. "Where, Nora? The room can barely hold the bassinet."

"Okay. Maybe no rocking chair," I say.

"We also need to pack up the *Phantom of the Opera* cloak." He points to the mannequin, presently protected under a drop cloth.

"We're months out, Jacob."

"I don't know what you see when you look at this room," says Jacob, "but I see a tiny depressing cell with a lot-lined window and *The Scream* on the ceiling." Our gazes lift to look at the stain, which really does look like it might have been an early Munch sketch.

"The tester guy came back and said *The Scream* was just a stain. Not asbestos."

"I know what the tester guy said. I don't believe it." Jacob takes a long swig from his water bottle. "I'm gonna shower and walk Nick."

"If it's bothering you, we can get a second opinion."

"I don't need a second opinion to know I hate this shitty apartment. I never thought we'd have to raise our child in it."

"But we're not raising our child in it," I say. "This is our starter apartment."

"We're barely out of the woods on the IVF debt," says Jacob, "and now we're getting knocked sideways by obstetrician bills. Big picture, we never move forward. We're never rolling out of here—not in the next few years, anyway."

"Bigger picture, this baby is our dream come true. So what if we can't fit a dresser? We are a couple who talks about bassinets and rocking chairs. These are champagne problems."

"Asbestos isn't a champagne problem," he snaps. "It's like you shame me—when all I want is our baby to have a decent room, which this is clearly not."

"I don't shame you, Jacob, and we're not going to argue about something this stupid," I say, and then I go out to the living room, where I sit on the couch and unhappily pretend to read a book as I wait for Jacob to leave the apartment—*slam*!

After he's gone, I fill a glass of water and return to the nursery.

I pull off the drop cloth to look at the cloak.

It's wildly beautiful, like we trapped a peacock in our apartment. I get my phone and recover my Bryce email. Like a kid with an F paper crushed in the bottom of my book bag, all I've done is wish it would just go away, but I know it won't, and at some point I have to deal with it.

Somewhere I read that an object holds its true worth only when it's being bought or sold. The Bergessen cloak will always hold the worth of my love for it and for Evelyn. Her big heart and her abundant generosity. In a perfect world, I'd never need to think about another kind of value.

But obviously it's also impossible for Jacob and me to have one honest conversation about our future as long as I'm secretly holding this key to another version of it. I can't keep putting off telling him. It's been weeks since I saw Bryce—I probably shouldn't have left it longer than a day.

Could we find some time for me to visit? I text Meg. I really need to see you.

Thirty-Four

M eg and I make plans for me to spend Saturday night in Greenwich and to visit the house on 87 Brook Lane the next day. I've secured a Sunday appointment with the Realtor, Oscar Torrey, and Meg will drop me at the train station afterward.

I know we've done the "just looking" rodeo a thousand times but really feel like this could be your Goldilocks home, Meg texts me that morning.

Mostly I want to see you and Banks and the girls.

Then I send her Harry Styles carrying a Mickey Mouse suitcase through an airport. It feels like forever since our last weekend visit—and a lifetime since Meg and I first met as freshman at Phelps.

For plenty of families, a private liberal arts college is just another step in a life of everything going right, but my mom didn't start fixating on this lofty goal for our own little family unit until she got so sick that she spent most of her days bedridden and online. She was besotted by Phelps's quaintness, its fieldstone buildings and plush green lawns that could have been the village setting of a BBC detective show, and eventually she grew obsessed with her vision of me tucked safely in its custody after she was gone.

And so, with the same dedication she put into sewing me clothes for the kind of life she thought I should live, she applied for every financial aid scholarship she thought I deserved to get me into Phelps. She also specialized in finding grants for kids with terminally ill parents: Life Lessons, Life Happens, Cancer for College, Pink Roses. She wrote the essays and read me the drafts.

"Growing up, I thought my mom would always be there. She was the most positive role model in my life. What I remember most is how she loved to help others. The main thing I'd say about losing her is the feeling of emptiness that never goes away."

"Who are all these others that you love to help so much?" I asked.

"I guess you, for one!" she said, waggling her eyebrows at me. "I just know this school will open its arms."

When Phelps accepted me, my mom kept the printout on her bedside table, next to her blister packs of Zofran and cans of Ensure. She died six weeks later, and Gabi and Dad came to settle her affairs, and to bring me to Florida, where I worked at Cold Stone Creamery by day, played endless rounds of gin rummy with Gabi by night, and tried to process my life after the most important person in it had left. I'd decided to defer Phelps, but by August, all I could see was my mom in her bathrobe, hunched at our clunky beige home computer, or in bed poring over those stacks of applications.

So I got on a Greyhound and twenty-four hours later, I met Meg.

Six feet tall in rainbow socks and sporting a punk fade haircut, Meghan DeLuca—recruited to Phelps for field hockey and widely known on campus by her last name, though always Meg to me—had been getting our freshman dorm room ready all weekend by the time I showed up. She'd made it catalog friendly, with a furry blue rug, mini fridge, silver standing lamp, framed and matted Matisse goldfish print, and even a lime-green iMac and printer on the desk. I'd never been here before, and yet somehow, it secured in me a sense of homecoming I didn't know how much I'd missed until it was right here in front of me.

"We can share everything. I've got four older brothers, so most of my stuff is hand-me-downs," Meg said. "Too bad I'm so tall, or we could share clothes. Where'd you get those jeans?" Another way I'd been coping through this painful summer was by devoting myself to sewing and embroidery projects. I was proud of the way these jeans had turned out, its seams embellished in a feather stitch trelliswork of gold-and-silver snapdragons.

"I did the flowers myself," I said.

"Seriously? I don't know anyone who sews. Could you let down hems for me? Should we also go in on a full-length mirror?"

Mutely, I nodded yes to everything, calculating when I'd get my first work-study check, hoping that the cost of a mirror wouldn't sink me too badly—it wasn't until years later that Meg told me I'd looked completely panicked by her suggestion.

"Or, actually, who needs a mirror?" She shrugged. "Mirrors just mess with my head."

"We'll be the body-positive room that only needs each other to say we look fabulous before we go out," I suggested.

"So much better," she agreed.

Later, in this strange new day of our tentatively adult lives, we strolled into town for a bottle of cheap vodka to make Gatorade screwdrivers, and then we sprawled on the big blue sky of rug. I talked about losing my mom. Meg showed me photos of her oldest brother, Andrew, who died of AIDS when she was twelve. Meg learned my mom's birthday, I learned Andrew's, and in later years, when Phelps was long behind us, we texted hearts on those days to mark the bruises.

That first fall break, I tagged along with Meg to Narragansett, Rhode Island, and met her pack of brothers, who roved in and out of the family's lakefront home that shuddered with every slam of the screen door. Family extended to include uncles and aunts, cousins, and grandparents—there was always another lanky DeLuca meandering over for a swim, then staying for spaghetti dinner at their backyard table.

After graduation, we lived together for three years. Our lease ended right around the same time Meg got engaged to affable Banks Barnett, who was in Phelps's architecture program. A couple of years later, Becket was born. Two years later came Reed. Then Banks turned thirty-five, and the Barnett-family trust kicked in.

No more pretending to make ends meet in a two-bedroom in Hell's Kitchen, as the Barnetts whisked off into their actual adulthood in Greenwich—where, as soon as I deboard the train, Duke bounds up to cover me in slobbery kisses.

"Down, boy!" Meg slings my bag over her shoulder and leans in for a squeeze. "Salmon's marinating for the grill. Sancerre's chilling in the fridge. Banks brought a brownie cheesecake; I didn't even know brownies could hybrid with cheesecake. And Georgia peaches."

"Dreamy."

"The girls are super amped for Aunt Nora. It's been chaos since sunup. Fair warning."

But it's heartening to be with them again—to see Hailey cruising into her first steps while Reed and Becket ply me with crayoned cards and chain necklaces made from limp bluebells and dandelions. We all go for an afternoon dip in the pool, where I'm referee for competitive water ballet, followed by Becket's mice-versus-kittens game that I take extra seriously since Reed just wants to splash.

Afterward, I find a wheelbarrow in the tool shed for some afternoon garden work. The girls trot beside me, each harnessed into a pair of gossamer fairy wings I'd brought for them. They yank up yellow weeds and the odd worm. Next is dinner on the flagstone patio, followed by cheesecake and peaches and an inky dusk of fireflies—adults watching, children chasing.

Banks goes into Daddy duty, scooping Hailey up for her last bottle of the night and then corralling the older girls into nightgowns and teeth-brushing so that Meg and I can have some alone time.

"Ah, peace." Meg stretches the tanned, toned highways of her legs up onto the chair Banks just vacated. "It gives me such joy, to think of your baby growing up with my girls."

"Dreaming and scheming, just like us." I bite through the skin of my second perfect peach.

"Hey, Norsie," she says, and she makes that tense, throat-clearing sound she always does before she wants to speak seriously. "When you see Hailey, does it weigh on you at all? Like, does it remind you of last year, finding out I was pregnant after all of our planning?"

"It did, but it doesn't anymore," I tell her, always glad I can be honest with Meg. "All I see when I see Hailey is Hailey. Same as Reed and Becket."

"I figured." Meg's face takes on the softness that it does when she hears any of her daughters' names. "And Evelyn really seems to know what she's doing. I'm a big fan of EvvieDoesIt. Is it weird I check in with it every day? Her stories are just so dang charming, and I love her sense of humor and her jeuje billionaire style."

"She'd be quick to tell you she's not a billionaire—she's just a lotsa millions-aire."

"Well, I'm here for her millions," says Meg. "I crack up every time I see Bryce the Nice in the Stories. Remember how intimidated we were by her at Phelps?"

"Ah, but Bryce the Nice is kind of a shark. She's put me in a conundrum." I find my email and pass over my phone for Meg to read Bryce's offer while I keep working on my peach that tastes like summer.

After a minute, she sits up, alerted. "Wait, what? What is this? What does she want to buy?"

When I tell her, Meg looks floored. "Let me get this right. You're debating about whether you should sell a *coat* to buy a *house*?"

"Cloak, technically. And not just a coat, it's a Dior haute from his very last season. I know, I hear myself say it and it sounds bananas. But if you saw it—it's like jumping in a time machine, and I think selling it might break Evelyn's heart. I know it's sort of breaking mine.

But I also know what the answer is. How do I look away from that much money?"

"You don't. It's a coat. For a house."

"It's more like an artifact, or a piece of art—it belonged to the poet Frieda Bergessen, which adds a whole other dimension to why I love it. I've never owned anything so special."

"I don't care if it belonged to the poet William Shakespeare, you vintage nerd." Meg shakes her head. "For seventy-five thou, you and Frieda need to break up."

"Right, I know." I sigh. "I guess I feel emotional about it."

"If you need the Linus-blankety feeling of owning something gorgeous, go find your sewing kit. Remember my formals dress you copied from the photo of that Oscar de la Renta? How you sewed in all the gold beads? And I called it my Nora de la Renta?"

"It's not the same thing, Meg."

"That dress is tied with my wedding dress as my forever favorite."

"I know, and it was a great project." I can still see the rhinestone whorls of the pinwheel design I'd duplicated, and can feel the underside of the fabric as I set the pattern, the triangle of bent cloth between my fingers as I inched my way along the neck. "It also helped that you've got nine feet of legs." I toss my peach pit and listen to it land with a soft rustle in the hedgerow. "My stomach is a jumble just talking about this."

"Are you stumped about how you'd break it to Evelyn?"

"That's another thing. Bryce doesn't want us to tell her—but that feels strange, right? Obviously, I need to talk about it with Evelyn first."

"No, no." Meg shakes a finger at me. "You keep this wrap under wraps. Don't you dare tell her until after you do it. What's that old expression—*ask forgiveness, not permission*?"

I cringe. "That's not me, and it feels like the wrong move. Don't you think she'd understand that I'd be doing this to make a home for the baby?"

"She might. She might freak out. And then what? Why chance it?"

Meg has a way of saying everything so that it sounds like a simple, declarative truth, but it's hard to explain that my objection is based not only on my concern that I'd upset Evelyn but also on my profound, irrational reluctance to give up this one small claim on history. Nearly every night, I've drifted into the nursery just to look at it. I'm smitten as much by the detailing as by the lore. Its pristine beauty derived in part from its unlikelihood, as a mint-condition piece that has been treasured and preserved since its creation. It's like being an artist and owning your very own Picasso or being a musician with a Stradivarius, and I can't stand the thought of it leaving me.

But it's time to reshape my thinking. A house for a coat.

Put that way, it's hard to argue.

Thirty-Five

I see trees of green,'" Meg sings as she parks her Jetta directly in front of the house.

"That is the worst Louis Armstrong impression maybe ever?"

"'Red roses too.'"

"End this now."

"I think it's this house that makes me want to sing out loud."

"It's even better in person," I agree as we get out of the car and walk the path that bisects the slick green lawn of 87 Brook Lane.

"Brick chimneys give me life." Meg adjusts her Ray-Bans. "I'm in love already."

Me too. The appeal of this charming little house hits me with such a blast of feeling that I almost wish I hadn't come here to bear witness to it. The red climbing roses, the Delft Blue center door.

I wave at the balding, mustached man striding out of it. "That's Oscar."

"Hello, hello! Oscar Torrey!" he says as we meet him halfway up the walk, pumping us with handshakes. His smile lifts his mustache. "A house that sells itself. Come and get it!" He ushers us forward. "Here's your wraparound porch. The owner's got a green thumb—the real garden's out back. Follow me to the kitchen... Watch your step."

"You had me at *wraparound porch*," says Meg as we step onto it.

I take pictures of everything: the finial newel post, the stained-glass fanlights that throw a rainbow over the foyer, the second bathroom's basket-weave mosaic tiles. I can't even pick a favorite detail.

"One of the best things about leaving the city was all the extra space for clothes," says Meg when she finds me gaping at the primary bedroom closet. "You're lucky the bathrooms are small."

"You think the bathrooms are small?"

"And that kitchen's dark. I mean, there are some real issues. You can see why it hasn't been snapped up, even in this crazy housing market."

I tap the window glass. "They've got a swing set."

"You can take that out," says Meg.

But we could also keep it. And just the fact that we have more than one bathroom feels kingly. Maybe Meg has forgotten the size of Jacob's and my apartment.

Downstairs, Oscar Torrey needs to head to another showing. He tells us we're free to sit on the porch.

"Betcha they'd sell us this cute furniture," I say as we drop onto the wicker settee.

"Betcha they'd throw it in for free."

"Excellent school district. Five-minute walk from the station." I sigh. "My new dream life feels so manageable."

"Nobody could fault you for wanting this adorable home."

"It doesn't feel like a Faustian bargain?"

"Nora, no! That's so superstitious!"

"I guess I'm feeling superstitious these days."

Meg's voice goes easy on me. "But why aren't you allowed a home *and* a kid?"

"Because I've got so much," I say. "Jacob. My job and my friends—and now this baby that I never, ever thought would happen. If this money is a windfall, maybe we should save it. Doesn't it feel like break-glass-in-emergency cash?"

"Or maybe you deserve better than a fourth-floor walk-up that smells like fried fish."

I give her a look. "Wait, is that a metaphor? Or does our place smell like fish?"

"Last time I was there, the person down the hall was literally frying a fishy dish," says Meg. "But this house is between you, your seventy-five-thousand-dollar secret, and Jacob."

"But telling is selling, right?"

"Whatever gets you there," says Meg.

Jacob meets me at Grand Central. We decide on an early dinner at the Oyster Bar. Sitting at its long winding counter, we feast on bowls of New England clam chowder with crackers.

"Okay, had some time to think," says Jacob, "and, yes, I've got to stop sweating this tired idea about what the baby should have—whatever *should* means. Because this baby's already got everything."

"I'm so happy you're saying this."

"Also, two more teddy bears showed up today. Gabi didn't get the memo that we can't even fit a dresser. Champagne problems. We are a couple who talks about an abundance of teddy bears." We smile at each other. "Wanna show me the house?"

I've taken dozens of photos of 87 Brook Lane, and Jacob looks though them all. "It's pretty appealing as fixer-uppers go," he says. "Maybe we can ask for a bridge loan from Mom and Dad." But even as he says this, Jacob gives me a look like he wants to stuff those words in a pillowcase and hide them. "Anyway," he says, handing back my phone. "I'm more fired up for the baby we're getting than the house we're not."

"We might have a way to get the house without asking for the loan."

And then I tell him everything, stopping short of the fact that I've been sitting on Bryce's offer for weeks. "I've just spent a weekend with Meg in my ear repeating 'seventy-five thousand dollars' over and over,"

I say, "but I want you to recognize that this is complicated for me. Especially explaining it to Evelyn."

Jacob is quiet. "Evelyn got her dopamine high when she gave you the gift. What happens next isn't up to her. Why do you need to explain to her what we're doing?"

"Because I don't like being complicit with Bryce."

"You're not being complicit," says Jacob. "You're respecting Bryce's relationship with Evelyn."

"That isn't how it feels to me."

Later, in bed, Jacob rolls on his side to face me in the dark. "I can practically hear your thoughts scuttling around. Did you write Bryce?"

"I did," I say. "I'm sure I'll hear back tomorrow."

"So that part's done."

"Yes." I knew telling Meg and Jacob would force me to action, even if the rebellious, stubborn vintage nerd inside me doesn't think there's any amount of money that's bigger than my desire to hold on to my gift. "Unrelated, does our apartment smell like fried fish?"

"Only in the summer," he says, "and only when that lady down the hall cooks trout."

Thirty-Six

The very next morning, Bryce calls me at work.

"I'm thrilled!" she sings, and I can just see her, perky at her empty desk in her spotless, pastel-hued office. "You have no idea!"

"The only thing is that I want to tell Evelyn," I say. "I just don't feel comfortable lying to her. I want her to know how much you paid me—I hope that works for you."

"I guess it'll have to," says Bryce after a moment's pause. "Winnie can arrange the pickup sometime in the next couple of weeks. Whenever it's convenient for you."

"Great. I hope your grandmother loves it." I close my eyes. "I loved my year with it."

"It's been a long time since I looked forward to giving Opal a gift," says Bryce. "Thank you. I'll get Winnie to call and verify your routing number, and we'll let you know when she'll be over to collect the piece."

Winnie's follow-up call happens twenty minutes later. By lunchtime, the full seventy-five hits Jacob's and my joint checking account, as easy as if I rubbed a magic lamp.

All that afternoon, whenever I get a minute, I log in to First Republic and stare at this money. It's more cash than I've ever seen all at once.

Jacob sends me a spreadsheet where he's input mortgage rates on 87 Brook Lane, but he wants to go tour the house in person before we put in an offer. I text him a piggy, a bank, and a heart emoji. My mind is a fiery whirligig of elation and panic. I knew that once I called Bryce, I wouldn't be able to undo the deed, but I didn't expect it to happen quite this fast. Even the house feels too quick, like we've jumped out onto a ledge, when the money really should be guarding us.

"Are you okay?" Frankie asks a couple of times that day, and again after we've closed the shop and cashed out. I've run downstairs twice for plastic EAS security tags, only to forget what I'm doing and come back empty-handed.

"I'm fine!"

He gives me the frown that says he knows I'm lying. My third time down and up the stairs, Frankie is suspicious. "You've got the most spaced-out look on your face, and I can't quite read it. What's going on with you?"

I point to the love seat. We sit, and I spill. "The end of the story is the money just hit. Jacob and I aren't in the red for the first time in years." I hesitate. "Whenever I even think about telling Evelyn, I want to throw up."

"Nora, honey. That's a lot. And the Evelyn part's not even the worst of it."

"Wait—what the worst of it?"

"The part where the curdled old mogul gets your scrumptious Dior!"

"Frankie! Seriously? You think *that's* the worst part?"

"I do," says Frankie. "You're the karmic owner of that piece. The soul of the cloak is yours no matter who gets it," says Frankie. "Also, Opal Appell is America's tyrant. Everyone knows that. Everyone read the *Vanity Fair* article. Why does her nonagenarian ass need yet another piece of couture?"

"At least I had my time with it," I say. "The only other person who'd have loved it like I do is my mom."

"She'd have wanted you to have the cash even more," says Frankie. "If seventy-five thousand dollars isn't someone watching over you, Nore, what is?"

That night, Evelyn posts the *Weekend Journal* article about Camp Champion. The piece is centered by a luminous photo of Evelyn nuzzling a horse, with Henry male-gazing tenderly in a soft-focus background.

Jacob and I lie on opposite ends of the couch, sharing a spoon and passing a pint of Ben & Jerry's Half Baked back and forth.

"Skip the horse-rescue parts and get right to us," says Jacob.

"All right, hang on." I skim the descriptors of Camp Champion and Evelyn's pedigree as a Fitzroy and start in with the third paragraph.

Elliot's decision to become a compassionate surrogate is well documented on her popular social platform, EvvieDoesIt, that upends the traditional norms of a socialite lifestyle with Elliot's distinct brand of down-home millennial ease. "My body always feels like it can do incredible things." Elliot explains she feeds a crisp green apple to her newest adoptee, Shoelace Warrior, a two-time Rosemount winner who arrived last month. "Going the extra mile, for me, is a no-brainer. My friend and their partner are so dear to me and—"

"Ha!"

"What?" I look up.

Jacob is pointing the spoon at me. "*Their* partner? Don't you get it? She's trying to make the Intended Parents sound more fascinating, like she might be carrying for someone who's a big deal, like Lil Nas X. Also, she's comparing us with run-down retired horses."

"Let me keep reading," I say.

"I've always felt a deep need to leave everything a little better than I found it. That's why I want to give fresh air and space to Shoelace here." The purchase, board, and retraining care of a single thoroughbred racehorse is not chump change. It can cost up to half a million dollars, a price—

"Whoa, Nelly."

I look up. "What now?"

"How many horses does Evelyn have?"

"Didn't it say about a dozen?"

"So there's six million dollars' worth of retired horses on that farm? And you're worried about our little transaction?" Jacob lifts his arms and spreads them wide in a big exasperated stretch. "I don't think Evelyn's gonna blink an eye about the seventy-five. Especially if we can get her to think of us as two old horses who found our own little patch of the suburbs to call home."

Comments are already piling up, most of them about the impressive splendor of Camp Champion, but plenty of them remark on Evelyn's goodness and her great big heart. The cynic in me notes that, once again, Evelyn has figured out a virtue niche that showcases her money without explicitly bragging about it—though I'd never say this out loud, since Jacob will be too quick to agree, and my default position is always Team Evelyn. Besides, for a woman who was born into privilege and has had everything handed to her, Evelyn has walked a conscious path of kindness—and I don't see how that's up for debate.

"We could name the baby Shoelace Warrior Junior to get Evelyn sold on all of us moving out to pasture," I say, to lighten Jacob up, and for the rest of the night, we make a silly on-and-off game of being retired horses, wheeling and stamping around the kitchen and the bathroom, to make each other laugh.

Thirty-Seven

⧯⧯⧯⧯⧯⧯⧯⧯⧯⧯

E velyn arrives early Thursday morning from Long Island. She's already in the waiting room by the time Jacob and I get to the hospital.

I pause to stare at her through the door's beveled rectangle of window. She looks as radiant as a sunbeam. There's a new roundness in her face, a doubling of her chin as she reads her phone in one hand, the rose-tipped manicure of her other hand cupping her belly.

When she catches sight of me, she leaps to pull open the door herself.

The big benevolent warmth of her hug is like a dream. I haven't seen her in weeks, and I'm immediately consumed with how outright horrible it will feel when I tell her I sold the Dior.

"Henry sends his love, but he's deep in his art! He's sketching ideas for his new picture book. So I left him to his inspiration." She performs a mini catwalk, a hand-to-hip and foot pivot. "Did I tell you I'm in a paid partnership with Harper's? That's the dry oil company. My own little business is growing every week, slow and steady. Just like this little bell pepper in here!" She smooths the front of her pale linen sundress.

"Promoted from banana," I say. "The last ultrasound was a turnip, though to be honest, I don't really get the pregnancy food calendar. Sometimes bananas are bigger than bell peppers, or you can have tiny turnips and portly pears—or you can have baby watermelons, or even giant cantaloupes."

"Catch a breath, Spell! Listen to all this chatty nervous-mom talk from you!" Evelyn's smile is so generous that my betrayal whips back through me like a bitter wind. *I've sold our treasure, the gift that brought us together.*

"Sorry," I say. "Big day."

"You're doing great! Look at you, so chill," says Evelyn. "Some of the women who follow me on social are next level with their fears. I've got this one who's always pestering me about if being around my horses is safe for the baby."

"Ha, no kidding." Heat flares under my armpits. It's actually @marjigangle who's speaking up about those scary horse photos. Of course it's dangerous for pregnant women to be around all those big kicky horses—and @marjigangle knows it! She's always warning Evelyn about it—but does Evelyn suspect I'm @marjigangle? If she is, she's not letting on.

And now Bianca is here to lead us to our private room.

As Makebe dims the lights, Evelyn looks at me, mischief in her eye. "Did I tell you I know the gender?"

"What?" I can't hide my shock. Jacob and I planned to wait until the birth to learn the gender. My mother had waited until my birth to learn I was a girl, and deciding to play the game of wait-and-see is a small happy way to keep her memory close to me.

"Yep! I charmed it out of Bianca and Makebe," says Evelyn. "But I was ninety-nine percent sure. It was really to confirm."

"Ha, okay." Bianca and Makebe are both poker-faced and avoiding eye contact with me.

"But if you want to know—do you want to know?" asks Evelyn.

"Nope," says Jacob. "You're just gonna have to help us wait."

"It's a girl," says Evelyn. "Or maybe—it's a boy."

"We'll know in January," Jacob says, friendly but ending it.

"Did you see the invite for the baby shower?" she asks.

"Not yet. But I sent the Birth Plans and Options file. If you want to check it out."

"Sure, let me do that." Evelyn pulls out her phone, and for a minute, I think she's checking her Dropbox, but then I see she's just scrolling *Hamptons Diary*.

"Good morning, one and all," says Dr. Glass as she comes in. "Let's get a look at that baby."

All the books and photos and diagrams and online sites and Frankie's images from his twins' screenings tell me exactly what to expect. So I think I'm ready. But turns out I'm not. This baby isn't a fruit or a veggie. This creature is a bulb of head nodding over wispy limbs and joints. It has hands and feet, fingers and toes. This baby might not look entirely of this earth, but it's real.

"Hey, you," I whisper to the screen.

Every molecule of me works to absorb what is happening right now. I want nothing more than to feel like I'm more than just another viewer. I want to feel like the one real, true mother. But it's like watching something happen on another planet.

With the scan recording, Dr. Glass inches through the medical checklist. I try to guess from her closed face if she's pleased with what she sees. I grow more anxious every second, with Makebe quietly clicking us along, measuring every degree.

"The skin is formed along the outside of the spine," she says, breaking the silence.

"Oh! Was there—any doubt about that?" I feel loopy with sudden vertigo.

"Sharon, really?" scolds Evelyn. "What's the percentage chance that the skin wouldn't form over the outside of the spine?"

"Very rare," Dr. Glass admits.

"Nobody cares a lick about all the things that might've gone wrong but didn't, am I right?" asks Evelyn, which wins a snort of agreement from Jacob.

"Guess we were just assuming the baby's skin knew what to do," he says.

"How about you talk us through the good news as you go," suggests Evelyn.

"Of course," says Dr. Glass. "What I can see here is no cleft palate. The cerebellum is correctly shaped... All four chambers of the heart exist... The vertebra of the spine is in alignment." The checklist takes us through the diaphragm, abdomen, bladder, and to all the muscular and joint development. "So far, we're looking at a normal scan," she concludes.

But I'm reeling in the aftershock. I hadn't thought to fear any abnormalities, and now I feel retroactively horrified. How pitifully shortsighted of us to come traipsing in here, assuming the best! How daft! How careless!

Evelyn leans forward, as if she knows what I'm thinking. She rubs her knuckles slowly up and down against my forearm, back and forth.

"It's all right," she says. "Nothing is going wrong. Nothing."

"I know." *I don't know.*

"This baby is fine," she says. "I feel it. I'm certain."

Tension dissolves from my body. I nod. We all leave together. Jacob and I wait with Evelyn as her car inches around the corner. She deals us a last round of hugs, along with assurances about getting us her fall travel schedule and finding a date for us to come out to Montauk, *promise.*

"Hooray for that precious scan," she says, right as she slips into her black town car. "Not that we ever thought it would be any different."

Thirty-Eight

‹‹‹‹‹‹‹‹‹‹‹‹

"One baby, all its working parts, on the way," says Jacob as we're hurtling downtown on the subway, falling in love with our newest batch of ultrasounds on his phone. "Hey, can I get you off your sewing machine at least for Saturday to go look at the Brook Lane house? By now, that baby's got to have enough clothes for the next five years."

"I'd love that." I lean against him; he lightly knocks his knee against mine just as my phone pings.

It's Raquel's itinerary of Evelyn's fall travel. "That was fast." I look through the calendar.

Jacob leans back to stare at my phone's screen. "Venice Beach or the real Venice?"

"Italy." My stomach tightens. Does November feel late?

As if he can hear my thoughts, Jacob asks, "How late into the pregnancy should she travel?"

"Thirty-six, thirty-seven weeks? Hang on." I look it up on my phone. "Thirty-six for domestic travel, twenty-eight to thirty-five for international."

"And she'd be..."

I calculate. "Thirty-four weeks."

Jacob gives me a look.

"If you don't want Evelyn to travel overseas," I say, "you can speak up too."

"But according to you, she can travel until thirty-five weeks."

"Not according to me, Jacob. According to this information on the Mayo Clinic website."

"So, great. She's under the wire."

"I mean, sure. Officially."

"Do we want to approach Evelyn together?" Jacob asks after a minute. "Or is this yet another thing we're gonna slide under the rug?"

I don't answer. We sit in a hard, spiky silence for the rest of the ride.

As we walk home, Jacob says, "I think Ursula had a point the other week. About you being superstitious."

"Ursula didn't use the word *superstitious*."

"She got you to confess you think that if you piss off Evelyn, bad things might happen to the baby."

"She didn't get me to *confess*."

"She *heightened* your *awareness*. She also thought we didn't communicate as well as we could with Evelyn."

"Communicate whatever you want to Evelyn. You've got her number."

"You act like it's such a piece of cake. But if I questioned Venice, I'd be going rogue," he says.

"How so?"

"Because we're in it together. We both don't want a baby shower until we've got the baby. We both think it's too risky for Evelyn to go to Venice. We sold Cloak Van Winkle because we both want to put down a payment on our very own little green monopoly house. It's *telling* Evelyn that's the issue."

"How could I tell her any of these things during the anatomy scan?"

"You can't keep having panic attacks trying to figure out the perfect moment to give Evelyn bad news. No bad news for Evelyn! Because then what?"

"I don't know." I'm trying to find the tone of voice that addresses the rising anxiety inside me while resisting Jacob's attempt to egg me on into outrage.

"Because then she stops talking to us? Because then she runs off with the baby?"

"Obviously I don't think she's running off with the baby." Alert, attentive, slightly superior—yes, that's the tone.

"What's the consequence of being real with Evelyn?"

"I don't know!" Now I just sound growly. Privately, I agree with Jacob more than I'd admit to him, but I've been outwardly Team Evelyn for so long it's hard for me to open any natural space for doubt. "I'll tell her about Bryce as soon as I can find some private time," I say. "So maybe that's also when we give her our peer review. Everything we dislike about her surrogacy choices, the whole kitchen sink."

"I know you're being sarcastic, but it's not the worst idea," mutters Jacob. "Getting some of this out in the open."

"So the plan is to pivot from my apology right to our nitpicks about what we think she could do better?"

"Flying halfway around the world when she's about to give birth is bigger than a nitpick," says Jacob, but I'm tired of arguing with him, and so I slow my walk to let him go ahead of me.

As we turn onto our block, I see last night's garbage all over the curb. Compost scraps are strewn across the sidewalk, too shredded and flattened for me to pick up. The air is rancid with the smell of eggs.

Evelyn will send me a date for Montauk later this week. I know she will. We'll wrap up in deck chair blankets and we'll watch the sun set over the Sound. Then, when everything feels just right, I'll explain Bryce and 87 Brook Lane and how I needed to save the baby from bad ventilation and rancid sidewalk egg—and she'll completely understand.

Thirty-Nine

E velyn does not send me a weekend invitation to her house in Montauk. Instead, Raquel sends me an invitation to the baby shower, also at Evelyn's house in Montauk, for early December.

I RSVP yes and put it in the calendar, though I know Jacob will see it as just another bad example of how we waited too long to tell Evelyn that we didn't want a pre-baby baby shower, and now it's happening. I'm already halfway to convincing myself that it's a lovely gesture, and superstition never helped anybody, and bonus, maybe some of Evelyn's fancy Hamptons friends will start that baby nurse fund.

Early Saturday morning, we rent a car and take Nick along with us to see the house. When we stop for gas, I check in with my phone. Evelyn is at a party at Pauline's home in North Fork. Just a glimpse of Bryce in the background sends a scribble of nerves through my system. I drop my phone in the bottom of my bag and make myself look at the foliage, a riot of bonfire-bright orange maples that line Hutchinson River Parkway.

We park in the town square to walk Nick, stopping to caffeinate our bloodstream with to-go coffees and buttery croissants at the local bakery. The neighborhood reminds me of the villager homes in *Animal*

Crossing, my favorite distraction game of a few years back, only this time it's real, a waking dream of sidewalks banked in crab apple trees, where every lawn is tended, and every home is a separate force field of privacy.

When we meet up with Oscar, he guides us through the house, then settles himself out on the porch with his laptop so that we can tour it privately. Jacob keeps his hands in his pockets, absorbing the layout in his methodical way, pacing each room as I follow him, picking croissant crumbs from my sweater. He looks at the fuse box and the storm doors, and there isn't a single electrical outlet that fails to enchant him. He even breaks out the measuring tape, which he's brought along.

"We can fit the dresser in here," he says on our third lap of the upstairs, where we've come to stand in the nursery, a room of sloped eaves and dormer windows and possibilities. Back down in the living room, Jacob points to the corner. "Here's where we put the Christmas tree." In the backyard, he says. "My new Weber goes right there."

"Hint taken."

I let Nick off the leash in the fenced-in back, where she dashes around in circles like a lunatic, then snuffles along the perimeters, tracking old pee smells and tidbits of dead bugs. It'd be so great to give her a yard in her dotage. I imagine the spray of a backyard sprinkler on my hot skin. Our baby sleeping in the shade on a picnic blanket. Our child swinging up, up into the blue air. The stitches of a thousand ordinary moments that make up a single divine design.

"Let's keep this swing set," I say when Jacob joins me. "I always wanted one when I was a kid."

Our drive back into the city is pensive.

"When is Bryce's assistant coming to do the pickup?" Jacob asks.

"Winnie, the week after next."

"This feels just right to me."

"Me too."

"Want to put in an offer Monday?"

I nod. "I do."

Forty

〈〈〈〈〈〈〈〈〈〈〈〈〈

Raquel and I play phone tag all week before she catches up with me late one night. I'm in the nursery and bent over my Singer, my sewing table rippled with fabric. These days—though mostly nights—my basket and scissors are out all the time, along with my old sewing magazines and pattern books for baby clothes.

The rhythm of this work has been my refuge, an antidote to my anxiety and a way to find a bit of late-night peace. I feel my childhood in these hours, and the trust my mother had in me when she let me wield her scissors and cut my first Simplicity pattern. Even today, I sew the way she did, with her same idiosyncrasies—the way she bit a thread and wrapped her wrist pincushion, the way she sang along with her beloved Sade or Laura Branigan—a little louder for her favorite song. *"Glore-ya! Glor-ee-aa!"*—as each panel fit together to create a magnificent whole.

It's not until my phone buzzes that I see I've worked past midnight again and that Jacob must have gone to bed hours ago. I push away from the table.

"Sorry to call so late, but you said anytime," says Raquel. "It's been impossible to pin down Evelyn for next week. There's a tiny window when she's back from the Hamptons for the U.S. Open but before she and Henry drive Xander to Andover. Then she's home Sunday night, but then they're out early Monday, headed to Old Orchard. Maybe you could wait to see her the week after, at the next doctor's appointment?" Raquel's voice implies that I should do just that.

"Okay," I say, and the next morning, I text Evelyn.

Could we set up a time for in person?

Yes! Tea after the Dr. appt.?

Or even before? How about that day when you're home next week? Anytime!

Let me see what I can do!

On EvvieDoesIt, the content upload is breakneck—from Evelyn modeling caftans by her pool overlooking Georgica Pond to clips from her VIP seats at Arthur Ashe. She hosts a conversation with her acupuncturist, Dr. Pillay, who holds forth on the principals of balance and transferred energies, then gamely answers the pushback of comments, including @marjigangle's multiple concerns about needling in dangerous areas, risks of infection, and adverse fetal outcomes. Evelyn doesn't post about her night at the Wainscott Fiesta Forever clambake, though I FedExed her a selection of sundresses for it. The next day, she brings on a branding expert to live-chat name trends, and she's inundated with suggestions before she takes a vote. The winning names for my baby are Saige and Dorian.

But there's nothing from the real Evelyn. My prayers that I'll hear the ping of her text go unanswered, and after a while, I forcibly release my clutch on my phone by hiding it in my sewing basket.

Later that week, Evelyn sends me a photo of herself against an oyster-gray New England coastline.

"I believe this is what's called a consolation selfie," I tell Jacob.

"Meeting up with Evelyn doesn't change the outcome," he says. "We put the offer in—there's no undoing our decision. But let's tell her together, okay? I don't know if me being by your side makes it any easier, but I don't see how I make it worse."

"Okay." I nod. "We'll do it right after the next appointment."

Thursday, Winnie confirms the pickup for seven.

"Is it any worse for wear?" I ask that evening before she's due to arrive, stepping back from the mannequin, examining it with a hard eye.

"I don't remember wearing it," says Jacob, "except for a few casual Fridays."

"No, really look at it. I know we took good care of it, but antique fabrics can fade and age in unexpected ways."

"I don't see anything." Jacob walks around the garment slowly, scrutinizing it. "No moth holes, no mildew, no Nick pee-mark territory. She looks just fine to me. In her own melancholic, bride-of-Edgar-Allan-Poe way."

Winnie is here fifteen minutes early. She puts on a pair of surgical gloves, stuffs the pockets with tissue paper, wraps the fabric in more sheaves of tissue paper, and covers it all up in a plastic bag before hanging it on a thick hanger and zipping it up into the heavy dress bag she's brought with her. So much attention given to the piece makes it feel different, like a deposed queen returning to her kingdom after she's spent a year in her humble Brooklyn exile.

Jacob and I watch from the window as Winnie spirits off the bag in a long black car like it's entering the Witness Protection Program. Then we collapse on the couch.

"Feels like we just had a corpse removed," says Jacob.

"Barb says we can keep the mannequin."

"No thanks. All hers."

I shift my legs to deposit my feet on Jacob's lap. "Well done, us," I say, making light of it in an empty British accent, but my body is trembling, and my palms are damp with sweat. I did it. It's done.

Jacob takes hold of my right foot and knuckles an arch. "Not all heroes wear capes."

"Jacob."

"Kidding."

I close my eyes and let the heaviness of my action and all its possible consequences fall on me. Jacob rubs my feet and holds the quiet. He doesn't even turn on the television. I'm grateful that he gets it.

Forty-One

‹‹‹‹‹‹‹‹‹‹‹‹‹

Monday afternoon, Bryce calls me while I'm at work, wrestling Gigi and Bella into matching vintage Kamali, slippery gold lamé evening gowns with thigh-high slits and fishtail trains.

I sit in the window to pick up.

"Just to let you know! We had our family party this weekend," Bryce enthuses. "Grandy was so happy! She was wild about it. I gave it to her with an entire library of Frieda's first editions."

"I'm glad it all worked out." I imagine Opal, frail but resplendent. Her lizardly face sandwiched between her lychee-sized pearl earrings. Another Opal Appell quote is "After fifty, more jewelry, less makeup." In that *Vanity Fair* piece, Opal comes off brutal. A woman of such raw, gnawing ambition that Appell Inc. had to brand-distance itself from her flash temper.

But now I envision another Opal, who is tender with love for Bryce. A sentimental grandmother, a grateful granddaughter, a storybook birthday.

"I still think it's shocking that selfish old crook took your beautiful Dior," says Barb when I tell her. "If I make it to ninety, please remind me not to be that mean."

"Hey, but at least you get a house," says Frankie.

"We'll see," I say. "We're waiting on the counteroffer. Cross your fingers."

We lock up. It's a good day. The sunset is raspberry sherbet colors against the black buildings. Jacob and I bike to a new Mexican restaurant in Park Slope with an outdoor garden and farolito lights. We celebrate with a single enchiladas verdes to split, medium-spicy guacamole to start, and two frozen lime margaritas.

"Salt on the rim, please—but no tequila," I tell the waitress.

"I won't tell if you want a real drink," said Jacob. "We're celebrating, after all."

I shake my head. Evelyn loves a margarita as much as I do, but it makes me feel purposeful not to drink until the baby is born. Of course, once she knows I've sold the Bergessen cloak, she'll probably figure I'm also sneaking endless boozy cocktails. It's even likely that on some level, she'll never quite trust me again. My skin crawls with shame at the thought.

"Spell!" Evelyn's voice through the phone later that week sends me wheeling into panic.

"Is everything okay?" I motion to Barb that I need to take the call as I quickly step out of the shop and into the bone-melting September heat.

"Yes, all good! No emergency. Fit as a fiddle, baby and me." Evelyn's laid-back laughter lets me exhale. "I'm calling because my parents are desperate to meet you, and at this point, I think they'll beat me with a bag of apples if I tell them no."

"Are you still in Tennessee?"

"We are, and I want to fly you and Jacob out next weekend. Are you free?"

"That's generous of you." I'm caught off guard. "You don't have to pay for our trip."

"Don't be silly! You're facing Beau and Bitsy in their lair."

"Let me check in with Jacob first." As much as I'd love to see Evelyn, dropping Jacob into a weekend of Evelyn's parents, who've never sounded too rosy in any of Evelyn's stories, will be hard to sell.

"They do insist," says Evelyn. "It'd be helpful for me."

"We can probably get out there...if you really need us."

"Yes, I do," she says. "Thank you kindly. Raquel'll be in touch." She's off before I can say anything else, and a pair of round-trip tickets hits my email two hours later.

I wait until later that evening, after dinner, when Jacob and I are nestled into the couch with a bowl of buttered Newman's Own popcorn, and Jacob has queued up *Picard* after his coin-toss win over *Bridgerton*.

"Nope. Not gonna happen," he says. "I am not spending my weekend at Evelyn's parents' creepy Southern plantation."

"It's not a plantation; it's a farm."

"Old Orchard is a farm the way Rolex is a watch."

"This is a big deal," I say. "Command performance."

"I know all summer you've been hoping Evelyn will invite us somewhere," says Jacob, "but her parents summoning us for a once-over is not the same, and it's not a win. In fact, it feels like a stressful fast-track to us both getting bleeding ulcers. Hard pass." He tosses a piece of popcorn in the air and catches it in his mouth.

"I want to see her."

"If this is about Hocus Cloakus, I thought we were resolved to wait until she's back in New York?"

"Evelyn doesn't ask for much. We don't just get to say no thanks. The other thing is, I really miss her." I find a breath. "And I want to be near the baby. I miss the baby. I miss the baby most of all." I didn't know that I was going to say it out loud, but saying is feeling it. I miss the baby with a force that takes hold inside me with a painful imperative. I want the baby to hear my voice. I want to feel its proximity. It's been too many weeks. My hands are gripped into fists. "I'm going with or without you."

"Nore." But then Jacob puts down the bowl of popcorn, opens his arms, and closes me inside them. "With," he says. "Always with."

Forty-Two

〈〈〈〈〈〈〈〈〈〈〈

We fly direct on Friday afternoon. We're picked up at the Nashville International Airport by Hal, a sun-faded, good-natured gentleman cowboy who tips his Stetson before taking a grip on our bags and leading us to his black Range Rover SUV. Purring down the flat highway, me crunching breath mints as Jacob chipmunk-chews multiple sticks of Big Red, we're lulled by the icy air-conditioning and fiddly country music. Our windows flash with passing miles of split-rail fencing and quilted farmland extending to the mountain range on the horizon.

Beautiful as it is, my mind won't give me a break, and I can't stop hopscotching through all the different consequences of telling Evelyn.

Jacob, my ever-reliable mind reader, looks over. "Remember, we don't need to use this weekend to explain everything we've been up to this month."

"As in, no bad news for Evelyn?" I say lightly.

"It's possible to commit no errors and still lose," he intones.

I nod and give him the Vulcan sign, but I have every intention of using this weekend to free myself from the weight of this secret.

Past the gates, the farmland is an open, rolling landscape all the way to the big white wedding cake of a farmhouse. I recognize everything from the photographs. Over there, the two big red horse barns and the stone-gray pony barn. In back, the greenhouse and the henhouse. Down that sloping bend are the tennis courts. There, that clapboard fence surrounds the landscaped swimming pool and pool house invisible from the road, and I feel eerily transported back into days of horse-drawn carriages and hoop skirts.

A second personable cowboy is ready to greet us as we pull into the drive.

"I'm Walker," he says, opening the passenger-side door. "Let me show you through."

"Pretty sure he's the actual Walker, Texas Ranger," I whisper to Jacob as we follow Walker through the front door and down a wide hall of antiques and dark portraits. We pass through a formal sitting room, a high-beamed sunroom, and a set of French doors onto a veranda that's as flat and vast as a prairie.

"Well, bless your hearts, it's the Intended Parents. The IPs! That's the proper term, isn't it? Did I get it right?" Right away I recognize Bitsy Fitzroy-Boyle's girlish, ringing voice from the YouTube interview I'd found of when she chaired the Big Hats and Bow Ties Gala. Hands on her hips, she's staring us down, a tiny roadblock between us and the others—Evelyn and Henry, along with the surprise of Pauline and Keith, are all lounging in the shade of the far, furnished corner. "It's only recently I've been educated on all this," she says.

Jacob is ready with an offered hand. "Nice to meet you, Mrs.—"

"Aw, now you just go on and call me Bitsy!"

"Bitsy," Jacob and I say in unison.

"Hammonds!" she carols back at us. She waves off Jacob's hand to hold him by each forearm for a double kiss.

Bitsy is tended and petite, with plucked eyebrows and thin lips and pale, apricot-tinted hair pressed into a neat comma behind each ear.

Her office-safari look—khaki jumpsuit, belted in snakeskin—is rounded out with knobby gold jewelry.

"My baby's having your baby," she says. "How fun!" It really does feel like Bitsy hoped for fun with this observation, but it comes out sounding like a wail.

"Yes! We are so delighted," I tell her.

"'Course you are. 'Course I'm not, not really, since I don't get to keep my own grandbaby—oh, I'm just fooling, I suppose. I'm happy for you, 'course I am." Her eyes convey something more like confusion.

"Okay, Mom," Evelyn calls over. "It's too early to scare the guests." She links her thumbs and reaches her arms overhead to flap-wave at Jacob and me. "Easy flight?"

"Yup!" says Jacob as I lean past Bitsy to wave back.

"So easy." Now I try to move around Bitsy, but she sidesteps with me.

"Ev's always done exactly what she pleases," she says. "But this is a twist in the road."

Twist in the road—is that her best enigmatic phrase for the surrogacy? I feel disoriented, like someone just snapped off my blindfold and I'm nowhere near the piñata. This isn't how I thought it would be. How upset is Bitsy, really, about this situation?

"We're so grateful to Evelyn," I say. "I'm glad to get to tell you that in person. It's been an extraordinary journey for us."

"Oh, us, too. Not to mention everyone else. We're right up front for every gory detail, aren't we?" says Bitsy. I guess she's referring to the EvvieDoesIt reel from the other day on pregnancy gas—the burps and farts of it all. Bitsy's smile doesn't falter, but I sense the undercurrent of her disapproval.

"And thank you for inviting us to your home," Jacob says, blithely cordial. "Beautiful out here."

"Why, you are so very welcome." Bitsy presses her lips closed; we're dismissed as she finally moves aside so we can cross the porch to greet the others.

I lean down to give Evelyn a hug that turns into more of a shoulder press. "Sorry if I don't get up, Spell," she says with a yawn. "I'm in my confinement."

"Hello, again. Such a treat," says Pauline, leaning up to do the double kiss that Jacob handles with his usual confusion, as if he didn't see it coming—*why doesn't he ever see it coming?* Because it's a silly affect, probably—the opposite of Jacob's style. "You brought the nice weather."

"Oh, good!" I'm grinning my way through the small talk, hoping my smile conveys an ease that does not feel fully in my grasp.

"We did a morning ride. Ideal trails here. Do you ride?" asks Keith.

"We don't," says Jacob, and I resist saying that Jacob could learn in an hour, given the chance. Jacob and I both look so rumpled and wrong that I want to snap my fingers for a redo. My retro Hooverette wrap dress, plain but perky when I put it on this morning, feels drably costume-y now, like I'm a lesser suspect in an Agatha Christie mystery. In their silks and Lucchese boots, everyone else has the look of an off-hours CEO. Even Henry had to trade his threadbare rock tees for a cashmere sweater that's the cantaloupe complement to Keith's honeydew, and he's tamed his mad-scientist hair with a geeky little side part.

"I've put y'all in the coral room," says Bitsy, veering up to rejoin us. "We've got some real nice foothill paths, too. You'll want to stretch your legs before dinner."

"Or laze around like a sloth, like me," says Evelyn.

Bitsy's smile is trimmed in irritation. "You're seeing Evelyn in her natural habitat."

But seeing Evelyn is everything; I feel bewitched. This morning, she'd posted a snippet of her skincare regime to EvvieDoesIt, and her face looks so dewy, it's as if she's created a filter to activate for her real life. "I'm tired," she tells me through a yawn.

"It's the air," agrees Pauline, "like at the Stein Ericksen. Remember the other time?"

"Ah, the worst," says Evelyn. "When we got the leak in the ceiling and we had to move to the other place?"

"And we kept sending the concierge out for more Boost Oxygen cans. Insane!" finishes Pauline, and I'm still smiling in this hopeful, asinine way, like I can almost remember it too—*oh, those oxygen cans at the other place,* madness!

"Dinner's at seven thirty. Drinks before, in the Great Room," says Bitsy. "Any questions, anything you need, you just ask Walker."

And now Walker is here, ready to march us off.

On our way out, Jacob grabs a handful of mini pretzels from a bowl on a drinks cart. Neither of us have eaten in hours, except for the hand-out packages of Sun Chips on the plane. We did our best with the gum and breath mints in the Range Rover, but we're ravenous. I wince when a scattering of tiny pretzels drops to the ground and Jacob greedily bends and scoops them into his mouth with a boyish "Five-second rule!"

Nobody says anything, which makes it worse.

Walker leads us upstairs to the coral room. It's got a queenly four-poster bed, a fireplace, and an outstanding view of the mountains.

He sets our suitcase on the luggage rack and departs.

"You don't tip people in private houses, right?" asks Jacob.

"Of course not." But even as I say it, I'm not so sure.

"You're looking at me like you think I'm a yokel," says Jacob. "Was it the pretzels? I'm starving. I should ask Walker to make me a sandwich."

"It's not just the pretzels," I tell him. "It's the whole cringe de la cringe. It's Bitsy's low-key meltdown. It's everyone in horse-and-hounds outfits, and we look like we just finished karaoke night in Bushwick."

Jacob rolls his eyes. "Next time, we'll pack our best *valorize the oppressors* looks."

"The house isn't antebellum; it was built in the early nineteen hundreds. It's more of an Oldish Orchard," I tell him. "But I won't argue that it doesn't feel uncomfortable to be here. I get a sense Evelyn didn't tell her parents about us in a normal way. I think they strong-armed

Evelyn to invite us, and we've interrupted this private weekend the Elliots were enjoying with the Chens."

"I don't think anything happens in a normal way in this family," says Jacob. "I wouldn't take it personally."

"Okay." I pop open the suitcase locks. "Let's reset. Want to unpack and then do a hike? I bet we could even beg a couple of granola bars off Walker."

Jacob nods. "Sounds good."

But no sooner have we put away the suitcase than we both drop straight into bed, like two kids under a fairy-tale spell.

Forty-Three

꧁꧂

When we wake up, it's dark.

"Durn it," says Jacob. "Guess we were plum tuckered out."

"Don't joke, we're late! It's almost seven thirty! Hurry, hurry!" I lunge from bed in alarm, pulling out the olive crepe midi-dress I hung in the closet earlier. What was I thinking? This dress is as feedsack-y as the other one. Dust Bowl–chic never felt so wrong.

"I've got khakis," says Jacob, scrambling for them. "But the guys were in lunch khakis."

"Maybe with another shirt," I tell him. "What else did you pack?"

"My flannel. The yellow button-down."

"The yellow should work." Though when I see the buttons straining around Jacob's stomach, I'm doubtful. "Isn't that shirt from college?"

"Is that your way of saying it's too small?" Jacob is immediately testy. "Sorry if I can't pull out my hot college body to deliver to this extremely important weekend."

"Stop, you look great. Be on my side tonight."

"Do you think everyone'll be in sports jackets?"

"I don't know, I don't care. Unified front."

I still feel sleep-creased and disheveled when we head downstairs.

There's a rogue's gallery of taxidermy on the walls of the Great Room and a spit-roast of a fire in its medieval-looking stone hearth. Everyone is already here, finishing cocktails. Evelyn is on the opposite end of the room, giggling with Pauline. All the men are in sports jackets.

"It's like that nightmare of showing up to school in your underpants," whispers Jacob.

"It's fine," I whisper back, trying to stifle my nervous, mortified laughter—it does feel like the underpants dream—as Bitsy spies us hovering in the door and zeros in.

"We thought you'd gotten lost," she says, sweetly passive-aggressive. Then, in a hushed voice, she says something to the lurking Walker. He leaves the room and reappears holding a navy blazer.

It's huge on Jacob. Like a clown. I want to dissolve into a puddle of nonexistence. I should have asked Evelyn about the dress code—or she should have told me. Too late now.

"And here's my husband, Beau," says Bitsy, presenting Beau Fitzroy-Boyle, wide and fleshy, with a linebacker's shoulders.

"Ah, the poodle-skirt lady," Beau says to me. "Ev tells me you sell old clothes." He doesn't wait for confirmation from me on that, as he's already got a ferocious hand pump working for Jacob.

"Thanks for inviting us," I tell him.

"You have my wife to thank," Beau answers. "I'm getting orders on a last round of drinks. What can I do you for?"

When we both say just water, Beau looks dismayed. "I've batched up some old-fashioneds with Blue Label," he coaxes, and when we say water is fine, thanks, he leaves us and never returns. But there's plenty more Beau when we're seated for dinner a few minutes later. At the head of the table, plowing through a wedge salad followed by rib lamb chops, glazed baby carrots, and fingerling potatoes, and with Jacob and me trapped on either side of him, Beau pilots and steers every topic right back to his own interests. Game birds. Crimson Tide versus Ole Miss Rebels. His antique 1884 lever-action Winchester "chambered to

powder two cartridges" that he's just purchased. Late-season wildflowers on the property. The pretty good job he's doing with his cholesterol.
And, finally, as the fresh strawberry-topped shortcakes are served, his
thoughts on Jacob and me.

"You seem like decent folks, from what I can tell. Not that we got
a word from that one about the two of you," Beau says, with a frown
for his daughter, who is seated next to Jacob but spent most of dinner
angled away from our end of the table, in sidebar conversations with the
Chens. Beau's head moves back and forth in a heavy, animal way from
Jacob to me. "We've got to go onto the internet to learn about what that
one's up to these days." He raises his voice. "Isn't that right, Miss You
All the Way Over There?" He waggles a finger at Evelyn. His Ole Miss
college ring is the size of a walnut.

"Dad's being very boring," says Evelyn to Bitsy, whose only reaction
is the barest lift of her whisker-thin apricot eyebrows. "Tell him to mind
his own business."

"Oh, but being your daddy is too my business," says Beau.

"Nora and I are here to vouch for our decency," says Jacob, casting
his cheerful little net of company-man humor, hoping for a bite.

"Always something brewing with that one," says Beau. "Now she's hung
her shingle to shill foot cream on the internet—right, Evvie?" He guffaws.

"It's a high-end dry oil made from grape and sesame seed," says
Evelyn. "It goes on more than just your feet. For example, you could rub
it right onto your Pooh-Bear tummy, Dad, if you wanted."

"Always something. I'm thinking back to the perfume store. What
was that called?"

"Find My Fragrance," says Evelyn.

"Find My Fragrance," repeats Beau, like it's a punch line. "I do
wish you luck, selling your dry oil, whatever that is. Let's see if it's your
winning ticket. Selling oil or having babies for strangers." Beau's laugh
deteriorates into a coughing fit that he manages to catch back into a
laugh through sheer force of will.

"For everyone to see and give their two cents," chirps Bitsy.

"Open comments," says Evelyn. "That's democracy, folks." Then she shifts around so that her back is firmly to Beau and her head ducked against Bitsy, as she refocuses on her conversation with Pauline. I feel like I'm witnessing timeworn family dynamics.

Looking at me, Beau says, "We said to Evelyn, 'Get 'em both down here. Right this minute—the trust fund's at stake.'" He winks. "That's what we always say to her. You better bet it gets her moving. We're vetting you."

"Vetting? They're a long way down that road, Beau," says Keith.

"Never too late to have our say," says Bitsy brightly.

Beau picks up his drink and rattles its cubes. "Don't get us wrong. Bitsy and I believe in charity. 'Carry one another's burdens, and so fulfill the law of Christ.' That's Galatians."

"You can't shock us, Dad," says Evelyn, as Jacob and I send each other a look of *oh, but we're quite shocked, actually.*

"How's it come to pass, Nora, that you can't have your own baby?" Beau's voice drops; even he seems to know this line of questioning will invoke protest from the table. "You look healthy. I thought you'd be older. Are you a diabetic?" He pushes a sorrowful expression onto his face. "There's all sorts of rare diseases can cause those things."

"As a matter of fact," I say, just as softly and sorrowfully, "I've got this condition, Schiaparelli syndrome by proxy, and thankfully I'm in remission. But it's been a lot."

Beau nods and purses his lips, looking concerned and appalled and unsure if I'm telling him the truth. But he couldn't feel more aghast than I do in this moment, staring into his bloodshot eyes. My heart is beating fast; it's rare that I go the smart-ass route, but what a brute. Clearly Evelyn's strategy tonight—and perhaps perpetually—is detachment. I watch as Beau's squint refocuses on Jacob.

"Jake," he says, his voice booming across the table again, "you're in good shape. What's your sport?"

"Was. Lacrosse," Jacob answers.

"Lacrosse is what the East Coast boys play when they can't handle baseball."

"Ha," says Jacob. "Maybe. Never heard that one before."

"She always makes you two sound like a couple of gays, by the way," says Beau. "I was surprised to find out you were just husband-wife people." He lifts his voice. "You Down There. Do you get more dry oil if Evvie Does It for a gay couple?"

"Jesus, Beau. Enough," says Henry, but Beau's place in the family feels a bit like a sick old dog that's vomited so many times on the carpet you've stopped noticing both the rug and the hound, maybe because the illness itself isn't being treated so much as endured.

"Evelyn is doing something remarkable." My voice sounds more happy-claps kindergarten teacher than I'd wanted. "Her platform is so approachable, and she answers all the questions people have, and with such kindness, and everything feels positive and shared. So it's really not about dry oil at all—although it's fantastic that EvvieDoesIt has sponsors now."

"Platform," says Beau mockingly, as if it's the only word to extricate from my speech.

"And I suppose if you really didn't want to air your laundry in public," says Bitsy to me, "you'd have piped up by now."

"We're so grateful," I say.

"Thanks, Spell," says Evelyn in a sort of comic, pretend-sadsack voice, and I'm not sure I delivered the rescue I'd hoped.

"Henry does racket sports," Beau says to Jacob as if I didn't say anything at all. "That's what the East Coast boys play when they can't handle lacrosse."

"If you say so, Beau," says Henry.

"Cue this East Coast squash-playing boy's good night." says Keith as he and Pauline stand in sync, old pros at handling Beau. "Thanks for a delicious dinner. Early-morning ride tomorrow."

Evelyn yawns. "Good night, all."

It feels like a moment. I shoot Jacob a look that tells him I'm about to seize my opportunity. He shoots a look back that asks if I need him.

I don't. I can do this myself.

"I'm heading up," says Jacob.

I nod. "See you there." Then I reach across the table to Evelyn's place setting and tap it. "Can we get a little time?"

"Sure." She smiles. "Let's walk."

Forty-Four

W hat's that sweet little Frieda poem about a night breeze? I think she wrote it here," says Evelyn as she stands and refolds her cream-and-gold wrap. My mind tunes in to its details: last-season Bottega Veneta, silk-cashmere blend. Sixty-six hundred dollars. She hooks elbows with me as we leave the house, crossing the wide open plain of the veranda. "You know which one?"

Moon-charmed breeze through walnut trees. "I can't recall," I say. No need to invoke an amplified sentimental feeling for Frieda Bergessen this weekend.

"Maybe it'll come to me later. Ah, nice to get out. Now that you've met Beau and Bitsy, you can see how I'd need a breath of fresh air time and again." She sighs. "Old folks and their shenanigans."

Shenanigans feels like a whimsical spin on what felt closer to the experience of Beau's flat-out abuse of the table, but I sense Evelyn already knows that.

It's the soft end of twilight, everything mushroom-colored and getting darker by the minute. But Evelyn knows exactly where to go, and she leads us with precision.

"It must be wonderful to live in a house that's belonged to your family for so long," I say as we take the footpath toward the stables.

"I guess. I'd say Old Orchard does feel the most like mine. More than the Bahamas or San Sebastián, or the ranch in Wyoming, or even New York—the city or upstate."

I don't have a natural way into this sentiment, but I give it a whirl. "It's lucky for Jacob and me his parents are only an hour away. The baby won't have many options outside of our apartment." I pause. "It's feeling very small lately."

"I thought you loved your little walk-up. You're always saying you do."

"I do!"

"But the city can feel unfriendly with a baby."

"Yes." I can't see more than two feet in front of me. "Where are we going?"

"I'm whisking you off to my Wendy cottage." Purposefully, she shepherds us down a path that forks away from the stables.

A couple of minutes later, and we're inside a forest of tall trees. The Frieda poem beats in my head: *Gnarled oak ghosts stand solitary still.* I shiver.

"I'm glad we're having some private time," I tell her. "This feels *very* private."

"We haven't had a lot of it this summer," says Evelyn. "And I wanted to talk to you about something specific. I've been thinking about the extra expenses you and Jacob'll have once the baby's born. We both know Raquel's strength is in digital, but she's not a superstar when it comes to the nuts and bolts, booking my travel or submitting for insurance or scheduling flu shots or any of that. So I was thinking, it might be smart to hire another—"

"You want to give me the PA job?" I say, startled, as the penny drops in my brain.

"And I want to make you an offer you can't refuse," Evelyn says cheerfully. "What number would it take for you to quit the shop?"

"Please, no," I say. "Please don't say a number."

Evelyn laughs. "All right, I won't, but I'll take my chance I can give you double what you're—here we are!"

I squint. Through a parting in the trees, I see a diminutive Dutch Colonial cottage. Two-storied, its sloping roof is balanced by twin brick chimneys and a center door.

"What is this?" I feel a dazed sense of déjà vu. Did I ever dream about this house?

"My playhouse! My Wendy house!" Evelyn's voice is childlike with pleasure, as she drops my elbow and begins leapfrogging away from me. "Come look."

Following her up the porch stairs, now I see the architecture is almost identical to 87 Brook Lane, except that it's built to scale for a third grader.

"It's over a hundred years old," says Evelyn. "It was made for Great-Gran when she was a little girl." Evelyn opens the front door. I duck in and peer into the shadows of a living room. Wallpapered, fully furnished, ready for move-in. Evelyn presses a wall-panel button, and a pair of end table lamps switch on. The furniture is soft and elegant, the fabrics a tasteful mix of complementary colors.

"Well, that's something," she says. "They must've never cut off the electric. When I was little, I was here all the time. I'd run around pell-mell and find ways to get just a tiny bit lost. I'd work myself into such a fright, then I'd see the roof—hooray!"

"Very sweet," I say.

Evelyn surveys the room with satisfaction, as if she's cast an eye back to her childhood and found all her memories to be in joyful order. She switches off the light and closes the door. "Funny how just a bit of timber can make a child so happy. Let's sit here for a spell."

There's a porch swing. We ease ourselves onto it.

Now I know why it feels like a dream. This, here, is where the photo was taken. The one I'd seen of Frieda Bergessen stuck between Evelyn's great-grandparents.

The inside joke, I realize, is that the swing is child sized.

"I was the star of all my stories," says Evelyn. "Snow White. Gretel. Anything with a cottage."

"It's something." It's too much. It might even be grotesque, a fully operational house that remains up and running for a child who is decades past her childhood. Pristine and frozen in time, maintained on her parents' sentimental whim.

"When I got older, I brought boys," says Evelyn, using the toe of her shoe to rock the swing back and forth. "We'd laze around for hours and get high—and talk about how every problem in the whole wide world could be solved with good weed."

"I'll have to think about it," I say abruptly.

"Oh, no! The job, you mean?" She turns to me, eyes wide with hurt.

"It's not my talent," I say. "It's not my skill set."

"It might be a real leg up," says Evelyn. "Financially, I mean. You know how much I want to take care of you. I'm already invested, right?" She is speaking so kindly, almost pleading. "Walker, Hal, Anya, Tabitha, Max, Kristen, Raquel—they're all on a generous healthcare plan. And I could give you that, Spell. I want to give you that."

"It's very generous of you—but Jacob and I are already doing okay."

"The extra money means renting bigger, or even moving right out of the city! More money means—"

"We've come into some money," I say, cutting her off, though I'm alarmed with my lie as soon as it's out.

"Oh!" I can see that Evelyn is caught by surprise, even as she politely recovers. "Well, that's just super! I'm happy for you, Spell! That's some luck right there—how'd you come by it?"

"An...inheritance." Over the weeks, I've idly thought about possible little fibs I might tell Evelyn to explain how we got the money for the house. Plausible stories such as Jacob's big promotion, a death in the family, or my thriving new business sewing baby clothes—I've made plenty of onesies and sleep sacks these past months, though I have yet to try my hand at selling any of them.

"Whose side?" asks Evelyn.

"Jacob's great-uncle," I say. "His great-uncle...Buck."

"Were they close? I'm so sorry."

"He was old," I say quickly, "and we've had our eye on a house for a while—we even made an offer."

Evelyn sits back. "Jiminy Christmas, a house. Leaving the city too. That is some headline news."

"Yes."

"Rats about the job, though. I guess it felt like a way to keep us close."

"But you know I'm always here, no matter what, if you need me." I feel sorry for Evelyn's disappointment and molten with shame about Uncle Buck. There's no space in my jumbled mind to bring up Bryce tonight, and I don't trust the next anything that might come out of my disingenuous mouth, so I zip it.

As we head back to the house, Evelyn keeps our elbows linked. The only sound is our breath and the cereal crunch of dried pine needles under our feet. We say good night in the hall. I know better than to hug her while she's feeling so dismayed about my decision. Even if a hug is all I want, a moment of *bye-bye, baby,* before I go upstairs.

Evelyn pecks a kiss into the air near my temple and is gone.

Jacob is in bed, reading. "We got turndown service," he says, pointing to the crackling fire in the fireplace. "Also, Beau cornered me last minute for skeet shooting tomorrow. That dude is some unbearable jerkdom. Skeets aren't real things, right?" He scrutinizes my face. "What happened?"

I lean back against the wall and close my eyes. "Evelyn took me to her childhood cottage in the woods," I tell him. "It looked like an exact replica of Brook Lane."

"Okay, bizarre."

"She also offered me a job to be her PA."

"And?"

"I said I didn't need it because we inherited money from your rich uncle Buck."

"Uncle Buck?"

"I know. I just blurted it out—I'm such a bad liar, I almost said Fester."

He nods. "Right. Well. The rich-uncle inheritance. The obvious play."

I move to drop down next to Jacob on the bed, and I press the heels of my hands into my closed eye sockets. "Her playhouse was too weird. I wanted her to know I had my own job, and we had our own house, our own money, our own agency."

"I understand." Jacobs shifts his body so that we're aligned. "You might be squishing the chocolate they put on your pillow," he says as he prongs it out from under my shoulder.

"She said she'd pay me double, plus healthcare."

"Not too shabby."

"But I love the shop. I don't want to work for Evelyn."

"Sure, but...you *have* been working for Evelyn, on and off," says Jacob. "You style her outfits. You styled her Thanksgiving, even."

"Being Evelyn's PA isn't my life's calling."

"And now it doesn't have to be, ever since poor Uncle Buck got mauled by that grizzly. You aren't going to eat this chocolate, are you?" He's still holding it.

I shake my head. I turn onto my side to face Jacob as he turns onto his side to face me. He smooths my hair back from the crown of my head.

"I thought it was pretty badass, what you said to Beau at dinner," he says.

"I think it just embarrassed Evelyn," I say.

"You're a good friend. She knows that. And nothing terrible happens to our baby if you don't become her PA," he says, unwrapping the candy.

"I know. Sort of." I close my eyes. Jacob's chocolate breath and the heat of his body are making me feel drowsy. "I'll straighten out everything tomorrow."

Forty-Five

〈〈〈〈〈〈〈〈〈〈〈〈

We set alarms for six, but I'm up earlier. I draw the curtains and sit in the coral damask wingback chair to watch the sun rise over the mountain range. The beauty of the morning plucks up my courage for my truth reboot. Evelyn will understand. She's invested in our future; she said so herself.

Outside on the veranda, Jacob and I find a table set for breakfast. We sit down to starched linen and heavy silver, a carafe of hot coffee and a basket of warm pastries. Walker brings out a couple of walking sticks, points out some trail loops, and tells us the main breakfast will be in the pony barn.

"See, this is just the false-start breakfast," says Jacob once Walter's gone. "Old Orchard is all about try, try again." His good spirits lift mine.

We set out, and soon we're lost to the splendor of the mountains. We don't even speak until we reach the pinnacle, where we experience the view Walker promised. I feel exultant, looking over the Smokies, their peaks dusted in a light sugaring of snow against the big blue pour of cloudless sky.

"I need to hold on to this invincible feeling for the rest of the day."

"Oscar says the owners could counteroffer by next week," says Jacob, which he knows I know, as we start walking back. "One step closer to a kitchen island with a side of bar sink."

"A walk-in closet with a side of built-in drawers."

"Our sleepy street with a side of maple trees."

"Big front lawn with a side of bigger backyard."

We follow the bark-blazed white paint that marks the trail to the bluff. "See, but now that's *too* much front lawn," says Jacob as we stare out over the sweep of massive property. "Brook Lane? Just exactly enough."

The pony barn is a washed-wood, wide-planked dining hall, and this time breakfast is a buffet, with chafing dishes of eggs and bacon, grits and hash browns, waffles and French toast. Bitsy and Beau are already here, drinking their orange juice and spooning up their fruit cups and reading *The Tennessee Star*.

Keith and Pauline, right behind us, ask Walker if the chef would make them egg-white omelets with grilled tomatoes. But when Jacob orders a kale juice, Beau lights up and starts hurling jabs—amusing only to Beau—about Jacob being a kale-loving East Coast boy after all.

I watch Jacob's ire rising, even as he scrounges up a chuckle, complicit with Beau's unbearable jerkdom.

Evelyn and Henry are last to join, and Henry prepares two bowls of oatmeal with nuts and chia seeds. They bypass sitting at the table for the corner inglenook, an act of togetherness that also feels like a defense against gathered-family time.

While Beau tents his face behind his newspaper for the rest of breakfast, Bitsy watches Jacob and me with a slightly aggrieved expression, as if we're a wilting flower arrangement that is not her job to remove. The third time I catch her eye and smile, she seems to decide she ought to speak.

"Evelyn tells me you're a fan of Frieda Bergessen," she says, and suddenly my windpipe is sticking in a way that makes it hard to find air. I feel Jacob's micro-glance in my direction.

"Yes, I am."

"Nora, are you hosting another poetry recital tonight?" asks Keith, deadpan.

"Sadly, I'm retired."

"Evelyn says you sold her a first edition," says Bitsy.

"I did." My stomach is clenched in apprehension of where this talk will lead. What else does Bitsy know?

"We've held on to some correspondence between Frieda and my grandmother, if you want a peek at it," says Bitsy. "Just some sleepy little thank-you notes, as I recall, but I'll have them sent to your room after breakfast."

"I'd love to read those letters," I tell her. "That would be incredible."

"Shouldn't they be in a museum, Bits?" asks Pauline.

"No, thank you, ma'am. Belle Meade Museum does come poking around here now and again," says Bitsy. "But in my opinion, private treasures are overly shared."

"Mama's speaking in cursive, but what she really means is *don't put the letters online*," says Evelyn to me.

"I won't," I promise.

"Then you'll stay here with the letters," says Evelyn, nodding at me—and it's only now that I feel the frisson of last night, and her disappointment that I didn't take the PA job. "Pauline wants me to drive her into town so we can stick our noses in the shops."

"I've got to look for andirons," says Pauline, apologetic, like she's got herself in an andirons pickle. I'm guessing they're both glad I won't tag along into stores I can't afford, freeing Pauline to spend whatever extravagant amount she deems necessary for fireplace accessories.

Any private time for my take-two with Evelyn will have to wait until they're back.

With Beau capturing Jacob's morning, I leave the barn to tour around the gardens. I retrace the path back to Evelyn's playhouse in the woods, where I walk up the front steps and open the three-quarters-of-Brook-Lane-sized door. By the light of day, the house is even more stately; all it needs is its own article in *Architectural Digest Junior* to enthuse over its *farm-fresh, praline-and-vanilla palette and rustic-yet-stylish invitation to authentic play.*

Upstairs, one room has a pair of bunk beds; in the other, a brass bed.

I lie on my back on the brass bed and let my feet hang over the edge. Did I come here to reactivate some outrage about this playhouse? A quick reminder of all its extravagant overindulgences, ahead of confronting Evelyn? If I did, it's not working. All I can feel is that it's deliriously comfortable. And how much I like this clean, powdery scent in the coverlet. And how, if I curl up, I can shape myself to fit inside the bed frame—a wee adult in my scaled-down fairy tale. Almost immediately, I'm sleepy, and so I hop from the bed before my inner Goldilocks gets the better of me, and I leave the cottage in a rush, as if someone's chasing me out.

Forty-Six

‹‹‹‹‹‹‹‹‹‹‹‹‹‹

When I return to the main house, it's quiet. Our bedroom has been tidied. The packet of yellowing envelopes, addressed in a calligraphic hand to *Mrs. Evelyn S. Fitzroy, Old Orchard, Fairfax County, Tenn.* is waiting for me on the dresser.

There's no doubt these letters should go to a museum. At the least, they belong in some type of acid-free alkaline container, accessible to the curious-minded, the Bergessen buffs, the American Studies scholars, the excitable poets.

At the same time, I love this glimpse behind the curtain.

I sit at the small corner desk and unknot the ivory ribbon.

Through the window, I see Evelyn's Alfa Romeo zip around and down the drive.

Ostensibly, the letters are just what Bitsy said, a cache of thank-yous for weekends at Old Orchard or for trips the women enjoyed together at other Fitzroy homes, both here and abroad. But they are also mesmerizing: surprising and digressive, witty and alert. In some letters, Bergessen refers to enclosed reimbursement checks, payments for theater and train tickets. She is meticulous and proud when it comes to her accounting. She also lists, in rapturous and grateful detail, every Fitzroy-gifted piece of bespoke clothing made for her in Paris. One letter is a heady recap devoted to the details of a fitting with a new designer she refers to as the *prodige de 30 Montaigne*.

> *Such an extraordinary eye behind those spectacles! He is a firebrand, as playful as he is serious, as nonconforming as he is precise.*

I check the postmark on that one. September 1957. Bergessen's last hurrah to Europe. Her career is hanging by a thread of relevance at this point. In the next decade Frieda Bergessen will be as out of fashion as her buckle shoes. And yet I don't get a sense of melancholy in her next letters about packing up her Greenwich Village apartment or even her move to the Catskills. After she settles upstate, her letters thin to an annual few. There's a postcard from her solo trip to Yellowstone National Park. A final letter is postmarked June 1963, where Frieda declines an invitation:

> *No matter how reliably generous your bonhomie, my Evvie, I think it best I stay put this summer. A country life for me! Give Montepulciano tanti baci, and I will relish our bounty of memories that have nourished me every season since.*

Frieda doesn't sound at all nostalgic for those memories; her last five years' worth of letters convey mostly enchantment for her new friends and neighbors, along with warmhearted descriptions of her cats and her lumpy zucchini. She always ends with an invitation for the Fitzroys to visit her upstate. I don't sense it ever happened, but it's gratifying to feel that Frieda is living life on her terms right up until her last letter, written just a few months before her death.

Evelyn and Pauline aren't home by the time I restack the packet and tie the ribbon that holds the envelopes together.

I lie down on the bed to uncrick my stiff neck and check in with my phone.

Jacob sent a text about forty minutes ago that he and Beau are having lunch at Beau's shooting club. He's added a red rage-face emoji, so it seems that things went even worse than his low expectations. Something happened—I can't remember when Jacob has used this emoji, so boiled over in eyebrow-scrunching wrath.

I also missed a voicemail from Dean about an hour ago. I'd turned my ringer off at breakfast. When I play the message, Dean sounds animated and says he just read the article.

I sit up and call Dean. He picks up on the first ring.

"What article?"

"You don't know? The interview with Opal Appell in the *New York Times* Style section," says Dean. "What did you sell it for? Tell me everything."

"What interview? Sell what?" Except that the bottom of my stomach is already dropping into the ice-cold shock of knowing exactly what.

"It's a profile about Opal turning ninety. It's to highlight her retrospective at the Costume Institute at the Met," says Dean. "And it mentions the Dior piece."

"Opal's retrospective?" No, no, no. Not this. "*My* Dior piece? Opal Appell is exhibiting the Bergessen cloak?"

"Didn't you sell it to her?" asks Dean. "You sound shocked! She donated it."

There's a roar of noise in my head. "Send the link."

"Sending. Tell me when it comes through."

It feels like an eternity before I get the ping. "I'll call you back."

"I'm here all day, and I want to hear all about it," says Dean, "but now I'm trading the *Times* for *British Bake Off.*"

Off the phone, I devour the article.

"Après Appell" is accompanied by an unsmiling black-and-white photograph, in which every crack in Opal's skin is so delineated she looks prehistoric. Even the way she is staring at me through those famously hooded eyes—like a crocodile at the surface of the water, sizing up her prey—makes me feel tricked.

I skim through the first paragraphs. Born in Queens, the daughter of a shopkeeper, Opal sold her own recipe for J'Appelle face cream as a teenager while she was working in her father's store. She married her husband at age twenty, divorced him, and famously married his brother. Both husbands are long buried, but Opal endures, awake every morning at six for her morning swim, and then she takes a call from her CEO.

"Opal Appell blazes a path with klieg lights!" gushes Carol Foreman, CEO.

I keep skimming. Here it is.

The Age of Appell, to be unveiled next year at the Costume Institute at the Metropolitan Museum of Art, is an eclectic collection befitting its curator. Selected highlights include the prototype for the Appell Allure skincare line and the original jelly bean–pink blazer and tailored A-line skirt that distinguished an Appell "beauty adviser" from a salesgirl. Also on display are Haruto Tsubaki's architectural models of the New York and London flagship stores.

To expand a biography of herself as more than founder and factotum, Appell is contributing personal pieces, including her wedding dress from her second marriage—"the one that counted"—to husband Max Appell (1913–1986). Among her treasures, the flight instruments of aviation pioneer Amelia Earhart, a composition notebook owned by songwriter Billie Holiday, and a couture Dior evening cloak made for the poet Freida Bergessen to honor what would be her final appearance at Carnegie Hall.

"When I was a young woman, I got the chance to see Bergessen that night," says Appell. "I've always felt a connection with her feminism, as I, too, fought the status quo of male-dominated business. As a New Yorker, I'm pleased that my collection stays close!"

Appell today is a far cry from "Chernobyl Opal," a moniker coined during a period of blitzkrieg job-slashing and restructuring that left Appell Inc. in turmoil but helmed its rebound. Today Appell Inc. boasts an international portfolio that cements its position as a Fortune 500 company. Appell clearly knows how to separate business decisions from pleasure, as she plans to donate the entire collection, valued in total at thirty million dollars.

Thirty million dollars. I'm terrified and nauseated. I call Dean and the minute he picks up, I run him through the whole story.

"Will Gavin get you an itemization number?" I ask. Gavin Hussie, who works in the Met's Appraisals department, is a friend of Dean's from his days with Sotheby's.

"Sure. Was your own deal with Appell a handshake?" Dean's voice is somber to match my own. "Or did you sign a nondisclosure?" He knows the havoc wreaked by inheritance. There's nothing like a dearly departed's Degas getting listed in a New York auction house to send relatives into a vicious tizzy of tugs-of-war and lawyering up.

"Handshake," I answer softly. "I thought it was a personal gift. Sentimental. I never considered this outcome."

"That it was a capital gains strategy?"

"Or that it was a betrayal."

"I'll get you that number," says Dean, "but we both know that it's going to be a padded value."

"I know." The skin of my face and neck is so hot I feel like I could peel it off like a mask. "I wonder if Bryce was orchestrating this flip all along."

"I'll text you when I hear from Gavin."

I call Bryce and leave a message for her to call me back. Was this really her plan? Or is she feeling as duped as I am? A few minutes later she sends me a text: So sorry! It seems that Grandy pulled an Opal! Zero clue that was coming. I'll call you when I can.

At this point, it doesn't matter if Bryce calls me or not. But Evelyn should learn about the *Times* article from me. The Alpha Romeo motored up the drive while I was talking with Dean. I'll go find her; then Jacob and I can figure out how to handle the fallout.

"Evelyn, here's the thing—" I say to the mirror, practicing my confession, and then the bedroom door bursts open, and Jacob walks in, dressed like Elmer Fudd's dapper cousin. His face is as red as a reaper chili.

"We're changing our tickets," he growls. "I'm not staying here till Sunday. It was a bad idea, and now it's time to go home."

Forty-Seven

⫷⫷⫷⫷⫷⫷⫷⫷⫷⫷

I've been waiting to pounce, but Jacob has come in so hot that I let him go first, and I listen with dismay to his tale of how Beau, deigning Jacob unfit to appear at the Dunaway Club in his best Brooklyn nondescript separates, dragged him to Orvis to purchase the high-tone tweedy shooting outfit that he's currently inhabiting.

"The bill came to over two thousand. I had to use the Mastercard."

"You couldn't have said no?"

"It was too public, and Beau was making all these unfunny cracks about how I owe it to him to look respectable since his daughter was carrying my baby."

I wrinkle my nose. "Lovely."

"He was soused by breakfast," says Jacob. "That wasn't just orange juice he was drinking. I still think we should leave tonight."

"We can return all the clothes, easy," I say. "There's an Orvis in New York."

Jacob is already shedding them so that he can rinse off the indignities of the day, but I can't wait that long, so I follow him into the bathroom and give him my phone, which is opened to the article.

He wraps a towel around his waist, then sits on the toilet and reads. I hear the ping of a text alert.

"Is that Dean?" I ask.

"Yes. He just sent you a very large number."

"How much?"

"Two hundred fifty thousand dollars." Jacob looks up. "What does it mean?"

I cover my face with my hands and groan. "It's the Costume Institute's appraisal of the Bergessen piece."

Jacob leans back against the toilet tank. "How?"

"We saw this happen at Lineage. It's a tax strategy, semi-disguised as philanthropy."

"Is it even legal?"

"It shouldn't be, but it is. It's totally legal for Opal Appell to shelter thirty million dollars so that she can dodge inheritance taxes. That's nothing to her. It's also legal for the Costume Institute to bloat the value. So, yes. Legal. A legal scam." I press my hands around my neck, willing my pulse to decelerate.

"Okay, but there's a chance Evelyn doesn't see this article. These people aren't *Times* subscribers by a long shot. Let's kick this drama into next week when we're all home."

"Evelyn's here now. I'd rather rip off the Band-Aid."

"She was in that room with all the taxidermy. Would it be easier if I went with you?"

Easier would be if Jacob had an actual Uncle Buck and the untold riches of his estate that would save me from this next shameful and excruciating hour.

"No, it's fine," I tell him. "I'll take care of it."

As I force myself down the stairs again, I try to bolster my thoughts. Maybe there's a happy ending buried somewhere in here, one where I tell Evelyn the truth, and she thanks me for being candid and says she's sorry I got tricked by Opal Appell, a con artist of note, to the surprise of no one who read that *Vanity Fair* article.

Downstairs, Evelyn is alone in the den with her iPad. "Yay, there you are! Here's some fun news: I'm in a sponsorship with Linen and Ink," she says, "for a notebook journal called *Our Journey Together: A Surrogate's Guide for Intended Parents*. I'd write a line or two a day, and then I'd give it to you when the baby's born. So watch for me promoting and linking it, because they're gonna give me a percentage of sales." She wriggles in place. "It's just small potatoes—but sweet potatoes, too, right?"

"That's great. Evelyn, we need to talk."

She looks at me, frowns, and sets aside her iPad. "What's up?"

I make myself sit on the settee that faces her. "I've been getting up the nerve to tell you something," I begin. "And I can't figure out how to say it."

"Jacob's uncle wasn't your big news?"

"No, it's bigger news."

Evelyn's eyes widen as a smile breaks unexpectedly across her face. "Oh my gosh! Sweetie!" For a moment, she cups her hands around her nose and mouth; her eyes are starry. "Are you *pregnant*?"

"Pregnant?" I'm so caught off guard I yelp the words. "No!"

"Oh." She deflates a little. "That's just—it happens. I've read all about it. The surrogate gets pregnant, and the stress goes out the window, and then voilà—two babies, five months apart!"

"It's not a good thing, this news," I say, as unease surges through me, along with a crawling guilt that no matter how I might want to hold Evelyn to her shortcomings, she is also this person, so full of goodwill that she'd only be overjoyed by the surplus of an unexpected pregnancy.

But her smile is already slipping off. "All ears."

"First of all, Jacob's uncle is a lie," I say, and now the rest of it comes spilling out as I stammer and fumble my way through. "And in the end, Jacob and I decided to use the money to put in an offer on a house, for the baby," I finish, conscious of my thumping heart and the pinging in my temple that feels like the start of a headache.

Evelyn has been listening with the blank attention you might offer a middle school flute concert, but I'm not fooled. I know that face. As a person often watched by others, Evelyn spends her life in control of her expressions. "Seventy-five thousand? Jeez. Bryce sure got you over a barrel," she says.

"Opal's ninetieth," I say.

"Her ninetieth!" Now Evelyn sounds indignant. "So maybe the solution is we just buy it back when Opal dies next week?" She laughs that deep-down saucy Evelyn laugh.

"I wish that was the solution." I give her my phone so she can read the *Times* article.

This news hits different. Evelyn holds herself very still as she reads and her expression slowly changes.

"No, no, no," she says. "Oh no. My parents." She puts down the phone and briefly presses her fingers over her eye sockets. "Now this is a real, true nightmare. Bitsy just might fall out of her pants about this. She doesn't even know I gave the Dior away." She uncrosses and recrosses her arms in that same nervous habit I'd witnessed in her mother. She looks at me and looks away. "Did they appraise it?"

I nod. "A quarter million," I say in a low voice.

"A quarter million. *Shit.* My parents are going to kill me! A quarter million—and I just gave it away for free!"

"I didn't know this would happen, Evelyn."

"You kept this whole thing to yourself, and what a mess! Why didn't you say something to me before?"

"I'm sorry," I say. "I should have talked it through with you, obviously. It felt so private and sensitive, and I kept trying to find the right time."

"Find a time?" she repeats querulously. "You can call, text, email, DM, WhatsApp me—anytime. What do you mean, find a *time*?"

"In-person time, I mean."

Evelyn is silent, as if making a point not to overreact by not reacting at all. It's unnerving and I start babbling to fill the silence. "Because it was complicated, with Bryce. But you've been away these past weeks, so

I was going to tell you right after the next appointment. I don't want to get caught up in the travel and scheduling issues. All I really want to say is that I'm very sorry."

"Do you have issues with my traveling?" she asks, forcing a smile. "This is the first I've heard of any of that. What else are we not talking about here?" When I don't say anything, she adds, "Really. Let's have at it."

The pileup of everything I've wanted to tell Evelyn all these past weeks feels like a bucket of rocks she's just asked me to throw at her. But I also know this is the opening, and that there's no such thing as perfect timing anymore. "It's only that you're so focused on EvvieDoesIt," I tell her. "I know that it's demanding and requires a lot of you, and—"

"Because the baby requires a lot of me," she says. "And you benefit from EvvieDoesIt most of all. You get to check in on everything—vitamins, exercise, prenatal massages, advice on stretching—I've got Dr. Tiblini on my channel next week. She was just on Kelly Clarkson."

"Evelyn, that's not—"

"I'd think you'd be happy I'm so focused on it. PrimaMama just reached out, and I'm podcasting with *Fertility Now*." She is staring at me as if my lack of gratitude is so inane as to be incomprehensible. "All day, I'm right here, showing up for this journey."

"EvvieDoesIt is spectacular," I say, my nerve failing, almost lost. "And you know I'm your biggest fan. But it's me you're talking to—and you're not indivisible from Evvie. In fact, lots of times you're off the radar. When Tabitha posts your meals for social—you're not even in the city to eat half of them. Or when you did the reel on doulas and midwives, but we never even went to Carriage House? Or when you have a glass of beer like the one that's next to you? Honestly, that's fine by me, Evelyn—but I know that's not going onto EvvieDoesIt, either. Same as you not writing me a line a day in that *Our Journey Together* notebook."

We both know that's true—Evelyn only holds a pen to sign a check. "Beer is rich in folic acid, everyone knows that," she says, standing up so abruptly she reminds me of a boxer who's taken some knocks and is ready to land a couple of jabs of her own. "I was considering doing a post about it, but I've got a few loonies who follow me, and their comments can poison the well." She picks up her glass and moves away from me, coming to stand below the portrait of her parents above the mantel. Suddenly it feels like the whole gang of fighting Fitzroys are glaring down at me.

"We'd decided to give up alcohol just as a thing to do together," I say.

"No, *you* decided. I was never game for your zero-alcohol pact," she says, "or your doulas. Doulas are just crazy hippies, and I don't want any of 'em near me while I'm having a baby. Or ever, come to think." She takes a deliberate sip of the beer and sets it on the mantel.

Now I stand up and take a few steps closer to the door, though I'm unsure how to leave. I feel unhinged with regret for the awfulness of everything I've said, as well as for this pain in Evelyn's eyes, knowing that I've caused it. "I'm sorry. I'd thought us going dry would be helpful."

"How does that help?" she snaps. "What's the point? It's not like we share a liver."

"I don't know," I say, lifting my hands. But then I say, "How was it helpful when you went live with that celebrity naming expert and crowd-sourced names for the baby? Knowing that Jacob and I already have picked out baby names? We can't share a name, either."

"You're being so churlish," says Evelyn. "That was only a little fun."

"Except I don't think it's fun having strangers decide names for my baby!" I burst out. "I think it's creepy, to be honest!"

"Now *that* is just mean," says Evelyn. "All I've ever done is try to help you. Really, since the minute we met. And what do you do for me? You sell my beautiful gift, which will be a whole kerfuffle when my parents find out—and then on top of that, I'm getting an earful of how you think I'm failing you with my work schedule? I mean, for heaven's sake, Nora! It's ridiculous!"

My heart jumps to hear Evelyn call me by my real name. When was the last time she used it? The formality is punishing. "I never wanted to be a charity," I say. "And I'm very sorry that I was disingenuous with you." I'm hovering by the door. I sense Evelyn wants me to go, and yet I don't know how I can leave us like this.

"Well, since we're being honest, do you want to know something I think is ridiculous?" she asks. "Keeping this secret of if it's a girl or a boy!"

Is she serious? Her mouth is pressed downward, and for the first time, I see Evelyn's resemblance to her mother. "I get how that might be ridiculous to you. But at least we're talking about it—and I'm glad we're talking," I say, though my voice is trembling, a final indignity. "Because I think it's always best to get everything out in the open."

Evelyn puts up a hand, as if even this conversation is ridiculous, and she stays quiet until I'm almost out the door. "Well, then, if you really think everything's best out in the open, then I guess you should know it's a girl."

Forty-Eight

<<<<<<<<<<<<<

Jacob and I change our plane tickets for a flight the next morning. Leaving the Fitzroys' early means we have to do a layover in Chicago, but we'd have done five more if it meant getting out of there. Before we go, I find Bitsy and return the letters and give her my truly terrible excuse that our dog is sick. When the cab picks us up down by the gate, I feel like we're leaving the scene of a crime. Evelyn doesn't respond to my apology or goodbye texts, and I take the silence as her yes, we should get the hell out of Dodge. We get a room at a Red Roof Inn, and we spend the next morning drinking bottomless coffee in the airport Chili's.

"Nothing," says Jacob as we idle on the runway before takeoff.

"Nothing what?"

"Nothing is what happens to the baby, even if you and Evelyn aren't on good terms right now. It's all going to work out."

"You don't know that." I turn to look out the window, and the flat, faceless sameness of the runway. "This is uncharted territory."

"None of what we did was so bad that we can't get past it," says Jacob. "And Evelyn made mistakes, too. For example, she wins hands-down for worst gender-reveal party, but in the bigger scheme of things, all I want's a healthy baby." I told Jacob we were having a girl last night, in bed, between my sobbing jags and our all-night battle with how to stop the motel air conditioner from sounding like it was trying to digest a pile of sticks.

"What are you saying? You don't think I understand the bigger scheme of things?"

"We're both in bad moods, but let's not fight," he says.

"I'm not in a bad mood."

"Because it was always going to be a lose-lose for us. Even without the chef's kiss of us accidentally giving away a small fortune."

"Jacob, we didn't give away that money!"

"Sort of, we did," he says, stifling a yawn. "But even if this was just a plain old visit to meet Evelyn's parents, they were never too on-board about what she's doing, and we didn't help relations by being just these regular people."

"We are not 'just these regular people'!"

"I don't mean it that way," says Jacob. "But also, yes we are. Not that we should berate ourselves for it—they're somewhat icky people. Him especially."

My mood is not improving from this conversation. I put on headphones and watch an instantly forgettable rom-com for the rest of the trip, and I make a point to fake-laugh a lot, to show what a not-bad mood I'm in.

It's late afternoon when we get home, and I've just retrieved Nick from Tara downstairs when the text we've been waiting for all week from Oscar Torrey pops in: They've counter offered.

The counteroffer is twenty thousand dollars more than we expected.

"A little over what we estimated," says Jacob. "But doable."

"This is wayyy beyond the estimate."

"We can swing it," says Jacob. "We've got the money now."

"But then we've got nothing left over. We've got nothing to save us."

"Save us from what?"

"From I don't know what! From whatever is around the corner."

"There's nothing around the corner—we've been around all the corners!"

"Evelyn's a corner," I say.

"Evelyn's not a corner!"

"Evelyn's the biggest corner!"

5D thumps her fist against the wall for us to keep it down.

"Evelyn and Brook Lane don't have anything to do with each other," Jacob whispers loudly after a moment. "Feelings get hurt. Look how Bryce Appell stuck it to you—and you'll survive."

"Even factoring out Evelyn—how can you think about throwing more money at the house? Twenty thousand dollars over what we budgeted isn't a rounding error."

"It'd be tight, but we could swing it," he says.

"When did we turn into reckless spenders?" I ask. "Where's the guy who paid off my last student loan with me instead of doing the big hotel wedding that you'd wanted? Where's the guy who sold his racing bike so we could stop hemorrhaging interest fees?"

"That house is an investment," says Jacob. "Maybe this is the big chance we take."

"I can point to some big chances we're already taking! I don't want to go for broke on this house!"

Now it's my voice that causes 5D to thump again as a stony fury settles into Jacob's face—but before he can use the excuse of walking Nick to slam out the door, I grab the leash and slam out with her myself.

The day is overcast, with a mist that hangs low over the city. Nick and I take our route through the park. I stop and sit on the bench in the dog-friendly section, where Nick gets into a staring match with some bobbing pigeons and I watch the kids at the playground. For years, I've watched kids on these same slides and swings. I get older and the kids never do. Me, always hopeful for one of my own. Never counting on it.

I'm on the cusp of tears and also out of energy for crying. Twenty thousand dollars over the estimate! How can Jacob hurl us right back into this much exposure? I imagine myself saying these things at our Ursula meeting next week and Ursula nodding in deepest agreement, while Jacob is reduced to a silent, shamed lump on the other side of the love seat.

And Evelyn *is* a corner! The only corner that matters, really. Even if our last conversation was in some small way cathartic, the unintended consequence is that I've lost my foothold with Evelyn, and now I'm tumbling through this bottomless unknown, unable to feel any sense of the order that defined our relationship. I'm not on speaking terms with the woman who is carrying my baby. How could I have managed to let that happen?

Dusk is here, and the skyline is jagged against the flint-gray sky, apartment lights blinking on all around me, and now I want to go home and light up my own window. Jacob and I will work it out; we have to, especially when this rift with Evelyn feels like a seismic crack.

After I leave the park, I pick up Chinese from Chu Hua's. Jacob's still out when Nick and I get back to the apartment.

I set the table and pour the wonton soup from its cardboard tub into bowls. I take the moo shu pork from its paper container and arrange it nicely with the rice on a serving plate.

Just when I'm starting to worry about the food going cold, Jacob sends a text that he's at the movies. He doesn't come back until it's almost eleven.

By then I'm in bed, lights out. He moves around in the dark in extreme, exaggerated silence. As if the absolute worst thing he can imagine is if I woke up and he'd have to talk to me.

I stay pretend-asleep, but my heart is pounding.

When Jacob gets into bed, he scoots himself so far onto the opposite side he's practically over the edge of the mattress.

I don't move closer. We go to sleep not touching—a first.

Forty-Nine

By the time I wake up the next morning, Jacob has already been out to walk Nick, and on my phone is a brief text from him that he's gone to the Chelsea Piers to play basketball. I put a piece of bread in the toaster and then forget about it until the whole apartment smells like burnt toast, which in a way also smells like our fight.

I write and rewrite and send Evelyn a long heartfelt apology.

When Jacob comes back, the apartment feels too small for two sets of sharp elbows, and so I head into the city to work, even though I'm not on today. I run inventory and help Frankie pack up the latest Barb buys, a batch of stiffly textured and corseted Dolce & Gabbana gowns that she purchased on a recent work weekend getaway trip to Miami.

"She's lost her sense of the zeitgeist," Frankie comments. "Maybe we all do at some point, but in the meantime, where do we hide the cast of *Moulin Rouge*?"

"I think we can keep two Dolces on the floor," I say, "and stash the rest in the stockroom."

"Barb should give you more buyer's leverage," says Frankie. "Everything you find sells—even the stuff that's not on sale. Did you notice the mahogany beveled mirror you found last year at Hester Fair is missing?"

"You sold that?" I turn around. Sure enough. "Fantastic."

"So just let me know when you want to have an honest conversation with Barb."

"I might be shy of having another honest conversation with anyone right now," I say.

Frankie, who already got an earful of the Old Orchard weekend, nods. "Fine, but Barb's heading to ThriftCon in Vegas next weekend, and I will lie down in the street in protest if she comes back with a box of Ed Hardy."

I text Jacob that I'm getting takeout at work while Frankie and I finish the inventory, and Jacob texts that he's going out for dinner with some of his basketball friends—he doesn't say where.

That night, he gets back late, and the next morning, he's walked Nick and is out the door for work before I'm even awake. He calls me at the shop at lunchtime.

"We could lowball," he says, like this is a business call between colleagues. "Something that's so low we don't have a chance."

"Like five thousand," I say.

"I was thinking ten."

"Seventy-five hundred."

"And then we won't get it."

"I know."

We hold the line. Somebody needs to apologize, but we're too locked into our frustration, knowing this house is slipping through our fingers. That night, we speak to each other with a polite formality that makes for a strange, unprecedented mood and leaves me spinning morosely through all the worst-case scenarios of what would happen if Jacob and I go our separate ways after the baby is born. I'd stay here at the apartment, while he could move in with his parents and commute, and then if it's over for good, our daughter would grow up with the younger half siblings of Jacob's second marriage—probably to his high school girlfriend who's still living in Massapequa, and then he'd become one of those dads who'd forget his oldest child's birthday and be late for her dance recitals, even though she always gets the solos, and I wish Jacob and I would make up soon so that I can tell him all about my dreary projections, and we could get to the part where we laugh about it.

Evelyn never answers my letter, but on Tuesday, she launches her *Our Journey* journal. When I click the order link, it takes me to a Linktree and her new storefront of curated idea lists for everything from travel-toiletry bags to maternity casuals and belly tape—with 15 percent off if you type EVVIE as a promo code when you order a bottle of Harper's dry oil.

She responds to all the congratulatory comments—even mine—with hearts and thanks, so it's only when I want to send her a direct message that I just ordered a bottle of dry oil myself that I learn she's unfollowed me.

Got your message, I'm at the dentist, texts Meg in response to the howl of a voicemail I've left her. Agree it's immature but remember when you set the trap in the cupboard to see if I was the one eating your home-made trail mix?

We were in college!

Meg sends the shrug emoji and a tooth emoji and an xo.

On the morning of the doctor's checkup appointment, Evelyn posts a throwback photo of herself and toddler Xander, plus present-day Xander—today is his fourteenth birthday—that sets the comments section into a frenzy of approval for what a handsome young man he is and how he looks just like his mama, and how she must be so proud of him and how he must be so proud of her.

"I know you're nervous, but seeing her will make everything better," says Frankie that morning at the shop, where we're in the basement, hiding Barb's latest online fever-dream splurge of half a dozen Sonia Rykiel sailor dresses in a large haunted house–style brass-bound chest. The chest predates us and might have been here since the store was built. Until we pried it open this morning, we'd presumed it was full of dead bodies. Luckily, it's empty, and now we can fill it with Barb's newest assortment of *wow, nope.*

"Do you mind if I leave early?" I ask him. "I really want to get up there."

"Go ahead," he says. "I'm going to spend the day looking for more crawl spaces and trapdoors to stash inventory."

"Keep me posted."

"Same same."

I get to the hospital half an hour early, but it turns out I'm also late by a day.

Makebe and Bianca meet me in the waiting room, where both of them are wearing pained smiles.

"We thought you knew," says Makebe. "Evelyn changed the appointment. It was yesterday morning. She said she had a last-minute travel-schedule issue."

"Oh, right." I make a show of frowning at my phone. "My mistake," I say, as anxiety burns a brush fire over my skin. "Usually, I'm very up to date on everything."

"She and Henry flew out for a wedding today," says Makebe. "Bogotá, she said."

"I thought she said Cartagena," says Bianca.

"Aha." I shoot a text to Raquel. None of the trip details are on Slack, which is not surprising, since Raquel barely pays attention to the PA part of her job. It's confusing; usually Evelyn posts packing vlogs, sharing her globe-trotter's tips, but this time, she decided against it. Maybe she didn't want me to know she was on the move.

"Anyway, everything looks great on the scan! The baby is a beautiful twenty-four weeks," says Bianca. "I'll send you some images?"

My heart turns over. "Yes, please. I'd like that so much."

"The next checkup is in just under five weeks, the first Friday of November." Makebe is scrolling her iPad and now she adds a note. "There! I just put you on our call alert!"

"We can let you know if anything changes," says Bianca.

"Thanks. I'll be here." I walk out of Weill Cornell feeling crumpled and slightly deranged.

Evelyn, I'm just leaving the hospital. Looks like I missed you by a day.

No answer. Raquel's email is an autoreply that redirects me to Evelyn's contacts.

A while ago, Evelyn told me the name of her friend who is getting married in Bogotá. Jessica? Veronica? I can't remember. I don't even know where Evelyn is staying or for how long. I search *socialite wedding Cartagena Bogotá* online—nothing.

It's a terrible, disorienting feeling, that Evelyn suddenly isn't here, and I don't know where she is. That she is spelunking through South America, unaccountable to everyone beyond what Evelyn deigns to post on EvvieDoesIt. My last-ditch effort is to check in with Henry's Facebook; his most recent photo is still him holding a big dead fish from his most recent trip to Alaska three years ago.

I'm meeting Jacob in Midtown so we can walk together to join Meg and Banks. Meg's been on a quest to see *The Music Man*, and before she and Banks watch the show, the four of us are meeting for dinner at Sardi's. It's a hark back to the first time Meg's parents took us there to celebrate her twenty-first birthday. We saw *The Producers* afterward. It was my first Broadway show, and an evening where I'd felt projected into a galaxy of dazzling marquees and star power. At Sardi's, newly legal Meg and I drank multiple Bellinis and polished off platters of cannelloni, and we both have the same keepsake memento—a photo of us making wide-eyed fish-lips in front of the Sardi's caricature of Lucille Ball.

When I see Jacob across the street, I can tell by his face that he's also ready to make up. Evelyn's no-show trumps all. The strength of his hug is everything I need; it's incredible how one hug can contain inside it all the emotions we've just lived through. We cross Forty-Sixth Street together, holding hands and leaning into each other.

"She shouldn't have let you hike up to the hospital if she wasn't there."

"She's still upset. She just needs time," I say, making my weary pitch for Team Evelyn. "Also, Meg and Banks don't know what happened at Old Orchard."

"Got it."

As soon as we step into Sardi's pre-theater din, Meg jumps up, her long arms beckoning. Banks looks more dapper than when I'd seen him last, chasing his daughters and picking Duke poop off the lawn.

Visually, the Barnetts make a slightly odd couple. I don't usually notice this until we're out in public. Banks is short and paunchy, with pale eyes behind the type of delicate wire-frame eyeglasses that studious rabbits wear in children's books, and he's always slightly puddled in his baggy Brooks Brothers suits. Whereas Meg is taut and strong, and when it's time to dress up, she likes to tend the embers of her old straight-edge punk self. Tonight, she's layered strips of pink through her hair and temporary star tattoos up her bare arm.

"We've just put in an order for homemade mozzarella and pan-fried baby artichokes as table-share appetizers," she says. "Spray-on color," she adds, touching her hair. "Paris Hilton sold it to me."

"Paris sold it personally to Meg at 2 a.m. on Instagram," says Banks.

"Speaking of personally, you saw Evelyn live and in person today, right?" says Meg. "How's the baby? How is everyone's favorite surro-glam?"

"The baby's looking great on the scan, but I missed Evelyn," I say. "She moved the appointment up a day." I try for casual, but Meg knows my face too well.

"And she didn't tell you she changed it?" she asks pointedly.

"I think she was dealing with multiple scheduling issues." I swallow.

"Okay," says Meg with a hand-swipe gesture of *let's move on.*

But Banks shifts his gaze from me to Jacob and back.

"We'll catch her next month," I say.

"Don't wait, Nora," declares Banks. "We all saw *Say Anything*. Go to her, go stand under her window at midnight with your boom box cranked. But instead of *In Your Eyes*, you play *Twinkle, Twinkle, Little Star*."

"That would be tricky," I say, "since I believe she's in Bogotá."

"*Bogotá?*" Banks reaches up and pops a mini artichoke into his mouth after the waitress sets the appetizer plates on the table. "Seriously? The country?"

"It's a city," says Meg. "And maybe let's not focus on Evelyn tonight."

"The same Bogotá that's the drug and guns capital of the world?" presses Banks.

"Banks," says Meg. "Stop. Evelyn's not running guns."

"Exactly," says Jacob. "She has a concierge service that runs the guns for her."

We all allow a laugh for that, but I see the Barnetts exchange a husband-wife glance that feels like it's about Banks wanting to say something that Meg doesn't want him to say.

"Do you ever feel like Evelyn might not do right by you two?" asks Banks anyway while Meg throws eye daggers at him. "Go on a bender? Have that baby wherever she wants?"

"Nobody thinks that," says Meg quickly. "On EvvieDoesIt, Evelyn's like this total spokesperson-surrogate babe. She's a rock star; she's got all the answers."

Banks looks at me directly. "But the real Evelyn's off radar, correct? What are your rights? Do you ever feel like you need to call a lawyer just to get a heads-up on her jet-setting-without-borders? I mean, at least with a paid surrogate, you've got a modicum of being the boss."

"For God's sake, Banks. Excuse him," says Meg. "We don't get out much anymore."

"All I'm saying is, you think you know a person," says Banks. "But you don't *know* her know her."

"Dude," says Meg, "I thought I knew you too. But now I might ask the waiter to throw you out."

"Evelyn's not a sociopath, and she takes good care of herself," says Jacob, "so we've also never felt the need to dictate where she goes and what she does. But from that perspective, yeah, it's a trust exercise."

"And we *do* trust her. She's a very kind, levelheaded person." Then I say, "It was always going to be a complicated relationship." I sound too emotional. The table is suddenly weighted with it.

"I just wish it'd been me," blurts Meg after a moment, going for her wineglass.

"Me, too," says Banks. "That also would've saved us."

"Saved us from what?" Meg's voice is suddenly flint.

"What do you mean *from what*?" Banks's eyes widen, but his face turns red. "We all know Hailey was an accident."

Meg thrusts her shoulders back at her husband and lifts her chin, an attack posture that I remember from her years of playing field hockey at Phelps. "Really?" she asks in a voice that somehow sounds both friendly and frightening. "Are you really doing this now?"

"Chill out, DeLuca." Banks is all good-natured incredulity. "It's not like Hailey can hear me."

Meg says nothing, and the silence lies thick on the table until Jacob launches into a subject he knows almost nothing about—NBA draft picks—betting awkwardly but correctly that superfan Banks will take the bait.

But Banks's comments have landed hard. Meg looks tense. I droop. Banks seems to know it's on him, but we can't recover the mood. Banks also must have slipped his credit card to the waiter on his way to the restroom. When we're all at the door, he tells us he really does need to get out more, and he's very sorry he accidentally gifted the table with conversational fender-benders.

"It's fine," I tell him. "I think we'll all be relieved when the baby gets here safe."

"Thanks again for dinner. Us, next time," says Jacob before the Barnetts peel off in search of the Winter Garden Theatre.

I will install a Banks software update later tonight, Meg texts.

You know I love all versions of Banks.

Then I send her a GIF of Harry Styles in a shamrock-green jump-suit, blowing kisses with both hands.

"Now is when you privately reassure me that Evelyn isn't planning to have our baby somewhere in Colombia and never come back," I tell Jacob.

"What's she gonna do?" asks Jacob. "Run away with the baby, like in all the horror movies? Give me a break. You're letting Banks get to you." But there's an edge to Jacob's voice that sounds like Banks got to him too.

"I guess I'm scared," I admit. "Only because she's gone, and I can't talk to her, and I don't know what's in her head."

"She doesn't want our baby. That's not what's happening." Jacob fastens his arm around my waist. "And here's an idea," he says, with a forced lightness in his voice. "Why don't you go ahead and start enjoy-ing that one glass of wine at dinner? Since even our dear Evelyn has thrown in a small towel on the no-booze rule."

It didn't occur to me to have a drink tonight. *How does that help?* she'd asked. *What's the point of that?* No point, except that it felt like a connec-tion. Ultrasound images and Dropbox links never inch me any closer to the baby. Neither do these gestures. But they're also all I've got, and what do they count for, anyway, if I don't even know where Evelyn is?

Fifty

<<<<<<<<<<<<<<

When Oscar texts us that our offer has been accepted, the unexpected happy news is like a slice of chocolate cake after our week on gruel.

Jacob and I call Meg, our 87 Brook Lane house whisperer, and we put her on speakerphone.

"All my dreams of us living only fifty minutes away in light-to-moderate traffic are coming true!" She's so purely delighted it's contagious. Brook Lane—everything it is and everything we hope to do with it—is on our horizon, and it gives us a small respite from all the Evelyn anxiety. Over the weeks, I've stayed slow and cautious with her, hearting the Bogotá trip when she finally posted about it and sending a quiet but steady stream of DMs from @IllHaveSeconds—thankfully, Evelyn still follows the shop—that are links to items of clothing she might like.

Then I brave it one night and text, how's that baby doing?

Strong legs! A kicker, she texts back, and this is such a new dollop of information that I have to sit down, weak with happiness and relief.

During Jacob's and my next Ursula visit, when I relate this morsel of text exchange and how it sustained me all week, Ursula asks me how I'm feeling lately about Evelyn.

"Frankly, I'm exhausted," I tell her, "from feeling so many things, all the time, about Evelyn. I'm always trying to dissect her posts—or, even trickier, the silences between her posts—to read her moods. Usually I feel like I'm careening between gratitude and frustration—not to mention my guilt about why she's so upset with me in the first place."

"I take it she hasn't answered your letter?" asks Ursula.

I shake my head no. "She's got this reel about how to become a carrier, where she lays it all out very clearly. Health requirements, pros and cons, the importance of a support network. Late at night, I just watch it," I admit. "Over and over."

Ursula quirks an eyebrow. "Why?"

"Probably because we haven't put a formal agreement in place, and Nora and I want to reassure ourselves that Evelyn is stable," says Jacob.

It was Ursula who'd advised us to go to contract early, for our own peace of mind, back when Evelyn suggested that we sign an agreement only if we got a viable pregnancy. We never spoke of it again.

"Ah," says Ursula now. "No contract." And I feel like a fool, and I know that Jacob does too, because drafting a formal contract also meant spending thousands of dollars we just don't have, and since Evelyn was always so easygoing about it, we let it slide—until last week, when we retained a lawyer.

"No contract *yet*. The draft will be ready very soon," says Jacob.

"Everything will be fine," I say. "Evelyn's smart and competent." I set my mug on the coffee table and press my palms together, half declaration, half prayer. "The truth is, Evelyn will do whatever she wants, whenever she wants. But she's always been good to the baby, and the bottom line is we're so lucky to have her!"

"Even presuming we're so lucky to have Evelyn," says Jacob, "do we have to say we feel as lucky about EvvieDoesIt? Because I'm not sure about that part. All the sharing, all the praise-mongering." He shifts back on the sofa and pulls his hands through his hair. "Would EvvieDoesIt's followers want to know she's not even speaking to the Intended Parents?"

"She is so speaking to us," I say quickly. "Just not a lot."

"And we all can agree," Ursula says, after a moment, "that contract or not, so far, she's been very responsible around the pregnancy."

"Yes," I say.

"Yes," admits Jacob.

"Yes," Ursula concludes firmly, though now I wonder if Jacob and I seem silly and small-minded to her, unworthy of our free-spirited, large-hearted surrogate, whose fealty is clearly to doing the right, responsible thing and whose only crime is that she also wants people to watch.

Fifty-One

I've marked Friday, November 6, in green Sharpie pen that I'd attached with a string and a pushpin to Gabi's *Flowers of Guam* wall calendar hanging on the inside door of our broom closet. November is a photograph of blooming ginger. I've drawn a green line diagonally through each little square room, and now we're in the green-bordered room, at last.

I've written Evelyn that I'm looking forward to seeing her, which got me a thumbs-up, and I've checked in multiple times with Makebe and Bianca to make sure nothing was rescheduled. At work, I waste fifteen neurotic minutes composing and re-composing the perfect message to Evelyn before I send See you at 3 p.m.!

At two o'clock, I'm debating if I should take my raincoat—there's a chance of showers this afternoon—when I hear the ping, sent to both Jacob and me: I can do this alone, thanks.

"Oh!" My breath is short-circuiting.

"What?" Barb looks up from where she and Frankie are disagreeing about pieces for our upcoming trunk show book.

"Evelyn doesn't want us with her!"

"Again?" asks Frankie.

"Can she even do that?" asks Barb.

I'm still trying to grind out a response when Jacob calls, and I step out onto the street to take it. "This feels awful. Please tell me that everything is going to be okay with Evelyn."

"Well, I don't love that she still wants space from us."

"If we gave her more space," I say, "we'd be in different time zones."

"Let me text her for a change, and then she'll know you and I talked. I think we schedule a FaceTime and just lay it out for her. We've got to move past all the hurt feelings because this is our baby, and we need to be at these doctor's appointments. Okay? Right?"

"Okay. Right."

"I've gotta step back into this meeting. You good?"

"Yep." I don't feel so good.

"I'll see you tonight."

As soon as I get off, Jacob's text to Evelyn pops in: Sorry we don't get to see you. Please ask the team to send us the imaging/report? And let's get Raquel to schedule us a follow-up call for tomorrow. Thanks!

Sure, texts Evelyn.

When I come back inside, Barb is watching me. "Are you going up anyway?"

"We're doing a call later."

"Go see her," says Frankie. "Face-to-face will make a big difference. She can't be upset with you forever."

"Can't she?"

"Take it from me: you make up the surrogacy playbook as you go along," says Frankie. "But you do need to get in the game."

"Agree." Barb clap-claps her hands. Frankie is already unhooking my umbrella and coat.

I'm not sure if they're right, but there are two of them, and I want to go. I go.

At Union Square, the subways are backed up, delaying me. I emerge to a mist and realize I forgot my umbrella on the train. I walk the four blocks to Weill Cornell as my hair flattens to a damp, wilted salad. When I catch sight of the black car, Max at the wheel, I duck under the awning of the apartment building across the street and text Evelyn that I'm here, outside, and that I'd love to see her.

Twenty minutes later, Evelyn, in a shaggy fur pelt of a coat and matching ushanka hat, looking very much like an Icelandic conqueror, bursts through the hospital's outermost glass doors. I'm so happy to see her it feels like the floor has dropped out of my heart.

"Evelyn!" I shout.

She stops. It feels like an eternity before she signals for me to come over. I dash across the street as Max opens Evelyn's door. I open the other side door and slide in.

"I didn't see your messages till now," she says. "The due date is moved to the eighth. Scheduled induction. Nothing else to report. Everybody's healthy." She removes her hat, and I catch the cedar-peach scent of her shampoo. It's so good to be near her that it's all I can do not to blurt out how much I've missed her, but I don't trust that anything I say will come out the way I mean it. My whole body hurts with my desire to make everything right.

"January eighth," I say. The baby's new birthday. One is Jacob's lucky number. Eight is mine.

"We can drop you at Astor Place to pick up the four, if you want." Evelyn keeps her phone in front of her face as the car swooshes us down Park.

"Okay, great. Thank you."

Silence. Outside, all down the sidewalks, umbrellas are popping open. Other people, caught bareheaded, are tenting up their jackets and moving in clumsy bursts, dodging puddles.

I have to say something. After a minute, I ask, "What's the reason for moving the birth date?"

"Sharon's at a conference on the eleventh." Evelyn glances at me. "Three days is safe. The baby is thriving. Don't worry."

Gratitude bursts through me. Evelyn wants all the right things, and she has all the best plans, and Jacob and I have been such suspicious, small-minded people to think anything less.

"Listen, Evelyn, what I wrote—" I begin, but she stops me with a palm up.

"You should know, my parents are fit to be tied," she says. "They got hold of the estimate. They just cannot believe I gave away a precious family heirloom—they even met with lawyers."

"But they should be angry at me, not you."

Evelyn floats a dismissive hand. "They figured you were easy to dupe. It's been a whole family drama." She takes a bottled water from the cup holder and twists the cap. "The money's not the point, though— the money's not what bothers me most," she adds in a sudden, heated rush. "What bothers me most, is that I was planning to post on Frieda and her connection with my great-gran and how it tied with you and me—but how do I do that now? So maybe that's my fault, for overly projecting my hopes."

"We could still tell a happy version of the story," I say. "If it's just for social, right?"

"You just don't understand my followers." Evelyn's face is tight with dismay. "I can't be inauthentic with them. They count on me. Anyway, we'll see about you coming to the December checkup, and that'll be closer to three weeks than two, because we're away for Thanksgiving."

"All right," I say.

"Though it suited me a whole heck of a lot better to do today's visit by myself," says Evelyn. "To be honest, I just don't feel quite right with you yet."

All month I've been in a fever of anticipation for this checkup, for the endorphin rush of peeking in on my baby through the grainy fog of the ultrasound. I'd lost week twenty-four, and I've lost this one too, and to think I might be losing the next visit feels overwhelming, and my tears are coming hot and fast, and I can't stop them. I'm wiping my hands over my wet face like useless windshield wipers.

"Please stop crying," says Evelyn. "It's making me nervous."

"I'm sorry," I say, but I can't seem to stop, and what's even more devastating is how I can't ever seem to fix the chasm between Evelyn and me, nor can I bear the prospect of another month like this one. "I've been nervous too," I manage to blurt out. "When I didn't know where you were in Colombia—and then people started talking about, oh, such ridiculous things, about how we don't have the contract signed, and where you might go—"

"The *contract*?" Evelyn gives a short displeased laugh. "What are you imagining? That I'm running off with this baby to Monte Carlo? I'm legitimately upset with you, Nora, and I wanted a bit of time away from you—and now you think I'm a baby kidnapper?"

"No! I'm sorry!" I'm a mess. I'm the definition of blubbering tears, the last thing anybody ever wants to be.

"I'll keep you updated," says Evelyn after a moment, her voice neutral as a newscaster, "and I'll probably see you for the next checkup at the beginning of December."

Probably has to be okay. There's no other option on the table than okay. I nod agreement, blot my face with my sleeve, and try not to sniffle too loudly.

And now Max has pulled up to the corner of Astor Place at Cooper Station, and my Evelyn time is over. I jump out of the car and slam the door before the rain gets in.

Fifty-Two

⸨⸨⸨⸨⸨⸨⸨⸨⸨⸨⸨

When we arrive at the Hammonds late Wednesday night of Thanksgiving weekend, Sandy puts Jacob and me in his old bedroom as usual, with its double bed and mattress so shot it feels like we might sink through its saggy middle to its box spring. I prop my head into the crook of Jacob's elbow to stare through his boyhood window out onto his boyhood view. Rooftops and treetops and a dark slate of stars.

"Just think. Next Thanksgiving will be so different. We'll be parents," I whisper. "Maybe even *hosting*." I've been working to speak only positive, holiday-worthy thoughts, rather than the spoils of all my many Evelyn-related worst-case scenarios.

"Sounds nice," he whispers back. "But then what'll you do when you can't search engine phrases like *travel and placenta previa*?"

He knows me too well. "Meg says there's tons of scary stuff to look up. Hundreds on newborn rashes alone."

"Something to be thankful for." Jacob already sounds half-asleep, and when his breath is even, I reach for my phone and one last look to see if Evelyn's put up anything new in the past hour. Nothing, but I scroll back through her family recipe for stuffing—link in the bio—her immunity-booster tips reel, her cute "tag a preggo mama" post, and her story from this morning that's all about week thirty-three and this year's Friendsgiving in North Fork because it's Pauline's turn to host. I listen again to the part where Evelyn talks about how to feel comfortable with loving people in your own way.

Is she referencing Beau and Bitsy? Or could she mean Jacob and me?

I focus on what's good here: Evelyn's wearing a flecked Scottish Highlands sweater I'd sourced for her last month. Raquel has, officially, sent me an invitation to the next appointment for December fourth. Of course, Raquel being Raquel, the invite might have gone out without Evelyn's approval, but I'm optimistic.

Once we're back home, I'll Sharpie-cross off four more days of November. Two days later, I can flip the *Flowers of Guam* calendar page to its final photograph of bougainvillea. Box by box and baby steps.

I set my phone on the bedside table, and Jacob wraps himself around me, arranging himself to fit along the shape of my body. *We can all agree that so far, she's been responsible around the pregnancy.* It's my mantra.

The next morning, everyone's already in the kitchen by the time I'm up. In his *No Soup for You* chef's apron from the Hammonds' jokester-apron collection, Phil is brining the turkey. Peter and Marisol are at the island, immersed in comparative toaster oven shopping on her laptop.

"One of you kids needs to be my chopper for the salad," says Phil. "My next hour requires intense risotto focus."

"I'll chop," I say as Jacob serves me a coffee and plate of burnt hash browns.

"Thanks," says Phil. "You know where the veggies are."

Sandy, at the table, is deep in her crossword puzzle. "Seven letters. Starts with a C. A folded pizza."

"Calzone," I say.

"Yes." She smiles as she blocks it in. "I saw Evelyn had the loveliest post about Southern stuffing," she says. "And she's heading to her friend Pauline's for Thanksgiving. Only she calls it *Friendsgiving.* So cute."

"So cute," I agree.

"She must feel a little bit like family by now?" says Sandy.

"She does, she does," says Jacob briskly.

"I do hope we get to meet her," says Sandy.

"Yup. Who's on for full-contact Nerf in the great outdoors?" asks Jacob.

"Me," says Peter. He tips back in his chair to call into the study. "Oliver! Football! Get off your Switch."

"I'm off," calls Ollie.

Jacob briefly rests a hand on my shoulder as he leaves the kitchen with the others.

Marisol begins mixing up her sugar, eggs, and heavy whipping cream to make her banana cream pie while I tie myself into the Lionel Ritchie *Hello? Is It Me You're Cooking For?* apron and get to the pleasing zen of using a large knife to chop colorful vegetables on butcher block.

Eventually, Sandy folds the newspaper. "It's not a properly set table without my grandchild's turkey centerpiece, is it? I need to go find that box."

When I'm done with the veggies, I head outside to where Ollie, Jacob, Marisol, and Peter are in a loose-rules game of Nerf football. I settle with Nick on the porch step to watch.

A few minutes later, Sandy joins me. "Look what I found," she says as she sits.

It's a kindergartener-sized handprint turkey on soft and faded red construction paper. Each finger is colored in with a crayon, with extra-long skinny turkey legs on the run. "This is the cutest! Little Ollie—such a talent."

"Actually." Sandy smiles. "Little Jacob."

"Ah!" I take the faded paper from her to examine it. "Leave it to Jacob to put his turkey in sneakers."

"You can keep it, if you like."

"Yes! I'd love to. Thank you." I press my own hand over Jacob's small turkey hand.

It's a beautiful fall day. That will be one of the things I remember about it. The cloudless sky and the nip in the air. We watch Ollie tackle Jacob, who collapses exaggeratedly. Even Jacob's pratfalls have a panther's grace.

"Nora, your phone has been vibrating off and on." Marisol comes outside to stand behind me, holding my bag. "Sounds like someone's really trying to get hold of you."

I jump up to take it from her hand.

Eight missed calls. The first from over an hour ago. All of them are Henry's number.

"Evelyn is in labor," he says first thing when I call back.

Blood rushes from my head like a stopper suddenly unplugged. Everything around me looks too bright, and I taste something sharply acidic in the back of my throat. I'm aware of Jacob stopping the game. His eyes narrowed and hard on me. Sandy whispering, *What is it, Nora, what?*

"You there?"

"I'm here."

"We're on the road," says Henry. "I'm sending you the address with the doctor's information."

"I've already got her contact info in my phone. How far apart are her contractions? Could it be a false start?" My teeth are chattering, my voice feels disembodied.

"No, no, sorry, it's not Sharon Glass." Henry sounds like he's fielding multiple conversations. "Sorry, I'm driving. Evelyn's beside me. You're on speaker. Did you get the contact information? I just sent it."

My phone vibrates. "But I don't need—"

Dr. R. Saetang, MD. Heat blazes under my arms, along with a pinpricking sensation that there's a bigger problem here. "I don't understand. Who is this person? Isn't Dr. Glass available? I thought she'd be on call throughout all the holiday weekends."

"What is happening?" whispers Sandy.

The baby, I mouth.

"Phil!" Sandy shouts, racing inside the house. Jacob is running across the lawn to me.

"Contractions are about twelve minutes apart," says Henry.

Everyone is pressed in close around me—a hover of Hammonds. "We're maybe seventy-five minutes from Weill Cornell," I tell him.

"We'll come too," whispers Sandy.

"We'll take my car," says Phil. "I'll drive."

"Let's go," says Jacob. "We need to get moving."

"Thirty-three weeks, right?" says Marisol. "That's not—I mean, it's... you know."

No, I don't know. I don't know.

"Maybe we take two cars," says Sandy.

"We're leaving now," I say to Henry.

But Henry also has been speaking, and there's a push in his voice that I didn't catch the first time. "Nora, I need you to listen—we're not— we decided not to go to Long Island. We're not in North Fork."

"But that's what's on social. That's what Evelyn said on EvvieDoesIt." I am suddenly ice-cold. "Why aren't you with Keith and Pauline?"

"We *are* with Keith and Pauline," he says. "We're up at their lodge in Maine."

Fifty-Three

There is one direct flight from New York to Portland International Airport this afternoon. It leaves JFK at 2:16 and touches down at 3:48.

"And then we'd still need to pick up a car," says Jacob. "But if we're driving from here to there, we'd get to the hospital in just over six hours."

We agree to the drive. Less risk of unexpected delays, or so we hope.

Jacob and Peter each knocked back a couple of Sam Adams during Nerf, so I'll be taking the first leg. We repack our suitcase while Phil and Sandy seal plastic containers with whatever is ready of dinner, along with a large thermos of coffee.

I remember my toothpaste last minute and toss it in my purse. I feel like I'm moving through Nutella.

"Should we take Nick?" I ask.

"Nora, are you in shock?" asks Jacob. "Obviously we're not taking the dog."

It doesn't feel so obvious to me. I show Peter where I've stashed the Ziploc of kibble and explain Nick's pee habits.

"We know how to dog," says Peter. "Just go."

When Phil has too many last-second stipulations about his Buick,

Jacob says we'll use the rental we drove here in. Sandy still wants to come with us.

"I'll be a help," she says. "I'll figure out snacks, and I can do some of the driving."

"Worse idea than bringing Nick," says Jacob.

"Then at least take my car?" says Sandy. "It's a Subaru—it was voted most reliable!"

Sandy's Subaru also has the benefit of a full tank. I've never driven her car before, but it feels like the car version of Sandy. Exceptionally clean, and her Bluetooth is programmed to a big band oldies station. We back out to the tinny harmonies of The Andrews Sisters.

As I enter the highway, it occurs to me that I can't remember the last time I drove any long distance. Jacob loves driving and usually handles it. Me behind the wheel adds to a disorienting sense that today is more like a strange dream that starts with me inexplicably speeding off in my mother-in-law's sedan, set to a soundtrack of boogie-woogie.

After we get on the Cross Island Parkway and Henry still hasn't called us, I think I might have to stop the car and get my breath in order.

"I'm pretty sure I'm having a heart attack and a stroke at the same time," I tell Jacob. "My teeth won't stop chattering."

"You're going almost eighty," he says. "You're definitely giving me a stroke, plus a heart attack."

Every cell of my body is humming at this new frantic frequency. "I could get pulled over for anxiety."

"Also for plain old speeding."

I look over at him. "Why do you keep slapping at your face?"

"I can't tell if I'm still beer-buzzed or if I'm buzzed because she's really having this baby today."

"Seven weeks early! What happened?" Through my shock, a rumbling terror is gathering upward from deep inside me. I pound the steering wheel with the heels of my hands. "What in the world happened?!"

"We'll know when we get there." Jacob stops his slapping and blinks down at his phone. "From Henry. They're at the hospital. They're checking in." He's quiet a moment. "What's the fruit for thirty-three weeks? A cantaloupe? A spaghetti squash? What does that mean in baby?"

"Stop, I don't care! Pineapple," I add, remembering the recipe on the EvvieDoesIt "Recipes" highlight reel for pineapple crisp. She's a pineapple.

"Want me to take over?"

"No," I say. "I think the driving helps me to not focus on my fear."

We stop in Bridgeport, pulling in for gas and the restroom and to-go coffees at the crowded service area. It's been raining off and on since we got out of New York, and now the storm clouds are ominous. Both of our phones are bleeping issues for weather warnings. We'd ordered Starbucks on Jacob's mobile app, and as we pick up our coffees at the kiosk, we see lightning electrocute the sky, then hear a crack and sonic boom.

"A little on the nose." Jacob grimaces. "Stay tuned for hailstones and locusts at the state line. Want me to take over driving?"

"Not yet."

"We might need to do a car dash. It's about to pour. Ready? We're parked left of that divide. Shit, hang on." Jacob pulls out his phone. "Henry texted."

I read it out loud. "'Nine centimeters, transitioning.'" It stops me cold. I know what that means. I've read all the baby books.

"What?" Jacob is staring at me. "Tell me what."

"It means she's moving into the second stage of labor."

"Then we better move, too," says Jacob as the exit doors slide open.

The downpour starts right as Jacob takes off, but I can't make myself go. Standing there in a daze, I watch him *Mission Impossible* himself halfway across the parking lot in less than ten seconds, and then, seeing that I'm not with him, exasperatedly double-back to where I'm still standing under the canopy.

He's soaking wet. "What are you doing? Let's go! We're wasting time!" He dives forward and makes a grab for my free hand. I yank it back. "What?" Jacob's eyes are hollowed by the surrounding lights. He looks like a scared, sodden jack-o'-lantern.

"I need a minute."

"We don't have a minute! What is wrong with you?"

I feel light-headed, bereft with the sense of everything slipping away so fast, like disaster-flood footage, a world swept out from under us in a matter of seconds. Where were my signs? How is this day our reality and not my treasured, sacred, green-Sharpie-boxed January eighth? How is it that I'm gripping at air?

"I just never thought we wouldn't get there in time," I say.

"Nora, we can't *stop*." He's jogging in place. Like it will tempt me into motion.

"We're not stopping. We're pausing to regroup because we're too late."

"Not if we—"

"No, Jacob—not if we anything."

He takes in what I'm saying and slowly extricates himself from his own action movie. Then his arms fence tight around me as he brings his chin to rest on the top of my head. "Okay, okay. We're in a new story," he says close in my ear. "But it could be a good one."

"Tell it to me," I say, my words muffled in his arm.

"So it starts with Marisol's rocket fuel coffee and Mom doing the crossword and crowdsourcing answers. You hiding those greasy, burned hash browns under your napkin. Me and Pete and Ollie playing some kickass Nerf."

"Your mom wanting to come with us," I say.

"Dad being Dad about his car. Him and Mom sending us off with a month's supply of mashed potatoes."

"Driving in the rain with the radio tuned to the 1940s."

"Getting there when we get there."

We listen to rain pound the corrugated roof. We watch it fall in liquid walls around us.

"The baby just texted," says Jacob. "Apparently she's got nothing else on her calendar except being born."

"Aha, good to know."

"She cleared her schedule. Says she's looking forward to getting to know us."

"She's going to be so sick and tired of us telling her this story."

"Except what's better than the story you've heard a million times?" he asks. "Told by people who love you the most?"

Not the day we planned, but the day we got. This is our story. I get back in it.

Fifty-Four

<<<<<<<<<<<<<<

We don't have the clothes. It's almost eight o'clock at night, and it's bone-chilling cold, and all I can think about, racing in step with Jacob to the entrance of Mercy Lights Hospital, are all the little sleep sacks and nightgowns I've been sewing and washing and pressing these last months. Soft, pristine baby colors like a roll of Necco Wafers. Neatly layered in two flat stacks on the towel shelf, ready and waiting.

Of course, the hospital will supply these things, and how sad that jammies are all I could offer anyway, when clearly this baby needed so much from me, a protection I couldn't ever give her—and now this cord we've never shared has snapped without warning, catapulting us over a cliff into the gut-wrenching, terrifying unknown of whatever happens next.

We don't know where we need to go. We're moving on a jet stream of confusion as we dash through the doors and up the elevator, wheeling like Keystone Cops around all the corners of this plain-featured, no-frills little hospital.

Hand in hand, we careen into the maternity ward's circular desk.

The supervising nurse is not Bianca nor Makebe, but she knows who we are. Her name tag says *Kim*, and she is tall, with large dark eyes and short dark hair. She's waiting to hand us each a mask and lead us through to the lights and noise of the neonatal intensive care unit.

We stop first at the handwashing station, where we lather and scrub up our forearms, and then Kim leads us through to what she describes as the warming isolettes, and I'm trying to figure out which one is our baby as if by internal divining rod, but there are so many babies, and they all look exquisite and important, and I'm drawn to all of them. I could be the mother of any of them.

"Here's your baby," says Kim as she stops.

Here is our baby. Our baby.

She is two hours old, wrinkled and otherworldly, a tiny traveler from outer space. She looks wary to be here. She's wearing a knit cap and a white cotton sleeper, and attached to her chest are sticky sensors and string-thin lead lines that connect her to the screen of a stand-alone monitor. Her bright eyes lock in with mine as Kim lifts her up and smooths out the tangle of lines to give her to me.

At first my arms feel paralyzed, locked with tension, as if some part of me is still gripped over the steering wheel and hurtling endlessly forward. It's not until Jacob moves a half step closer to me, and I feel his hand come to rest at the small of my back, that I can force myself to relax enough to accept the bundle of baby.

"She's here," I say, wonder-smitten. I've yearned for this baby in abstraction for so long that her appearance—so unexpected and early and far from home—is also so flat-out shocking that she seems impossible.

"Gloria," says Jacob, trying out her name as if it's three syllables of a magic spell.

When I glance at him, his eyes are wide with the irrefutable fact of her.

But she weighs nothing! At just four pounds, she feels lighter than a bouquet of wildflowers in my arms. Holding her, I'm terrified I'll disturb her. I can't fathom her resilience. We still haven't moved when, a couple of minutes later, we're joined by a woman who introduces herself as Dr. R. Saetang, MD—Radha, the doctor who delivered her.

"These lead lines on your baby's chest and the ankle cuff are precautionary measures," Radha tells us. "She had a short episode of apnea about an hour ago. It's not unusual, but we're keeping an eye on it. Your baby has a slightly underdeveloped central nervous system."

I am listening so hard, and I know what this doctor just said is critical, but all I'm sure I hear in that stew of words is *your baby*.

"Is she okay?" I ask.

"She's still got some growing to do," says Radha, "but she has reserves." Young as she is, Radha seems like a person who was born serious. "This monitor tracks her respiratory rate and her oxygen saturation. It's protocol for premature infants. We're also watching for jaundice, kidney and liver function. The usual suspects." Even her smile is solemn. "We're on a bit of a roller coaster right now."

"We can do roller coasters," says Jacob.

"Your sister is a trooper," Radha tells me. "She's been sleeping, but I'm sure she'll want to see you when she wakes up."

Sister. I feel the light and dark and the weight of this word—my heartbreak and gratitude, my urgent need to see Evelyn—in sudden conflict with never, ever wanting to leave this baby.

"Do you know why she came early?" asks Jacob.

"We don't," says Radha. "It happens."

"But she's going to be okay, right?" I finally ask it. Gloria doesn't look like a chubby, healthy newborn. She looks too thin, like a tiny wizard, her head overly large in proportion to her tender body.

"I can vouch that she's got a good team," says Radha, "but we're not out of the woods."

Radha leaves us to Kim, who shows us how to change the baby and weigh the diaper, before we tuck her back into the isolette. I cannot stop looking at her, at the fragile rose-petal boneless wobbly pudding softness of her. *You are my best thing.* My mother's hand in mine, her last words to me, and now it's my turn to love my own best thing, and at least this part feels easy. *All you had to do was get here. Now all you need to do is stay.*

Fifty-Five

<<<<<<<<<<<<<

The neonatal intensive care unit is a dizzying, overbright, spinning top of activity around us. Hospital workers swoosh in and out through the heavy pneumatic doors, while attendants in scrubs stop to speak with parents who stand at dazed attention over their babies' ventilators or bassinettes. Larger groups of doctors in lab coats gather with families by the far-wall ventilators and high-tech incubator beds. They look like futuristic pods on wheeled pedestals, with monitor screens on top that display numbers and waveforms in different colors. I'm already enormously thankful that Gloria has crossed one finish line here, in that she doesn't need the sequestered protection of those sealed cocoons. Tiny as she is, she is big enough to be out in the world, where she can be picked up and touched as an actual being.

I wave when I see Henry across the floor.

There are tiredness dents under his eyes. When he hugs me, he smells so un-Henry, like skin and sweat.

"They called me down to verify the birth certificate—you still need to sign it." He looks sheepish. "But I don't know Gloria's middle name. They left it blank."

"We can handle that," says Jacob. "We've got it from here."

"Evelyn's asking for you," Henry tells me.

"Now?"

He nods. "She's about to get something for pain. It's a good window. She was a warrior." His eyes on me are focused, like he's trying to figure out what I'm thinking, but then he just shakes his head. "She'll tell you."

Her room is down the hall. Henry leaves me at the open door.

Evelyn is sitting up in bed, in a mint-green hospital nightgown, staring out the night-dark window. Her left arm is hooked into an IV and her right hand is holding a fork as if someone has placed it between her fingers and poised it, like a marionette, over the tray table set in front of her. The tray holds a plastic carafe of water and a plate of sad Thanksgiving; beige disk of pressed turkey, a tousle of green beans, and a runny blob of cranberry sauce.

I enter the room, but she doesn't look over until I softly say her name. Mascara is crumbed beneath her eyes, and she's wearing heavy pearl-knot earrings. The loose ends of a day that started very differently.

"Hey," she says. "Did you hear? I just had a baby."

"A holiday baby," I say. "I don't know anyone else who was born on Thanksgiving."

She blinks, nods, takes me in. "They've got me on something really good," she says. "But a nurse came by earlier and said Gloria didn't want a bottle? They're asking me to pump." Though we know it's not the plan. Right from last spring, that wasn't the plan, when Evelyn explained to me about her difficulty breastfeeding Xander. How she'd tried and tried, and finally had to put him on formula.

"We're going to try the Similac again soon." I glance at my watch, aware it might be the first time I've had to prioritize time ahead of Evelyn. "I'm happy to see you," I say, "but you must be so tired. I'm sure you want to rest."

"This wasn't supposed to happen." Her voice is unexpectedly thick with emotion; it startles me.

"Hey," I say, "it's all right."

"It's not," she says. "It's so far from all right. I thought it'd be the same as Xander. My strength—I was so strong for him. I knew exactly what I was doing when I had Xander." She tips back her head as if to observe the room from a more critical distance. "We're not even in the right hospital." Her fork points accusingly at the window, the wall-mounted TV.

"The important thing is that she's here."

Evelyn shakes her head. The silence lengthens between us. "She's little," she says.

"The doctor says she has reserves." I'm holding hard on to that statement, clutching it against me like a love letter.

"It's not like I'm super-religious," says Evelyn, "but I always felt such a lot of faith in myself. My health, you know? My health was always a blessing." Her fork is still hovering over her food choices.

"Your health *is* a blessing." I say.

She frowns. "Just...be yourself, okay, Nora? Be angry. Be whatever."

I lean against the wall and let go of my smile. "I'm not angry."

Evelyn sets down her fork, dismissing the whole idea of this meal as food. She leans back against the pillows. "You should be."

"How would you know you'd go into labor today? Even the doctor doesn't know why."

Evelyn suddenly pushes back the tray arm. "I can't, with this."

I pick up the tray and leave the room, where a passing nurse takes it from my hands without breaking step.

"What I'm trying to tell you is, I screwed up," Evelyn says as soon as I come back in. "I got on that plane, and I shouldn't have."

My knees buckle. There's a chair. I take it. "Tell me."

She nods, barely. "The water boiler blew at Pauline's house in North Fork," she says. "That whole property—it's always one thing or another going wrong. I said I didn't want to deal with no hot water, and I pushed it because we had the plane, and Kennebunk is nicer. It's picturesque. Also, I'd already done North Fork this summer. Maine was somewhere new, visually. It was only a little over an hour's flight. Not a big risk."

Visually. She means for content, I realize; for EvvieDoesIt. The impact of Evelyn making this choice slams me sideways. "Okay," I say.

She looks uncomfortable, and her eyes shift to the window, straining to see past the night's frigid, opaque blackness. "Everything was fine at first, and I felt the way I always do, which is great, and I'd just posted my thirty-three-week update and everyone was saying such sweet things, so many nice comments about—"

"Don't," I interrupt. "Do not tell me about your comments section. It's just us now."

She looks down, nods. "When I felt the stitch in my side, we hadn't taken off yet," she continues quietly. "It wasn't bad at first—not really. But it was different. It felt like a warning. I was even saying it to myself. *Get off this plane.* But I was also thinking that I could source a concierge doctor once we got to Portland. That it was probably a Braxton Hicks." She looks at me. "But I should have gotten off the plane and gone right to the hospital. Sharon could have kept me from going into labor."

"You don't know that."

"I do, though," she says, her voice firm. "There's steroids, there's all kinds of ways—you can look them up, later."

I take a breath. "So, the stitch got worse."

"Ten minutes in, I had to tell Henry. We mapped the hospital. But then we had weather issues and couldn't land, and once we did, it still wasn't over because of all the horrible traffic, and I started to lose it. I didn't know what to expect. Waiting on those tests, waiting for the heartbeat. If it all had gone wrong—the real wrong. I was so scared." Even telling it, she looks stunned and frightened and confused. She closes her eyes. "This wasn't how any of it was supposed to be."

I don't know what to say, and there are no do-overs, and I'm intensely grateful that it's not worse—not so far, anyway—and I also want to scream my head off for Evelyn's total abnegation of responsibility. Her haphazard, childish travel plans and their underthought consequences. But it's also the most extraordinary unburdening that I don't have to stay in this room and figure out how to make things right for Evelyn.

That, in fact, I ought to leave. Because I need to be with this baby, who needs me right back.

I stand up. "I'll let you sleep," I tell her.

Jacob is standing in the same place where I left him, staring into the isolette. He looks a little bit wild—I'm sure that I do too, in this late and foggy hour of a day that came at us so fast and fierce. I join him and feel as if we're two halves made whole, staring down at this brand-new life that still feels impossible, even as my heart brims with its proof.

"Radha and Kim came by," says Jacob. "Last round before the shift change. She says we can count on spending a few weeks here."

"Weeks?"

"Realistically, a month. Kim says there's a motel in walking distance, right across the highway."

"Okay." I inhale. "We'll figure it out." I'll wait to tell him about the plane. It's crushing, but also it doesn't matter. Now is what matters.

Suddenly, the machine screeches a whining, high-pitched alarm, and a nurse dashes over to check on the baby and the lead lines while Jacob and I stand, vibrating in terror. The alarm stops.

"Apnea," says the nurse, whose name tag reads *Ann*. "It's a pause in the breathing. You'll hear the same alerts for bradycardia—we call them bradys for short—when the heartbeat slows. Sometimes with these little ones, they get stressed or they're overtired, and that's when the bradys happen. It'll be easier once you learn how to read the monitors."

Since we're sticking around, Ann finds us a couple of rocking chairs from on the floor. We pull them up to the isolette, and we fall into them, downshifting from panic to simmering anxiety that Gloria's heart will pause again, and I wonder if this is the NICU in a nutshell: large, soft rocking chairs arranged next to bone-rattling alarms.

Ann comes back to check on us and asks me if I want to try giving a feed.

"Evelyn just pumped." She gives me a searching look. "Is that okay by you, Mom? Or would you rather try with the formula?"

Mom. The word slivers through the shock of this day, striking the center of my heart. "Okay by me," I tell her. "I'm the mom now," I whisper to Jacob when Ann leaves to get the bottle.

"You were always the mom," says Jacob, and my eyes prick. Ann returns and shows Jacob and me how to give the bottle. The rocker is built wide and low. Holding this fragile baby crooked in one arm, her doll-sized bottle of milk in the other, I feel awkward with uncertainty, worried that somehow Gloria will sense it and that my doubts will imprint onto her fragile baby psyche and she'll reject me as an impostor.

"Maybe you should do it," I tell Ann. Maybe I'm not the mom. Not just yet.

"Just try. Don't be anxious if she refuses at first," says Ann. "Newborns will test-drive a dozen different bottles and nipples before they settle on one."

But Gloria takes to her feeding at once. As if she's been waiting for me. She finishes the entire bottle, and I'm washed over in exhaustion and delight, and I feel like I can do anything.

Fifty-Six

〈〈〈〈〈〈〈〈〈〈〈〈〈

The first day is daunting. Whenever I'm taught anything new—how to change a diaper the size of a cocktail napkin or retape the floss of a lead line—I can't shake that initial stumbling feeling that I'm a fraud, a pretender. I'm Bugs Bunny in a nurse's cap and stethoscope. But it isn't long before Jacob and I grasp the basics of Gloria's feed and sleep schedule, and we've learned the language of her ECG lines, her core and peripheral temperature, her pulse oximeter, and her blood pressure.

And then there's the language of the baby herself. Her irascible sleepy cry, her feisty, eyes-scrunched hungry face. Her kicky right leg when she's overstimulated. We watch our baby so that we don't focus on the NICU, its harsh lights and competing alarms, its rows of incubators holding babies the size of your hand. There are no chunky, happy newborns here, no congratulatory flowers or balloons. As the revolving shifts of nurses and doctors, residents and fellows, neonatologists and pulmonologists explain everything we can't control and might go wrong, we hold hard to the belief that our presence here will sustain Gloria and keep her safe until we can get her home.

A few times that day, I also visit Evelyn's room. She's still feeling drowsy and loopy on hormones and painkillers, but she's got the doctor's okay to be discharged late afternoon. Xander is with the Chens, and Evelyn and Henry want to get in a couple of days with him before he heads back to school. Evelyn speaks to me with burnt-out detachment, and I sense that she doesn't want any company other than Henry's. She smiles only when she mentions Xander or when she hears the baby took her breakfast bottle. She doesn't ask to see any photos, and so I don't offer them.

They'll stop by the hospital again tomorrow, Henry assures me, to say goodbye.

In between AirDropping batches of Gloria pictures to every-one, I reflexively go onto EvvieDoesIt, and the last posted photo of Evelyn. She looks so beautiful, the sage green in her Scottish sweater emphasizing the deeper green of her eyes, and yet her carefree confidence also feels naive of what's to come. I reread her lovely piece about her thirty-third week, followed by the thick plant of hashtags: #pregnant, #pregnancy, #surrojourney, #surrogacy, #gestationalsurrogate, #gestationalcarrier, #motherly, #surrgatemother, #surrogatemom, #surrogatesupport, #surrogatemoms, #surrogatecommunity.

It feels like the dreamy and incongruous tale of *before* that has nothing to do with this baby in the NICU. In one day, EvvieDoesIt has tipped and fallen and receded far behind me as I press forward into the demands of an entirely different reality.

Sunday morning, both Elliots, wrapped in shearling coats that make them look like they've dropped in from some après-ski mingle, arrive back at the hospital, as promised, to say their goodbyes.

"I can pump for three months, if that works," Evelyn tells me. In her high-heeled boots, she towers over most of us, formidable and out of place. "It'll come to you frozen and FedExed. Those La Leche people have a whole system."

"Thank you," I say. "I'm extremely grateful for this. I know it wasn't the plan."

"Thirty-three weeks also wasn't the plan," she says, and I sense her frustration and the freight of her grief as she hugs me goodbye.

When she lets me go, her release on me feels profound.

It breaks my heart to imagine my life without Evelyn, but that's not up to me.

Later, Jacob and I watch the baby sleep until we get shooed out for shift change, and we walk across the highway to the misnamed Harbor Inn, the budget motel where we've been staying that is unremarkable in every aspect except for its daily homemade soup. In the dining room, we order dinner and talk through the next steps. Jacob needs to be in-office this month, but they're giving him Fridays off, so he'll fly here for long weekends. Meanwhile, just as she'd done for Frankie, Barb's pulled in her friend Tina Mendelson to cover for me so that I'm free to stay here until the baby is, as Barb put it on our last phone call, "fully built."

"I hate to go," Jacob says as our bowls of minestrone arrive, along with buttered potato rolls and even-more-buttered string beans. "Especially since I'm leaving you to live in a motel off the side of the highway while caring for our sick baby around the clock."

"It only sounds grim when you put it truthfully like that." But then I slip my hand in his. "You know I got her."

"I do."

We scroll through photos, and we send the ones where she looks healthiest to every person who ever expressed even half an interest in seeing pictures of our baby.

Then we move on to the task at hand. We work through different financial projections of this month. The baby's insurance, the astonishing hospital bills, Jacob's travel expenses commuting back and forth to Maine, the cost of motel living, and the gasp of the new bill from the lawyer who drew up the surrogate contract that just landed in our inbox. Finally, I make myself say it. "Jacob, we're going to sink if we don't make some changes. I think we need to walk away from Brook Lane."

The devastation is rigid in Jacob's face. But I've known him so long, and I know that he's also been preparing for this. "We forfeit the security deposit," he says.

"But the money we save will go a long way. These bills are real—and the hits'll keep on hitting."

"Our home," he says, and his voice cracks a little.

"That's not our home," I tell him. "*Home*'s only another word for *us*, right?"

He nods. "Let me see if the kitchen can fill me a coffee thermos before I take off." But then he catches sight of something across the room, and his eyes crinkle with his smile.

I turn, following his gaze.

Standing in the doorway next to her tapestry-print suitcase, a modern-day Nanny McPhee holding her umbrella and zipped into a puffer coat the shape and color of a baked potato—is Gabi.

Fifty-Seven

G abi also likes the minestrone.

"I was hungry!" she exclaims over her second bowl. "I haven't been on an airplane in a few years. When did they stop serving those nice meals with brownies at the end?"

"Gabi, that's some pre-Y2K memories you're sharing," says Jacob.

"I'm so happy to see you." I can't stop saying it. "How long are you here for?"

"Till she's bigger," Gabi answers. "I said to Fred, I'm a nurse after all. I know my way around a pediatric hospital floor, and I've done my fair share of shifts in a neonatal. So let me go and see if I can help— because Nora won't ask for it."

Later, I walk Jacob out to the reliable Subaru. He'll fly back here Thursday nights, and then he'll drive up to Portland as soon as the baby is ready so that we can bring her home.

I watch the car until it's out of sight. When I go back inside, Gabi introduces me to the front desk clerk. "Mahmud's granddaughter was born at twenty-eight weeks," she says triumphantly.

"Is that right?"

"She's all grown up now," says Mahmud. "But we've been through it."

Gabi shows Mahmud some photos of Gloria under the phototherapy light. Mahmud proudly hands over his phone so we can scroll through Amy's basketball-team pictures and some of her jump shots.

"My wife and I used to take Amy's clothes home from the hospital," says Mahmud. "It made us feel better, using our own detergent. We'd bring back the clean clothes in the morning." He hands me a card key. "Second floor, laundry room." Then he tells us to be down before seven if we want the free blueberry muffins.

The next morning, Gabi beats me to the early-bird breakfast bar. She's wearing scrubs under her puffy jacket, and she shows me the three-ring binder she's brought with her. "We need to write down everything," she says. "Writing it down makes people accountable. Ready?"

"Ready." But then I need to sit again. My throat aches, and my game face is crumpling.

"We're here for weeks, you know," I tell her. "And you should know, she looks a lot bigger in the photos. In real life she's so skinny, and her eyes look tired, and even finishing a bottle is really effortful, and when she's done feeding, it's like she just collapses, and we have to watch her color and her numbers on the chart, and everyone's always checking to make sure she doesn't get an infection—because hospitals are actually pretty germy, no matter how much you sterilize everything and no matter how careful you are—and it's actually just really shocking to see her, Gabi."

"Shocking for *you*, maybe," says Gabi, her voice as calm as a pillar. "You think I've never seen a premature baby before, Nora? That's why I'm here. There should be therapists for any family staying long-term in a hospital—usually it's the nurses who end up taking on that role." She sits down next to me. "Let's reset here a minute. I brought my Bicycles." She produces a pack of playing cards from her pocketbook. "So how about some gin rummy, you and me," she says, "before we start in on this day. Okay?"

We play a few rounds, the way we did all those years ago, that first summer without my mom. Holding the same soft cards, betting my odds, I feel my body relax as my brain stops buzzing and my breath slowly comes back to me. And then I'm ready, and then we go.

Fifty-Eight

〈〈〈〈〈〈〈〈〈〈〈〈〈

G abi and I do the baby's laundry at night, and it sparks our sense of purpose, to spring into the hospital each morning with clean clothes to place on the share-shelf of Gloria's area. We print and tape pictures of Jacob and me, both sets of grandparents, and probably too many of Nick—who can't take a bad photo—to the side of the crib.

At the gift shop, we buy glitter paper and we cut out letters spelling *G L O R I A* and Blu-Tack them onto the wall above Gloria's crib. There's a magic in her name that compels everyone who sees it to sing it.

And we've got to sing. We've got to hold our optimistic notes, especially for those days when doctors can't tell us everything is going to be okay. We keep vigil on this baby, on perpetual watch for jaundice, pneumonia, anemia, sepsis. We celebrate every finished feed and extra ounce of weight. When she's sleeping, we rock her until we are falling asleep ourselves. One day, Gabi and I take an infant-CPR class. Another afternoon, we attend a seminar to learn about precautions against SIDS. Jacob mails a box of the baby's clothes, and we have so much extra that we give away pajamas and onesies to other NICU families. This month, the very best-dressed babies are right here at Mercy Lights Hospital.

Our Gloria area is so festive that I send a photo to Meg, texting her that it reminds me of when I first saw our freshman dorm room.

In answer, she sends Harry Styles dancing in a fuchsia pantsuit.

"As soon as Gabi needs to leave, I'm coming up for a visit," Meg tells me one night on the phone. "New England winters don't scare this Narragansett girl."

"That's bonkers," I say. "Also it's too luxurious here on Interstate 95's best-kept secret. If you come, you'll never go. Possibly because you'll freeze in your bed."

"Are you trying to scare me? Tell my goddaughter to get ready."

Gabi's week turns into two, until she has to be near my dad and the sun and the ocean again—it's been their longest time apart as a couple.

"I can't imagine doing these two weeks without you," I tell Gabi that Sunday, when she hands over the three-ring binder.

"Family's family, Nora," she says in that same pragmatic voice that has been marshaling medical staff and asking dozens of questions and generally making sure that our presence here is known. "Your father and I, we never..." she begins, and then she stops. Gabi is not exactly a serving platter of her feelings, and she's never spoken to me about not having children. I wait, but behind her eyes, I sense secrets that are too personal, too private. "Don't forget to send me photos," she says instead. It's not until Jacob and Gabi have left in the cab that I find, tucked into the side pocket of the binder, she's left me her pack of Bicycles.

In what feels like a coordinated plan, Meg arrives the very next morning, a thrilling surprise that presumably meant some Jenga-like moves with Barnett childcare. She comes straight to the hospital, where she takes custody of the spare rocking chair and assures me right away that no, Gloria doesn't look one jot like Baby Yoda—an opinion exuberantly voiced by Ollie the last time Peter and Marisol FaceTimed us.

"She's bigger than I'd imagined," says Meg, and her conviction is a balm for my worry. Meg melts into the hospital rhythms like it's a dance she's always known, and our time together reverts to our college days, one long conversation from sunup into the small night hours, when the NICU's lights are lowered and we quietly pass Gloria between us so that she is always held, skin-on-skin contact upping her success odds on everything from temperature regulation to weight gain.

"Any word from Evelyn?" Meg asks one night, as she takes her turn rocking the sleeping baby while I knit yet another pair of baby shoes.

"No," I say. "I've texted her a few times. Henry texted that they were upstate for a while. It crushes me that I can't make any of this easier for her."

"This isn't exactly the most joyous birth story for anyone," says Meg. "Not for Evelyn, not for you and Jacob, and especially not for the baby."

"That's not how it feels to me," I say. "Yes, those first two weeks were scary, but the baby's coming through it, and every time I look at her, I always feel so thankful for Evelyn." My eyes are smarting. "Always."

Meg's three-day visit is over too soon. By the end of that week, Gloria leaps one whole ounce to clear the five-pound mark. She is vaulting every obstacle that she needs to come home. By now, she can glug sixty milliliters of milk on a single feed. She passes the car-seat test—her breathing and oxygen monitored for almost two hours while she sits semi-reclined in the throne of her SnugRider—and collects her green sticker.

Christmas Day, Jacob is here with the Subaru.

We give out presents to our primary nurses, whom we've gotten to know and adore—Kim, Ann, Sally, Abbe, Jean, Nancy, Stacey, and Summer—and we celebrate with sparkling cider in paper cups, the drink of choice in the NICU that I'm starting to get a taste for, because it always means we've hit a milestone. I've knit dozens of doll-sized caps and booties for the NICU parents, and we give them out as gifts, bonded by our collective awareness that while this isn't the Christmas any of us imagined, we're in it together.

Gloria Evelyn Hammond is ready to leave Mercy Lights three days later.

We say goodbyes to Mahmud and drive home on a snow-dusted morning, and by the time we arrive in Brooklyn, it's night. Entering the apartment, I feel like I've been gone for a year. In the nursery, the bassinet is assembled, the rainbow wall mural is up, the shades are installed, and Jacob's boyhood duck lamp is placed just so on the nightstand.

"A soft landing after all," I say, as we nestle Gloria into her bassinet.

Jacob rolls in his lips like he might be on the verge of a counterpoint, but then he just jerks a thumb upward.

I squint as I look up. "Did you draw around *The Scream*?"

"I did, and see how I also turned it into Nick?"

The big eyes, the hands like floppy dog ears against the face. Our very own Nick Munch Charles. "Impressive."

"I work on commission. I'll send you my contact info."

Nick chooses to sleep on the nursery rug, and every time I enter, she thumps her tail, calm but alert, serious in her new role as the baby's watchdog. That first night, I must get up a hundred times to make sure that Gloria is still breathing, and I wonder how long it will take before I stop thinking she might be snatched away from me at any moment. Maybe all new parents feel some threat of the baby-stealing, fairy-tale witch lurking in the shadow, and maybe the witch's lurking seems lurkier— and possibly more potent—if a baby feels like she got here by magic.

By the pale light of the next morning, as soon as Gloria's rustling awakens me, I scoop her up. Small as she is, I think she's got some of Jacob's personality in her already: she's open and direct, a communicator, a pleaser. Even if Jacob says that's all babies—because how else do you get your needs met if you can't talk? But I know what I know.

On the roof across the street, a woman in thermals is doing sunrise yoga. I've never seen her before. Then again, I've never been up this early.

The woman waves, and I wave back.

She points to Gloria and makes a heart with her hands, and in this one simple gesture, I can feel how different this year will be from all the years that came before. We're in the bloom of a new season, where Gloria's presence is enormous and everywhere. Her clothing and diapers and blankets, her fish tub that takes up all the kitchen counter space, her high chair and ExerSaucer and glider swing that are cumbersome enough be legitimate pieces of furniture. How ironic to think of all the time Jacob and I spent agitating about the confines of the nursery space because our entire apartment is Gloria's realm. Then again, it's not surprising. Sometimes it feels like we didn't know anything before Gloria.

That night, I delete all my photos of 87 Brook Lane, with its wraparound porch and dogwood trees and summer hammock. It hurts, it does hurt. But a couple of weeks later, after her shots, we bundle up the baby for her first carriage ride, and bumping along the sidewalk, I feel exultant. Gloria will grow up a city kid; she'll know the piers and parks and museums, and this whole town will be her backyard. We take her to Chu Hua's since you can't get anything even close to as good as Chu Hua's in the suburbs. It's sunny and warm enough that we decide on takeout and we eat at a bench in the park, the baby carriage parked in front of us, luxuriating in the ease of our first day as pee-on-a-stick parents.

Evelyn's milk arrives via FedEx all through January. On EvvieDoesIt, she posts a brief clip informing her quarter million followers that the baby was born healthy and she's taking a break from social. She also texts me that she and Henry have decided to move up to Saratoga Springs for the year, where he can focus on his art and she can take care of her horses and just be in my life.

When she asks me to give her regular Gloria updates, my heart flips over.

Late at night, with Jacob sleeping beside me, I send Evelyn the day in baby photos. Then I make myself turn off my phone so I don't go nuts watching to see if she's put a heart on them, and by morning, she always has.

Fifty-Nine

❮❮❮❮❮❮❮❮❮❮❮❮

The same week in March that Opal Appell dies in her sleep and is the feature of countless international headlines and obituaries, Barb quietly survives a stroke that lands her at NYU Langone.

The news about Opal doesn't affect me at all at first. But Barb's illness immediately changes everything.

"I'm retiring," she tells us when Frankie and I visit her as soon as we're allowed. We came bearing things Barb loves most—matzo ball soup from Eli's and a box of pistachio macaroons from Sant Ambroeus.

"You're too young to retire!" Frankie and I protest in unison.

"What are you talking about? I'm eighty-four," says Barb.

"You're only seventy-nine," I remind her. Barb never seems to age; for as long as I've known her, she's had that same smooth, plump face. It's only the context of a bright, antiseptic hospital room that makes her look frail.

"Seventy-nine is my professional age," she says. "Anyway, I want my time! Time to make huckleberry cobbler and scrub the mold off my grout and repot my spider ferns and take my grandson to Six Flags. So, effective as soon as my lawyer calls me back, I'm transferring ownership of the shop to you two."

"The shop," I say, dumbfounded.

"To us," says Frankie, equally stunned.

"Who else?" asks Barb. "You've both got a similar aesthetic and lots of passion, and you don't mind the nitty gritty."

That's us. Still, it takes us a while to believe this isn't the whimsical impulse of a stroke victim.

"I've still got some of my wits," says Barb, when she tires of our questioning along these lines. "And you need to make the shop your own. It hasn't felt like mine for a while now."

"Possibly because we hide all your inventory," I tell her.

"Ha, I suspected that was happening. And don't count on making any money," she warns us. "I never did. Now is the time for you two to be appropriately solemn with gratitude."

"We are so incredibly appropriately solemn with gratitude," Frankie says solemnly.

But once Frankie and I leave the hospital and hit the street, we just stare at each other.

"Are we even the people Barb thinks we are?" I ask. "Or are we going to ultimately turn out to be a tremendous disappointment?"

"We've just got to keep calm and bet on ourselves," he answers.

The calm part is too hard, but we take the bet. We lose the next weeks to an ongoing conversation of what the shop should be and won't be and might be. Do we want to expand to menswear? What do we define as eclectic decor or antique handicrafts? Should we do share-shelves and pop-ups? Teens and preteens?

All spring, Frankie and I take long walks and daydream and reimagine. We mentally fill the shop with everything we love, and then we empty it out again. We debate space to sell some of my homemade baby clothes. We consider adding a selection of perfumes, and a selection of tights and stockings. We debate whimsical touches like a coffee bar and handwritten tags. Walking, always walking—Frankie with his double stroller and me wearing my carrier pouch of inward-facing Gloria, all round observant eyes and rebel swoop of hair that looks like a cartoon punch line every time I pop off her cotton cap.

"What do you think, Glory Be?" I ask her. "What do you imagine for this shop?"

In answer, she makes her signature bird sound. I've kept her close in this pouch, as if I can make up for all the months when I didn't carry her. Strapped to my body in her padded nest, I can fixate for hours on the delirious pleasures of her—her Bambi eyelashes, the downy wisps of her dark hair, the soft nub of her button nose, her milky smell, her magnetic gaze. We know each other well now; I'm fluent in Gloria's moods and demands and the feed-burp-change-comfort cycle of our conversations. I watch and respond, affirm and soothe, guess and worry, and then do it all over again the next day.

At the end of the summer, when Frankie and I relaunch the shop, it's a catchall of what we love best—a curated mix of independent designers and better-known names, a cabinet of curiosities filled with everything from carved wooden fans to pearl-beaded barrettes to unusual iPhone cases. We've got a shelf of rare books and a back corner area of baby clothes—including my selection of Glory Be separates—anchored by a rocking chair. Finally, we offer a select array of our favorite showpiece haute, just waiting to receive that one-in-a-million wildcard customer and to give us a reason to stay open late. We've named the shop everything from Violet Femmes to Room for Thirds, but by the time we reopen for business, we've settled on Pineapple.

Sixty

Evelyn's text pops up late May—a photo of Xander at his cross-country meet.

Handsome, so tall now! I write.

She sends a smile emoji.

A week later, she texts me an image of herself with Life of the Party, her newly adopted old racehorse, who, at this point in his life, is probably fine to be just a Bystander at the Party. But Evelyn looks clear-eyed and happy.

I put a heart on the horse photo.

During restaurant week, Evelyn sends a link about a fusion restaurant Jacob and I should try. She's got our names down for a special pass if we want to go. We go, and it's great, and I send her a thank-you note.

A few weeks later, she AirDrops me Henry's finished art for his new picture book.

I love it but tell the truth is Braggy Badger your dad?

Ha. I can almost hear her burst of low laughter; it makes me smile.

When Meg throws Jacob and me a baby shower, Evelyn sends us a baby Baghera sports car in hunter green. At ten months, Gloria's fat little feet dangle far from the car's pedals. But she can sit upright, and so I prop her into the driver's seat for a photo shoot. Gloria is a wriggler and a smiler and, lately, very much a drooler.

It takes time, and some chin-wiping, before I get the right photo.

She doesn't say our names yet, but she can say Nick.

Evelyn sends a heart. Later that night, she writes, that night when you told off my dad was why I always wanted a sister.

I put a heart on her words, and later that afternoon, I send my own father a photo of Gloria, who is just starting to eat rice cereal, though most of it ends up smeared all over her face like a baby facial treatment mask.

In return, Dad sends me a photo of Siesta Beach as the sun is sinking. Won't be long before I can teach her to surf.

For all that we didn't have, my father never found happiness hard to come by.

A couple of days later, Evelyn texts again. Raquel's directing a short film for the Tribeca Film Festival.

Go, Raquel! That's incredible.

I have an eye for other people's talent.

I don't answer, but the next day, I write, You carried and delivered a baby I love so much my heart could crack, and I hope you'll want to meet her one day.

She doesn't answer.

A few days later, she writes. Does she have asthma? I read it's a preemie thing.

No asthma. She has good lungs and she uses them.

How big is she? What are her baby stats?

For a few seconds, I consider—then reject—the pros of not quite telling Evelyn the truth so that she doesn't worry.

Right now Gloria's only in the tenth percentile for height and weight. It'll take a few years for her to catch up.

I watch the dots of Evelyn typing and typing but then she drops off, and I don't hear from her until late September when she picks up the thread by giving me the recipe for her secret vinaigrette that she admits is really Tabitha's—I'd always figured. When she asks for Gloria's percentile stats again, this time I've got better news. In October, she sends me a link to a spoken-verse play about Jean-Paul Sartre underwritten by the Fitzroy Foundation, and we both decide that we won't ever go see it.

Sixty-One

Y ou know what we should do?" I ask Jacob one night over the chickpea meat loaf. "We should host Thanksgiving right here. In our apartment."

"Are you kidding me?" He tips all the way back in his chair, which sets Gloria, strapped in her own little high chair, into a fit of appreciative burbling noises for her daredevil father. "See, even Glory Be thinks it's hilarious," he says. "This apartment is the size of a lobster trap. The baby monitor gives us a feedback screech unless we keep the volume at zero."

Gloria, her dad's best audience, woots and bangs her wooden spoon on her tray.

"Oh, come on. It's our home," I tell him. "Even if the space is small, the city is big. We can invite Gabi and Dad, and they'd love it. It'll give them a chance to hang with Gloria on the long weekend of her first birthday. Gabi hasn't seen the baby in a year, and Dad's never even met her."

Jacob is still shaking his head, but I feel the idea moving toward me, taking shape and heft. We could call it Gloria's Thanksbirthday. We could get card tables and folding chairs. We could prepare the basics but also make it a potluck.

"I love the city in the fall," says Meg when I tell her my plan. "I get so nostalgic. Do you want a big slobbery pack of Barnetts to come too? We could take the girls to the Macy's Parade, and I'd bring a baked ziti."

"I'd love that," I say. "The more the merrier." Though, in this instance, with our space limitations, I'm not sure if that trope is completely true.

Gloria proves to be an excellent carrot. My parents say yes immediately, and they start looking for nearby hotels. Jacob's parents want to come for the day; Peter, Marisol, and Ollie will drive in with them. Phil says he'll bring his risotto. Frankie and Seth want to visit so they can meet my parents, and Seth is bringing his mom.

Thanksbirthday, ha ha ha! writes Evelyn. Pauline and I'd been thinking we'd turn Friendsgiving into Friendsnothing this year and do a spa thing.

Come celebrate with us instead.

We'll see.

I don't push it. I slip R. Xenakis in 5D an invitation because if she's here, this will be one noisy event, and so she might as well join us instead of knocking on the wall in protest. She stops by to accept her invitation in person. We've been hall neighbors for more than five years, and I don't think I've ever seen her except in profile, retrieving her mail. Now we learn her name is Reyna and she tells us she'll bring a Mediterranean cheeseboard.

"Thanksgiving *and* a birthday party? You don't have the room," Reyna tells us.

"So maybe we'll stick half the party in your apartment," says Jacob kiddingly.

"That's one idea," she answers. "Let me think about it."

"At least she's not bringing over a plate of her fried fish special," says Jacob when she's gone.

Dad and Gabi decide they'll make a weekend of it. They've booked three nights at the nearby Court Street Marriott, flying in late Wednesday with plans to come over to the apartment early the next morning and take the birthday girl to watch the Thanksgiving Day Parade. True to their word, they show up at 7:00 a.m. with a bag of takeout muffins and egg-and-cheese sandwiches. Gloria's favorite things in the world after Nick are food and new people, and so her party is already off to a roaring start.

Jacob and I've spent this year so quietly, nestled-in and swept along on the schedule of our baby's needs, that it's a marvel to see Gloria in this new public light, presented to her grandparents to admire. She's immediately won over by the shiny foil wrapping of her birthday gift, though less enchanted by her new sunflower-print birthday overalls. I dress her in them and then clip her hair with the matching tiny sunflower barrette. Later, when I see her in Gabi's arms, she looks so grown up that I'm jolted by panic. She is a full one year old today, a big girl in denim coveralls. It's over already, and I can't bring it back. No matter how many photos I've taken and stories Jacob and I will retell each other, so many memories are lost already, and Gloria is moving in only one direction, away from us.

In the meantime, she's ready for the day. We bundle her up against the cold, and my parents leave with plans to meet up with the Hammonds and the Barnetts at a designated spot somewhere in the thick of Midtown. It already feels a little bit chaotic, and when everyone assures me it's completely under control, I have to wonder if they're humoring me.

Frankie and Seth, along with Mrs. Tanaka and the double stroller of Abe and Claudia, show up a bit later—in true New Yorker fashion, they have no desire to be anywhere near a parade. We set up the twins' Pop 'N Go in the nursery, and now we're out of square feet in that room. Mrs. Tanaka takes the good armchair and declares that's where she stays. Frankie's got a diaper bag filled with the entire contents of the world. He settles the twins with snack cups full of puffed mango stars and a sticker book. Soon the twins are applying stickers onto the sides of Nick, who handles this indignity by going to sleep.

Jacob is catching up on drinks orders, and I'm sliding out the baking sheets of roasted brussels sprouts when Keith and Pauline—plus their son, Louis, and young daughters, Emma and Grace—all arrive. Right behind them are Henry, Evelyn, and Xander, who is now as tall as his mom, with an almost-man's voice that makes him seem like a new person.

Evelyn is holding a glass bowl shaped like an orange that's filled with clementines. She sets it in the middle of the table.

"I saw this, and I thought of your mom," she says. "Free oranges, right? Wouldn't she have loved it?"

I need a second. "She would have," I say. "It's a perfect gift."

Henry passes around early copies of *The Kindest Kangaroo*, his book about different animals lending a helpful paw or pouch or hoof, except for the boastful, undermining badger, who is clearly modeled on Beau Boyle—though Henry swears he doesn't see it.

Soon there's more commotion at the door, and now the apartment is crammed with both sets of grandparents, along with Barnetts and Hammonds. There's so much jostling and tilting that the space feels like a ship at sea, only all of the sailors here need a beverage or the bathroom—and everyone wants to meet Evelyn, who might not have signed on for this many hugs or strangers coming at her but soon relaxes into the role. It isn't long before she's got Gloria on one hip.

"Actually, we've been friends for a long time, baby," she tells her, and Gloria seems to get it. She cranes to look at Evelyn's face from every different angle, as if mapping a print into her memory.

"She might not be *heavy*, exactly," says Evelyn, with some relief in her voice, "but she's not *nothing*, either."

At some point, Reyna is here. She's wearing a long skirt with a T-shirt that reads DO NOTHING in rainbow block letters, though clearly she's been doing plenty in terms of preparing her cheeseboard—feta and Manchego cheeses, whipped hummus, olives and sun-dried tomatoes, and marinated artichokes.

"I was right," says Reyna, looking around. Her expression is a somber told-you-so. "We'll have to share space." When she takes me next door into the calm of 5D, it feels like a respite, and it looks like she was planning for this moment all along. Her apartment is neat and clean, with popcorn in bowls and *Toy Story 3* teed up on her TV screen. We call the kids to let them know about the extra room, and they drift in and settle as if summoned by a Pied Piper flute.

"This is such a save," I tell Reyna. "Thank you. Next time we have people over, we won't go past capacity."

"Aren't you all planning to move?" Reyna looks at me, skeptical. "People with babies always move. My place is the same as yours, and it even feels small for only me."

Maybe it's because Reyna's space is so tidy, but now I see that she's right. Her unit is identical to ours, with the same low ceiling and hardwood floors, the same boxy windows with their view of grimy rooftops across the street, and yet minus the whole messy overspill of all that is Gloria, the apartment is also startlingly different.

"No, we're not moving anytime soon," I answer, "so I'm glad we get to be neighbors."

We leave the children settled for the movie and call them over when dinner is ready though one small oven means nothing is the right temperature, and so the meal is haphazard. We serve Mrs. Tanaka's udon noodles, then Phil's risotto and Keith's fish congee, and then Meg's baked ziti with room-temperature brussels sprouts. Pies are baked and set in the windowsills: pumpkin, apple, and a lemon meringue for Jacob. It's rowdy and messy, and Nick is in perpetual motion trawling all the food that spills on the rug. There will never be an encore of this Thanksbirthday, but when I catch Evelyn's amused eye down the table, I'm also happy I did it.

After the pies, while kids are peeling clementines and Jacob is taking orders for coffee and tea, Louis finds a cardboard paper towel tube.

"Ah, yes, the annual poetry recital," says Keith. "It's almost a tradition."

Louis's voice has also changed from two years ago. It adds extra texture to the monologue about survival he's chosen from *The Batman*. Next to grab the microphone tube is Reed Barnett, who speed-recites *The Lorax* before breaking off midsentence to burst into tears and hide under the table.

We pause on the talent show when Jacob brings out Gloria's birthday cake, centered by a crooked candle in the shape of a number one. Gloria, on Sandy's lap, lurches forward and waves her hands in an attempt to catch the flame. When she's not allowed to touch the fire, her fingers find her barrette, and she looks over at me for a moment, scowling, as she yanks it off. She might not be a braids girl, after all, I realize. She might be a whole new vintage.

Grace, Pauline's youngest, has taken hold of the paper towel tube, and now she's belting out the chorus to the *Toy Story* theme.

"Your turn, grown-ups!" calls Grace. "You've got a friend in me! Join in!" And we all do our best to sing it together.

Epilogue

≪≪≪≪≪≪≪≪≪≪

When *The Age of Appell: Icon and Influences* opens in December, Winnie sends me a link to special opening-day passes. Frankie and I close shop so we can go up to the Costume Institute and check it out. When we arrive, the crowd is at a glitzy overflow. We traverse the vaulted glass-and-marble space, divided by decades and commemorated with enormous blowup portraits of Opal as captured by the lenses of Horst, Avedon, Warhol, and Leibovitz.

We stop before the pleated glass prototype bottle of *Belle by Appell*. "Everyone wore this scent in high school," I tell Frankie. "No matter what people might say about Opal Appell, she leaves a huge legacy."

"Except nobody has anything good to say about Opal Appell," says Frankie, plucking a couple of mini-burger sliders from a caterer's passing tray and tucking them into his cocktail napkin. "Which begs the question—would you rather be a terrible human with a big fancy retrospective or someone decent who people say cool shit about after you die?"

"I don't think you get to choose," I say.

"I'm getting more of these teeny burgers. That's my choice," Frankie says. "They're next level. Want to go hunting with me? We haven't been downstairs yet."

"Sure." The downstairs—the Influences section—is given over to Opal's personal collections. We examine with awe the encased displays of the Bessie Smith notebook, the Earhart flight instruments, Jacqueline Kennedy's Cassini inaugural ball gown, and Opal's own (second) wedding dress by Adolfo.

"But where's your Dior?" Frankie asks. "I don't see it anywhere."

I've been looking for it too. "It wasn't on the main floor either."

"Did Bryce ever tell you it was rejected? Maybe it just wasn't famous enough."

"Maybe." I feel a prickling in my skin when I see Bryce herself across the room. She's seen me too, and I watch her expression flicker from reserved to resolutely cheerful once she makes real eye contact with me and beckons me to come over.

This will be fine. I let go of the tension in my shoulders. "Come with me to meet Bryce," I tell Frankie, and we cross the room together.

"Nora!" she exclaims. "I just read about your shop! Congratulations!"

"Thanks, we're really happy about it." Frankie and I made a recent roundup of *New York* magazine's 25 Best New Boutiques list, and we've been enjoying a smattering of publicity, helped by the arty photo of Frankie holding a bottle of champagne and looking oh-so-suave.

Now I introduce Frankie, who acts like he needs no introduction, and Bryce is suitably charmed. She looks atypically casual in her blazer and dark jeans, reminding me of another Opal Appell quote: *A lady should never chew gum or wear denim.* I can't help but speculate if Bryce's relaxed demeanor, like her outfit, has anything to do with the End of the Age of Appell.

"Baby pics, please," Bryce says, and I don't need to be asked twice. She looks at them all and asks about Gloria's latest tricks, which I'm happy to rattle off: she can drink from a cup, she can wave goodbye, she's got two teeth, we're pretty sure she can say *Nick.*

"You must be so proud," Frankie says to Bryce, raising his plastic glass to indicate the exhibit.

"I'm sorry your grandmother couldn't be here to see it," I add.

Bryce nods. Her face is composed, her tone neutral. "When you live in a family with a personality as big as Opal's, you never imagine it will just end." She lowers her voice. "And I'm sure you noticed we had to pull the Bergessen."

"Yes," I say, my heart speeding up. "I mean, I noticed its absence."

Bryce inclines her head to Frankie that she'd like to speak with me privately, and we step closer together as he darts off murmuring about sliders. "I'd planned tell you if I saw you in person," Bryce says, "because as it turned out, that piece—it wasn't a Dior."

My eyes widen. "What do you mean?"

"I mean, it's a forgery," she says. "Beautiful in its own right, but it's not the original."

"Wait—what?" I ask. "When did you learn this?"

"The Costume Institute contacted me a few months ago." Bryce's voice is low and quick. "It wasn't until they'd started putting the show together that they discovered it. It's not even a mid-twentieth-century piece. Nora, it's the strangest thing. I've been up and down all the possibilities of what might have happened."

I look at her closely. "Do you have a theory?"

"I think I might," Bryce answers, "though unfortunately, I'm pretty sure the swap was made on our watch. Because I saw the Dior for the very first time right on the night of my grandmother's birthday party. Of course, it was just spectacular—and I do know my haute." She pauses for me to nod affirmation. "After the party, we had it stored in one of our Midtown facilities. This summer, it was brought out in preparation for the exhibit, and that's when I got the call. I went to see it, and the discrepancies were pretty obvious."

"But who would do that?" I ask. "And why?"

Bryce looks troubled. "I feel terrible to make an accusation," she says quietly, "but the only finger I can point is at Evelyn's family. It would have been easy for them to pay off a security guard; it's not as if these storage buildings are Fort Knox. And they were so sour about the *Times* article—last year, they'd even threatened legal action, and just imagine if they'd followed through! Opal would have jumped right into that fight." She grimaces. "And I don't even want to think about what she'd have done if she'd found out about the forgery."

"But if your grandmother never knew," I say tentatively, "maybe it was the joy of giving her the gift that counts?"

"Yes! Exactly! That's what I think too. It was a special birthday—in the moment." Bryce looks rueful. "Opal wasn't known for taking the high road, but I'd like to put this business behind us. Let the Fitzroys think they've won." She's trying for an easy tone, but her eyes on me are worried. "And I'm sorry, Nora. I've always felt guilty for forcing you to sell the piece. Opal never apologized for anything."

"Well, thanks," I say. "I appreciate that. And what about Evelyn? Have you spoken with her about any of this?"

"Actually, I practiced my apology on her first," says Bryce. "She either played innocent about the swap, or it was all her parents' doing— but do you want to know something? I just don't care. I really don't. It's only *things*. And things don't matter, not the same way as friendship." Suddenly she looks hopeful. "Do you know if Evelyn's coming to this?"

I shake my head. "She's upstate."

"I saw that Camp Champion's getting very popular on social," she says.

"'A second chance on a forever home,'" I say, quoting the Camp Champion bio. "I look in on it every day. If anyone can get thousands of people invested in her causes, it's Evelyn."

I bought the velvet first, that night of the same day Bryce made her offer. She'd priced me out; of course I'd have to give up the piece. The fabric was on a vintage deadstock site, and on the same site, I bought three yards of cherry-red silk. I didn't have a fixed plan, but I had my knock-off bottle of Libre d'Orange and knew the thrill it gave me, the nostalgia it unlocked. Over the years, Meg has often mentioned how she treasures her Nora de la Renta. A good fake can be a real joy. Maybe, I thought, I could trick myself into thinking I still owned my Dior, simply by recreating it.

I learned everything about the architecture of clothing from my mother, and right from the first slice of my scissors through that midnight velvet, I could feel her guiding this project, and my muscle memory held all her best tricks. I sensed her watching me as I whipstitched the frog closures and marked the configurations for the textured embroidery, and in those late-night hours, I found calm in this challenge, and I kept my hand steady even when my mind went rogue with anxiety, as it often did those months. The duplicate, when I'd finished it, was no Dior, but it was, as my mother might have put it, a real piece of work.

Jacob never suspected a thing—not even when I asked him to examine it.

The Appells weren't on the lookout for a counterfeit, either. Opal saw only her triumph of acquisition. Bryce was merely on watch for her grandmother's approval.

It was Dean who kept me informed of the backstage antics after Opal donated the piece. When Gavin Hussie told Dean the Costume Institute planned to wait until Opal died to stage her retrospective—it is a mercenary truth that death elevates value—I breathed easier. But not even Dean knows my part in this drama. Or if he has an inkling, he's decided it's easier to think the Fitzroys made the swap and to file it under *Rich Folk and Their Shenanigans*.

Unsurprisingly, Bryce misremembers what she saw that night of her grandmother's birthday party. She doesn't know her haute well enough not to need the eye of an appraiser, someone like Dean, Gavin, or me to point out the rayon thread and the machine-made stitches, the slight puckering in the inside hem, or the inked letters of the tag, all the style marks of a forgery.

In the way of the moneyed class, Bryce is just used to being right.

Later, when I'm back at the shop, I go upstairs to Barb's cold storage, where I've kept the cloak all year, slipped in with those posturing Bob Mackies.

I take it off its hanger and drop it over my shoulders.

That night, when I'd watched Winnie leave with the duplicate, I'd figured it would be spirited off into some undisclosed cavern of riches where the Appells keep their spare Old Masters and Egyptian artifacts. What's another item of haute to Opal Appell? Especially this piece. By the late 1950s, Dior's New Look was old hat, and his collections were no longer the stuff of fable.

It was a moment's impulse, to hold onto the original—*my* original because it belonged to me in a way that my forgery never could capture. Winnie arrived early, while the mannequin was still wearing my creation. I watched her pack it up and go, and in the moment, it seemed right that she have it and that I should keep mine. It's impossible to regret the decision.

Then I read the Bergessen letters, and that's when learned that I didn't have a Dior on my hands after all; I had something even more fascinating. *The wunderkind of 30 Montaigne*, Bergessen referred to him that afternoon she'd met Yves Saint Laurent, only twenty-one years old in the spring of 1958 when he took over from Dior, who'd died just months before. It was a transitional moment at 30 Montaigne, reflected in the cloak itself, its drop-shoulder silhouette offering a hint of Saint Laurent's "trapeze" style that would define his first collection.

Perhaps that's why I've always loved the cloak so intensely, not only as a work of art wrought from a point of intersection but as the launch of Saint Laurent, a talismanic young designer who would revolutionize haute. It thrills me to picture him, his narrow face, his eyes bright behind his thick square-cut glasses as he bends to examine these very beaded sequences. How does he imagine this cloak, folded in on itself like a chrysalis? And what does Bergessen feel that night, crowd-shy and armored in velvet, stepping from her car for one last brush with her public—*my way to you was not a lie.*

I slip off the cloak and replace it on its hanger and carefully close the door on my secret.

Downstairs, a woman is outside the shop, knocking on the glass. She's got a look of money, and I know better than to keep her out.

"You're the absolute best," she says as I unlock the door and she steps inside, bringing in the cold. "I need something that says *wow*, in a size twelve."

We've got that. A mid-'90s Gaultier acetate cocktail dress that gives her the edge she's been chasing. We stare at her and agree that it's a *wow*, that it works. It's also seventy-eight hundred dollars, and she doesn't blink.

Frankie will swoon. Next month's rent, all paid.

As I open the mini fridge to see if we have anything for a toast, I remember last week we decided to stock up, and Frankie has all the bottles neatly arranged—sparkling ciders pyramided with a generous supply of champagne, ready to celebrate whatever might be our next moment of good fortune.

Reading Group Guide

1. Describe Nora and Evelyn's first meeting. How do those first impressions shape the dynamic of their friendship?

2. How does Nora's love of vintage clothing shape her outlook on life?

3. Why does Jacob feel threatened by Evelyn? How does he handle his feelings? What effect does his discomfort have on Nora?

4. When asking her for styling, do Evelyn's references to Nora's savings feel empathetic or manipulative?

5. What role does Nora's mother play throughout the book? How do her dreams influence Nora's life?

6. How does Evelyn handle rejection? Why do you think she behaves that way?

7. Evelyn is happy to use the pregnancy to boost her standing on social media. How did you feel about EvvieDoesIt? Would you have pushed back if you were in Nora's shoes?

8. Nora is superstitious about believing anything positive about the pregnancy. How does superstition protect us from bad news?

9. How does Nora's attempt to be tactful by discussing the Bergessen cape in person backfire? Can you remember a time when waiting for "the right moment" to discuss a problem made it worse in the long run?

10. Where does Nora and Evelyn's friendship stand at the end of the book? What do you think is next for them?

A Conversation
with the Author

What was the inspiration for *The Favor*?

My children were both born via surrogacy, and I'm fortunate that my personal experiences were so positive. But I remember the push and pull of that time, of being deeply emotionally invested while physically so disconnected. My surrogates were literally my lifeline. But what if it had been a different experience? What if my surrogate never kept me in the loop? What if I wasn't even a priority? Those were some of the questions that kicked off my early outline.

What's the first thing you decide on when you start writing a new book?

First, I buy a 5 x 7 lined notebook. For the next weeks, I'm writing down everything I sense about this maybe-novel. I gather scraps—names, scenes, settings, a feel for the trajectory—all in my scribbly longhand. Also, I try not to blurt out my idea to everyone, but I always do.

There are so many great details about the history of fashion and the world of vintage styling throughout the book. How did you connect with those worlds? What did your research process look like?

Many of us who love wearing vintage fashion connect with the sense that we inhabit other stories and a shared life—I've got a closet full of other people's histories. So research was a delight. Rapt hours steeped in online vintage sites? Yes, please. I'm also a big fan of memoirs and documentaries about designers. Writing about fashion was a happy, natural burrow down well-known rabbit holes.

As many of Nora's and Evelyn's acquaintances point out, the stories we hear most about surrogacy are horror stories of kidnapping and protracted lawsuits. Did those well-known fears change the way you wrote *The Favor*?

My oldest is fifteen, so I've had surrogacy conversations for a while now. Generally, I find that people know more about surrogacy now than they did sixteen years ago. At the time, we fielded some pretty wild questions. People didn't get it—but they wanted to get it. That's what I remember best—how friends and strangers tried to understand the process and wanted to be part of a conversation about how my family came to be. I hope the book caught some of that bewildered curiosity.

Evelyn and Nora are back in contact by the end of the book, but they're nowhere near as close as they were when they first became friends. Do you think this is the beginning of finding each other again, or will they remain friends only distantly?

I'd like to believe that both answers are true. I think in the evolution of this friendship, Nora and Evelyn come to a hard-won, genuine understanding of each other. At the same time, they're more respectful and honest about the boundaries of this relationship. They've found their balance.

Nora's cape switch is a big surprise. When did you decide that she should keep the original?

I'd hoped to give Nora the last laugh, and I'm drawn to writing about privilege bubbles—people wanting things for the sake of wanting them, people who get their way and say. Nora's switch makes me happy because she knows precisely why she values this piece. It's a feisty move but not out of character—and I'm always cheering for Nora.

How did writing *The Favor* compare to writing books for younger readers? What surprised you the most?

It was a journey! I'd written YA for many years, and the structure of coming-of-age novels is usually about figuring out arcs and resolutions of first love, first loss, first real look at that giant horizon of your future. By the time I jumped into Nora's life, she's already had a lot of her firsts, she's made some big decisions, she's got her view established. The other surprise is that while I've been writing fiction for a long time, the experience of finding and exploring Nora's voice was so different that *The Favor* feels like a debut. Was not expecting that!

Acknowledgments

‹‹‹‹‹‹‹‹‹‹‹‹‹‹

The acknowledgments is a "don't forget to thank" page I'll revisit a dozen times before I can let go. It's the happiest real estate in the book as a space to shout my thanks for so many friends and colleagues who gave their time and thoughts, insights and advice, encouragement and expertise to what eventually became *The Favor*.

In writing about mid-twentieth-century fashion, I read several excellent books for research and inspiration; in particular, *What Shall I Wear?* by Claire McCardell, *Fashion Is Spinach* and *It's Still Spinach* by Elizabeth Hawes, and *Christian Dior: The Illustrated World of a Fashion Master* by Megan Hess. For the curated aesthetic and wisdom of fashion/vintage platforms I've learned from and loved following for years, I am also indebted to @decadesinc, @drjustinefancypants, @duroolowu, @foundingfabric, @gabriellak_j, @ladybugvintage, @polkadot.pink, @superettevintage, @thevintageshow, @thewaywewore, @thiswasfashion, @whatgoesaroundnyc, @ysl, @1stdibs, and @90senchanting.

I feel fortunate to count on so many friends who keep my writing day (and day-to-day) perpetually electric; in particular, Julie Buxbaum, Anna Carey, Julia DeVillers, Sarah Enni, Maurene Goo, Jenny Han, Sarah Mlynowski, Rebecca Serle, Courtney Sheinmel, Siobhan Vivian, and Robin Wasserman. For her generous reading of early drafts and a steadfastness when I wasn't even sure this book existed, I am profoundly grateful to Jen E. Smith. Special thanks to Morgan Matson for her insights, edits, and landing that title. A big thank you to Jodi Fodor and Emily Ohanjanians for their invigorating feedback through the tricky spots. My heartfelt appreciation to Emma Straub, J. Courtney Sullivan, and Meg Wolitzer for their support when I needed it most. Thank you Michelle Gagnon, Stuart Gibbs, Farrin Jacobs, Leslie Margolis, and Abbi Waxman, my favorite LA neighbors who all made this west coast move so joyful.

I have enduring appreciation for Emily van Beek for her clear-eyed advice and guidance, and to Erin Harris for her energetic readiness to take on *The Favor* from the starting line. Hooray for Team Sourcebooks and especially Shana Drehs for her wholehearted embrace of this story.

While *The Favor* is fiction, writing about surrogacy was also a daily exercise in gratitude, as my own little family never would have happened if it weren't for the grace and great big hearts of our surrogates: Holly, Terri, and Amanda. And finally, thank you to my family. I am so grateful for your love.

About the Author

© Andreas Neumann

Adele Griffin is the acclaimed author of more than thirty books. Her works include the National Book Award finalists *Sons of Liberty* and *Where I Want to Be*. Her novel *The Unfinished Life of Addison Stone* was named a YALSA Best Book, an Amazon Best Book of the Year, a *Booklist* Top Ten Arts Books for Youth, a JLG selection, a *Romantic Times* finalist for Book of the Year, and a *School Library Journal* Top Fiction pick. She lives in Los Angeles with her family.